PENGUIN CLASSICS

SUNSET SONG

LEWIS GRASSIC GIBBON was born James Leslie Mitchell in 1901 at Hillhead of Seggat, Auchterless, Aberdeenshire, the county in which both parents had strong farming roots. The Mitchell family moved south to Kincardine and in 1908 settled in the remote croft of Bloomfield, Arbuthnott in the Howe of the Mearns. Following eight productive years at Arbuthnott School and an unhappy year at Mackie Academy in Stonehaven, Leslie Mitchell found employment in 1917 as cub reporter with the *Aberdeen Daily Journal*, quickly gaining promotion to the post of Junior Reporter with the *Scottish Farmer* for the first six months of 1919, when his left-wing political sympathies were tempered by his exposure to social deprivation in Glasgow. For the next ten years, Mitchell suffered recurrent bouts of unemployment accompanied by severe depression, promoting desperate recourse to the military. His first period of service, for four years, with the Royal Army Service Corps, offered the chance to travel to Egypt, Persia and Mesopotamia. His second spell, six years spent as a clerk in the Royal Air Force based in the South of England, witnessed his first appearance in print with the prizewinning story 'Siva Plays the Game' in 1924, as well as his marriage to his former classmate Rebecca Middleton in 1925. Spurred on by further publishing success with his first full-length volume, *Hanno: or the Future of Exploration*, in 1928 and serialisation of his exotic story-cycle *Polychromata* in the *Cornhill* from 1929, Mitchell committed himself to the career of professional writer. With the birth of his children in 1930 and 1934, Mitchell settled in the London satellite town of Welwyn Garden City. Throughout his last six years, Mitchell published sixteen full-length volumes of astonishing range, from social realism to romance, as well as the historical novel *Spartacus* (1933) and the dystopian fantasy *Gay Hunter* (1934). The appearance of 'Lewis Grassic Gibbon' with *Sunset Song* in 1932 cemented his reputation in Scotland and the United States in particular. Gibbon's output became equally impressive, encompassing sequels in his *Scots Quair* trilogy, a biography of the Scottish explorer Mungo Park, *Scottish Scene, or the Intelligent Man's Guide to Albyn* (1934), his fiery miscellany co-authored with the poet Hugh MacDiarmid, and his biographical study of exploration, *Nine Against the Unknown* (1934), attributed to Gibbon and Mitchell. In December 1934, Mitchell suffered severe stomach pains, and on 4 February 1935 he underwent an emergency operation and died three days later, a week before his thirty-fourth birthday. Following cremation, his ashes were carried back by his widow to his native North-east, to be buried at Arbuthnott Kirkyard.

DR WILLIAM K. MALCOLM graduated Ph.D. from the University of Aberdeen in 1982. His critical analysis of the work of Lewis Grassic Gibbon, *A Blasphemer & Reformer: A Study of James Leslie Mitchell / Lewis Grassic Gibbon*, was published in 1984. For the past two decades, he has promoted modern Scottish literature as writer, broadcaster, teacher and consultant and is a long-standing director of The Grassic Gibbon Centre at Arbuthnott.

ALI SMITH was born in Inverness in 1962 and lives in Cambridge. She is author of *Free Love, Like, Other Stories and Other Stories, Hotel World, The Whole Story and Other Stories* and *The Accidental*.

LEWIS GRASSIC GIBBON

Sunset Song
A Novel

Edited with Notes by WILLIAM K. MALCOLM
with an Introduction by ALI SMITH

PENGUIN BOOKS

PENGUIN CLASSICS

Published by the Penguin Group
Penguin Books Ltd, 80 Strand, London WC2R ORL, England
Penguin Group (USA) Inc., 375 Hudson Street, New York, New York 10014, USA
Penguin Group (Canada), 90 Eglinton Avenue East, Suite 700, Toronto, Ontario, Canada M4P 2Y3
(a division of Pearson Penguin Canada Inc.)
Penguin Ireland, 25 St Stephen's Green, Dublin 2, Ireland
(a division of Penguin Books Ltd)
Penguin Group (Australia), 250 Camberwell Road, Camberwell, Victoria 3124, Australia
(a division of Pearson Australia Group Pty Ltd)
Penguin Books India Pvt Ltd, 11 Community Centre, Panchsheel Park, New Delhi – 110 017, India
Penguin Group (NZ), 67 Apollo Drive, Rosedale, North Shore 0632, New Zealand
(a division of Pearson New Zealand Ltd)
Penguin Books (South Africa) (Pty) Ltd, 24 Sturdee Avenue, Rosebank, Johannesburg 2196, South Africa

Penguin Books Ltd, Registered Offices: 80 Strand, London WC2R ORL, England

www.penguin.com

First published 1932
This edition first published in Penguin Classics 2007

013

Editorial material copyright © William K. Malcolm, 2007
Introduction copyright © Ali Smith, 2007
All rights reserved

Map artwork: Andrew Farmer

Set in 10.25/12.25 pt PostScript Adobe Sabon
Typeset by Rowland Phototypesetting Ltd, Bury St Edmunds, Suffolk
Printed in England by Clays Ltd, St Ives plc

ISBN: 978-0-141-18840-9

www.greenpenguin.co.uk

Contents

Chronology   vii
Introduction   xi
Further Reading   xxiv
Note on the Text   xxvi

SUNSET SONG   1

Maps   263
Notes   269
Glossary   290

Chronology

1901 *13 February* Born James Leslie Mitchell at Hillhead of Seggat, Auchterless, Aberdeenshire, son of James McIntosh Mitchell and Lilias Grant Gibbon, and half-brother to George and John

1907 *May* Family moves to Aberdeen

1908 *May* Family moves to croft of Bloomfield, Arbuthnott, Kincardineshire, in the Mearns. *18 May* Admitted to Arbuthnott School

1916 *22 August* Admitted to Mackie Academy, Stonehaven

1917 Reporter with the *Aberdeen Daily Journal*

1919 *February* Junior Reporter on the *Scottish Farmer* in Glasgow. *June* Dismissed for falsifying business expenses. *Summer* Recuperation at Bloomfield after nervous breakdown. *26 August* Enlists in Royal Army Service Corps

1923 *22 March* Discharged from army, following service in Egypt, Persia and Mesopotamia. *April–August* Spends summer as recluse at Bloomfield. *31 August* Enlists as clerk in Royal Air Force, based in the South of England

1924 *18 October* First published story, 'Siva Plays the Game', wins first prize in *T.P.'s and Cassell's Weekly*

1925 *15 August* Marries Rebecca Middleton (later Ré, Rhea or Ray) at Fulham Registry Office. *August* Posted to RAF Kenley

1926 *January–February* Ray convalescent at Purley Cottage Hospital following serious miscarriage. *June* Transferred to Uxbridge

1927 *December* Stationed at RAF Upavon, Wiltshire; Mitchells move to Shepherds Bush

1928 *June* Publication of first book, *Hanno: or the Future of Exploration, An Essay in Prophecy*

1929 *January* Publication of 'For Ten's Sake', first of series of short stories to appear in the *Cornhill*. *31 August* Discharged from RAF

1930 *17 March* Birth of daughter, Rhea Sylvia. *September* Publication of first novel, *Stained Radiance: A Fictionist's Prelude*. *October* Attempts to establish Society of Militant Pacifists, anarchist political group dedicated to aim of abolishing war

1931 *January* *The Thirteenth Disciple, Being Portrait and Saga of Malcom Maudslay in his Adventure through the Dark Corridor*. *July The Calends of Cairo*, Introduction by H. G. Wells and Leonard Huxley; published in USA as *Cairo Dawns: A Story Cycle with a Proem*. *December* Mitchells move to Welwyn Garden City, Hertfordshire. In 1931, applies twice, unsuccessfully, to join the Communist Party of Great Britain

1932 *January* *Three Go Back*. *July The Lost Trumpet*. *August* Lewis Grassic Gibbon, *Sunset Song* (first use of Scots pseudonym, adapted from his maternal grandmother's name of Lilias Grassick Gibbon), first volume of trilogy *A Scots Quair*. *November Persian Dawns, Egyptian Nights*, with a Preface by J. D. Beresford

1933 *March* *Image and Superscription: A Novel*. *May* Lewis Grassic Gibbon, *Cloud Howe* (second volume of *A Scots Quair*). *August Spartacus*

1934 *February* Lewis Grassic Gibbon, *Niger: The Life of Mungo Park*. *February The Conquest of the Maya*, with a Foreword by G. Elliot Smith. *16 March* Birth of son, Daryll Allan Leslie. *May Gay Hunter*. *June* Hugh MacDiarmid and Lewis Grassic Gibbon, *Scottish Scene, or the Intelligent Man's Guide to Albyn*. *November* J. Leslie Mitchell and Lewis Grassic Gibbon, *Nine Against the Unknown: A Record of Geographical Exploration*; published under sole authorship of Mitchell in USA as *Earth Conquerors: The Lives and Achievements of the Great Explorers*. *November* Lewis Grassic Gibbon, *Grey Granite* (third volume of *A Scots*

Quair). *December* Suffers acute stomach pains, diagnosed as
gastritis
1935 4 *February* Undergoes operation at Queen Victoria Hospital, Welwyn, for perforated gastric ulcer. 7 February: Dies,
age 33 years, 11 months

Introduction

(New readers are advised that this Introduction makes details of the plot explicit.)

'How funny were folk! Chris thought . . . You knew them, saw through them, tied them up in little packets stowed away in your mind, labelled COARSE or TINKS or FINE; and they came tumbling from the packets at the very first shake, mixed and up-jumbled, she'd never known a soul bide neat and sure in his packet yet' (p. 144).

Sunset Song, the first novel of Lewis Grassic Gibbon's 1930s trilogy, *A Scots Quair*, has always been a paradox of its own versatility. A scorching piece of literary cunning, it is the opening act in an astonishing fictional work which traces, in an unlikely reconciliation of lyrical and polemical, the effect of the coming of war and mass industrialisation to the north-east of Scotland in the early decades of the twentieth century.

Held in massive affection in Scotland, where it consistently tops nationwide polls like the one which, in 2005, named it Best Scottish Book of All Time, *Sunset Song*, and the other parts of the trilogy, *Cloud Howe* (1933) and *Grey Granite* (1934) – books 'in their different way as great a departure from the run of Scottish novels as James Joyce's Ulysses from the run of Irish novels', as Hugh MacDiarmid put it[1] – invite comparison with the achievements of writers as different as Thomas Hardy, D. H. Lawrence, Willa Cather and William Faulkner, and yet are so little known and read outside Scotland that it's a near crime.

But for more than seventy years *Sunset Song*'s readers have passionately loved this unflinching yearn of a book and its evocation of adolescence and coming of age. Its loamy sensuality and its heightened language evoke a rare kind of reader-intoxication. Its strange hybrid of melodrama, romance and realism caused a huge stir of excitement on its appearance in 1932, when it was widely critically lauded – and withheld from general circulation in, among several of the Scottish libraries, Aberdeen Public Library, where you could only read a copy if you asked the Reference librarian, because it rather too sensually called a spade a spade, as the *Kirriemuir Free Press* put it, 'when there is no need whatever to refer to the implement at all'.[2]

It has been claimed, among other things, as a classic diffusionist text, a classic Marxist text, a classic Scottish Nationalist text, a classic humanist text; it even has the arguable (and intriguing) makings of a classic feminist text.[3] It's a novel that has meant so many things to so many people; its heroine being so notable a creation that she has had to represent, over time, a daunting list of romanticised entities from Woman as Archetype, to Woman as Enduring Natural Cycle, to a romanticised version of The Land, to Scotland itself.

Yet *Sunset Song* consistently survives all its critical and political and simplified and romanticised packaging. It has been shaking off easy categorisation since its first publication, when the journalist George Malcolm Thomson, shocked enough by the pioneering drive of the book to call it 'perhaps the first really Scottish novel', wrote to the writer Helen Cruickshank: 'if you have not already done so, get hold of a novel Sunset Song by L. G. Gibbon, whoever he or she may be'.[4]

Such fluidity of gender would presumably have delighted James Leslie Mitchell who gloried, as a writer, in an identity critics have always chosen to call divided but one which could equally be called multiple or multivocal. He used the pen name Lewis Grassic Gibbon (adapted from his maternal grandmother's name) to write the more obviously 'Scottish' of his fiction and his birth name to write what is referred to as his more 'English' work; he himself identified these two 'selves' as relatives: 'my distant cousin', 'my English cousin'. (For the purpose of this introduction I'm going to use his more Scottish name throughout.)

Gibbon was a phenomenon of energy, creativity and versatility. He died a far-too premature death in 1935, just a week before his thirty-fourth birthday, having published in only seven years of literary output seventeen works – novels, essays, biography and short fiction set all over the world and covering an incredible range of discursive, anthropological, historical, archaeological, sci-fi, political and literary ground. On his deathbed he left a number of dizzyingly ambitious plans for future works.

He was born into a small crofting family in Auchterless in the Scottish north-east in 1901 and spent his most formative years in the parish of Arbuthnott, a rural community about twenty-five miles south-west of Aberdeen, where he was seen by locals as both shining lad o' pairts and a wee bit too smart for his own good. Precocious enough to have found and read Darwin's *Origin of Species* at thirteen, fascinated by exploration, archaeology and history, and avidly keen, after he left school, to educate himself further and eventually to make a living by writing, he refused to take a fee in local farming and went very rebelliously into journalism instead, first in Aberdeen, then in Glasgow. After this he spent time in the service corps, travelled in Egypt and the Middle East; then, having married a childhood friend, he settled in Welwyn Garden City (arguably environmentally about as far as you could get, on the same island, from rural Arbuthnott) where he began writing full time.

With his knack for somehow turning up right at the political centre of things (in his teens as a cub reporter sent to write up the founding of the local Aberdeen Soviet, he'd found himself actually elected on to its Council), he was soon at the core of the debates about what has come to be called the Scottish Literary Renaissance, with writers such as MacDiarmid, Edwin Muir and Neil Gunn arguing and writing about what would constitute the 'new' Scotland. *A Scots Quair* was written in under three years in the south-east of England where its writer was more than aware, both politically and personally, of the complexity of what it meant to be Scottish at a time when one in four were out of work in Scotland (in some places half the people were unemployed) and where home was the place he'd become nothing but scandalous; 'the speak of the place', as his shamed mother put it to him on his visit north after the publication of *Sunset Song*.[5]

Sunset Song opens with a 'Prelude' which Gibbon actually advised his American readers, in the transatlantic edition, to skip if they found it too foreign or hard-going (see Glossary, note 1), telling them to go straight to the body of the novel, The Song. But the Prelude is a rhetorical masterpiece. Its subject is history, seen here as a hurtling succession of wars and power struggles (and if you compare this and the shattered, calm Epilude at the end of the novel for a full view on what 'makes' history, it is clear how important this framing device is to the workings of the novel).

This is, at the very least, an unusual history of a place and a community. It is idiomatic. It is individual, choosy. It creates a different kind of authority. At the same time it's delivered in a second-person 'you' of a narratorial voice. This makes it not simply one voice but the fluid reportage of several voices at once – a communal voice. The voice is deeply and entertainingly judgemental, but also crucially ever-shifting in its own judgement (which suggests to a reader to allow his or her views to be at least a bit fluid too).

This communal 'you' is Gibbon's real technical achievement. It's a voice which challenges all the given versions, even challenges its own conservatism. It makes short shrift of every belief and ideal while it crams the whole history of eight centuries (including quick histories of class and of the growth of crofting) into four and a half pages, a virtuoso piece of time-melt full of casual violence and hilarity, which rushes us up to the novel's present day, 1911, the tiny community of Kinraddie still there under its long-time rulers of Meikle House and kirk (both, incidentally, empty when this story begins) and its main characters, players in their own history. Then, in the first chapter of The Song, the 'you' focuses tightly in on just one family mentioned in the common history, the Guthries, and on just one member of that family, sixteen-year-old Chris.

So far, then, the simple word 'you' has come to mean many

things, often all of them at once – the community voice, the folk-voice, and also, skilfully, its reader, the 'you' holding and reading this book. By Chapter I it comes to mean Chris – and it delivers her with a surprising intimacy to the reader, who is at one and the same time inside and outside the book's central consciousness.

Involvement and detachment are important concepts in Gibbon's writing. His inspired use of this tiny word, 'you', signals an openness in the face of things more usually kept closed, like intimate selves, communities, localities. This very localising also suggests exclusion. 'You' can also mean 'not-you'; 'you' signals all the precariousness of belonging or not belonging, and how the rules of belonging work. In *Sunset Song* fictional structure and voice shift lithely between exclusion and inclusion, between communal and individual states of being. They do this as the narrative subjects both its community and Chris, its individual protagonist, to several tough chronological processes – the cyclic farming seasons; the inevitable hardening shift from innocence to knowledge, both personal (burgeoning sexual growth for Chris) and historical (the First World War looms unseen over this still-innocent time and place); and the arrival of the future, initially in the comic shape of the occasional, laughable, rich, rare motor-car in the rural landscape, more invidiously throughout as the changes in industry and the demands of history alter the crofting life for good.

Gibbon's choice of a central female protagonist in a largely male landscape is radical throughout the *Quair*, and in *Sunset Song* this choice is immediately radical within his own narrative. By the end of just the first chapter, Chris's blithe, sweet mother, Jean Guthrie, with her spark of independence against Chris's father, John Guthrie, and the dark authorities of sexual and religious tyranny which form him, is maddened, poisoned and dead. But the survival of the sensual and intelligent 'you' at the centre of the novel is the book's hope from the very beginning. In a repeated patterning of the concepts of involvement and detachment, which in turn give way to understanding, *Sunset Song* asks questions about what constitutes a self –

and especially a female self, as each chapter brings something particular and formidable for a girl or woman to have to deal with.

Chris, like the novel, is a versatile creation, at once integrated and detached. She's a creature of unified mind and body, a clever book-lover who is also totally sensual, regardless of the abusive religion of her father and forefathers and the she's-no-better-than-she-ought-to-be view of the local community. She's an argumentative fusion – an identity both created and fractured by different countries and languages. Gibbon suggests this most clearly by reference to language, particularly language that signals questions of communal (and inherited) involvement:

> . . . two Chrisses there were that fought for her heart and tor-mented her. You hated the land and the coarse speak of the folk and learning was brave and fine one day; and the next you'd waken with the peewits crying across the hills, deep and deep . . . You saw their faces in firelight, father's and mother's and the neighbours' . . . you wanted the words they'd known and used, forgotten in the far-off youngness of their lives, Scots words to tell to your heart how they wrung it and held it, the toil of their days and unendingly their fight. And the next minute that passed from you, you were English, back to the English words so sharp and clean and true – for a while, for a while, till they slid so smooth from your throat you knew they could never say anything that was worth the saying at all. (pp. 41–2)

Language, Chris finds, is also a question of hierarchy: 'you felt fine and tingly and above all the rest of the queans who weren't learning Latin or anything else, they were kitchen-maids in the bone'. She knows to answer to a different impulse, a different set of aspirations. 'The English . . . couldn't speak right' (p. 43).

Later in the novel, at Chris and Ewan's wedding, Long Rob of the Mill compares the meanings of the English word 'sunset' and the Scottish word 'gloaming' and ponders on how their meanings can never equal each other; and at the very end of the novel a repeated emphatic use of the word 'sunset', in the

Reverend Colquohoun's war-memorial speech, marks a place of the dead.

Throughout this novel, whose title places its lament firmly in the 'English' context, the life of a language argues back at its own impending death. Like MacDiarmid, but with his own remarkable originality, Gibbon re-evaluated and reinvented not just written Scots but written English too. At the time of his writing this novel, Scots was the 'speech of bed and board and street and plough, the speech of emotional ecstasy and emotional stress', perceived, Gibbon noted in his essay 'Literary Lights', even among most of its own literary users, as 'low and common and loutish, a matter for laughter ... to be quoted in vocal inverted commas ... an inadequate and pitiful and blunted implement'.[6] He often refers to language as an implement or a tool in his essays. Arguably his own most versatile implement is this creation of subtle idiomatic Scots, heightened and literary yet rhythmically and aurally based on the spoken voice; connected to rather than rejective of English but with its own fluid and rhythmic authority. Gibbon loved English too, 'that lovely and flexible instrument, so akin to the darker Braid Scots which has been the Scotsman's tool of thought for a thousand years'.[7] He recognised what was an exciting 'essential foreignness' in every approximation between Scots and English.[8] He famously and objectively described his own method as being 'to mould the English language into the rhythms and cadences of Scots spoken speech, and to inject into the English vocabulary such minimum number of words from Braid Scots as that remodelling requires'.[9]

The language of *Sunset Song*, poetic and realist and soaring and dark and local and strange all at once, is lyrically the riskiest and richest by far of the three books of the *Quair*. Its hybrid of English and Scots stretches what language can and is usually expected to do. Its sentences, resembling a meandering, live thought process, are far longer than the average physical breath, but still all about breathing, about how the heart works. The language is so rich that the comic spite of its folk-voice is often a sheer relief. Its most often repeated refrain is 'folk said ...' It presents a community in which talk is more than reality or entertainment – it is a survival tactic, a rare richness in a position of poverty and a pure power.

Sunset Song seems, on the surface, to write off the very notion of itself as a book. Throughout, books are referred to with some suspicion, 'coarse' or 'stite'. The communal 'you' knows there's no good in and no point in books. At the same time books are acknowledged as immensely powerful. '*Learning in books it was sent the wee red daftie at Cuddiestoun clean skite, they say*' (p. 56), and reading them, Chris knows, is something which can take you 'to a magic land', away from reality, 'out and away and south' (p. 40). *Sunset Song* repeatedly declares it has no allegiance to them at all – at exactly the same time as it places itself succinctly on a specific literary map.

'The new minister, him they chose early next year, he was to say it was the Scots countryside itself, fathered between a kail-yard and a bonny brier bush in the lee of a house with green shutters.' Gibbon closes his Prelude with a literary reference to very contemporary Scottish fiction – to the seminal argument, in the last decade of the nineteenth and the first of the twentieth century, between what was known as Kailyard (or cabbage-patch) literature, a genre which made use of extremely senti-mental views of Scottish locality and sold particularly well to expatriates across the Atlantic, making its writers, like J. M. Barrie and Ian Maclaren, very rich men, and what came to be known as Anti-Kailyard literature whose stories, in novels such as *The House with the Green Shutters* by George Douglas Brown (1901) and *Gillespie*, by J. MacDougall Hay (1914), were bloody, dark, gothic and powerfully unpleasant views of Scottish small community life.

Gibbon deeply hated 'the scum of Kailyard romance' and its patronising, reductive and sentimentalising powers.[10] *Sunset Song*'s blend of fury and kindness, heat and cold, melodrama and realism and its constant dialogue between romance and viscera, between the lyrical and the debunking of lyricism, all make it a brand-new thing in Scottish writing – a conscious hybrid of Kailyard and Anti-Kailyard.

Of the three books in the *Quair* it is (aptly for its focus on this time in its protagonist's lifespan) by far the most innocent, burgeoning and adolescent, and by far the most overtly sensual and narratively teasing. It rejects Kailyard – and at the same time is the closest to Kailyard of the three. It is as if it knows, and trades on, its own youthful adolescence and folk-nostalgia. This is deeply fitting, too, for its place in the trilogy, which purposefully traces the hardening of a people over time. *Sunset Song*, much more than the others, goes straight for the emotional jugular. It does this calculatedly. It is a lament, a ceremonial mourning of loss.

But this mourning is its own vitality. Versatile as ever, Gibbon's is a prose that can hold, at one and the same time, a description of the bullet-riddled dead Ewan, returning as a ghost, shot open and 'laired with glaur', and a high emotional romanticism, as Chris welcomes home the grotesque, bloodied, real-life ghost, 'the light in his eyes that aye she could bring' (p. 244).

The effect of this heightened prose fusion was and still is violently powerful, both emotionally and politically.

'I hate capitalism; all my books are explicit or implicit propaganda.'[11] Critics will probably argue about Gibbon and his politics until the end of time. Was he a nationalist? Is the *Quair* a Communist creed? Was he a Humanist–Marxist–Anarchist–Socialist-believing non-believer? 'I have amused myself with many political creeds – the more egregious the creed the better', he wrote in his essay 'Glasgow', in itself a passionate and angry rejection of any belief system or culture which might, in actuality, result in any more misery or poverty for human beings. 'There is nothing in culture and art that is worth the life and elementary happiness of one of those thousands who rot in the Glasgow slums. There is nothing in science or religion.' Gibbon was an uneasy nationalist at best. 'A time will come when nationalism, with other cultural aberrations, will have passed from the human spirit, when Man, again free and unchained, has all the earth for his footstool, sings all his epics in a language moulded from the best on earth.'[12]

Although there's no denying that the impetus behind *Sunset*

Song is to narrate the negotiation of a Scottish existence, mark
the vitality of a country and a people whose way of life is being
subsumed, the book and the rest of the trilogy refute every
-ism a reader might apply in exactly the way the folk-voice
characterises the figure of Faith in the stained-glass windows of
the kirk in the opening Prelude: 'One of the queans was Faith,
and faith she looked a daft-like keek for she was lifting up her
hands and her eyes like a heifer choked on a turnip' (p. 16).
Faith lies, instead, in the turn of phrase that takes Faith's capital
F away and makes it a marker of common voice: 'and faith she
looked . . .'

'I am a jingo patriot of planet earth: "Humanity right or
wrong!"'[13] he wrote, in an essay called 'The Land', and for all
the romanticised critical lauding of soil or Land in *Sunset Song*,
and of Gibbon's supposed rural idyllising of it throughout his
work, land in his writing most often simply means clay, and
clay most often comes to mean the very people who work the
earth and have worked it over the centuries, so that the earth
itself is a stratification of the lives of the lost individuals who
lived briefly on its surfaces.

So much of Chris's own adolescent consciousness is con-
cerned with the brevity of life, what it's like to live, to have a
feeling-and-thinking body, and to know that, however imposs-
ible it seems, too soon she herself, along with every 'you' there's
ever been in the world, will be 'dead and still under grass, down
in the earth that smelt so fine and you'd never smell . . . seeing
never again the lowe of burning whins or hearing the North
Sea thunder beyond the hills' (p. 55).

Sunset Song's considerable political force lies in its being a
narrative which creates and makes vividly alive an individual
and a community of like individuals – and then demonstrates
the decimation of that life, that community. This is at its strong-
est when, at the end of the novel, Gibbon shows us the war-lost
names, carved in the standing stone, of characters with whom
the reader has closely shared the story. It poignantly recalls,
and provides a whole new perspective on, Chris and Ewan's
first 'romantic' afternoon at Dunottar Castle earlier in the novel
and the anonymous names which Chris sees carved in the

Covenanting memorial there. The history and brevity of these lives, the unknowability of these people – once, it's inferred, as local and knowable as the reader has 'known' Long Rob, Chae Strachan and Ewan Tavendale – is at the heart of *Sunset Song*'s lament.

'Yes, horrors do haunt me,' Gibbon wrote to his friend Helen Cruickshank on the subject of his (English-persona-authored) historical novel, *Spartacus* (1933):

> That's because I'm in love with humanity. Ancient Greece is never the Parthenon to me: it's a slave being tortured in a dungeon of the Athenian law-courts; Ancient Egypt is never the Pyramids: it's the blood and tears of Goshen; Ancient Scotland is never Mary Queen; it's those serfs they kept chained in the Fifeshire mines a hundred years ago.[14]

This book gives history back to the individuals whose lives history took. Coolly conceived, coolly achieved, it gives voice and hot-blooded life back to the lost anonymous.

Gibbon thought of himself as 'a revolutionary writer',[15] and he was. He politically questioned and redressed the power of literature. He wrote at a time of great historical upheaval, directly addressing the upheaval, and in recording both place and time he reinvigorated language and genre. He created a language whose blend of artifice and authenticity and whose lyrical achievement are still unparalleled in British writing. He invented a means to display a kind of democracy of voice – many voices held in the one voice – and this dilemma of multivocality still resonates in the preoccupations and narrative voice play of most modern Scottish (and not just Scottish) fiction today.

He wrote cunningly original and gripping fiction which took both contemporary history and fiction apart and, rather than dating, seems to have strengthened, to have become more versatile and adaptable over time.

Sunset Song, wrenchingly moving, ingeniously conceived and above all humane, sets up the multiplicities and paradoxes of a single self against the foulness and inevitability of a simplifying and belittling history. It is a balance of life force and bleakness, kindness and harshness. It is a ceremony of endings and loss. But – and this is only part of its studied kindness – *Sunset Song* is, after all, about beginnings. This vital, visceral book, 'perhaps the first really Scottish novel' and one so preoccupied with the ends of things, will always embody all the potency of beginnings and brings this potency back to raging life every time it is read or reread.

Ali Smith

NOTES

1. Hugh MacDiarmid, *Selected Essays*, ed. Duncan Glen (London: Cape, 1969), p. 190.

2. *Kirriemuir Free Press*, 28 October 1932, quoted in *Leslie Mitchell: Lewis Grassic Gibbon* by Ian S. Munro (Edinburgh: Oliver & Boyd, 1966), p. 76.

3. See '"Women's Time": Reading the Quair as a Feminist Text' by Alison Lumsden, in *A Flame in the Mearns: Lewis Grassic Gibbon, A Centenary Celebration*, ed. Margery Palmer McCulloch and Sarah M. Dunnigan (Glasgow: Association for Scottish Literary Studies, 2003). This collection of essays is full of tremendously useful responses to Gibbon, including a sharp re-reading of his female protagonist in comparison with those created by his much less feted contemporaries, Nan Shepherd and Willa Muir, in 'Gibbon's Chris: A Celebration with some Reservations' by Isobel Murray.

4. Letter from George Malcolm Thomson to Helen Cruickshank, 17 August 1932, quoted in Munro, *Leslie Mitchell*, p. 74.

5. Munro, *Leslie Mitchell*, p. 99.

6. Lewis Grassic Gibbon, 'Literary Lights', *Smeddum: A Lewis Grassic Gibbon Anthology*, ed. Valentina Bold (Edinburgh: Canongate, 2001), p. 126.

7. Gibbon, 'Glasgow', *Smeddum*, p. 107.

8. 'Literary Lights', *Smeddum*, p. 125.

9. Ibid., p. 135.

10. Gibbon, 'The Land', *Smeddum*, p. 85. See Prelude, note 35.

11. Letter from Gibbon to *Left Review*, *Smeddum*, p. 739.

12. 'Glasgow', *Smeddum*, pp. 101–2.
13. 'The Land', *Smeddum*, p. 95.
14. Letter from Gibbon to Helen Cruickshank, 18 November 1933, National Library of Scotland, MS 26109.
15. Letter to *Left Review*, *Smeddum*, p. 738.

Further Reading

The remaining volumes in Lewis Grassic Gibbon's *A Scots Quair*, *Cloud Howe* (1933) and *Grey Granite* (1934), which follow Chris Guthrie's life, are essential reading. They are available in paperbacks, edited by Tom Crawford (Edinburgh: Canongate, 1989, 1990). There is a single-volume edition of the trilogy (Canongate, 1995). In 2006, Polygon (Edinburgh) published *Sunset Song*, edited by Ian Campbell, singly and in the whole trilogy, as part of their exhaustive Lewis Grassic Gibbon series.

Gibbon's stories and essays from *Scottish Scene* (1934) are collected in *Smeddum: A Lewis Grassic Gibbon Anthology*, ed. Valentina Bold (Canongate, 2001). This also includes the fiction fragment of 'The Speak of the Mearns', unpublished in his lifetime, as well as selected synopses and manuscripts, poetry, essays and early Mitchell short stories. A more concise collection of Gibbon's fiction and non-fiction is *The Speak of the Mearns*, ed. Ian Campbell (Polygon, 1994).

Polygon plans to bring Gibbon's complete published works back into print. Most noteworthy is *Spartacus* (1933), his highly politicised reconstruction of the slave revolt from the first century BC, and his first two novels, published under his own name of J. Leslie Mitchell, *Stained Radiance* (1930) and *The Thirteenth Disciple* (1931).

Major critical works on Gibbon include Ian S. Munro's workmanlike biography *Leslie Mitchell: Lewis Grassic Gibbon* (Edinburgh: Oliver & Boyd, 1966), my comprehensive critical study *A Blasphemer & Reformer: A Study of James Leslie Mitchell / Lewis Grassic Gibbon* (Aberdeen: Aberdeen University Press, 1984), and Ian Campbell's succinct monograph *Lewis Grassic Gibbon* (Edinburgh: Scottish Academic Press, 1985).

Cairns Craig sensitively places Gibbon within a modern Scottish literary context in *The Modern Scottish Novel: Narrative and the National Imagination* (Edinburgh: Edinburgh University Press, 1999), while sympathetic treatments of his achievement within a broader cultural context are provided by Valentine Cunningham in *British Writers of the Thirties* (Oxford: Oxford University Press, 1988), and by H. Gustav Klaus in *The Literature of Labour: 200 Years of Working Class Writing* (Brighton: Harvester Press, 1985). The most reliable contemporary analyses of Scottish history are Christopher Harvie's *No Gods and Precious Few Heroes: Twentieth-Century Scotland* (London: Edward Arnold, 1987) and T. M. Devine's *The Scottish Nation 1700–2000* (London: Penguin Books, 1999).

Among the wealth of criticism generated by Gibbon's writing, there is a useful collection of essays, published to commemorate the centenary of his birth, *A Flame in the Mearns: Lewis Grassic Gibbon, A Centenary Celebration* (Glasgow: Association for Scottish Literary Studies, 2003), ed. Margery Palmer McCulloch and Sarah M. Dunnigan, which includes a full primary bibliography of Gibbon's published works by Hamish Whyte.

A comprehensive listing of secondary criticism, regularly updated, is available on the website of The Grassic Gibbon Centre at Arbuthnott, at www.grassicgibbon.com. The Centre, which has a permanent display and mounts temporary exhibitions related to his life and work, publishes a twice-yearly newsletter exploring contemporary issues concerning the author.

Note on the Text

The text used for this Penguin Classics edition of *Sunset Song* is the first edition (cheaper edition, September 1933) published by Jarrolds in London in August 1932, with a few minor emendations.

The first edition is substantially free of the misprints that crept into subsequent editions published by Jarrolds, including the 1937 Jackdaw paperback and the 1946 and 1950 resettings for the single volumes of the trilogy *A Scots Quair*. The 1950 text is bowdlerised, including the silent removal of the tink's crude sexual boast to Chris in the barn in Drilling. These accidental and deliberate distortions continue to be found in some recent editions.

The American history of *Sunset Song* has some infelicities. While the first edition published by the Century Company in New York in 1933 corrects punctuation and spelling errors that slipped through in the first edition, it excised some of the more sexually explicit references (see Seed-Time, note 1 in the Notes).

Details of the principal textual variants of the trilogy can be found in Jeremy Idle, 'The Bowdlerisation of Lewis Grassic Gibbon's *A Scots Quair*', *Bibliotheck*, 17 (1990/91), pp. 63–9.

The 75 page fragment of Gibbon's original typescript for *Sunset Song*, with his papers in the National Library of Scotland (NLS MS26040), are made up of the end of the Prelude, the opening of Ploughing and the end of Harvest, and the end of the Epilude, with a further 5 pages surviving on the versos of a typescript in MS26052, from the middle of Ploughing. The extant pages confirm the reliability of the first edition, very much in keeping with the author's efficient and accurate working methods which produced typescripts requiring minimal revision. Indeed, the typescript reveals that the Jarrolds typesetting perpetuates verbatim the rare slips in Gibbon's own typing. Of the 80 pages that survive of Gibbon's original 412-page typescript, 39 are identical to the published text. The author's own distinctive ink revisions are evident throughout, usually picking up typing errors, in spacing and in spelling, indicating that this was the first completed version as Gibbon composed it, at white heat, directly on to his typewriter, duly revised before delivery to the publisher. The changes made to the final published text are judicious, if relatively minor in character, generally polishing punctuation and syntax and tightening expression. Of the 68 changes made in the first edition of the novel from the extant typescript – presumably at Gibbon's behest – 24 are the substitution of more felicitous words or phrases, 14 minor revisions in punctuation, 12 the deletion of extraneous words, 9 the addition of fresh words, 7 spelling changes, and 1 removes italicisation, with 1 further change to the author's word order.

While preparatory notes for the subsequent volumes of the trilogy exist in both handwritten and typed form, none remains for *Sunset Song* beyond Gibbon's sketch of the topography of Kinraddie (see Maps) and his insertion of the three fictive locales for the trilogy in the John Bartholomew map, as described in Prelude, note 1 in the Notes. Gibbon's intention to provide a definitive revised single-volume edition of the trilogy, as reported in his letter of 19 November 1934 to fellow novelist Neil M. Gunn (NLS Dep. 209), was left unfulfilled.

Gibbon's style strays idiosyncratically from grammatical orthodoxy, but obvious errors in spelling and punctuation have been emended and lapses in consistency have been standardised within the present text, as recorded below. Where readings are adopted from his typescript, the source is given (TS). In five instances the first edition lacks a word – a preposition, an article, an incomplete verb – and these have been supplied in square brackets. Line endings are indicated by an oblique stroke. (A few typesetting problems of broken letters and spacing that did not affect meaning are not recorded, e.g. 'heardof'.)

Page:line number	Penguin	1st edition
18:20	*give*	*gave*
18:23	well liked	well-liked
23:34	gowkèd-like	gowkéd-like
25:5	everybody	every body
25:28	shown	show
28:29	forgot	forget
29:29	concert [from]	concert
36:34	everybody	every body
37:10	she'd	she's
37:32	ploughing match	ploughing-match
39:5	then	then,
39:22	the herds (TS)	herds
40:12	oat-cake	oatcake
46:28	carts,	carts
46:29	harvest-home,	harvest-home
49:9	find	fine
50:10	*you've*	*you're*
55:9	evening,	evening
62:1	chance [for]	chance
68:9	maybe	maybe'd
69:4	her,	her
76:38	its	it's
78:20	been [for]	been
87:14	They	They they
88:19	*Drumlithie–Galt*	*Drumlithie-Galt*
90:18	kitchen door	kitchen-door
93:3	Auchinblae	Auchenblae
93:29	collie	colie
95:11	over-young	over young
95:30	bare-footed	barefooted
105:7	Gourdon	Gourdon;
105:25	began	begun
106:6	see	seeing
107:34	then	than
126:2	over-old	over old
127:26	train	trains
129:31	*Yes, just that;*	Yes, just that;

130:21	11.00	11.0
131:29	led	lead
132:4	besiegers	beseigers
132:25	XI	II
134:16	sleekèd	sleekéd
135:26	over-young	over young
135:27	over-many	over many
137:25	Mains –	Mains,—
142:24	should [be]	should
147:6	*memento*	*momento*
150:16	*won't*	*wont*
150:29	kin	kiln
154:10	cart-shaft	cartshaft
154:25	than	then
155:11	liked	like
159:6	over-bright	over bright
161:2	over-much	over much
162:6	kin	kiln
164:8	of	off
166:7	Sunday best	Sunday-best
166:35	*with all* (TS)	*with*
167:6	*your*	*you're*
172:1	kitchen door	kitchen-door
174:2	*Your*	*You're*
174:23	outgoing	out-going
175:13	fog-horn	foghorn
175:34	larch wood (TS)	larch-wood
177:31	larch woods (TS)	larch-woods
179:8	though (TS)	though,
179:22	again and (TS)	again, and
179:22	again, and (TS)	again
179:37	from off (TS)	from
179:38	fog-horn	foghorn
180:1	drookèd	drookéd
180:16	shining (TS)	shining,
181:4	things (TS)	thing
181:6	her again, (TS)	her,
189:9	iron-blue	iron blue

193:24	nearby	near-by
194:23	*wait down* (TS)	*wait*
194:26	*it's*	*its*
194:36	farmhouse (TS)	farm-house
195:7	night-gown	nightgown
206:27	his	this
210:29	forever	fore-/ ever
211:8	over-much	over much
211:15	near-cut	near cut
218:29	*over-much*	*over much*
219:7	Mollie's	Molly's
219:10	Mollie	Molly
219:24	Mollie	Molly
219:37	*Mollie*	*Molly*
223:26	*over-much*	*over much*
224:3	Auchinblae	Auchenblae
229:8	*like* [*a*]	*like*
238:10	there	their
241:37	*happèd*	*happéd*
248:21	public house	public-house
249:6	over-much	overmuch
261:2	[musical notation correct]	[musical notation upside-down]

The last two lines of the musical notation for 'The Flowers of the Forest' (p. 262) were originally printed upside-down, and escaped correction by Gibbon at proof stage. He freely owned his responsibility for this oversight, confessing to his friend James Barke in 1933: 'So *that* was why you didn't like the Flowers of the Forest version in Sunset Song – you know something about these things. Me – nix' (letter dated 11 May 1933, Mitchell/ Gibbon papers, Mitchell Library, Glasgow). (The upside-down lines are found in all reprints until the 1971 Longman version.)

House styling has been applied to dashes (spaced N-dashes for the first edition's heavier, longer M-dash) and regular spacing of ligatures ('ae' for 'æ').

Grateful acknowledgement is made to Mrs Rhea Martin, Alasdair Barke, Edinburgh University Library, the Harry Ransom Humanities Research Center at the University of Texas at Austin, the Mitchell Library in Glasgow and the Trustees of the National Library of Scotland in Edinburgh for granting permission to cite manuscript work by James Leslie Mitchell / Lewis Grassic Gibbon in this edition. Grateful thanks are due also to Lindeth Vasey for providing expert and informed advice in editing the present volume.

Sunset Song

A Novel

A Note

If the great Dutch language disappeared from literary usage and a Dutchman wrote in German a story of the Lekside peasants, one may hazard he would ask and receive a certain latitude and forbearance in his usage of German. He might import into his pages some score or so untranslatable words and idioms – untranslatable except in their context and setting; he might mould in some fashion his German[1] to the rhythms and cadence of the kindred speech that his peasants speak. Beyond that, in fairness to his hosts, he hardly could go: to seek effect by a spray of apostrophes would be both impertinence and mistranslation.

The courtesy that the hypothetical Dutchman might receive from German a Scot may invoke from the great English tongue.

L. G. G.

Contents

PRELUDE

THE UNFURROWED FIELD 9

THE SONG

  I PLOUGHING   35
  II DRILLING   72
 III SEED-TIME 114
 IV HARVEST   186

EPILUDE

THE UNFURROWED FIELD 247

THE PRELUDE

PRELUDE

The Unfurrowed Field

Kinraddie lands[1] had been won by a Norman childe, Cospatric de Gondeshil, in the days of William the Lyon, when gryphons[2] and such-like beasts still roamed the Scots countryside and folk would waken in their beds to hear the children screaming, with a great wolf-beast, come through the hide window, tearing at their throats. In the Den of Kinraddie one such beast had its lair and by day it lay about the woods and the stench of it was awful to smell all over the countryside, and at gloaming a shepherd would see it, with its great wings half-folded across the great belly of it and its head, like the head of a meikle cock, but with the ears of a lion, poked over a fir tree, watching. And it ate up sheep and men and women and was a fair terror, and the King had his heralds cry a reward to whatever knight would ride and end the mischieving of the beast. So the Norman childe, Cospatric, that was young and landless and fell brave and well-armoured, mounted his horse in Edinburgh Town and came North, out of the foreign south parts, up through the Forest of Fife and into the pastures of Forfar and past Aberlemno's Meikle Stane[3] that was raised when the Picts beat the Danes; and by it he stopped and looked at the figures, bright then and hardly faded even now, of the horses and the charging and the rout of those coarse foreign folk. And maybe he said a bit prayer by that Stone and then he rode into the Mearns, and the story tells no more of his riding but that at last come he did to Kinraddie, a tormented place, and they told him where the gryphon slept, down there in the Den of Kinraddie.

But in the daytime it hid in the woods and only at night, by a path through the hornbeams, might he come at it, squatting in bones, in its lair. And Cospatric waited for the night to come and rode to the edge of Kinraddie Den and commended his soul to God and came off his horse and took his boar-spear in his hand, and went down into the Den and killed the gryphon. And he sent the news to William the Lyon, sitting drinking the wine and fondling his bonny lemans in Edinburgh Town, and William made him the Knight of Kinraddie, and gave to him all the wide parish as his demesne and grant to build him a castle there, and wear the sign of a gryphon's head for a crest and keep down all beasts and coarse and wayward folk, him and the issue of his body for ever after.

So Cospatric got him the Pict folk to build a strong castle there in the lithe of the hills, with the Grampians[4] bleak and dark behind it, and he had the Den drained and he married a Pict lady and got on her bairns and he lived there till he died. And his son took the name Kinraddie, and looked out one day from the castle wall and saw the Earl Marischal come marching up from the south to join the Highlandmen in the battle that was fought at Mondynes,[5] where now the meal-mill stands; and he took out his men and fought there, but on which side they do not say, but maybe it was the winning one, they were aye gey and canny folk, the Kinraddies. And the great-grandson of Cospatric, he joined the English against the cateran Wallace,[6] and when Wallace next came marching up from the southlands Kinraddie and other noble folk of that time they got them into Dunnottar Castle that stands out in the sea beyond Kinneff,[7] well-builded and strong, and the sea splashes about it in the high tides and there the din of the gulls is a yammer night and day. Much of meal and meat and gear they took with them, and they laid themselves up there right strongly, they and their carles, and wasted all the Mearns that the Cateran who dared rebel against the fine English king might find no provision for his army of coarse and landless men. But Wallace came through the Howe right swiftly and he heard of Dunnottar and laid siege to it and it was a right strong place and he had but small patience with strong places. So, in the dead of one night, when the thunder of the sea drowned the noise of his feint, he climbed the Dunnottar rocks and was over the wall, he and the vagabond

Scots, and they took Dunnottar and put to the slaughter the
noble folk gathered there, and all the English, and spoiled them
of their meat and gear, and marched away.

Kinraddie Castle that year, they tell, had but a young bride
new home and she had no issue of her body, and the months
went by and she rode to the Abbey of Aberbrothock[8] where the
good Abbot, John, was her cousin, and told him of her trouble
and how the line of Kinraddie was like to die. So he lay with
her, that was September, and next year a boy was born to the
young bride, and after that the Kinraddies paid no heed to wars
and bickerings but sat them fast in their Castle lithe in the hills,
with their gear and bonny leman queans and villeins libbed for
service.

And when the First Reformation came and others came after
it and some folk cried *Whiggam!* and some cried *Rome!* and
some cried *The King!*[9] the Kinraddies sat them quiet and decent
and peaceable in their castle, and heeded never a fig the arguings
of folk, for wars were unchancy things. But then Dutch William
came, fair plain a fixture that none would move, and the Kinraddies were all for the Covenant[10] then, they had aye had
God's Covenant at heart, they said. So they builded a new kirk
down where the chapel had stood, and builded a manse by it,
there in the hiddle of the yews where the cateran Wallace had
hid when the English put him to rout at last. And one Kinraddie,
John Kinraddie, went south and became a great man in the
London court, and was crony of the creatures Johnson and
James Boswell;[11] and once the two of them, John Kinraddie and
James Boswell, came up to the Mearns on an idle ploy and sat
drinking wine and making coarse talk far into the small hours
night after night till the old laird wearied of them and then they
would steal away and as James Boswell set in his diary, *Did get
to the loft where the maids were, and one* Πεγγί Δυνδας ωας
φατ ιν τηε βυττοςκς ανδ I διδ λιε ωιτη ηερ.

But in the early days of the nineteenth century it was an ill
time for the Scots gentry, for the poison of the French Revolution came over the seas and crofters and common folk like
that stood up and cried *Away to hell!* when the Auld Kirk
preached submission from its pulpits. Up as far as Kinraddie

came the poison and the young laird of that time, and he was Kenneth, he called himself a Jacobin and joined the Jacobin Club of Aberdeen and there at Aberdeen was nearly killed in the rioting, for liberty and equality and fraternity,[12] he called it. And they carried him back to Kinraddie a cripple, but he would still have it that all men were free and equal and he set to selling the estate and sending the money to France, for he had a real good heart. And the crofters marched on Kinraddie Castle in a body and bashed in the windows of it, they thought equality should begin at home.

More than half the estate had gone in this driblet and that while the cripple sat and read his coarse French books; but nobody guessed that till he died and then his widow, poor woman, found herself own no more than the land that lay between the coarse hills, the Grampians, and the farms that stood out by the Bridge End above the Denburn, straddling the outward road. Maybe there were some twenty to thirty holdings in all, the crofters dour folk of the old Pict stock,[13] they had no history, common folk, and ill-reared their biggings clustered and chaved amid the long, sloping fields. The leases were one-year, two-year, you worked from the blink of the day you were breeked to the flicker of the night they shrouded you, and the dirt of gentry sat and ate up your rents but you were as good as they were. So that was Kenneth's leaving to his lady body, she wept right sore over the pass that things had come to, but they kittled up before her own jaw was tied in a clout and they put her down in Kinraddie vault to lie by the side of her man. Three of her bairns were drowned at sea, fishing off the Bervie braes they had been, but the fourth, the boy Cospatric, him that died the same day as the Old Queen,[14] he was douce and saving and sensible, and set putting the estate to rights. He threw out half the little tenants, they flitted off to Canada and Dundee[15] and parts like those, the others he couldn't move but slowly. But on the cleared land he had bigger steadings built and he let them at bigger rents and longer leases, he said the day of the fine big farm had come. And he had woods of fir and larch and pine planted to shield the long, bleak slopes, and might well have retrieved the Kinraddie fortunes but that he married a Morton quean with black blood in her, she smitted him and drove him to drink and death, that was the best way out. For his son was clean daft, they locked him up at last in an asylum, and that was the end of Kinraddie family, the Meikle House that stood where the Picts had builded Cospatric's castle crumbled to bits like a cheese, all but two-three rooms the trustees held as their offices, the estate was mortgaged to the hilt[16] by then.

So by the winter of nineteen eleven there were no more than nine bit places left the Kinraddie estate, the Mains the biggest of them, it had been the Castle home farm in the long past times. An Irish creature, Erbert Ellison was the name, ran the place for the trustees, he said, but if you might believe all the stories you heard he ran a hantle more silver into his own pouch than he ran into theirs. Well might you expect it, for once he'd been no more than a Dublin waiter, they said. That had been in the time before Lord Kinraddie, the daft one, had gone clean skite. He had been in Dublin, Lord Kinraddie, on some drunken ploy, and Ellison had brought his whisky for him and some said he had halved his bed with him. But folk would say anything. So the daftie took Ellison back with him to Kinraddie and made him his servant, and sometimes, when he was real drunk and the fairlies came sniftering out of the whisky bottles at him, he would throw a bottle at Ellison and shout *Get out, you bloody dish-clout!* so loud it was heard across at the Manse and fair affronted the minister's wife. And old Greig, him that had been the last minister there, he would glower across at Kinraddie House like John Knox at Holyrood, and say that God's hour would come. And sure as death it did, off to the asylum they hurled the daftie, he went with a nurse's mutch on his head and he put his head out of the back of the waggon and said *Cockadoodledoo!* to some school bairns the waggon passed on the road and they all ran home and were fell frightened.

But Ellison had made himself well acquaint with farming and selling stock and most with buying horses, so the trustees they made him manager of the Mains, and he moved into the Mains farmhouse and looked him round for a wife. Some would have nothing to do with him, a poor creature of an Irishman who couldn't speak right and didn't belong to the Kirk, but Ella White she was not so particular and was fell long in the tooth herself. So when Ellison came to her at the harvest ball in Auchinblae and cried *Can I see you home to-night, me dear?* she said *Och, Ay.* And on the road home they lay among the stooks and maybe Ellison did this and that to make sure of getting her, he was fair desperate for any woman by then. They were married next New Year's Day, and Ellison had begun to think himself a gey man in Kinraddie, and maybe one of the gentry. But the bothy billies, the ploughmen and the orra men of the Mains, they'd never a care for gentry except to mock at them and on the eve of Ellison's wedding they took him as he was going into his house and took off his breeks and tarred his dowp and the soles of his feet and stuck feathers on them and then they threw him into the water-trough, as was the custom. And he called them *Bloody Scotch savages*, and was in an awful rage and at the term-time he had them sacked, the whole jing-bang of them, so sore affronted he had been.

But after that he got on well enough, him and his mistress, Ella White, and they had a daughter, a scrawny bit quean they thought over good to go to the Auchinblae School, so off she went to Stonehaven Academy[17] and was taught to be right brave and swing about in the gymnasium there with wee black breeks on under her skirt. Ellison himself began to get well-stomached, and he had a red face, big and sappy, and eyes like a cat, green eyes, and his mouser hung down each side of a fair bit mouth that was chokeful up of false teeth, awful expensive and bonny, lined with bits of gold. And he aye wore leggings and riding breeks, for he was fair gentry by then; and when he would meet a crony at a mart he would cry *Sure, bot it's you, thin, ould chep!* and the billy would redden up, real ashamed, but wouldn't dare say anything, for he wasn't a man you'd offend. In politics he said he was a Conservative but everybody in Kinraddie knew that meant he was a Tory and the bairns of Strachan, him that farmed the Peesie's Knapp, they would scraich out

Inky poo, your nose is blue,
You're awful like the Turra Coo![18]

whenever they saw Ellison go by. For he'd sent a subscription
to the creature up Turriff way whose cow had been sold to pay
his Insurance, and folk said it was no more than a show off,
the Cow creature and Ellison both; and they laughed at him
behind his back.

So that was the Mains, below the Meikle House, and Ellison
farmed it in his Irish way and right opposite, hidden away
among their yews, were kirk and manse,[19] the kirk an old,
draughty place and in the winter-time, right in the middle of
the Lord's Prayer, maybe, you'd hear an outbreak of hoasts fit
to lift off the roof, and Miss Sarah Sinclair, her that came
from Netherhill and played the organ, she'd sneeze into her
hymn-book and miss her bit notes and the minister, him that
was the old one, he'd glower down at her more like John Knox
than ever. Next door the kirk was an olden tower, built in the
time of the Roman Catholics, the coarse creatures, and it was
fell old and wasn't used any more except by the cushat-doves
and they flew in and out the narrow slits in the upper storey
and nested there all the year round and the place was fair
white with their dung. In the lower half of the tower was
an effigy-thing of Cospatric de Gondeshil, him that killed the
gryphon, lying on his back with his arms crossed and a daft-like
simper on his face; and the spear he killed the gryphon with
was locked in a kist there, or so some said, but others said it
was no more than an old bit heuch from the times of Bonny
Prince Charlie.[20] So that was the tower, but it wasn't fairly a
part of the kirk, the real kirk was split in two bits, the main
hall and the wee hall, and some called them the byre and the
turnip-shed, and the pulpit stood midway. Once the wee hall
had been for the folk from the Meikle House and their guests
and such-like gentry but nearly anybody that had the face went
ben and sat there now, and the elders sat with the collection
bags, and young Murray, him that blew the organ for Sarah
Sinclair. It had fine glass windows, awful old, the wee hall, with

three bit creatures of queans, not very decent-like in a kirk, as
window-pictures. One of the queans was Faith, and faith she
looked a daft-like keek for she was lifting up her hands and her
eyes like a heifer choked on a turnip and the bit blanket round
her shoulders was falling off her but she didn't seem to heed,
and there was a swither of scrolls and fiddley-faddles all about
her. And the second quean was Hope and she was near as unco
as Faith, but had right bonny hair, red hair, though maybe
you'd call it auburn, and in the winter-time the light in the
morning service would come splashing through the yews in the
kirkyard and into the wee hall through the red hair of Hope.
And the third quean was Charity, with a lot of naked bairns at
her feet and she looked a fine and decent-like woman, for all
that she was tied about with such daft-like clouts.

But the windows of the main hall, though they were coloured,
they had never a picture in them and there were no pictures
in there at all, who wanted them? Only coarse creatures like
Catholics wanted a kirk to look like a grocer's calendar. So it
was decent and bare-like, with its carved old seats, some were
cushioned and some were not, if you weren't padded by nature
and had the silver to spend you might put in cushions to suit
your fancy. Right up in the lithe of the pulpit, at angles-like to
the rest of the kirk, were the three seats where the choir sat and
led the hymn-singing; and some called it the calfies' stall.

The back door, that behind the pulpit, led out across the
kirkyard to the Manse and its biggings, set up in the time of
the Old Queen, and fair bonny to look at, but awful damp said
all the ministers' wives. But ministers' wives were aye folk to
complain and don't know when they're well off, them and the
silver they get for their bit creatures of men preaching once or
twice a Sunday and so proud they hardly know you when they
meet you on the road. The minister's study was high up in the
house, it looked out over all Kinraddie, at night he'd see from
there the lights of the farmhouses like a sprinkling of bright
sands below his window and the flagstaff light high among the
stars on the roof of the Meikle House. But that nineteen eleven
December the Manse was empty and had been empty for many
a month, the old minister was dead and the new one not yet

voted on; and the ministers from Drumlithie and Arbuthnott and Laurencekirk they came time about in the Sunday fore-noons and took the service there at Kinraddie; and God knows for all they had to say they might well have bidden at home.

But if you went out of the kirk by the main door and took the road east a bit, and that was the road that served kirk and Manse and Mains, you were on to the turnpike then. It ran north and south but opposite to the road you'd just come down was another, that went through Kinraddie by the Bridge End farm. So there was a cross-roads there and if you held to the left along the turnpike you came to Peesie's Knapp, one of the olden places, no more than a croft of thirty-forty acres with some rough ground for pasture, but God knows there was little pasture on it, it was just a fair schlorich of whins and broom and dirt, full up of rabbits and hares it was, they came out at night and ate up your crops and sent a body fair mad. But it wasn't bad land the most of the Knapp, there was the sweat of two thousand years in it, and the meikle park behind the biggings was black loam, not the red clay that sub-soiled half Kinraddie.

Now Peesie's Knapp's biggings were not more than twenty years old, but gey ill-favoured for all that, for though the house faced on the road – and that was fair handy if it didn't scunner you that you couldn't so much as change your sark without some ill-fashioned brute gowking in at you – right between the byre and the stable and the barn on one side and the house on the other was the cattle-court and right in the middle of that the midden, high and yellow with dung and straw and sharn, and Mistress Strachan could never forgive Peesie's Knapp because of that awful smell it had. But Chae Strachan, him that farmed the place, he just said *Hoots, what's a bit guff?* and would start to tell of the terrible smells he'd smelt when he was abroad. For he'd been a fell wandering billy, Chae, in the days before he came back to Scotland and was fee'd his last fee[21] at Netherhill. He'd been in Alaska, looking for gold there, but damn the bit of gold he'd seen, so he'd farmed in California till he was so scunnered of fruit he'd never look an orange or a pear in the face again, not even in a tin. And then he'd gone on to South Africa and had had great times there, growing real chief-like with the head one of a tribe of blacks, but an awful decent man for all that. Him and Chae had fought against Boers[22] and British both, and beaten them, or so Chae said, but folk that didn't like Chae said all the fighting he'd ever done had been with his mouth and that as for beaten, he'd be sore made to beat the skin off a bowl of sour milk.

For he wasn't well liked by them that set themselves up for gentry, Chae, being a socialist creature[23] and believing we should all have the same amount of silver and that there shouldn't be rich and poor and that one man was as good as another. And the silver bit of that was clean daft, of course, for if you'd all the same money one day what would it be the next? – Rich and Poor again! But Chae said the four ministers of Kinraddie and Auchinblae and Laurencekirk and Drumlithie were all paid much the same money last year and what had they this year? – Much the same money still! *You'll have to get out of bed slippy in the morning before you find a socialist tripping and if you give me any of your lip I'll clout you in the lug, my mannie.* So Chae was fell good in argy-bargying and he wasn't the quarrelsome kind except when roused, so he was well liked, though folk laughed at him. But God knows, who is it they don't laugh at? He was a pretty man, well upstanding, with great shoulders on him and his hair was fair and fine and he had a broad brow and a gey bit coulter of a nose and he twisted his mouser ends up with wax like that creature the German Kaiser,[24] and he could stop a running stirk by the horns, so strong he was in the wrist-bones. And he was one of the handiest billies in Kinraddie, he would libb a calf or break in a horse or kill a pig, all in a jiffy, or tile your dairy or cut the bairns' hair or dig a well, and all the time he'd be telling you that socialism was coming or if it wasn't then an awful crash would come and we'd all go back to savagery, *Damn't ay, man!*

But folk said he'd more need to start socialising Mistress Strachan, her that had been Kirsty Sinclair of Netherhill, before he began on anybody else. She had a fell tongue, they said, that would clip clouts and yammer a tink from a door, and if Chae

wasn't fair sick now and then for his hut and a fine black quean
in South Africa damn the hut or the quean had he ever had.
He'd fee'd at Netherhill when he came back from foreign parts,
had Chae, and there had been but two daughters there, Kirsty
and Sarah, her that played the kirk organ. Both were wearing
on a bit, sore in the need of a man, and Kirsty with a fair
let-down as it was, for it had seemed that a doctor billy from
Aberdeen was out to take up with her. So he had done and left
her in a gey way and her mother, old Mistress Sinclair, near
went out of her mind with the shame of it when Kirsty began
to cry and tell her the news. Now that was about the term-time
and home to Netherhill from the feeing market who should old
Sinclair of Netherhill bring but Chae Strachan, with his blood
warmed up from living in those foreign parts and an eye for
less than a wink of invitation? But even so he was gey slow to
get on with the courting and just hung around Kirsty like a
futret round a trap with a bit meat in it, not sure if the meat
was worth the risk; and the time was getting on and faith!
something drastic would have to be done. So one night after
they had all had supper in the kitchen and old Sinclair had gone
pleitering out to the byres, old Mistress Sinclair had up and
nodded to Kirsty and said *Ah well, I'll away to my bed. You'll
not be long in making for yours, Kirsty?* And Kirsty said No,
and gave her mother a sly bit look, and off the old mistress
went up to her room and then Kirsty began fleering and flirting
with Chae and he was a man warm enough and they were alone
together and maybe in a minute he'd have had her couched
down right well there in the kitchen but she whispered it wasn't
safe. So he off with his boots and she with hers and up the
stairs they crept together into Kirsty's room and were having
their bit pleasure together when *ouf!* went the door and in burst
old Mistress Sinclair with the candle held up in one hand and
the other held up in horror. *No, no,* she'd said, *this won't do
at all, Chakie, my man, you'll have to marry her*. And there
had been no escape for Chae, poor man, with Kirsty and her
mother both glowering at him. So married they were and old
Sinclair had saved up some silver and he rented Peesie's Knapp
for Chae and Kirsty, and stocked the place for them, and down

they sat there, and Kirsty's bairn, a bit quean, was born before seven months were past, well-grown and finished-like it seemed, the creature, in spite of its mother swearing it had come fair premature.

They'd had two more bairns since then, both laddies, and both the living spit of Chae, these were the bairns that would sing about the Turra Coo whenever they met the brave gig of Ellison bowling along the Kinraddie Road, and faith, they made you laugh.

Right opposite Peesie's Knapp, across the turnpike, the land climbed red and clay and a rough stone road went wandering up to the biggings of Blawearie. *Out of the World and into Blawearie* they said in Kinraddie, and faith! it was coarse land and lonely up there on the brae, fifty-sixty acres of it, forbye the moor that went on with the brae high above Blawearie, up to a great flat hill-top where lay a bit loch that nested snipe by the hundred; and some said there was no bottom to it, the loch, and Long Rob of the Mill said that made it like the depths of a parson's depravity. That was an ill thing to say about any minister, though Rob said it was an ill thing to say about any loch, but there the spleiter of water was, a woesome dark stretch fringed rank with rushes and knife-grass; and the screeching of the snipe fair deafened you if you stood there of an evening. And few enough did that for nearby the bit loch was a circle of stones from olden times, some were upright and some were flat and some leaned this way and that, and right in the middle three big ones clambered up out of the earth and stood askew with flat, sonsy faces, they seemed to listen and wait. They were Druid stones[25] and folk told that the Druids had been coarse devils of men in the times long syne, they'd climb up there and sing their foul heathen songs around the stones; and if they met a bit Christian missionary they'd gut him as soon as look at him. And Long Rob of the Mill would say what Scotland wanted was a return of the Druids, but that was just a speak of his, for they must have been awful ignorant folk, not canny.

Blawearie hadn't had a tenant for nearly a year, but now there was one on the way, they said, a creature John Guthrie from up in the North. The biggings of it stood fine and compact one side of the close, the midden was back of them, and across the close was the house, a fell brave house for a little place, it had three storeys and a good kitchen and a fair stretch of garden between it and Blawearie road. There were beech trees there, three of them, one was close over against the house, and the garden hedges grew as bonny with honeysuckle of a summer as ever you saw; and if you could have lived on the smell of honeysuckle you might have farmed the bit place with profit.

Well, Peesie's Knapp and Blawearie were the steadings that lay Stonehaven way. But if you turned east that winter along the Auchinblae road first on your right was Cuddiestoun, a small bit holding the size of Peesie's Knapp, and old as it, a croft from the far-off times. It lay a quarter-mile or so from the main road and its own road was fair clamjamfried with glaur from late in the harvest till the coming of Spring. Some said maybe that accounted for Munro's neck, he could never get the glaur washed out of it. But others said he never tried. He was on a thirteen years' lease there, Munro, a creature from down south, Dundee way, and he was a good six feet in height but awful coarse among the legs, like a lamb with water on the brain, and he had meikle feet that aye seemed in his way. He was maybe forty years or so in age, and bald already, and his skin was red and creased in cheeks and chin and God! you never saw an uglier brute, poor stock. For there were worse folk than Munro, though maybe they were all in the jail, and though he could blow and bombast till he fair scunnered you. He farmed his bit land in a then and now way, and it was land good enough, the most of it, with the same black streak of loam that went through the Peesie parks, but ill-drained, the old stone drains were still down and devil the move would the factor at Meikle House make to have them replaced, or mend the roof of the byre that leaked like a sieve on the head of Mistress Munro when she milked the kye on a stormy night.

But if anybody, chief-like, were to say, *God, that's an awful byre you have, mistress*, she would flare up in a minute *It's fine, and good enough for the like of us*. And if that body, not

knowing better, poor billy, were to agree that the place was
well enough for poor folk, she'd up again *Who's poor? Let me
tell you we've never needed anybody come to our help, though
we don't boast and blow about it all over the countryside, like
some I could mention.* So the body would think there was no
pleasing of the creature, and she was right well laughed at in
all Kinraddie, though not to her face. And that was a thin one
and she had black hair and snapping black eyes like a futret,
and a voice that fair set your hackles on edge when she girned.
But she was the best midwife for miles around, right often in
the middle of the night some poor distracted billy would come
chapping at her window *Mistress Munro, Mistress Munro, will
you get up and come to the wife?* And out she'd get, and into
her clothes before you could whistle, and out into the cold of
Kinraddie night and go whipping through it like a futret, and
soon be snapping her orders round the kitchen of the house
she'd been summoned to, telling the woman in childbed she
might easily be worse, and being right brisk and sharp and
clever. And the funny thing about the creature was that she
believed none spoke ill of her, for if she heard a bit hint of such,
dropped sly-like, she'd redden up like a stalk of rhubarb in a
dung patch and look as though she might start to cry, and the
body would feel real sorry for her till next minute she'd be
screeching at Andy or Tony, and fleering them out of the little
wits they had, poor devils.

Now, Andy and Tony were two dafties that Mistress Munro
had had boarded out on her from an Asylum in Dundee, they
weren't supposed to be dangerous. Andy was a meikle slummock of a creature, and his mouth was aye open, and he
dribbled like a teething foal, and his nose wabbled all over his
face and when he tried to speak it was just a fair jumble of
foolishness. He was the daftest one, but fell sly, he'd sometimes
run away to the hills and stand there with his finger at his nose,
making faces at Mistress Munro, and she'd scraich at him and
he'd yammer back at her and then over the moor he'd get to
the bothy at Upperhill where the ploughmen would give him
cigarettes and then torment him till he fair raged; and once
tried to kill one with an axe he caught up from a hackstock.

And at night he'd creep back to Cuddiestoun, outside he'd make a noise like a dog that had been kicked, and he'd snuffle round the door till the few remaining hairs on the bald pow of Munro would fair rise on end. But Mistress Munro would up and be at the door and in she'd yank Andy by the lug, and some said she'd take down his breeks and skelp him, but maybe that was a lie. She wasn't feared at him and he wasn't feared at her, so they were a gey well-matched pair.

And that was the stir at Cuddiestoun, all except Tony, for the Munros had never a bairn of their own. And Tony, though he wasn't the daftest, he was the queer one, too, right enough. He was small-bulked and had a little red beard and sad eyes, and he walked with his head down and you would feel right sorry for him for sometimes some whimsy would come on the creature, right in the middle of the turnpike it might be or half-way down a rig of swedes, and there he would stand staring like a gowk for minutes on end till somebody would shake him back to his senses. He had fine soft hands, for he was no working body; folk said he had once been a scholar and written books and learned and learned till his brain fair softened[26] and right off his head he'd gone and into the poorhouse asylum. Now Mistress Munro she'd send Tony errands to the wee shop out beyond the Bridge End, and tell him what she wanted, plain and simple-like, and maybe giving him a bit clout in the lug now and then, as you would a bairn or a daftie. And he'd listen to her and make out he minded the messages and off to the shop he'd go, and come back without a single mistake. But one day, after she'd told him the things she wanted, Mistress Munro saw the wee creature writing on a bit of paper with a pencil he'd picked up somewhere. And she took the paper from him and looked at it and turned it this way and that, but feint the thing could she make of it. So she gave him a bit clout in the lug and asked him what the writing was. But he just shook his head, real gowkèd-like, and reached out his hand for the bit of paper, but Mistress Munro would have none of that and when it was time for the Strachan bairns to pass the end of the Cuddiestoun road on their way to school down there she was waiting and gave the paper to the eldest, the quean Marget, and told her to show it to the Dominie and ask him what it might mean. And at night she was waiting for the Strachan bairns to come back and they had an envelope for her from the Dominie; and she opened it and found a note saying the writing was shorthand and that this was what it read when put in the ordinary way of writing: *Two pounds of sugar The People's Journal*[27] *half an ounce of mustard a tin of rat poison a pound of candles and I don't suppose I can swindle her out of tuppence change for the sake of a smoke, she's certainly the meanest bitch unhung this side of Tweed.* So maybe Tony wasn't so daft, but he got no supper that night; and she never asked to see his notes again.

Now, following the Kinraddie road still east, you passed by Netherhill on your left, five places had held its parks in the crofter days before Lord Kenneth. But now it was a fair bit farm on its own, old Sinclair and his wife, a body that was wearing none so well – soured up the creature was that her eldest daughter Sarah still bided all unwed – lived in the farmhouse, and in the bothy was foreman and second man and third man and orra lad. The Denburn lay back of the Netherhill, drifting low and slow and placid in its hollow, feint the fish had ever been seen in it and folk said that was just as well, things were fishy enough at Netherhill without the Denburn adding to them. Through the rank schlorich of moor that lay between the place and Peesie's Knapp were the tracks of an old-time road, some said it was old as Calgacus, him that chased the Romans all to hell at the battle of Mons Graupius,[28] others said it was a Druid work, laid by them that set the stones above Blawearie loch. And God! there must have been an unco few idle masons among the creatures, they'd tried their hands at another stone circle in the Netherhill moor, right midway the old-time road. But there were no more than two-three stones above the ground in this later day, Netherhill's ploughmen swore the rest must have been torn up and broadcast over the arable land, the parks were as tough and stony as the heart of the old wife herself.

But it was no bad place for turnips and oats, the Netherhill, sometimes the hay was fair to middling but the most of the

ground was red clay and over coarse and wet for barley, if it
hadn't been for the droves of pigs old Mistress Sinclair fed and
sold in Laurencekirk maybe her man would never have sat
where he did. She came of Gourdon stock,[29] the old wife, and
everybody knows what they are, the Gourdon fishers, they'd
wring silver out of a corpse's wame and call stinking haddocks
perfume fishes and sell them at a shilling a pair. She'd been a
fishing quean before she took up with old Sinclair, and when
they settled down in Netherhill on borrowed money it was she
that would drive to Gourdon twice a week in the little pony
lorry and come back with it stinking out the countryside for
miles around with its load of rotten fish to manure the land.
And right well it manured it and they'd fine crops the first six
years or so and then the land was fair bled white and they'd to
stop the fish-manure. But by then the pig-breeding was fine and
paying, their debts were gone, they were coining silver of their
own. He was a harmless stock, old Sinclair, and had began to
doiter and Mistress Sinclair would push him into his chair at
night and take off his boots and put slippers on him there in
front of the kitchen fire and say to him *You've tired yourself
out again, my lad.* And he'd put his hand below her chin and
say *Och, I'm fine, don't vex yourself. . . . Aye your lad still, am
I, lass?* And they'd look at each other, daft-like, two wrinkled
old fools, and their daughter Sarah that was so genteel would
be real affronted if there were visitors about. But Sinclair and
his old wife would just shake their heads at her and in their bed
at night, hiddling their old bones close for warmth, give a bit
sigh that no brave billy had ever shown inclination to take
Sarah to *his* bed. She'd hoped and peeked and preened long
years, and once there had seemed some hope with Long Rob of
the Mill, but Rob wasn't the marrying sort. God! if Cuddiestoun's dafties were real dafties what would you say of a man
with plenty of silver that bided all by his lone and made his
own bed and did his own baking when he might have had a
wife to make him douce and brave?

But Rob of the Mill had never a thought of what Kinraddie
said of him. Further along the Kinraddie road it stood, the Mill,

on the corner of the side-road that led up to Upperhill, and for
ten years now had Rob bided there alone, managing the Mill
and reading the books of a coarse creature Ingersoll that made
watches and didn't believe in God.[30] He'd aye two-three fine
pigs about the Mill had Rob, and fine might well they be for
what did he feed them on but bits of corn and barley he'd
nicked out of the sacks folk brought him to the Mill to grind?
Nor could a body deny but that Long Rob's boar was one of
the best in the Mearns; and they'd bring their sows from as far
afield as Laurencekirk to have them set by that boar of his, a
meikle, pretty brute of a beast. Forbye the Mill and his swine
and hens Rob had a Clydesdale and a sholtie beast he ploughed
his twenty acres with, and a cow or so that never calved, for
he'd never time to send them to the bull though well might he
have taken the time instead of sweating and chaving like a daft
one to tear up the coarse moorland behind the Mill and turn it
into a park. He'd started that three years before and wasn't half
through with it yet, it was filled with great holes and ponds and
choked with meikle broom-roots thick as the arm of a man,
you never saw a dafter ploy. They'd hear Rob out in that
coarse ground hard at work when they went to bed, the rest of
Kinraddie, whistling away to himself as though it were nine
o'clock in the forenoon and the sun shining bravely. He'd
whistle *Ladies of Spain* and *There was a young maiden* and
The lass that made the bed to me,[31] but devil the lass he'd ever
taken to his bed, and maybe that was as well for the lass; she'd
have seen feint the much of him in it beside her.

For after a night of it like that he'd be out again at the keek
of day, and sometimes he'd have the Clydesdale or the sholtie
out there with him and they'd be fine friends, the three of them,
till the beasts would move off when he didn't want them or
wouldn't move when he did; and then he'd fair go mad with
them and call them all the coarsest names he could lay tongue
to till you'd think he'd be heard over half the Mearns; and he'd
leather the horses till folk spoke of sending for the Cruelty,
though he'd a way with the beasts too, and would be friends
with them again in a minute and when he'd been away at the
smithy in Drumlithie or the joiner's in Arbuthnott they'd come

running from the other end of the parks at sight of him and he'd get off his bicycle and feed them with lumps of sugar he bought and carried about with him. He thought himself a gey man with horses, did Rob, and God! he'd tell you stories about horses till you'd fair be grey in the head, but he never wearied of them himself, the long, rangy childe. Long he was, with small bones maybe, but gey broad for all that, with a small head on him and a thin nose and eyes smoky blue as an iron coulter on a winter morning, aye glinting, and a long mouser the colour of ripe corn it was, hanging down the sides of his mouth so that the old minister had told him he looked like a Viking and he'd said *Ah well, minister, as long as I don't look like a parson I'll wrestle through the world right content*, and the minister said he was a fool and godless, and his laughter like the thorns crackling under a pot. And Rob said he'd rather be a thorn than a sucker any day, for he didn't believe in ministers or kirks, he'd learned that from the books of Ingersoll though God knows if the creature's logic was as poor as his watches he was but a sorry prop to lean on. But Rob said he was fine, and if Christ came down to Kinraddie he'd be welcome enough to a bit meal or milk at the Mill, but damn the thing he'd get at the Manse. So that was Long Rob and the stir at the Mill, some said he wasn't all there but others said Ay, that he was, and a bit over.

Now Upperhill rose above the Mill, with its larch woods crowning it, and folk told that a hundred years before five of the crofter places had crowded there till Lord Kenneth threw their biggings down and drove them from the parish and built the fine farm of Upperhill. And twenty years later a son of one of the crofters had come back and rented the place, Gordon was the name of him, they called him Upprums for short and he didn't like that, being near to gentry with his meikle farm and forgetting his father the crofter that had cried like a bairn all the way from Kinraddie that night the Lord Kenneth drove them out. He was a small bit man with a white face on him, and he'd long, thin hair and a nose that wasn't straight but peeked away to one side of his face and no moustache and wee

feet and hands; and he liked to wear leggings and breeks and
carry a bit stick and look as proud as a cock on a midden.
Mistress Gordon was a Stonehaven woman, her father had been
a bit post-office creature there, but God! to hear her speak
you'd think he'd invented the post office himself and taken out
a patent for it. She was a meikle sow of a woman, but aye
well-dressed, and with eyes like the eyes of a fish, fair cod-like
they were, and she tried to speak English and to make her
two bit daughters, Nellie and Maggie Jean, them that went to
Stonehaven Academy, speak English as well. And God! they
made a right muck of it, and if you met the bit things on the
road and said *Well, Nellie, and how are your mother's hens
laying?* the quean would more than likely answer you *Not very
meikle*[32] *the day* and look so proud it was all you could do to
stop yourself catching the futret across your knee and giving
her a bit skelp.

Though she'd only a dove's flitting of a family herself you'd
think to hear Mistress Gordon speak that she'd been clecking
bairns a litter a month since the day she married. It was *Now,
how I brought up Nellie* – or *And the specialist in Aberdeen,
said about Maggie Jean* – till folk were so scunnered they'd
never mention a bairn within a mile of Upperhill. But Rob of
the Mill, the coarse brute, he fair mocked her to her face and
he'd tell a story *Now, when I took my boar to the specialist in
Edinburgh, he up and said 'Mister Rob, this is a gey unusual
boar, awful delicate, but SO intelligent, and you should send
him to the Academy and some day he'll be a real credit to you.'*
And Mistress Gordon when she heard that story she turned as
red as a fire and forgot her English and said Rob was an orra
tink brute.

Forbye the two queans there was the son, John Gordon, as
coarse a devil as you'd meet, he'd already had two-three queans
in trouble and him but barely eighteen years old. But with one
of them he'd met a sore stammy-gaster, her brother was a
gardener down Glenbervie way and when he heard of it he
came over to Upperhill and caught young Gordon out by the
cattle-court. *You'll be Jock?* he said, and young Gordon said
Keep your damned hands to yourself, and the billy said *Ay, but*

first I'll wipe them on a dirty clout, and with that he up with a
handful of sharn and splattered it all over young Gordon and
then rolled him in the greip till he was a sight to sicken a sow
from its supper. The bothy men heard the ongoing and came
tearing out but soon as they saw it was only young Gordon
that was being mischieved they did no more than laugh and
stand around and cry one to the other that here was a real fine
barrow-load of dung lying loose in the greip. So the Drumlithie
billy, minding his sister and her shame, wasn't sharp to finish
with his tormenting, young Gordon looked like a half-dead cat
and smelt like a whole-dead one for a week after, a sore affront
to Upperhill's mistress. She went tearing round to the bothy
and made at the foreman, a dour young devil of a Highlandman,
Ewan Tavendale, *Why didn't you help my Johnnie?* and Ewan
said *I was fee'd as the foreman here, not as the nursemaid*, he
was an impudent brute, calm as you please, but an awful good
worker, folk said he could smell the weather and had fair the
land in his bones.

Now the eighth of the Kinraddie places you could call hardly a
place at all, for that was Pooty's, midway along the Kinraddie
road between the Mill and Bridge End. It was no more than a
butt and a ben, with a rickle of sheds behind it where old Pooty
kept his cow and bit donkey that was nearly as old as himself
and faith! twice as good-looking; and folk said the cuddy had
bided so long with Pooty that whenever it opened its mouth to
give a bit bray it started to stutter. For old Pooty was maybe
the worst stutterer ever heard in the Mearns and the worst of
that worst was that he didn't know it and he'd clean compel
any minister creature organising a concert [from] miles around
to give him a platform part. Then up he'd get on the platform,
the doitered old fool, and recite *Weeeee, ssss-leek-ed, cccccccow-
ering TIMROUS BEASTIE*[33] or such-like poem and it was
fair agony to hear him. He'd lived at Pooty's a good fifty years
they said, his father the crofter of the Knapp before that time,
hardly a soul knew his name, maybe he'd forgotten it himself.
He was the oldest inhabitant of Kinraddie and fell proud of it,
though what there was to be proud of in biding all that while

in a damp, sour house that a goat would hardly have stopped to ease itself in God knows. He was a shoemaker, the creature, and called himself the Sutor, an old-fashioned name that folk laughed at. He'd grey hair aye falling about his lugs and maybe he washed on New Year's Days and birthdays, but not oftener, and if anybody had ever seen him in anything but the grey shirt with the red neck-band he'd kept the fact a dead secret all to himself.

Alec Mutch was farmer of Bridge End that stood beyond the Denburn head, he'd come there up from Stonehaven way, folk said he was head over heels in debt, and damn it you couldn't wonder with a slummock of a wife like that to weigh him down. A grand worker was Alec and Bridge End not the worst of Kinraddie, though wet in the bottom up where its parks joined on to Upperhill. Two pairs of horses it was stabled for but Alec kept no more than three bit beasts, he'd say he was waiting for his family to grow up before he completed the second pair. And fast enough the family came, if she couldn't do much else, Mistress Mutch, fell seldom a year went by but she was brought to bed with a bairn, Mutch fair grew used to dragging himself out in the middle of the night and tearing off to Bervie for the doctor. And the doctor, old Meldrum he was, he'd wink at Alec and cry *Man, Man, have you been at it again?* and Alec would say *Damn it, you've hardly to look at a woman these days but she's in the family way.*

So some said that he must glower at his mistress a fell lot, and that was hard enough to believe, she was no great beauty, with a cock eye and a lazy look and nothing worried her, not a mortal thing, not though her five bairns were all yammering blue murder at the same minute and the smoke coming down the chimney and spoiling the dinner and the cattle broken into the yard and eating up her clean washing. She'd say *Ah well, it'll make no difference a hundred years after I'm dead*, and light up a bit cigarette, like a tink,[34] for aye she carried a packet of the things about with her, she was the speak of half the Mearns, her and her smoking. Two of the five bairns were boys, the oldest eleven, and the whole five of them had the Mutch face, broad and boney and tapering to a chinny point, like the face of an owlet or a fox, and meikle lugs on them like the handles on a cream-jar. Alec himself had such lugs that they said he flapped them against the flies in the summer-time, and once he was coming home on his bicycle from Laurencekirk, and he was real drunk and at the steep brae above the Denburn bridge he mistook the flow of the water for the broad road and in between coping and bank he went and head over heels into the clay bed twenty feet below; and often he'd tell that if he hadn't landed on a lug he might well have been brained, but Long Rob of the Mill would laugh and say *Brained? God Almighty, Mutch, you were never in danger of that!*

So that was Kinraddie that bleak winter of nineteen eleven and the new minister, him they chose early next year, he was to say it was the Scots countryside itself, fathered between a kailyard and a bonny brier bush in the lee of a house with green shutters.[35] And what he meant by that you could guess at yourself if you'd a mind for puzzles and dirt, there wasn't a house with green shutters in the whole of Kinraddie.

THE SONG

I

Ploughing

Below and around where Chris Guthrie lay the June moors whispered and rustled and shook their cloaks, yellow with broom and powdered faintly with purple, that was the heather but not the full passion of its colour yet. And in the east against the cobalt blue of the sky lay the shimmer of the North Sea, that was by Bervie,[1] and maybe the wind would veer there in an hour or so and you'd feel the change in the life and strum of the thing, bringing a streaming coolness out of the sea. But for days now the wind had been in the south, it shook and played in the moors and went dandering up the sleeping Grampians, the rushes pecked and quivered about the loch when its hand was upon them, but it brought more heat than cold, and all the parks were fair parched, sucked dry, the red clay soil of Blawearie gaping open for the rain that seemed never-coming. Up here the hills were brave with the beauty and the heat of it, but the hayfield was all a crackling dryness and in the potato park beyond the biggings the shaws drooped red and rusty already. Folk said there hadn't been such a drought since eighty-three and Long Rob of the Mill said you couldn't blame *this* one on Gladstone,[2] anyway, and everybody laughed except father, God knows why.

Some said the North, up Aberdeen way, had had rain enough, with Dee[3] in spate and bairns hooking stranded salmon down in the shallows, and that must be fine enough, but not a flick of the greve weather had come over the hills, the roads you walked down to Kinraddie smithy or up to the Denburn were fair blistering in the heat, thick with dust so that the motor-cars went shooming through them like kettles under steam. And

serve them right, they'd little care for anybody, the dirt that
rode in motors, folk said; and one of them had nearly run over
wee Wat Strachan a fortnight before and had skirled to a stop
right bang in front of Peesie's Knapp, Wat had yowled like a
cat with a jobe under its tail and Chae had gone striding out
and taken the motorist man by the shoulder. And *What the hell
do you think you're up to?* Chae had asked. And the motorist,
he was a fair toff with leggings and a hat cocked over his eyes,
he'd said *Keep your damn children off the road in future*. And
Chae had said *Keep a civil tongue in your head* and had clouted
the motorist man one in the ear and down he had flumped in
the stour and Mistress Strachan, her that was old Netherhill's
daughter, she'd gone tearing out skirling *Mighty, you brute,
you've killed the man!* and Chae had just laughed and said
Damn the fears! and off he'd gone. But Mistress Strachan had
helped the toff up to his feet and shook him and brushed him
and apologised for Chae, real civil-like. And all the thanks she
got was that Chae was summonsed for assault at Stonehaven
and fined a pound, and came out of the courthouse saying there
was no justice under capitalism, a revolution would soon sweep
away its corrupted lackeys. And maybe it would, but faith!
there was as little sign of a revolution, said Long Rob of the
Mill, as there was of rain.

  Maybe that was the reason for half the short tempers over
the Howe. You could go never a road but farmer billies were
leaning over the gates, glowering at the weather, and road-
menders, poor stocks, chapping away at their hillocks with the
sweat fair dripping off them, and the only folk that seemed to
have a fine time were the shepherds up in the hills. But they
swore themselves dry when folk cried that to them, the hill
springs about a shepherd's herd would dry up or seep away all
in an hour and the sheep go straying and baying and driving
the man fair senseless till he'd led them weary miles to the
nearest burn. So everybody was fair snappy, staring up at the
sky, and the ministers all over the Howe were offering up
prayers for rain in between the bit about the Army and the
Prince of Wales'[4] rheumatics. But feint the good it did for rain;

and Long Rob of the Mill said he'd heard both Army and rheumatics were much the same as before.

Maybe father would have done better to keep a civil tongue in his head and stayed on in Echt, there was plenty of rain there, a fine land for rain, Aberdeen, you'd see it by day and night come drenching and wheeling over the Barmekin and the Hill of Fare[5] in the fine northern land. And mother would sigh, looking out from Blawearie's windows, *There's no land like Aberdeen or folk so fine as them that bide by Don.*

She'd bidden by Don all her life, mother, she'd been born in Kildrummie,[6] her father a ploughman there, he'd got no more than thirteen shillings a week and he'd had thirteen of a family, to work things out in due ratio, maybe. But mother said they all got on fine, she was never happier in her life than those days when she tramped bare-footed the roads to the little school that nestled under the couthy hills. And at nine she left the school and they packed a basket for her and she bade her mother ta-ta and set out to her first fee, no shoes on her feet even then, she hadn't worn shoes till she was twelve years old. It hadn't been a real fee that first one, she'd done little more than scare the crows from the fields of an old bit farmer and sleep in a garret, but fine she'd liked it, she'd never forget the singing of the winds in those fields when she was young or the daft crying of the lambs she herded or the feel of the earth below her toes. *Oh, Chris, my lass, there are better things than your books or studies or loving or bedding, there's the countryside your own, you its, in the days when you're neither bairn nor woman.*

So mother had worked and ran the parks those days, she was blithe and sweet, you knew, you saw her against the sun as though you peered far down a tunnel of the years. She stayed long on her second fee, seven or eight years she was there till the day she met John Guthrie at a ploughing match at Pittodrie.[7] And often once she'd tell of that to Chris and Will, it was nothing grand of a match, the horses were poor and the ploughing worse and a coarse, cold wind was soughing across the rigs and half Jean Murdoch made up her mind to go home. Then it

was that it came the turn of a brave young childe with a red
head and the swackest legs you ever saw, his horses were laced
in ribbons, bonny and trig, and as soon as he began the drill
you saw he'd carry off the prize. And carry it off he did, young
John Guthrie, and not that alone. For as he rode from the park
on one horse he patted the back of the other and cried to Jean
Murdoch with a glint from his dour, sharp eye *Jump up if you
like*. And she cried back *I like fine!* and caught the horse by its
mane and swung herself there till Guthrie's hand caught her
and set her steady on the back of the beast. So out from the
ploughing match at Pittodrie the two of them rode together,
Jean sitting upon the hair of her, gold it was and so long, and
laughing up into the dour, keen face that was Guthrie's.

So that was beginning of their lives together, she was sweet
and kind to him, but he mightn't touch her, his face would go
black with rage at her because of that sweetness that tempted
his soul to hell. Yet in two-three years they'd chaved and saved
enough for gear and furnishings, and were married at last, and
syne Will was born, and syne Chris herself was born, and
the Guthries rented a farm in Echt, Cairndhu it was, and sat
themselves down there for many a year.

Winters or springs, summers or harvests, bristling or sunning
the sides of Barmekin, and life ploughed its rigs and drove its
teams and the dourness hardened, hard and cold, in the heart
of Jean Guthrie's man. But still the glint of her hair could rouse
him, Chris would hear him cry in agony at night as he went
with her, mother's face grew queer and questioning, her eyes
far back on those Springs she might never see again, dear and
blithe they had been, she could kiss and hold them still a
moment alone with Chris or Will. Dod came, then Alec came,
and mother's fine face grew harder then. One night they heard
her cry to John Guthrie *Four of a family's fine; there'll be no
more*. And father thundered at her, that way he had *Fine? We'll
have what God in His mercy may send to us, woman. See you
to that*.

He wouldn't do anything against God's will, would father,
and sure as anything God followed up Alec with the twins,
born seven years later. Mother went about with a queer look

on her face before they came, she lost that sweet blitheness that was hers, and once, maybe she was ill-like, she said to father when he spoke of arranging a doctor and things, *Don't worry about that. No doubt your friend Jehovah*[8] *will see to it all*. Father seemed to freeze up, then his face grew black, he said never a word, and Chris had wondered at that, seeing how mad he'd been when Will used the word, thoughtless-like, only a week before.

For Will had heard the word in the kirk of Echt where the elders sit with shaven chins and the offering bags between their knees, waiting the sermon to end and to march with slow, sleeked steps up through the pews, hearing the penny of penury clink shy-like against the threepenny of affluence. And Will one Sunday, sitting close to sleep, heard fall from the minister's lips the word *Jehovah*, and treasured it for the bonniness and the beauty of it, waiting till he might find a thing or a man or beast that would fit this word, well-shaped and hantled and grand.

Now that was in summer, the time of fleas and glegs and golochs in the fields, when stirks would start up from a drowsy cud-chewing to a wild and feckless racing, the glegs biting through hair and hide to the skin below the tail-rump. Echt was alive that year with the thunder of the herds, the crackle of breaking gates, the splash of stirks in tarns, and last with the groans of Nell, the old horse of Guthrie's, caught in a daft swither of the Highland steers and her belly ripped like a rotten swede with the stroke of a great, curved horn.

Father saw the happening from high in a park where the hay was cut and they set the swathes in coles, and he swore out *Damn't to hell!* and started to run, fleetly as was his way, down to the groaning shambles that was Nell. And as he ran he picked up a scythe-blade, and as he neared to Nell he unhooked the blade and cried *Poor quean!* and Nell groaned, groaning blood and sweating, and turned away her neck, and father thrust the scythe at her neck, sawing till she died.

So that was the end of Nell, father waited till the hay was coled and then tramped into Aberdeen and bought a new horse, Bess, riding her home at evening to the raptured starings of Will. And Will took the horse and watered her and led her into

the stall where Nell had slept and gave to her hay and a handful
of corn, and set to grooming her, shoulder to heel, and her fine
plump belly and the tail of her, long and curled. And Bess stood
eating her corn and Chris leant against the door-jamb, her Latin
Grammar[9] held in her hand. So, working with fine, strong
strokes, and happy, Will groomed till he finished the tail, and
then as he lifted the brush to hit Bess on the flank that she might
move to the other side of the stall and he complete his grooming
there flashed in his mind the fine word he had treasured. *Come
over, Jehovah!* he cried, smiting her roundly, and John Guthrie
heard the word out across the yard and came fleetly from the
kitchen, wiping oat-cake from his beard, and fleetly across the
yard into the stable he came—

But he should not have stricken Will as he did, he fell below
the feet of the horse and Bess turned her head, dripping corn, and
looked down at Will, with his face bloody, and then swished her
tail and stood still. And then John Guthrie dragged his son aside
and paid no more heed to him, but picked up brush and curry-
comb and cried *Whoa, lass!* and went on with the grooming.
Chris had cried and hidden her face but now she looked again,
Will was sitting up slowly, the blood on his face, and John
Guthrie speaking to him, not looking at him, grooming Bess.

*And mind, my mannie, if I ever hear you again take your
Maker's name in vain, if I ever hear you use that word again,
I'll libb you. Mind that. Libb you like a lamb.*

So Will hated father, he was sixteen years of age and near a
man, but father could still make him cry like a bairn. He would
whisper his hate to Chris as they lay in their beds at night in
the loft room high in the house and the harvest moon came
sailing over the Barmekin and the peewits wheeped above the
lands of Echt. And Chris would cover her ears and then listen,
turning this cheek to the pillow and that, she hated also and
she didn't hate, father, the land, the life of the land – oh, if only
she knew!

For she'd met with books, she went into them to a magic
land far from Echt, out and away and south. And at school
they wrote she was the clever one and John Guthrie said she

might have the education she needed if she stuck to her lessons. In time she might come out as a teacher then, and do him credit, that was fine of father the Guthrie whispered in her, but the Murdoch laughed with a blithe, sweet face. But more and more she turned from that laughter, resolute, loving to hear of the things in the histories and geographies, seldom thinking them funny, strange names and words like Too-long and Too-loose[10] that convulsed the classes. And at arithmetic also she was more than good, doing great sums in her head so that always she was first in the class, they made her the dux and they gave her prizes, four prizes in four years she had.

And one book she'd thought fair daft, *Alice in Wonderland* it was, and there was no sense in it. And the second, it was *What Katy did at School*, and she loved Katy and envied her and wished like Katy she lived at a school, not tramping back in the spleiter of a winter night to help muck the byre, with the smell of the sharn rising feuch! in her face. And the third book was *Rienzi, the Last of the Roman Tribunes*, and some bits were good and some fair wearying. He had a right bonny wife, Rienzi had, and he was sleeping with her, her white arms round his neck, when the Romans came to kill him at last. And the fourth book, new given her before the twins came to Cairndhu, was *The Humours of Scottish Life*[11] and God! if that stite was fun she must have been born dull.

And these had been all her books that weren't lesson-books, they were all the books in Cairndhu but for the Bibles grandmother had left to them, one to Chris and one to Will, and in Chris's one were set the words *To my dawtie Chris: Trust in God and do the right*. For grandmother, she'd been father's mother, not mother's mother, had been fell religious and every Sunday, rain or shine, had tramped to the kirk at Echt, sitting below some four-five ministers there in all. And one minister she'd never forgiven, for he'd said not GAWD, as a decent man would, but GOHD, and it had been a mercy when he caught a bit cold, laid up he was, and quickly passed away; and maybe it had been a judgment on him.

So that was Chris and her reading and schooling, two Chrisses there were that fought for her heart and tormented her. You hated the land and the coarse speak of the folk and learning was brave and fine one day; and the next you'd waken with the peewits crying across the hills, deep and deep, crying in the heart of you and the smell of the earth in your face, almost you'd cry for that, the beauty of it and the sweetness of the Scottish land and skies. You saw their faces in firelight, father's and mother's and the neighbours', before the lamps lit up, tired and kind, faces dear and close to you, you wanted the words they'd known and used, forgotten in the far-off young-ness of their lives, Scots words to tell to your heart how they wrung it and held it, the toil of their days and unendingly their fight. And the next minute that passed from you, you were English, back to the English words so sharp and clean and true – for a while, for a while, till they slid so smooth from your throat you knew they could never say anything that was worth the saying at all.

But she sat for her bursary, won it, and began the conjugating Latin verbs, the easy ones only at first, *Amo, amas, I love a lass* and then you laughed out loud when the Dominie said that and he cried *Whist, whist* but was real pleased and smiled at you and you felt fine and tingly and above all the rest of the queans who weren't learning Latin or anything else, they were kitchen-maids in the bone. And then there was French, fair difficult, the u was the worst; and an inspector creature came to Echt and Chris near dropped through the schoolroom floor in shame when he made her stand out in front of them all and say *o-oo, o-oo, o-oo-butin*. And he said *Put your mouth as though you were going to weesel, but don't do it, and say 'o-oo, o-oo, o-oo.'* And she said it, she felt like a hen with a stone in its thrapple, after the inspector creature, an Englishman he was with an awful belly on him and he couldn't say whistle, only weesel. And he went away, down to the gig that was waiting to drive him to the station he went, and he left his brave leather bag behind, and the Dominie saw it and cried *Whist, Chrissie, run after the Inspector man with his bag.* So she did and caught him up at the foot of the playground, he gowked at her and said *Haw?* and then gave a bit laugh and said *Haw?* again and then *Thenks.* And Chris went back to the Dominie's room, the

Dominie was waiting for her and he asked if the Inspector had given her anything, and Chris said *No*, and the Dominie looked sore disappointed.

But everybody knew that the English were awful mean and couldn't speak right and were cowards who captured Wallace and killed him by treachery. But they'd been beaten right well at Bannockburn, then, Edward the Second hadn't drawn rein till he was in Dunbar, and ever after that the English were beaten in all the wars, except Flodden and they won at Flodden by treachery again, just as it told in *The Flowers of the Forest*.[12] Always she wanted to cry when she heard that played and a lot of folk singing it at a parish concert in Echt, for the sadness of it and the lads that came back never again to their lasses among the stooks, and the lasses that never married but sat and stared down south to the English border where their lads lay happed in blood and earth, with their bloodied kilts and broken helmets. And she wrote an essay on that, telling all how it happened, the Dominie said it was fine and that sometime she should try to write poetry; like Mrs Hemans.[13]

But then, just after writing the essay, the twins were born and mother had as awful a time as she'd always had. She was sobbing and ill when she went to bed, Chris boiled water in kettles for hours and hours and then towels came down, towels clairted with stuff she didn't dare look at, she washed them quick and hung them to dry. The doctor came in with the evening, he stayed the whole night, and Dod and Alec shivered and cried in their room till father went up and skelped them right sore, they'd something to cry for then but they didn't dare. And father came down the stairs again, fleet as ever, though he hadn't been in bed for forty hours, and he closed the kitchen door and sat with his head between his hands and groaned and said he was a miserable sinner, God forgive him the lusts of the flesh. Something about the bonny hair of her also he said and then more about lust, but he hadn't intended Chris to hear for he looked up and saw her looking at him and he raged at her, telling her to spread a table with breakfast for the doctor – *through in the parlour there, and boil him an egg*.

And then mother began to scream, the doctor called down the stairs *Man, it's a fair tough case, I doubt I'll need your help*, and at that father turned grey as a sheet and covered his face again and cried *I dare not, I dare not!* Then the doctor childe called him again *Guthrie man, do you hear me?* and father jumped up in a rage and cried *Damn't to hell, I'm not deaf!* and ran up the stairs, fleet as ever, and then the door in the room closed fast and Chris could hear no more.

Not that she wanted to hear, she felt real ill herself, cooking the egg and laying a meal in the parlour, with a white cloth spread above the green plush cloth and all the furniture dark and shadowed and listening. Then Will came down the stair, he couldn't sleep because of mother, they sat together and Will said the old man was a fair beast and mother shouldn't be having a baby, she was far too old for that. And Chris stared at him with horrified imaginings in her mind, she hadn't known better then, the English bit of her went sick, she whispered *What has father to do with it?* And Will stared back at her, shamed-faced, *Don't you know? What's a bull to do with a calf, you fool?*

But then they heard an awful scream that made them leap to their feet, it was as though mother were being torn and torn in the teeth of beasts and couldn't thole it longer; and then a little screech like a young pig made followed that scream and they tried not to hear more of the sounds above them, Chris boiled the egg over and over till it was as hard as iron. And then mother screamed again, Oh God! your heart stopped to hear it, and that was when the second twin came.

Then quietness followed, they heard the doctor coming down the stairs, the morning was close, it hung scared beyond the stilled parks and listened and waited. But the doctor cried *Hot water, jugs of it, pour me a basin of water, Chris, and put plenty of soap near by it*. She cried *Ay, doctor*, to that but she cried in a whisper, he didn't hear and was fell angry. *D'you hear me?* And Will said to him, calling up the stair, *Ay, doctor, only she's feared*, and the doctor said *She'll have a damned sight more to fear when she's having a bairn of her own. Pour out the water, quick!* So they poured it and went through to

the parlour while the doctor passed them with his hands held
away from them, and the smell of his hands was a horror that
haunted Chris[14] for a day and a night.

That was the coming of the twins at Cairndhu, there'd been
barely room for them all before that time, now they'd have to
live like tinks. But it was a fell good farm, John Guthrie loath
to part with it though his lease was near its end, and when
mother came down from her bed in a fortnight's time with the
shine of the gold still in the sweet hair of her and her eyes clear
eyes again, he raged and swore when she spoke to him. *More
rooms? What more room do we want than we have? Do you
think we're gentry?* he cried, and went on again to tell that
when he was a bairn in Pittodrie his mother had nine bairns all
at home, nought but a butt and ben they had and their father
nought but a plough-childe. But fine they'd managed, God-
fearing and decent all he'd made them, and if one of Jean
Murdoch's bairns were half as good the shame need never
redden the face of her. And mother looked at him with the little
smile on her lips, *Well, well, we're to bide on here, then?* and
father shot out his beard at her and cried *Ay, that we are,
content yourself.*

But the very next day he was driving back from the mart, old
Bob in the cart, when round a corner below the Barmekin came
a motor-car spitting and barking like a tink dog in distemper.
Old Bob had made a jump and near landed the cart in the ditch
and then stood like a rock, so feared he wouldn't move a step,
the cart jammed fast across the road. And as father tried to
haul the thrawn beast to the side a creature of a woman with
her face all clamjamfried with paint and powder and dirt, she
thrust her bit head out from the window of the car and cried
You're causing an obstruction, my man. And John Guthrie
roused like a lion: *I'm not your man, thank God, for if I was
I'd have your face scraped with a clart and then a scavenger
wash it well.* The woman nearly burst with rage at that, she
fell back in the car and said *You've not heard the last of this.
Take note of his name-plate, James, d'you hear?* And the shover
looked out, fair shamed he looked, and keeked at the name-plate

underneath Bob's shelvin, and quavered *Yes, madam*, and they
turned about and drove off. That was the way to deal with dirt
like the gentry, but when father applied for his lease again he
was told he couldn't have it.

So he took a look at the *People's Journal* and got into his
fine best suit, Chris shook the moth-balls from it and found
him his collar and the broad white front to cover his working
sark; and John Guthrie tramped into Aberdeen and took a train
to Banchory to look at a small place there. But the rent was
awful high and he saw that nearly all the district was land of
the large-like farm,[15] he'd be squeezed to death and he'd stand
no chance. It was fine land though, that nearly shook him, fine
it looked and your hands they itched to be at it; but the agent
called him *Guthrie*, and he fired up at the agent: *Who the hell
are you Guthrie-ing? Mister Guthrie to you*. And the agent
looked at him and turned right white about the gills and then
gave a bit laugh and said *Ah well, Mr Guthrie, I'm afraid you
wouldn't suit us*. And John Guthrie said *It's your place that
doesn't suit me, let me tell you, you wee, dowp-licking clerk*.
Poor he might be but the creature wasn't yet clecked that might
put on its airs with him, John Guthrie.

So back he came and began his searchings again. And the
third day out he came back from far in the south. He'd taken
a place, Blawearie, in Kinraddie of the Mearns.

Wild weather it was that January and the night on the Slug
road smoring with sleet when John Guthrie crossed his family
and gear from Aberdeen into the Mearns.[16] Twice the great
carts, set with their shelvins that rustled still, stray binder-twine
from September's harvest-home, laired in drifts before the ascent
of the Slug faced the reluctant horses. Darkness came down like
a wet, wet blanket, weariness below it and the crying of the twins
to vex John Guthrie. Mother called him from her nook in the
leading cart, there where she sat with now one twin at the breast
and now another, and her skin bare and cold and white and a
strand of her rust-gold hair draped down from the darkness
about her face into the light of the swinging lantern: *We'd
better loosen up at Portlethen and not try the Slug this night*.

But father swore at that *Damn't to hell, do you think I'm made of silver to put up the night at Portlethen?* and mother sighed and held off the wee twin, Robert, and the milk dripped creamily from the soft, sweet lips of him: *No, we're not made of silver, but maybe we'll lair again and all die of the night.*

Maybe he feared that himself, John Guthrie, his rage was his worriment with the night, but he'd no time to answer her for a great bellowing arose in the road by the winding scurry of peat-moss that lined the dying light of the moon. The cattle had bunched there, tails to the wind, refusing the Slug and the sting of the sleet, little Dod was wailing and crying at the beasts, Polled Angus and Shorthorns and half-bred Highland stirks[17] who had fattened and fêted and loved their life in the haughs of Echt, south there across the uncouthy hills was a world cold and unchancy. But John Guthrie dropped the tarpaulin edge that shielded his wife and the twins and the furnishings of the best room and gear good and plentiful enough; and swiftly he ran past the head of the horse till he came to where the cattle bunched. And he swung Dod into the ditch with one swipe of his hand and cried *Have you got no sense, you brat?* and uncoiled from his hand the length of hide that served him as a whip. Its crackle snarled down through the sting of the sleet, the hair rose in long serrations across the backs of the cattle, and one in a minute, a little Highland steer it was, mooed and ran forward and fell to a trot, and the rest followed after, slipping and sprawling with their cloven hooves, the reek of their dung sharp and bitter in the sleet smore of the night. Ahead Alec saw them coming and turned himself about again, and fell to a trot, leading up the Slug to Mearns and the south.

So, creaking and creaking, and the shelvins skirling under the weight of their loads, they passed that danger point, the carts plodded into motion again, the first with its hooded light and house gear and mother suckling the twins. In the next, Clyde's cart, the seed was loaded, potato and corn and barley, and bags of tools and implements, and graips and forks fast tied with esparto twine and two fine ploughs and a driller, and dairy things and a turnip machine with teeth that cut as a guillotine cuts. Head down to the wind and her reins loose and

her bonny coat all mottled with sleet went Clyde, the load a
nothing to her, fine and clean and sonsy she marched, following
John Guthrie's cart with no other thing or soul to guide but
that ever and now, in this half-mile and that she heard his voice
cry cheerily *Fine, Clyde, fine. Come on then, lass.*

Chris and Will with the last cart, sixteen Will and fifteen
Chris, the road wound up and up, straight and unwavering,
and sometimes they hiddled in the lithe and the sleet sang
past to left and right, white and glowing in the darkness. And
sometimes they clambered down from the shelvins above the
laboured drag of old Bob and ran beside him, one either side,
and stamped for warmth in their feet, and saw the whin bushes
climb black the white hills beside them and far and away the
blink of lights across the moors where folk lay happed and
warm. But then the upwards road would swerve, right or left,
into this steep ledge or that, and the wind would be at them
again and they'd gasp, climbing back to the shelvins, Will with
freezing feet and hands and the batter of the sleet like needles
in his face, Chris in worse case, colder and colder at every turn,
her body numb and unhappy, knees and thighs and stomach
and breast, her breasts ached and ached so that nearly she wept.
But of that she told nothing, she fell to a drowse through the
cold, and a strange dream came to her as they plodded up
through the ancient hills.

For out of the night ahead of them came running a man,
father didn't see him or heed to him, though old Bob in the
dream that was Chris's snorted and shied. And as he came he
wrung his hands, he was mad and singing, a foreign creature,
black-bearded, half-naked he was; and he cried in the Greek
The ships of Pytheas![18] *The ships of Pytheas!* and went by into
the smore of the sleet-storm on the Grampian hills, Chris never
saw him again, queer dreaming that was. For her eyes were
wide open, she rubbed them with never a need of that, if she
hadn't been dreaming she must have been daft. They'd cleared
the Slug, below was Stonehaven and the Mearns, and far
beyond that, miles through the Howe, the twinkling point of
light that shone from the flagstaff of Kinraddie.

*

So that was their coming to Blawearie, fell wearied all of them were the little of the night that was left them, and slept late into the next morning, coming cold and drizzly up from the sea by Bervie. All the darkness they heard that sea, a shoom-shoom that moaned by the cliffs of lone Kinneff. Not that John Guthrie listened to such dirt of sounds, but Chris and Will did, in the room where they'd made their shake-down beds. In the strangeness and cold and the sighing of that far-off water Chris could find no sleep till Will whispered *Let's sleep together*. So then they did, oxtering one the other till they were real warm. But at the first keek of day Will slipped back to the blankets of his own bed, he was feared what father would say if he found them lying like that. Chris thought of that angrily, puzzled and angry, the English Chris as sleep came on her again. Was it likely a brother and a sister would do anything if they slept together? And besides, she didn't know how.

But Will back in his bed had hardly a minute to get warm or a wink of sleep when John Guthrie was up and about the place, rousing them all, and the twins were wakened and crying for the breast, and Dod and Alec trying to light the fire. Father swore up and down the strange Blawearie stairs, chapping from door to door, weren't they sick with shame lying stinking in bed and half the day gone? Then out he went, the house quietened down as he banged the door, and he cried back that he was off up the brae to look at the loch in Blawearie moor – *Get out and get on with the breakfast and get your work done ere I come back else I'll warm your lugs for you.*

And faith! it was queer that the notion took father to climb the brae at that hour. For as he went up through the broom he heard a shot, did John Guthrie, cracking the morning so dark and iron-like, and he stood astounded, was not Blawearie his and he the tenant of it? And rage took him and he ceased to dander. Up through the hill among the dead broom he sped like a hare and burst in sight of the loch, grass-fringed and chill then under the winter morning, with a sailing of wild geese above it, going out east to the sea. All but one winged east in burnished strokes under the steel-grey sky, but that one loped and swooped and stroked the air with burnished pinions, and

John Guthrie saw the feathers drift down from it, it gave a wild
cry like a bairn smored at night below the blankets, and down
it plonked on the mere of the loch, not ten yards from where
the man with the gun was standing. So John Guthrie he went
cannily across the grass to this billy in the brave leggings and
with the red face on him, and who was he standing so sure-like
on Guthrie's land? He gave a bit jump, hearing Guthrie come,
and then he swithered a laugh inside the foolish face of him,
but John Guthrie didn't laugh. Instead, he whispered, quiet-like,
Ay, man, you've been shooting, and the creature said *Ay, just
that*. And John Guthrie said *Ay, you'll be a bit poacher, then?*
and the billy said *No, I'll not be that, I'm Maitland, the foreman
at Mains*, and John Guthrie whispered *You may be the arch-
angel Gabriel, but you're not to shoot on MY land, d'you hear?*

The Standing Stones reared up above the two, marled and
white-edged with snow they were, and a wind came blowing fit
to freeze the chilblains on a brass monkey as they stood and
glowered one at the other. Then Maitland muttered *Ellison at
Mains will see about this*, and made off for all the world as if
he feared the crack of a kick in the dowp of him. And right
fairly there, midmost his brave breeks John Guthrie might well
have kicked but that he restrained himself, cannily, for the
goose was still lying by the side of the loch, jerking and slobber-
ing blood through its beak; and it looked at him with terror in
its slate-grey eyes and he waited, canny still, till Maitland was
out of sight, syne he wrung the neck of the bird and took it
down to Blawearie. And he told them all of the meeting with
Maitland, and if ever they heard a shot on the land they were
to run to him at once and tell him, he'd deal with any damn
poacher – Jew, Gentile, or the Prince of Wales himself.

So that was how father made first acquaintance with the
Standing Stones, and he didn't like them, for one evening in
Spring after a day's ploughing and tired a bit maybe, he went
up on a dander through the brae to the loch and found Chris
lying there, just as now she lay in the summer heat. Tired
though he was he came to her side right fleet enough, his
shoulders straight and his frightening eyes on her, she had no
time to close the story-book she read and he snatched it up and

looked at it and cried *Dirt! You've more need to be down in the house helping your mother wash out the hippens.* And he glanced with a louring eye at the Standing Stones and then Chris had thought a foolish thing, that he kind of shivered, as though he were feared, him that was feared at nothing dead or alive, gentry or common. But maybe the shiver came from his fleetness caught in the bite of the cold Spring air, he stood looking at the Stones a minute and said they were coarse, foul things, the folk that raised them were burning in hell, skin-clad savages with never a skin to guard them now. And Chris had better get down to her work, had she heard any shooting that evening?

But Chris said *No*, and neither she had, nor any other evening till John Guthrie himself got a gun, a second-hand thing he picked up in Stonehaven, a muzzle-loader it was, and as he went by the Mill on the way to Blawearie Long Rob came out and saw it and cried *Ay, man I didn't mind you were a veteran of the '45.*[19] And father cried *Losh, Rob, were you cheating folk at your Mill even then?* for sometimes he could take a bit joke, except with his family. So home he brought the old gun and loaded it up with pellets and stuffed in wadding with a ramrod; and by night he would go cannily out in the gloaming, and shoot here a rabbit and there a hare, no other soul must handle the gun but himself. Nor did any try till that day he went off to the mart at Laurencekirk and then Will took down the gun and laughed at the thing and loaded it and went out and shot at a mark, a herring box on the top of a post, till he was fell near perfect. But he wished he hadn't, for father came home and counted his pellets that evening and went fair mad with rage till mother grew sick of the subject and cried *Hold your whist, you and your gun, what harm was in Will that he used it?*

Father had been sitting at the neuk of the fire when he heard that, but he got to his feet like a cat then, looking at Will so that the blood flowed cold in Chris's veins. Then he said, in the quiet-like voice that was his when he was going to leather them, *Come out to the barn with me, Will.* Mother laughed that strange, blithe laugh that had come out of the Springs of

Kildrummie with her, kind and queer in a breath it was, looking pityingly at Will. But Chris burned with shame because of him, he was over-old for that, she cried out *Father, you can't!*

As well have cried to the tides at Kinneff to keep away from the land, father was fair roused by then, he whispered *Be quiet, quean, else I'll take you as well.* And up to the barn he went with Will and took down his breeks, nearly seventeen though he was, and leathered him till the weals stood blue across his haunches; and that night Will could hardly sleep for the pain of it, sobbing into his pillow, till Chris slipped into his bed and took him into her arms and held him and cuddled him and put out her hand below his shirt on to his body and made gentle her fingers to pass and repass across the torn flesh of his body, soothing him, and he stopped from crying after a while and fell asleep, holding to her, strange it seemed then for she knew him bigger and older than she was, and somehow skin and hair and body stranger than once they had been, as though they were no longer children. She minded then the stories of Marget Strachan, and felt herself in the darkness blush for shame and then think of them still more and lie awake, seeing out of the window as it wore on to midnight a lowe in mauve and gold that crept and slipt and wavered upon the sky, and that was the lowe of the night-time whin-burning up on the Grampians; and next morning she was almost too sleepy to stiter into her clothes and set out across the fields to the station and the College train for Duncairn.[20]

For to the College she'd been sent and found it strange enough after the high classes in Echt, a little ugly place it was below Duncairn Station, ugly as sin and nearly as proud, said the Chris that was Murdoch, Chris of the land. Inside the main building of it was carved the head of a beast like a calf with colic, but they swore the creature was a wolf on a shield, whatever the brute might be doing there.

Every week or so the drawing master, old Mr Kinloch, marched out this class or that to the playground in front of the wolf-beast; and down they'd all get on the chairs they'd brought and try and draw the beast. Right fond of the gentry was

Kinloch, if you wore a fine frock and your hair was well brushed and your father well to the fore he'd sit beside you and stroke your arm and speak in a slow sing-song that made everybody laugh behind his back. *Noooooooooooo, that's not quate raight*, he would flute, *More like the head of one of Chrissie's faaaaaaaather's pigs than a heraaaaaaaaaaaldic animal, I'm afraaaaaaaaaaaaaaaaid*. So he loved the gentry, did Mr Kinloch, and God knows he was no exception among the masters there. For the most of them were sons and daughters of poor bit crofters and fishers themselves, up with the gentry they felt safe and unfrightened, far from that woesome pit of brose and bree and sheetless beds in which they had been reared. So right condescending they were with Chris, daughter of a farmer of no account, not that she cared, she was douce and sensible she told herself. And hadn't father said that in the sight of God an honest man was as good as any school-teacher and generally a damned sight better?

But it vexed you a bit all the same that a creature like the Fordyce girl should be cuddled by Mr Kinloch when she'd a face like a broken brose-cap and a voice like a nail on a slate. And but little cuddling her drawing warranted, her father's silver had more to do with it, not that Chris herself could draw like an artist, Latin and French and Greek and history were the things in which she shone. And the English master set their class an essay on *Deaths of the Great* and her essay was so good that he was forced to read it aloud to all the class, and the Fordyce quean had snickered and sniffed, so mad she was with jealousy.

Mr Murgetson was the English master there, not that he was English himself, he came from Argyll and spoke with a funny whine, the Highland whine, and the boys swore he had hair growing up between his toes like a Highland cow, and when they'd see him coming down a corridor they'd push their heads round a corner and cry *Moo!* like a lot of cattle. He'd fly in an awful rage at that, and once when they'd done it he came into the class where Chris was waiting her lesson and he stood and swore, right out and horrible, and gripped a black ruler in his hands and glared round as if he meant to murder a body. And maybe he would if the French teacher, her that was bonny and brave, hadn't come simpering into the room, and then he lowered the ruler and grunted and curled up his lip and said *Eh? Canaille?* and the French teacher she simpered some more and said *May swee*.[21]

So that was the college place at Duncairn, two Chrisses went there each morning, and one was right douce and studious and the other sat back and laughed a canny laugh at the antics of the teachers and minded Blawearie brae and the champ of horses and the smell of dung and her father's brown, grained hands till she was sick to be home again. But she made friends with young Marget Strachan, Chae Strachan's daughter, she was slim and sweet and fair, fine to know, though she spoke about things that seemed awful at first and then weren't awful at all; and you wanted to hear more and Marget would laugh and say it was Chae that had told her. Always as Chae she spoke of him and that was an unco-like thing to do of your father, but maybe it was because he was socialist and thought that Rich and Poor should be Equal. And what was the sense of believing that and then sending his daughter to educate herself and herself become one of the Rich?

But Marget cried that wasn't what Chae intended, she was to learn and be ready for the Revolution that was some day coming. And if come it never did she wasn't to seek out riches anyway, she was off to be trained as a doctor, Chae said that life came out of women through tunnels of pain and if God had planned women for anything else but the bearing of children it was surely the saving of them. And Marget's eyes, that were blue and so deep they minded you of a well you peeped into, they'd grow deeper and darker and her sweet face grow so solemn Chris felt solemn herself. But that would be only a minute, the next and Marget was laughing and fleering, trying to shock her, telling of men and women, what fools they were below their clothes; and how children came and how you should have them; and the things that Chae had seen in the huts of the blacks in Africa. And she told of a place where the bodies of men lay salted and white in great stone vats till the doctors needed to cut them up, the bodies of paupers they were – *so*

*take care you don't die as a pauper, Chris, for I'd hate some
day if I rang a bell and they brought me up out of the vat your
naked body, old and shrivelled and frosted with salt, and I
looked in your dead, queer face, standing there with the scalpel
held in my hand, and cried 'But this is Chris Guthrie!'*

That was awful, Chris felt sick and sick and stopped midway
the shining path that led through the fields to Peesie's Knapp
that evening in March. Clean and keen and wild and clear, the
evening, ploughed land's smell up in your nose and your mouth
when you opened it, for Netherhill's teams had been out in that
park all day, queer and lovely and dear the smell Chris noted.
And something else she saw, looking at Marget, sick at the
thought of her dead body brought to Marget. And that thing
was a vein that beat in Marget's throat, a little blue gathering
where the blood beat past in slow, quiet strokes, it would never
do that when one was dead and still under grass, down in the
earth that smelt so fine and you'd never smell; or cased in the
icy darkness of a vat, seeing never again the lowe of burning
whins or hearing the North Sea thunder beyond the hills, the
thunder of it breaking through a morning of mist, the right
things that might not last and so soon went by. And they only
were real and true, beyond them was nought you might ever
attain but a weary dream and that last dark silence – Oh, only
a fool loved being alive!

But Marget threw her arms around her when she said that,
and kissed her with red, kind lips, so red they were that they
looked like haws, and said there were lovely things in the world,
lovely that didn't endure, and the lovelier for that. *Wait till you
find yourself in the arms of your lad, in the harvest time it'll be
with the stooks round about you, and he'll stop from joking –
they do, you know, and that's just when their blood-pressure
alters – and he'll take you like this – wait, there's not a body to
see us! – and hold you like this, with his hands held so, and
kiss you like this!*

It was over in a moment, quick and shameful, fine for all
that, tingling and strange and shameful by turns. Long after she
parted with Marget that evening she turned and stared down
at Peesie's Knapp and blushed again; and suddenly she was

seeing them all at Blawearie as though they were strangers
naked out of the sea, she felt ill every time she looked at father
and mother. But that passed in a day or so, for nothing endures.

Not a thing, though you're over-young to go thinking of that,
you've your lessons and studies, the English Chris, and living
and eating and sleeping that other Chris that stretches your toes
for you in the dark of the night and whispers a drowsy *I'm you*.
But you might not stay from the thinking when all in a day,
Marget, grown part of your life, came waving to you as you
neared the Knapp with the news she was off to Aberdeen to
live with an auntie there – *it's a better place for a scholar, Chae
says, and I'll be trained all the sooner.*

And three days later Chae Strachan and Chris drove down
to the station with her, and saw her off at the platform, and
she waved at them, bonny and young, Chae looked as numb as
Chris felt. He gave her a lift from the station, did Chae, and on
the road he spoke but once, to himself it seemed, not Chris: *Ay,
Marget lass, you'll do fine, if you keep the lads at bay from
kissing the bonny breast of you.*

So that was your Marget gone, there seemed not a soul in
Kinraddie that could take her place, the servant queans of an
age with Chris were no more than gowks and gomerils a-screech
round the barn of the Mains at night with the ploughmen
snickering behind them. And John Guthrie had as little use for
them as Marget herself. *Friends? Stick to your lessons and let's
see you make a name for yourself, you've no time for friends.*

Mother looked up at that, friendly-like, not feared of him at
all, she was never feared. *Take care her head doesn't soften
with lessons and dirt, learning in books it was sent the wee red
daftie at Cuddiestoun clean skite, they say.* And father poked
out his beard at her. *Say? Would you rather see her skite with
book-learning or skite with* – and then he stopped and began
to rage at Dod and Alec that were making a noise in the kitchen
corner. But Chris, a-pore above her books in the glow of the
paraffin lamp, heeding to Caesar's coming in Gaul[22] and the
stour the creature raised there, knew right well what father had
thought to speak of – *lust* was the word he'd wanted, perhaps.

And she turned a page with the weary Caesar man and thought of the wild career the daftie Andy had led one day in the roads and woods of Kinraddie.

Marget had barely gone when the thing came off, it was fair the speak of the place that happening early in April. The sowing time was at hand, John Guthrie put down two parks with grass and corn, swinging hand from hand as he walked and sowed and Will carried the corn across to him from the sacks that lined the rigs. Chris herself would help of an early morning when the dew had lifted quick, it was blithe and lightsome in the caller air with the whistle of the blackbirds in Blawearie's trees and the glint of the sea across the Howe and the wind blowing up the braes with a fresh, wild smell that caught you and made you gasp. So silent the world with the sun just peeking above the horizon those hours that you'd hear, clear and bright as though he paced the next field, the ringing steps of Chae Strachan – far down, a shadow and a sunlit dot, sowing his parks behind the steadings of Peesie's Knapp. There were larks coming over that morning, Chris minded, whistling and trilling dark and unseen against the blaze of the sun, now one lark, now another, till the sweetness of the trilling dizzied you and you stumbled with heavy pails corn-laden, and father swore at you over the red beard of him *Damn't to hell, are you fair a fool, you quean?*

That morning it was that the daftie Andy stole out of Cuddiestoun and started his scandalous rampage through Kinraddie. Long Rob of the Mill was to say he'd once had a horse that would do that kind of thing in the early Spring, leap dykes and ditches and every mortal thing it would if it heard a douce little mare go by. Gelding though it was, the horse would do that, and what more was Andy, poor devil, than a gelding? Not that Mistress Ellison had thought him that – faith, no!

It was said she ran so fast after her meeting with the daftie she found herself down two stone in weight. The coarse creature chased her nearly in sight of the Mains and then scrabbled away into the rough ground beyond the turnpike. She'd been out fell early for her, Mistress Ellison, and was just holding along the road a bit walk to Fordoun[23] when out of some bushes

Andy jumped, his ramshackle face all swithering and his eyes all hot and wet. She thought at first he was hurted and then she saw he was trying to laugh, he tore at her frock and cried *You come!* She nearly fainted, but didn't, her umbrella was in her hand, she broke it over the daftie's head and then turned and ran, he went louping after her along the road, like a great monkey he leapt, crying terrible things to her. When sight of the Mains put an end to that chase he must have hung back in the hills for an hour or so and seen Mistress Munro, the futret, go sleeking down the paths to the Mains and Peesie's Knapp and Blawearie, asking sharp as you like, as though she blamed every soul but herself, *Have you seen that creature Andy?*

While she was up Blawearie way he must have made his road back across the hills, high up above the Cuddiestoun, till Upperhill came in sight. For later one of the ploughmen thought he'd seen the creature, shambling up against the skyline, picking a great bunch of sourocks and eating them. Then he got into the Upperhill wood and waited there, and it was through that wood at nine o'clock that Maggie Jean Gordon would hold her way to the station – close and thick larch wood with a path through it, where the light fell hardly at all and the cones crunched and rotted underfoot and sometimes a green barrier of whin crept up a wood ditch and looked out at you, and in the winter days the deer came down from the Grampians and sheltered there. But in the April weather there were no deer to fright Maggie Jean, even the daftie didn't frighten her. He'd been waiting high in the wood before he took her, but maybe before that he ran alongside the path she was taking, keeping hidden from view of the lass, for she heard a little crackle rise now and then, she was to remember, and wondered that the squirrels were out so early. Gordon she was, none the better for that it might be, but a blithe little thing, thin body and bonny brown hair, straight to walk and straight to look, and you liked the laugh of her.

So through the wood and right into the hands of the daftie she went, and when he lifted her in his hands she was frightened not even then, not even when he bore her far back into the wood, the broom-branches whipped their faces and the wet of the dew sprayed on them, coming into a little space, broom-surrounded, where the sun reached down a long finger into the dimness. She stood up and shook herself when he set her down, and told him she couldn't play any longer, she must really hurry else she'd miss her train. But he paid no heed, crouching on one knee he turned his head this way and that, jerking round and about, listening and listening, so that Maggie Jean listened as well and heard the ploughmen cry to their horses and her mother at that moment calling the hens to feed – *Tickie-ae! Tickie-ae!* – *Well, I must go*, she told him and caught her bag in her hand and hadn't moved a step when he had her in his hands again; and after a minute or so, though she wasn't frightened even then, she didn't like him, telling him mother only was allowed to touch her there, not anyone else, and please she'd have to go. And she looked up at him, pushing him away, his mad, awful head, he began to purr like a great, wild cat, awful it must have been to see him and hear him. And God alone knows the next thing he'd have done but that then, for it was never such a morning before for that bright clearness, far away down and across the fields a man began to sing, distant but very clear, with a blithe lilt in the voice of him. And he broke off and whistled the song and then he sang it again:

> Bonny wee thing,
>   Canty wee thing,
> Lovely wee thing,
>   Wert thou mine
> I would clasp thee
>   In my bosom
> Lest my jewel
>   I should tyne![24]

And at that, crouching and listening, the daftie took his hands from Maggie Jean and began to sing the song himself; and he took her in his arms again, but gently, fondling her as though she were a cat, and he set her on her feet and tugged straight the bit frock she wore; and stood up beside her and took her hand and guided her back to the path through the larch wood.

And she went on and left him and once she looked back and saw him glowering after her; and because she saw he was weeping she ran back to him, kind thing, and patted his hand and said *Don't cry!* and she saw his face like that of a tormented beast and went on again, down to the station. And only when she came home that night did she tell the story of her meeting with Cuddiestoun's Andy.

But as the day wore on and Long Rob, working in that orra field above the Mill, still sang and sweated and swore at his horses, the singing must have drawn the Andy creature down from the larch wood, by hedges creeping and slipping from the sight of the Upperhill men in the parks. And once Rob raised his head and thought he saw a moving shadow in a ditch that bounded the orra ground. But he thought it a dog and just heaved a stone or so in case it was some beast in heat or on chicken-killing. The shadow yelped and snarled at that, but was gone from the ditch when Rob picked up another stone; so he went on with his work; and the daftie, tearing along the Kinraddie road out towards the Bridge End, with the blood red trickling down his woesome face, was all unseen by him.

But right at the corner, close where the road jerked round by Pooty's place, he near ran full tilt into Chris herself, coming up from Auchinblae she was with the messages her mother had sent her on, her basket over her arm and her mind far off with the Latin verbs in *-are*. He slavered at her, running towards her, and she screamed, though she wasn't over-frightened; and then she threw the basket clean at his head and made for Pooty's. Pooty himself was sitting just inside the door when she reached it, the louping beast was close behind, she heard the pant of his breath and was to wonder often enough in later times over that coolness that came on her then. For she ran fleet as a bird inside the door and banged it right in the daftie's face and dropped the bar and watched the planks bulge and crack as outside the body of the madman was flung against them again and again. Pooty mouthed and stuttered at her in the dimness, but he grew real brave when she made him understand, he sharpened two of his sutor's knives and prowled trembling from window to window – the daftie left them untouched. Then Chris took a

keek from one window and saw him again; he was raking about
in the basket she'd thrown at his head, he made the parcels dirl
on the road till he found a great bar of soap; and then he began
to eat that, feuch! laughing and yammering all to himself, and
running back to throw himself against the door of Pooty's
again, the foam burst yellow through the beard of him as he
still ate and ate at the soap.

But he soon grew thirsty and went down to the burn, Pooty
and Chris stood watching him, and then it was that Cuddiestoun himself came ben the road. He sighted Andy and cried out
to him, and Andy leapt the burn and was off, and behind him
went Munro clatter-clang, and out of sight they vanished down
the road to Bridge End. Chris unbarred the door in spite of
Pooty's stutterings and went and repacked the bit basket, and
everything was there except the soap; and that was down poor
Andy's throat.

Feint the thing else he'd to eat that day, he was near the end
of his tether; for though he ran like a hare and Cuddiestoun
behind him was more than coarse in the legs, yet luck would
have it that Mutch of Bridge End was just guiding his team
across the road to start harrowing his yavil park when the two
runners came in sight, real daft-like both of them, Andy running
near double, soap and madness a-foam on his face, Cuddiestoun
bellowing behind. So Mutch slowed down his team and called
out to Andy, *Ay, man, you mustn't run near as fast as that*, and
when Andy was opposite threw out a foot and tripped him up,
and down in the stour went Andy, and Cuddiestoun was on
top of him in a minute, bashing in the face of him, but Alec
Mutch just stood and looked on, maybe working his meikle
ears a bit, it was no concern of his. The daftie's hands went up
to his face as the bashings came and then Cuddiestoun gripped
him right in the private parts, he screamed and went slack, like
a sack in Cuddiestoun's hands. And that was the end of Andy's
ploy, for back to the Cuddiestoun he was driven and they said
Mistress Munro took down his breeks and leathered him sore;
but you never know the lies they tell, for others said it was
Cuddiestoun himself she leathered, him having let the daftie
out of the house that morning to scandalise her name with his

coarse on-goings. But he'd no chance [for] more of them, poor stock, next day the asylum officials came out and took him away in a gig, his hands fast tied behind his back; and that was the last they ever saw of Andy in Kinraddie.

Father raged when he heard the story from Chris, queer raging it was, he took her out to the barn and heard the story and his eyes slipped up and down her dress as she spoke, she felt sickened and queer. *He shamed you then?* he whispered; and Chris shook her head and at that father seemed to go limp and his eyes grew dull. *Ah well, it's the kind of thing that would happen in a godless parish like this. It can hardly happen again with the Reverend Gibbon in charge.*

Three minister creatures came down to Kinraddie to try for its empty pulpit. The first preached early in March, a pernickety thing as ever you saw, not over five feet in height, or he didn't look more. He wore a brave gown with a purple hood on it, like a Catholic creature, and jerked and pranced round the pulpit like a snipe with the staggers, working himself up right sore about *Latter-Day Doubt in the Kirk of Scotland.*[25] But Kinraddie had never a doubt of *him*, and Chris coming out of the kirk with Will and father heard Chae Strachan say he'd rather sit under a clucking hen than *that* for a minister. The second to try was an old bit man from Banff, shaking and old, and some said he'd be best, he'd have quietened down at his age, not aye on the look for a bigger kirk and a bigger stipend. For if there's a body on earth that would skin a tink for his sark and preach for a pension in purgatory it's an Auld Kirk minister.

But the poor old brute from Banff seemed fair sucked dry. He'd spent years in the writing of books and things, the spunk of him had trickled out into his pen, forbye that he read his sermon; and that fair settled his hash to begin with. So hardly a soul paid heed to his reading, except Chris and her father, she thought it fine;[26] for he told of the long dead beasts of the Scottish land in the times when jungle flowered its forests across the Howe and a red sun rose on the steaming earth that the feet of man had still to tread: and he pictured the dark, slow tribes that came drifting across the low lands of the northern seas, the great bear watched them come, and they hunted and fished and loved and died, God's children in the morn of time; and he brought the first voyagers sailing the sounding coasts, they brought the heathen idols of the great Stone Rings, the Golden Age was over and past and lust and cruelty trod the world; and he told of the rising of Christ, a pin-point of the cosmic light far off in Palestine,[27] the light that crept and wavered and did not die, the light that would yet shine as the sun on all the world, nor least the dark howes and hills of Scotland.

So what could you make of that, except that he thought Kinraddie a right coarse place since the jungles had all dried up? And his prayers were as short as you please, he'd hardly a thing to say of the King or the Royal Family at all, had the Reverend Colquohoun. So that fair put him out with Ellison and Mutch, they were awful King's men both of them, ready to die for the King any day of the week and twice on Sundays, said Long Rob of the Mill. And his preaching had no pleasure at all for Chae Strachan either, he wanted a preacher to praise up socialism and tell how Rich and Poor should be Equal. So the few that listened thought feint the much of the old book-writer from Banff, he stood never a chance, pleasing Chris and her father only, Chris didn't count, John Guthrie did, but his vote was only one and a hantle few votes the Banff man got when it came to the counting.

Stuart Gibbon was the third to make try for Kinraddie manse, and that Sunday when Chris sat down in the kirk and looked up at him in the pulpit she knew as well as she knew her own hand that he was to please all of them, though hardly more than a student he was, with black hair on him and a fine red face and shoulders strong and well-bulked, for he was a pretty man. And first his voice took them, it was brave and big like the voice of a bull, and fine and rounded, and he said the Lord's Prayer in a way that pleased gentry and simple. For though he begged to be forgiven his sins as he forgave those that sinned against him – instead, as was more genteel, crying to be forgiven his trespasses as he forgave those that trespassed against him[28] – still he did it with a fine solemnity that made everybody that heard right douce and grave-like; and one or two joined in near the end of the prayer, and that's a thing gey seldom done in an Auld Kirk kirk. Next came his sermon, it was out of the *Song of Solomon*[29] and well and rare he preached on it, showing that the Song had more meaning than one. It was Christ's description of the beauty and fine comeliness of the Auld Kirk of Scotland, and as such right reverently must it be read; and it was a picture of womanly beauty that moulded itself in the lithe and grace of the Kirk, and as such a perpetual manual for the women of Scotland that so they might attain to straight and fine lives in this world and salvation in the next. And in a minute or so all Kinraddie kirk was listening to him as though he were promising to pay their taxes at the end of Martinmas.

For it was fair tickling to hear about things like that read out from a pulpit, a woman's breasts and thighs and all the rest of the things, in that voice like the mooing of a holy bull; and to know it was decent Scripture with a higher meaning as well. So every body went home to his Sunday dinner well pleased with the new minister lad, no more than a student though he was; and on the Monday Long Rob of the Mill was fair deaved with tales of the sermon and put two and two together and said *Well, preaching like that's a fine way of having your bit pleasure by proxy, right in the stalls of a kirk, I prefer to take mine more private-like*. But that was Rob all over, folk said, a fair caution him and his Ingersoll that could neither make watches nor sense. And feint the voter it put off from tramping in to vote for Kinraddie's last candidate.

So in he went with a thumping majority, the Reverend Gibbon, by mid-May he was at the Manse, him and his wife, an English creature he'd married in Edinburgh. She was young as himself and bonny enough in a thin kind of way, with a voice as funny as Ellison's, near, but different, and big, dark eyes on her, and so sore in love were they that their servant quean said they kissed every time he went out a bit walk, the minister. And one time, coming back from a jaunt and finding her waiting him, the minister picked up his wife in his arms and ran up the stairs with her, both cuddling one the other and kissing, and laughing in each other's faces with shining eyes; and into their bedroom they went and closed the door and didn't come down for hours, though it was bare the middle of the afternoon. Maybe that was true and maybe it wasn't for the servant quean was one that old Mistress Sinclair had fee'd for the Manse in Gourdon, and before a Gourdon quean speaks the truth the Bervie burn will run backwards through the Howe.

Now every minister since Time was clecked in Kinraddie had made a round of the parish when he was inducted. Some did it quick, some did it slow, the Reverend Gibbon was among the quick. He came up to Blawearie just after the dinner hour on a Saturday and met in with John Guthrie sharpening a hoe in the close, weeds yammered out of Blawearie soil like bairns from a school at closing time, it was coarse, coarse land, wet, raw, and red clay, father's temper grew worse the more he saw of it. So when the minister came on him and cried out right heartily *Well, you'll be my neighbour Guthrie, man?* father cocked his red beard at the minister and glinted at him like an icicle and said *Ay, MISTER Gibbon, I'll be that.* So the minister held out his hand and changed his tune right quick and said quiet-like *You've a fine-kept farm here, Mr Guthrie, trig and trim, though I hear you've sat down a bare six months.* And he smiled a big, sappy smile.

So after that they were chief enough, sitting one the other on a handle on the sharn-barrow right in the middle of the close, the minister none feared for his brave, black clothes; and father told him the coarse land it was in Kinraddie, and the minister said he well believed him, it was only a man from the North could handle it so well. In a minute or so they were chief as brothers, father brought him over into the house, Chris stood in the kitchen and father said *And this quean's my daughter, Chris.* The minister smiled at her with his glinting black eyes and said *I hear you're right clever, Chrissie, and go up to the Duncairn College. How do you like it?* And Chris blushed and said *Fine, sir*, and he asked her what she was to be, and she told him a teacher, and he said there was no profession more honourable. Then mother came ben from putting the twins to sleep and was quiet and friendly, just as she always was with loon or laird, crowned with gold with her lovely hair. And she made the minister some tea and he praised it and said the best tea in his life he'd drunk in Kinraddie, it was the milk. And father asked whose milk they got at the Mains and the minister said *The Mains*, and father shot out his beard and said *Well may it be good, it's the best land in the parish they've a hold of, the dirt*, and the minister said *And now I'll have to be dandering down to the Manse. Come over and see us some evening, Chrissie, maybe the wife and I'll be able to lend you some books to help in your studies.* And off he went, swack enough, but no more fleet than father himself who swung along side him down to where the turnip-park broke off from the road.

Chris made for the Manse next Monday night, she thought maybe that would be the best time, but she said nothing to father, only told mother and mother smiled and said *Surely*; far-off she seemed and dreaming to herself as so often in the last month or so. So Chris put on the best frock that she used for Sundays, and her tall lacing boots, and prigged out her hair in front of the glass in the parlour, and went up across the hill by Blawearie loch, with the night coming over the Grampians and the snipe crying in their hundreds beyond the loch's grey waters – still and grey, as though they couldn't forget last summer nor hope for another coming. The Standing Stones pointed long shadow-shapes into the east, maybe just as they'd done of an evening two thousand years before when the wild men climbed the brae and sang their songs in the lithe of those shadows while the gloaming waited there above the same quiet hills. And a queer, uncanny feeling came on Chris then, she looked back half-feared at the Stones and the whiteness of the loch, and then went hurrying through the park paths till she came out above kirkyard and Manse. Beyond the road the Meikle House rose up in its smother of trees, you saw the broken walls of it, the flagstaff light was shining already, it would soon be dark.

She unsnecked the door of the kirkyard wall, passing through to the Manse, the old stones rose up around her silently, not old when you thought of the Standing Stones of Blawearie brae but old enough for all that. Some went back to the old, unkindly times of the Covenanters, one had a skull and crossed bones and an hour-glass on it and was mossed half over so that but hardly you could read the daft-like script with its esses like effs,[30] and it made you shudder. The yews came all about that place of the oldest stone and Chris going past put out her hand against it and the low bough of a yew whispered and gave a low laugh behind her, and touched her hand with a cold, hairy touch so that a daft-like cry started up on her lips, she wished she'd gone round by the plain, straightforward road, instead of this near-cut she'd thought so handy.

So she whistled to herself, hurrying, and just outside the kirkyard stood the new minister himself, leaning over the gate looking in among the stones, he saw her before she saw him and his voice fair startled her. *Well, Chrissie, you're very gay*, he said, and she felt ashamed to have him know she whistled in a kirkyard; and he stared at her strange and queer and seemed to forget her a minute; and he gave an unco half-laugh and muttered to himself, but she heard him, *One's enough for one day*. Then he seemed to wake up, he mooed out at her *And now you'll be needing a book, no doubt. Well, the Manse is fair in a mess this evening, spring-cleaning or something like that, but if you just wait here a minute I'll run in and pick you something light and cheerful.*

Off he set, she was left alone among the black trees that bent over the greyness of the kirkyard. Unendingly the unseen grasses whispered and rustled above the stones' dim, recumbent shapes, and she thought of the dead below those stones, farmers and ploughmen and their wives, and little bairns and new-born babes, their bodies turned to skeletons now so that if you dug in the earth you'd find only their bones, except the new-buried, and maybe there in the darkness worms and awful things crawled and festered in flesh grown rotten and black, and it was a terrifying place. But at last came the minister, not hurrying at all but just drifting towards her, he held out a book and said *Well, here it is, and I hope you'll like it.* She took the book and looked at it in the dying light, its name was *Religio Medici*,[31] and she mastered her shyness and asked *Did you, sir?* and the minister stared at her and said, his voice just even as ever, *Oh, like hell!* and turned about and left her to go back through the terror of the yews. But they didn't terrify at all, climbing home and thinking of that word he used, swearing it had been and nothing else, should she tell of it to father?

No, that wouldn't do, a minister was only a man, and he'd loaned her a book, kind of him though he looked so queer. And besides, father didn't know of this errand of hers down to the Manse, maybe he'd think she was trying to hold in with gentry and would swear himself. Not that he swore often, father, she told herself as she hurried across the brae, and, hurrying, climbed out of the dimness into the last of the May daylight with the sunset a glow and a glimmer that danced about her feet, waiting for her; not often, except when things went clean over him, as that day in the sowing of the park below Blawearie when first the cart-shaft had broken and then the hammer had broken and then he'd watched the rain come on, and he'd gone nearly mad, raging at Will and Chris that he'd leather them till they hadn't enough skin to sit a threepenny bit on; and at last, fair skite, he'd shaken his fist at the sky and cried *Ay, laugh, you Mucker!*[32]

Chris took a bit peep or so in *Religio Medici* and nearly yawned her head off with the reading of it, it was better fun on a spare, slow day to help mother wash the blankets. In the sun of the red, still weather Jean Guthrie had every bed in Blawearie cleared and the blankets piled in tubs half-filled with lukewarm water and soap, and Chris took off her boots and her stockings and rolled her knickers far up her white legs and stepped in the grey, lathered folds of blankets and tramped them up and down. It felt fine with the water gurgling blue and iridescent up through your toes and getting thicker and thicker; then into the next tub while mother emptied the first, lovely work, she felt she could trample blankets forever, only it grew hot and hot, a red forenoon while they did the washing. So next time mother was indoors she took off her skirt and then her petticoat and mother coming out with another blanket cried *God, you've stripped!* and gave Chris a slap in the knickers, friendly-like, and said *You'd make a fine lad, Chris quean*, and smiled the blithe way she had and went on with the washing.

But John Guthrie came home from the fields then, him and Will, and as soon as he saw her, father's face went all shrivelled up and he cried *Get out of that at once, you shameful limmer, and get on your clothes!* And out she got, white and ashamed, shamed more for father than herself, and Will turned red and led off the horses, awkward-like, but John Guthrie went striding across the close to the kitchen and mother and began to rage at her. *What would folk say of the quean if they saw her sit there, near naked? We'd be the speak and laughing-stock of the place.* And mother looked at him, sweet and cold, *Ah, well, it wouldn't be the first time you've seen a naked lass yourself; and if your neighbours haven't they must have fathered their own bairns with their breeks on.*

Father had been in a fair stamash at that, he left mother and went out with his face dead-white, not red, and he didn't say another word, he didn't speak to mother all that evening nor all the next day. Chris went to her bed that night and thought of the happening, lying close-up and alone, it had been as though she saw a caged beast peep from her father's eyes as he saw her stand in the tub. Like a fire that burned across the close, it went on and on as though she still stood there and he glowered at her. She hid her face below the blankets but she couldn't forget, next morning she was able to bear thinking of it no longer, the house had quietened with the folk gone out, she went to mother and asked her straight, she'd never asked anything of the kind before.

And then an awful thing happened, mother's face went grey and old as she stopped from her work at the kitchen table, she went whiter and whiter second on second, Chris near went out of her mind at the sight. *Oh, mother, I didn't mean to vex*, she cried and flung her arms round mother and held her tight, seeing her face then, so white and ill-looking it had grown in the last month. And mother smiled at her at last, putting her hands on her shoulders. *Not you, Chris quean, just life. I cannot tell you a thing or advise you a thing, my quean. You'll have to face men for yourself when the time comes, there's none can stand and help you.* And then she said something queerer, kissing Chris, *Mind that for me sometime if I cannot thole it longer* – and stopped and laughed and was blithe again. *We're daft, the two of us, run out and bring me a pail of water.* And Chris went out with the pail, out and up to the pump in the hot red weather, and then something came on her, she crept back soft-footed and there mother stood as she'd left her, white and lonely and sad, Chris didn't dare go into her, just stood and looked.

Something was happening to mother, things were happening to all of them, nothing ever stayed the same except maybe this weather and if it went on much longer the Reverend Colquohoun's[33] bit jungles would soon be sprouting back across the parks of the Howe. The weary pleiter of the land and its life while you waited for rain or thaw! Glad she'd be when she'd finished her exams and was into Aberdeen University, getting her B.A.[34] and then a school of her own, the English Chris, father and his glowering and girning forgotten, she'd have a brave house of her own and wear what she liked and have never a man vexed with sight of her, she'd take care of that.

Or maybe she wouldn't, queer that she never knew herself for long, grown up though she was, a woman now, near. Father said that the salt of the earth were the folk that drove a straight drill and never looked back, but she was no more than ploughed land still, the furrows went criss and cross, you wanted this and you wanted that, books and the fineness of them no more than an empty gabble sometimes, and then the sharn and the snapping that sickened you and drove you back to books—

She turned over on the grass with a jerk when she came to that troubled thinking. The sunset was painting the loch, but hot as ever it was, breaking up for one of those nights when you couldn't bear a blanket above you and even the dark was a foul, black blanket. It had died off, the wind, while she lay and thought, feint the loss was that, but there was sign of nothing in the place of it, the broom stood up in the late afternoon, not moving, great faces massed and yellow like the faces of an army of yellow men, looking down across Kinraddie, watching for the rain. Mother below would be needing her help, Dod and Alec back from the school already, father and Will soon in from the fields.

There somebody was crying her already!

She stood up and shook out her frock and went through the grass to the tail of the brae, and looked down and saw Dod and Alec far below waving up at her. They were crying her name excitedly, it sounded like the lowing of calves that had lost their mother, she went slow to tease them till she saw their faces.

It was then, as she flew down the hill with her own face white, that the sky crackled behind her, a long flash zig-zagged across the Grampian peaks, and far across the parks by the hills she heard the hiss of rain. The drought had broken at last.

II

Drilling

Lying down when her climb up the cambered brae was done, panting deep from the rate she'd come at – skirt flying and iron-resolute she'd turn back for nothing that cried or called in all Blawearie – no, not even that whistle of father's! – Chris felt the coarse grass crackle up beneath her into a fine quiet couch. Neck and shoulders and hips and knees she relaxed, her long brown arms quivered by her side as the muscles slacked away, the day drowsed down an aureal light through the long brown lashes that drooped on her cheeks. As the gnomons of a giant dial the shadows of the Standing Stones crept into the east, snipe called and called—

Just as the last time she'd climbed to the loch: and when had that been? She opened her eyes and thought, and tired from that and closed down her eyes again and gave a queer laugh. The June of last year it had been, the day when mother had poisoned herself and the twins.

So long as that and so near as that, you'd thought of the hours and days as a dark, cold pit you'd never escape. But you'd escaped, the black damp went out of the sunshine and the world went on, the white faces and whispering ceased from the pit, you'd never be the same again, but the world went on and you went with it. It was not mother only that died with the twins, something died in your heart and went down with her to lie in Kinraddie kirkyard – the child in your heart died then, the bairn that believed the hills were made for its play, every road set fair with its warning posts, hands ready to snatch you back from the brink of danger when the play grew over-rough. That died, and the Chris of the books and the dreams died with it, or you folded them up in their paper of tissue and laid them away by the dark, quiet corpse that was your childhood.

So Mistress Munro of the Cuddiestoun told her that awful night she came over the rain-soaked parks of Blawearie and laid out the body of mother, the bodies of the twins that had died so quiet in their crib. She nipped round the rooms right quick and pert and uncaring, the black-eyed futret, snapping this order and that, it was her that terrified Dod and Alec from their crying, drove father and Will out tending the beasts. And quick and cool and cold-handed she worked, peeking over at Chris with her rat-like face. *You'll be leaving the College now, I'll warrant, education's dirt and you're better clear of it. You'll find little time for dreaming and dirt when you're keeping the house at Blawearie.*

And Chris in her pit, dazed and dull-eyed, said nothing, she minded later; and some other than herself went searching and seeking out cloths and clothes. Then Mistress Munro washed down the body that was mother's and put it in a night-gown, her best, the one with blue ribbons on it that she hadn't worn for many a year; and fair she made her and sweet to look at, the tears came at last when you saw her so, hot tears wrung from your eyes like drops of blood. But they ended quick, you would die if you wept like that for long, in place of tears a long wail clamoured endless, unanswered inside your head *Oh, mother, mother, why did you do it?*

And not until days later did Chris hear why, for they tried to keep it from her and the boys, but it all came out at the inquest, mother had poisoned herself, her and the twins, because she was pregnant again and afraid with a fear dreadful and calm and clear-eyed. So she had killed herself while of unsound mind, had mother, kind-eyed and sweet, remembering those Springs of Kildrummie last of all things remembered, it may be, and the rooks that cried across the upland parks of Don far down beyond the tunnels of the years.

A month later Dod and Alec went back to school and as they left to go home that night first one scholar cried after them and others took it up *Daftie, daftie! Whose mother was a daftie?*

They ran for Blawearie and came stumbling into the house weeping and weeping, father went fair mad at the sight of them and skelped them both, but skelping or not they wouldn't go back to the school next day.

And then Will spoke up, he cared not a fig for father now. All in a night it seemed the knowledge had come on him father wouldn't dare strike him again, he bought an old bicycle and would ride off in an evening as he pleased, his face cold and hard when he caught the glint of father's eye. Of a morning John Guthrie grumbled and girned at him, crying *Where do you wander each night like a tink?* But Will would say never a word, except once when John Guthrie made at him and then he swung round and whispered *Take care*. And at that father stopped and drew back, Chris watched them with angry eyes, angry and frightened in a breath as now when Will spoke up for his brothers.

Why should they go back? I wouldn't. Oh, and you needn't glower at me. You take damn good care you never go near a mart or a market yourself nowadays – I've to do all your dirty work for you!

Father louped to his feet at that, Will was on his as well, they stood with fists clenched in the kitchen and Dod and Alec stopped from their greeting and stared and stared. But Chris thrust the table in between the two, she made out she wanted it there for baking; and they dropped their fists and John Guthrie swore, but soft; and Will reddened up and looked foolish.

But father that night, he said never a word to the rest of them in Blawearie, he was over-proud for that, wrote off to his sister Janet in Auchterless[1] and asked that she take Dod and Alec in her care and give them an Aberdeen schooling. In a week she was down from the North, Auntie Janet and her man, Uncle Tam he was, big and well-bulked and brave, and his watch-chain had rows and rows of wee medals on it he'd gotten for playing quoits. And they were fell kind, the two of them, Alec and Dod were daft with delight when they heard of the Auchterless plan. But Auntie and Uncle had never a bairn of their own and soon made plain if the boys went with them it would be for aye, they wanted to adopt the pair of them.

Father sneered and thrust out his beard at that *So you'd like to steal the flesh of my body from me?* and Auntie Janet nodded, right eye to eye, *Aye, John, just that, we've never a wean of our own, though God knows it's not for want of the trying;* and father said *Ill blood breeds ill;* and Auntie said *Ay, it'll be long ere I have to kill myself because my man beds me like a breeding sow;* and father said *You dirty bitch.*

Chris stuck the dirl of the row till her head near burst and then ran out of the kitchen, through the close into the cornyard, where Will was prowling about. He'd heard the noise and he laughed at them, but his eyes were angry as his arm went round her. *Never heed the dirty old devils, one's bad as the other, father, auntie, or that midden that's covered with its wee tin medals. Come off to the park with me and we'll bring home the kye.*

Deep in clover the cows as they came on them, Chris and Will; and they went in no hurry at all, unanxious to be back in Blawearie. And Will seemed angry and gentle and kind all at once. *Don't let them worry you, Chris, don't let father make a damned slave of you, as he'd like to do. We've our own lives to lead.* And she said *What else can I do but bide at home now?*

He said he didn't know, but he'd be libbed and pole-axed and gutted if *he* did for long, soon as he'd saved the silver he was off to Canada, a man was soon his own master there. Chris listened to that with eyes wide opened, she caught at the hope of it and forgot to smack at the kye that loitered and boxed and galumphed in their cloverful-foolishness up the brae. *Oh, Will, and you could send for me as your housekeeper!* He turned a dull red and smacked at the kye and Chris sighed and the hope went out, he'd no need to answer *Ay, maybe, but maybe it would hardly suit you.*

So then she knew for sure he'd a lass somewhere in Drum-lithie, it was with her he planned to share a bed and a steading in the couthy lands of Canada.

And when they got back to Blawearie they found the row ended, father'd given in to his sister Janet, ill the grace though he did it with. In three days time but three of them were sitting to

meat at the kitchen table, Chris listened for days for voices of
folk that were dead or gone, both far enough from Blawearie.
But even that lost strangeness in time, the harvest drew on, she
went out to the park to help with it, lush and heavy enough it
had sprung and yellowed with the suns and rains of the last
two months.

He'd no binder, father, wouldn't hear of the things, but he'd
brought an old reaper from Echt and with that they cut the
corn; though Will swore he'd be the fool of Kinraddie seen
driving a thing like that. Father laughed at him over his beard,
like a spitting cat, *If Kinraddie's laughing can make you a
bigger fool than nature made you it'll be a miracle; and don't
fret the sark from your dowp, my mannie, I'LL do the driving.*
And though Will muttered at that he gave in all the same, for
every harvest there came something queer and terrible on father,
you couldn't handle the thing with a name, it was as if he grew
stronger and crueller then, ripe and strong with the strength of
the corn, he'd be fleeter than ever and his face filled out, and
they'd hear him come up from the parks, astride the broad back
of Bess, singing hymns, these were the only things that he ever
sang, singing with a queer, keen shrillness that brought the
sweat in the palms of your hands.

Now in the park below Blawearie, steading and house, the
best crop, and that was the ley, was the first they cut, a great
swither of a crop with straw you could hardly break and twist
into bands for sheaves. Sore work Chris found it to keep her
stretch of each bout cleared for the reaper's coming, the weather
cool and grey though it was. But a sun was behind the greyness
and sometimes when you raised your head from the sheaves
you'd see a beam of light on the travel far over the parks of
Upperhill or lazing across the moor or dancing a-top the Cuddiestoun stooks, a beam from the hot, grey haze of that sky that
watched and waited above the sweat of the harvesting Howe.

First ere the cutting in the ley began there'd been roads to
clear all round the corn, wide bouts that father scythed himself,
he swore that the scythe would yet come back to its own when
the binders and reapers rotted in rust and folk bred the old
breed again. But its time was past or was yet to come, the

scythe's, out the reaper was driven and yoked, Chris followed down at the tail of it. The best of weather for harvest, folk said, it was ill to cut in a swither of heat; and so still was the air by morn and noon it reminded you of the days in Spring, you'd hear the skirl of the blades ring down the Howe for mile on mile, the singing of Long Rob of the Mill, the Cuddiestoun creatures swearing at Tony as he stood and gowked at the stooks. Then Blawearie's reaper clanged in through the gates with Bess and Clyde at the pole, and the blades flashed and brightened like the teeth of a beast and snarled in a famished freedom. And then John Guthrie cried *Get up!* and swung the horses down the bout, and the hungry snarl changed to a deep, clogged growling as the corn was driven on the teeth by the swinging reaper flails; and down the bout, steady and fine, sped the reaper, clean-cutting from top to bottom, with never a straggling straw as on other farms, John Guthrie saw to that.

But feint the time had you for glowering at rig or reaper, soon as the horses were off and the flail drove the first sheaf from the tail-board Chris had pounced on that sheaf and gathered and bound it and flung it aside before you could say *Glenbervie!* and had run to the next and twisted its band, and gathered and bound and bound and gathered with her hands like a mist below her eyes, so quick they were. Midway the bout Will met with her, working up from the foot, and flicking the sweat from his face. And just as they straightened and stretched and looked up to the head of the park the clong, clong of the empty reaper would change to the snarling engaging whirr as father guided the horses to the cutting again. Still the sun smouldered behind its mists and out by Kinneff the fog-horn moaned all hours, you felt like moaning like that yourself long ere the day was out and your back near cracked and broke with the strain of the bending.

But in three days time the ley was cut, the yavil glowed yellow across the dykes and they moved to that without stop. And then suddenly the mists cleared up and the fog-horn stopped from its droning, it came on real blistering weather of heat, but hardly you'd bear to touch on the wood of the reaper shaft when you loosed the horses, so hot it grew. Kinraddie gasped and then bent to its chaving again, this heat wouldn't last, the rain was due, God help the crops that waited cutting then.

The second day of the yavil cutting a tink climbed up the Blawearie road[2] from the turnpike and cried to John Guthrie for work, and father said *Maybe, maybe. Let's see the work that you've in you first,* and the tink said *Ay, fine that.* And he off with his coat and took the middle of the bout, and was up it in a jiffy, gathering and binding to the manner born, you might say, and giving Chris a bit smile when he met with her. So, coming down the next bout father cried to the tink that he'd take him on for a day or so, if the weather held; and Chris could get up to the house and see to the supper – *no idling, quean, mind that.* He was a black-like, gypsy childe, the tink, father wouldn't have him into the kitchen for meat, the creature might be all lice; and he wouldn't have him sleep in the house.

So Chris made him a shake-down out in the barn, he said he was real content with that. But when she carried him his supper over to the barn the first night she felt shamed for him suddenly, and told him she'd have had him eat in the house if it hadn't been [for] father. And he said *Don't let that fash you, lass, I'm as little anxious for his company as he is for mine. Forbye, he's only a Kinraddie clown!* Chris felt her face flame at that, it just showed you there was no good doing kindness to tinks, but she made out she hadn't heard and turned back to go over the close. Then it was the tink put out his arm, round her legs before she could move, almost he pulled her down on the hay beside him. *You've never lain with a man yet, lass, I can see, and that's a sore waste of hot blood like yours. So mind I'm here if you want me, I've deflowered more queans than I've years to my name and sent none of them empty away.* He loosed her then, laughing low, she couldn't do anything but stare and stare at him, sick and not angry, something turned in her stomach and her knees felt weak. The tink put out his hand and patted her leg again, *Mind, if you want me I'll be here,* and Chris shook her head, she felt too sick to speak, and slipped out of the barn and crossed the close and washed and washed at her hands and face with hot water till father lowered his paper and asked *Have you gone clean daft?*

But up in her room that night, the room that was hers and hers only now, Will slept where his brothers had slept, she saw a great moon come over the Grampians as she undressed for bed. She opened the window then, she liked to sleep with it open, and it was as though the night had been waiting for that, a waft of the autumn wind blew in, it was warm and cool and it blew in her face with a smell like the smell of late clover and the smell of dung and the smell of the stubble fields all commingled. She leant there breathing it, watching the moon with the hills below it but higher than Blawearie, Kinraddie slept like a place in a picture-book, drifting long shadows that danced a petronella across the night-stilled parks. And without beginning or reason a strange ache came in her, in her breasts, so that they tingled, and in her throat, and below her heart, and she heard her heart beating, and for a minute the sound of the blood beating through her own head. And she thought of the tink lying there in the barn and how easy it would be to steal down the stairs and across the close, dense black in its shadows, to the barn.

But it was only for a second she thought of that, daftly, then laughed at herself, cool and trim and trig, and closed the window, shutting out the smells of the night, and slowly took off her clothes, looking at herself in the long glass that had once stood in mother's room. She was growing up limber and sweet, not bonny, perhaps, her cheek-bones were over high and her nose over short for that, but her eyes clear and deep and brown, brown, deep and clear as the Denburn flow, and her hair was red and was brown by turns, spun fine as a spider's web, wild, wonderful hair. So she saw herself and her teeth clean-cut and even, a white gleam in that grave brown stillness of face John Guthrie's blood had bequeathed to her. And below face and neck now her clothes were off was the glimmer of shoulders and breast and there her skin was like satin, it tickled her touching herself. Below the tilt of her left breast was a dimple, she saw it and bent to look at it and the moonlight ran down her back, so queer the moonlight she felt the running of that beam along her back. And she straightened as the moonlight grew and looked at the rest of herself, and thought herself sweet and cool and fit for that lover who would some day come and kiss her and hold her, so.

And Chris saw the brown glimmer of her face grow sweet and scared as she thought of that – how they'd lie together, in a room with moonlight, and she'd be kind to him, kind and kind, giving him all and everything, and he'd sleep with his head here on her breast or they'd lie far into the mornings whispering one to the other, they'd have so much to tell! And maybe that third and last Chris would find voice at last for the whimsies that filled her eyes, and tell of rain on the roof at night, the terror and the splendour of it across the long slate roofs; and the years that faded and fell, dissolved as a breath, before those third clear eyes; and mother's face, lying dead; and the Standing Stones up there night after night and day after day by the loch of Blawearie, how around them there gathered things that wept and laughed and lived again in the hours before the dawn, till far below the cocks began to crow in Kinraddie and day had come again. And all that he'd believe, more than so often she believed herself, not laugh at, holding and kissing her, so. And faith! no more than a corpse he'd hold if she didn't get into her bed-gown and into her bed, you may dream of a lad till you're frozen as a stone, but he'll want you warmer than that.

So that was the harvest madness that came on Chris, mild enough it had been, she fell fast asleep in the middle of it. But it scored her mind as a long drill scores the crumbling sods of a brown, still May, it left neither pleasure nor pain, but she'd know that track all the days of her life, and its dark, long sweep across the long waiting field. Binder and reaper clattered and wheeped through the brittle weather that held the Howe, soon the weather might break and the stooking was far behind in Blawearie. But Will would have nothing to do with night-time work, he laughed in John Guthrie's face at the mention of it and jumped on his bicycle and rode for Drumlithie evening on evening. Father would wander out by the biggings and stare at the parks and then come glinting into the house and glower at Chris, *Get off to your bed when you've milked the kye*; and

she made little protest at that, she was tired enough at the end
of a day to nearly sleep in the straw of the byre.

But one night she didn't dare sleep, for up in the room he'd
shared with mother she heard John Guthrie get out of bed and
go slow padding about in his stocking soles, like a great cat
padding there, a beast that sniffed and planned and smelled at
the night. And once he came soft down the cowering creak of
the stairs and stopped by her door, and she held her breath,
near sick with fright, though what was there to be feared of?
And she heard his breath come quick and gasping, and the
scuffle of his hand on the sneck of the door; and then that
stopped, he must have gone up or down, the house was quiet,
but she didn't dare sleep again till Will came clattering home
in the still, small hours.

For the harvest madness was out in Kinraddie if Chris had
been quick to master hers. And though a lad and a quean might
think their ongoings known to none but themselves, they'd
soon be sore mistaken, you might hide with your lass on the
top of Ben Nevis[3] and have your bit pleasure there, but ten to
one when you got up to go home there'd be Mistress Munro or
some claik of her kidney, near sniggering herself daft with
delight at your shame. First it was Sarah Sinclair and the foreman at Upperhill, Ewan Tavendale he was, that the speak rose
round: they'd been seen coming out of the larch wood above
the Upperhill, that wood where the daftie had trapped Maggie
Jean, and what had they been doing there on their lone? It was
Alec Mutch of Bridge End that met them, him taking a dander
over the moor to the smithy with a broken binder-blade for
mending. The two hardly saw him at first, Miss Sinclair's face
was an unco sight, raddled with blushing it was like the leg of a
tuberculous rabbit when you skinned the beast, Ewan slouched
along at her side, hang-dog he looked as though it was his
mother he'd bedded with, said Alec, and maybe that's how it
had felt. Alec cried a *Good night!* to the pair, they near jumped
out of their skins, and went on with the story to the smithy
beyond the moor. And from there you may well be sure it went
through Kinraddie fast enough, the smith could tell lies faster
than he could shoe horses; and he was fell champion at that.

Truth or no, Chae Strachan got hold of the story and went over to Upperhill to see Ewan Tavendale and ask in a friendly way what he meant to do about Sarah, his sister-in-law, the daft old trollop. And maybe he'd have settled things canty and fine but that he came on Ewan at the wrong bit minute, he was sitting outside the bothy door with the rest of the bothy billies; and when Chae came up there rose a bit snigger, that fair roused Chae, he stopped bang in front of them and asked what the hell they were laughing at? And Sam Gourlay said *Little, damned little*, looking Chae from head to foot; and Ewan said he felt more in the way of weeping than laughing at such a sight, and he spoke in a slow, impudent way that fair roused Chae's dander to the boiling point. So, being a fell impatient man, and skilly with his hands, he took Sam Gourlay a clout in the lug that couped him down in the stour and then before you could wink he and Ewan were at it, ding-dong, like a pair of tinks, all round the Upperhill close; and Upprums came running in his leggings, the creature, fair scandalised, but he got a shove in the guts that couped him right down in the greip where once his son Jock had been so mischieved; and that was the end of *his* interfering. In a minute or so it was plain that Ewan, fight though he might, was like to have the worst of the sett, he was no match for that madman Chae. So the rest of the bothy lads up and went for Chae; and when he got back to Peesie's Knapp he'd hardly a stitch on his back. But Ewan, the coarse, dour brute, had a cut in the face that stopped *his* mouth for a while, and a black eye big enough to sole the boots on Cuddiestoun's meikle feet, folk said.

And faith! if it shouldn't be Cuddiestoun himself that began the next story, running into the middle of it himself, you might say, going up to the Manse to get a bit signature on some paper or other for his lawyer man. But Mr Gibbon they told him wasn't at home, Mistress Gibbon herself came out to tell him that, kind and fine as she was, but he didn't like her, the English dirt. So, fair disgruntled he turned from the door, maybe the poor brute's big sweating feet were fell sore already with a hot day's stooking. But just down at the end of the Manse's garden, where the yews bent thick above the lush grass their boughs that had sheltered the lost childe Wallace in the days before the coarse English ran him to earth and took him to London and there hanged and libbed him and hewed his body in four to hang on the gates of Scotland – there, in that grass in the half-dark was a rustling and squealing as though a drove of young pigs was rootling there. And Cuddiestoun stopped and picked up a handful of gravel from the minister's walk and flung it into the grass and cried *Away with you!* for maybe it was dogs in heat that were chaving there, big collies are none so chancy to meet when the creatures are set for mating. But instead of a collie up out of the grass rose the Gourdon quean, her that old Mistress Sinclair had fee'd for the Manse; and Munro saw her face then with a glazed look on it, like the face of a pig below the knife of its killer; and she brushed the hair from her face, daft-like, and went trailing past Munro, without a word from her, as though she walked half-asleep. But past him, going into the Manse, she began to whistle, and laughed a loud scraich of a laugh – as though she'd tried right desperately for something, and won, and beaten all the world in the winning of it. So it seemed to Cuddiestoun, and faith! you couldn't put that down to imagination, for he'd never had any, the ugly stock; so fair queer it must well have been, he stood and stared after her, dumbfoundered-like, and was just turning at last, to tramp down to the road, when he found Mr Gibbon himself at his elbow.

It had grown fell dark by then but not so dark that Cuddiestoun couldn't see the Minister was without a hat and was breathing in great deep paichs as though he'd come from the running of a race. And he barked out, *Well, speak up, man, what do you want?* Munro was sore took aback at hearing a fine childe like the minister snap at him that way. So he just said *Well, well, Mr Gibbon, you've surely been running a bit race?* and then wished he hadn't, for the minister went by him without another word, and then flung over his shoulder *If you want me, come to-morrow.*

And into the Manse he went and banged the door with a clash that fair made Cuddiestoun loup in his meikle boots. So there was nothing for him but to taik away home to Mistress

Munro, and faith! you might well believe the story lost nothing
in the telling she gave it, and soon every soul in Kinraddie had
a different version, Long Rob's was cried to John Guthrie as he
went by the Mill. He never spread scandal about folk, Long
Rob – only horses, was the joke they told of him – but maybe
he classed ministers lower than them.

It seemed like enough to John Guthrie, the story, though he'd
no coarse notions like Rob and his Ingersoll, the world was
rolling fast to a hell of riches and the old slave days come back
again, ministers went with it and whored with the rest. For the
bitterness had grown and eaten away into the heart of him in
his year at Blawearie. So coarse the land proved in the turn of
the seasons he'd fair been staggered, the crops had fared none
so bad this once, but he saw in a normal year the corn would
come hardly at all on the long, stiff slopes of the dour red clay.
Now also it grew plain to him here as never in Echt that the
day of the crofter was fell near finished, put by, the day of folk
like himself and Chae and Cuddiestoun, Pooty and Long Rob
of the Mill, the last of the farming folk that wrung their living
from the land with their own bare hands. Sign of the times he
saw Jean Guthrie's killing of herself to shame him and make of
his name a by-word in the mouths of his neighbours, sign of a
time when women would take their own lives or flaunt their
harlotries as they pleased, with the country-folk climbing on
silver, the few, back in the pit, the many; and a darkness down
on the land he loved better than his soul or God.

And next it was Will himself that started the claiks of Kinraddie,
him and his doings in Drumlithie. But Chris met the story ere
it reached Kinraddie, she met it in Drumlithie itself, in the yard
of the gardener Galt. The tink had been gone from Blawearie
that day she set out with her basket, no sign of the rain showed
even then, the heat held still as the white, dull heat from a
furnace door. Down in the turnpike the motor-cars went whipping by as she set her feet for Mondynes, there where the battle
was fought in the days long syne. Below the bridge went the
wash of the burn west to the Bervie Water, bairns cried and
splashed in the bridge's lithe, they went naked there when they

dared, she saw them glance white and startled in the shelter of the stones. Soon the heat grew such that she took off her hat and swung that in her hand and so climbed the road, and there to the left rose Drumlithie at last, some called it Skite to torment the folk and they'd get fell angry at that in Skite. No more than a rickle of houses it was, white with sunshine below its steeple that made of Skite the laugh of the Howe, for feint the kirk was near it. Folk said for a joke that every time it came on to rain the Drumlithie folk ran out and took in their steeple, that proud they were of the thing, it came from the weaver days of the village when damn the clock was there in the place and its tolling told the hour.

So that was Skite, it rose out of its dusts and its ancient smells, the berries hung ripe in the yard of the gardener Galt and he looked at Chris in a queer kind of way when he heard her name. Syne he began a sly hinting and joking as he weighed her berries, a great sumph of a man the creature was, fair running with creash in that hot weather, you near melted yourself as you looked at him. *And how's Will?* he asked, *We haven't seen much of him here of late – faith, the roses are fair fading from Mollie Douglas' cheeks.* And Chris said *Oh?* right stiff-like, and then *And I'll have two pounds of your blackberries too.* So he packed her that, hinting and gleying like a jokesome fat pig, she could have taken him a clout in the face, but didn't, it would only stir up more scandal, there seemed enough and to spare of that. Whatever could Will have been doing; and what had he done to his quean that he'd left her?

Right glad she was to be out from the stink of Skite with the road of Mondynes in front of her. Then she heard the bell of a bicycle far down the road behind and drew to one side, but the thing didn't pass, it slowed down and somebody called out, timid-like, *Are you Will Guthrie's sister?* Chris turned and saw her then, knew her at once Will's quean, young and white-faced and fair, and heard her own voice near troubled as the eyes that looked at her as she answered, *Yes; and you'll be Mollie Douglas?*

The face of the girl blushed slow at that, slow and sweet, and she looked away back at the steeple of Skite as though she feared the thing spied on them: and then suddenly, near crying, she was asking Chris to tell Will he must ride over and see her again, come again that night, she couldn't bear it longer – she didn't care were she shameless or not, she couldn't! And then she seemed to read the question in Chris's eyes, the blood drained off from her face in a minute and then came back, it seemed to Chris she must be blushing all over under her clothes, right down to the soles of her feet as she herself sometimes blushed. But she cried *Oh, you think THAT, like all of them, but it isn't true!* Staring at her surprised and shamed Chris found she just couldn't speak up and deny that THAT was indeed what she'd thought, what else was a body to think? Then she found Mollie Douglas' face bent close to hers, sweet and troubled and shamed as her own. And Mollie tried to look at her and then looked away, blushing as though she'd sink into the ground, such a fool of herself she was making. *It's not that at all, only I love him so sore I can't live if I don't see Will!*

So there they were in the middle of the road, so shamed to look one at the other they'd nothing to say; and then a gig came spanking along from the station, at sight of it Mollie jumped on her bicycle again, and wheeled it about, and looked over her shoulder with a smile you couldn't forget, and stammered and cried *Ta-ta!*

But Chris couldn't forget that look in her eyes, she went home with that in her mind and at supper that night couldn't take her own eyes from Will. She saw him then for the first time in years, almost a man, with his fair hair waving across his head and spreading to his cheeks in a rust-red down, like the down on a new-hatched chick; and his eyes blue and dark as a quean's, and kind when they looked at her, sulky when they turned on father. Not that they turned there often, there was never a word between Will and father unless they were clean compelled to it; like dumb folk working and eating together that needed no speech for hate.

Father ate his supper and climbed down the hill with his gun, Will loitered from door to window, whistling and idle, till he saw right across the Howe, up on Drumtochty hills,[4] something that rose and coiled ash-grey and then darker against the autumn sky, a great shape like a snake there in the quiet of the evening air, with its tail a glimmer that wasn't the sunset, burning up red in the lithe of the hills. *Whin-burning*, he called to Chris, *they're burning the whins up Drumtochty way, come on up the moor and have a try at ours. They're damned sore in the need of it.—But I've my jelly to make, you gowk!—Oh, to hell with your jelly, we'll soon be jelly and bones in a grave ourselves, come on!*

So she went, they gathered great piles of old papers for twisting in torches, and made up the brae to the moor. They sat down on the grass and breathed a while, Kinraddie below them all cut and close-stooked, waiting the coming of the night, the lowe of the Bervie lights as the glow of another whin-burning there by the sea. They spread out to left and right below the moor-gate, Chris held to the left and ran through the whins, stopping to kick holes down close to the ground wherever a meikle bush rose up. Then far round the knowe Will cried he was starting, she saw him a long way off with the sky behind him, and called back *All right!* and knelt by the biggest bush she'd struck; and kindled her torch and set its light to the crackling dryness of the grass.

It whoomed in an instant, the whin, she set her torch into it and ran to the next and fired that: and so in and out, backwards and forwards worked round the brae, you'd to speed quick as your legs could carry you to fire the frontward bushes when those behind raged out with their flames and smoke at your hair. In the dry, quiet evening the fire crackled up and spread and roared through the bushes and caught on the grass and crept and smoked on quick, searching trains to bushes unlit, and fired them, half you thought those questing tongues alive and malignant as they lapped through the grass. By the time Chris met with Will at the moor-gate there spread before them a park like an upland sea on fire, sweeping the hill, now the sun had quite gone and the great red roaring beast of a thing hunted and postured unchallenged, all Kinraddie was lit with its glare.

Will was black as a nigger, his eyebrows scorched, he pulled Chris down to rest on the grass. *By God, I hope the fire doesn't*

*catch on the fence up there, else old Guthrie will be casting me
out of Blawearie for bringing his grey hairs in sorrow to the
grave!*

He said that sneering-like, mocking at father's Aberdeenshire
voice, and Chris stirred half-angry, and sighed, and then asked
What would you do if he did put you out? and Will said *Go.—
Would you get a fee?—Damn the fears of that.*

But he didn't sound over-confident, Chris knew right well
that he'd find it none so easy if it came to the push, with the
harvest over now in the Howe. And then, for she'd clean forgot
her in the excitement of the fires, she minded the quean Mollie
Douglas – it was as though she saw her white face by Will's in
the firelit dark. *I met Mollie Douglas in Drumlithie to-day, she
asked me to ask you to go down and see her.*

He sat stock-still, he mightn't have heard, she pushed at his
elbow *Will!* And at that he shook off her hand, *Oh, I hear.
What's the good? I can't have a quean like other folk – I haven't
even a fee.—Maybe she doesn't want your fee, just you. Will,
they're saying things about her and you in Drumlithie–Galt and
coarse tinks like that.—Saying things? What things?—What
they aye say – that she's with a baby to you and you're biding
away from her now.—Galt said that?—Hinted at it, but he'll
do more than hint when he's not speaking to a sister of yours.*

She'd never heard him swear as he did then, jumping to his
feet with his fists tight-clenched. *That about Mollie – they said
that, the orra swine! I'll mash that bloody Galt's head till his
own mother won't know it!* But Chris told him that wouldn't
help much, folk would just snigger and say there was something,
sure, in the story of Mollie's condition. *Then what am I to do?*
Will asked, raging still, and Chris blushed and said *Wait. Do
you love her, Will?* But she might have known well enough
how he'd take that question, maybe he blushed himself in the
lithe of the dark, he threw down the paper torches he'd saved
and muttered *I'm away to Drumlithie*, and was running down
the hill before she could stop him.

Maybe, as he told Chris later, he went with no other intention
than seeing his Mollie herself. But as luck would have it, who
should he near run down with his bicycle outside the Drumlithie

Hotel but Galt himself, the great creash, gey drunk, and Alec
Mutch in his company. And Alec cried, *Fine night, Will,* but
Galt cried *Don't take her out to-night, Will lad, the grass is
overwet for lying on.* Will stopped and jumped off and left his
bicycle lying in the road and went up to Galt – *Speaking to me?*
And the fat creash, panting like a sow in litter and sweating all
down the great face of him, hiccoughed drunken-like *Who
else?*—*Well take that then,* Will said and let drive at the great
belly of Galt; but Mutch caught his arm and cried *Young
Guthrie, you've fair gone daft, the man's old enough to be your
father.* Will said if he'd a father like that he'd kill him and then
go and drown himself; and tried to break away from Mutch
and get at the Galt creash again. But Galt was right unkeen for
that, in a minute he'd turned, for all his fat, and made off like
a hare up the Drumlithie lanes, real swack with his girth and
all, and was out of sight in a second.

Well, sure you may be there were claiks enough in Skite for
Mutch to get all the story and drive home with it to the Bridge
End. In a day or so it was all about the place, Will was the
laughing-stock of Kinraddie. Father heard it first from the postman, who waved him down to the road to tell him, and soon's
he heard it John Guthrie went back to Will stooking in the yavil
field and said *What's this that I hear about you and some orra
tink bitch in Drumlithie?*

Now Will had been in a fair fine temper all that day from
seeing his Mollie again: and she'd made him swear he'd not fly
in a rage or go making a fool of himself if he heard their coarse
hinting at her. So he just went on with the stooking and said
What the devil are you blithering about? Father shot out his
beard and cried *Answer my question, Will!* and Will said *Put a
question with sense in it, then. How am I to know what you've
been hearing? I'm not a thought-reader,* and father said *Damn't
to hell, you coarse brute, am I to stand your lip as well as
your whoring every night? Is't true there's a tink called Mollie
Douglas that's with a bairn by you?* and Will said *If you call
Mollie Douglas a tink again, I'll knock the damned teeth down
the throat of you, father though you be.*

And they stopped their stooking, glaring at each other, and

father made to strike at Will but Will caught his arm and cried
Mind! So father lowered his arm, white as a ghost he'd turned,
and went on with the stooking, Will stared at him, white himself, and then went on with the stooking as well. And that might
well have been the end of it so far as Blawearie went; but that
evening they heard a clatter outside in the close and there was
the minister's bicycle and Mr Gibbon himself new off it; and
into the kitchen he came and said *Good evening, Chris, good
evening Mr Guthrie. Can I have a word with Will?*

So Chris was sent to bring Will from the byre where he
bedded the kye, he came back with her grey in the gills, there
sat the minister and father, solemn as two owls in the loft of a
barn, it was plain they'd been taking the matter through hand
together. Father said *Chris, go to your room*, and there was
nothing else for her but go; and what happened after that she
was never sure, for Will wouldn't tell her, but she heard the
sound of the three of them, all speaking at once and Will getting
in a rage: and then suddenly the kitchen door banged and there
was Will striding across the close to the barn where he stored
his bicycle. Mr Gibbon's voice cried after him, angry-like, with
a boom, *Just a minute, Will, where are you going?* and Will
looked back and said *You're so anxious I should lie with my
lass and get her with a bairn that I'm off to try and oblige you.*
And he wheeled his bicycle out by the honeysuckle hedge and
pedalled away down the road and didn't come back to Blawearie till one o'clock in the morning.

Chris hadn't been able to sleep, she lay listening for him, and
when she heard him come up the stairs she cried his name in a
whisper *Will!* He stopped uncertain outside her door and then
lifted the sneck and came in soft-footed and sat on the side of
her bed. Chris raised herself on an elbow and peered at him,
there was little light in the room and no moon that night though
the sky was white with stars, and Will no more than a shadow
hunched on her bedside there, with a whitish blotch for a face.
And Chris whispered *Will, I heard what you said when you
went away. But you didn't do it?* and Will gave a low laugh,
he wasn't in a rage, *It wouldn't be for want of prigging by
half the holy muckers in Kinraddie if I had. But you needn't*

be feared for that, I'd as soon cut my own throat as do hurt to – HER.

So the minister's interfering brought no harm, faith! he'd more need to roust round his own bit byre with a clart if Cuddiestoun's story of the Gourdon quean were true. And soon enough after that a worse scandal went on the rounds about him, folk shook their heads and made out they were fell affronted: all but Long Rob of the Mill, and he swore B'God, it was the best he'd heard since Nebuchadnezzar went out to grass![5]

And the way of it was that in early November a bit daughter was born to the Manse, and the Reverend Gibbon was proud as punch, he preached a grand sermon that Sunday, *For unto us a child is born;*[6] and it was so affecting that old Mistress Sinclair of the Netherhill broke down and cried in her hanky about it; but Long Rob of the Mill, when he heard that, said: *She shouldn't take whisky sweeties to the kirk with her.* Everybody else was fell impressed, folk who'd been a bit off the Manse for months agreed he'd maybe his faults, the Gibbon childe, but who hadn't these days? and feint the many could wag a pow like that in a Mearns pulpit. But damn't! if the next day he didn't go off and spoil the whole thing, the Monday it was, he was just setting out for the train to Aberdeen, Mr Gibbon, when the nurse cried out to him he might bring a small chamber-pot for the girlie, none in the Manse was suitable. He gave a bit blush, the big, curly bull, and said *Very well, nurse,* in a bull-like voice, and off to the station he went, it was Fordoun, and left his bicycle there and caught his train.

About what happened after that some told one thing and some another and some told both together. But it seems that fair early in the day in Aberdeen the Reverend Gibbon fell in with some friends of his; and they'd have it that a dram there must be to celebrate the occasion. So off the whole lot of them went to a public house and had their dram and syne another on top of that to keep the first one down, syne two-three more to keep the wind out, it was blowy weather on the edge of winter. Some said that midway the carouse Mr Gibbon had got up to make a bit prayer: and one of the barmaids had laughed at him and he chased her out of the bar up to her room and finished his prayer with her there. But you couldn't believe every lie you heard.

Sometime late in the afternoon he minded his train, the minister, and hired a cab and bought the bit chamber, and caught the train by the skin of the teeth. No sooner was he down in his carriage than, fell exhausted, he went fast asleep and blithely snored his way south through many a mile, right dead to the world he was.

Most of the story till then was maybe but guessing, ill-natured guessing at that, but the porter at the Bridge of Dunn, a good twenty miles south from Fordoun, swore to the rest. He was just banging the doors of the old 7.30 when out of a carriage window came a head, like a bull's head out of the straw, he'd fair a turn, had the porter, when he saw the flat hat that topped it. *Is this Fordoun?* the meikle head mooed, and the porter said *No, man, it's a damned long way from being that.*

So he opened the door for Kinraddie's minister, and Mr Gibbon came stumbling out and rubbed his eyes, and the porter pointed to a platform where he'd find a slow train back to Fordoun. This platform lay over a little bridge and the minister set out to cross: and the first few steps he managed fell well, but near the top he began to sway and missed his footing and flung out his hands. The next thing that the porter saw was the chamber-pot, burst from its paper, rolling down the steps of the bridge with the minister's hat in competition and the minister thundering behind.

And then, when the porter had picked him up and was dusting him, the Reverend Gibbon broke down and sobbed on the porter's shoulder what a bloody place was Kinraddie! And how'd the porter like to live 'tween a brier bush and a rotten kailyard in the lee of a house with green shutters? And the minister sobbed some more about the shutters, and he said you couldn't lie down a minute with a quean in Kinraddie but that some half-witted clod-hopping crofter began to throw stones at you, they'd feint the respect for God or kirk or minister down in Kinraddie. And the porter said it was awful the way the world went, he'd thought of resigning from the railway himself and taking to preaching, but now he wouldn't.

Syne he helped the minister over to an up-going train and
went home to his wife and told her the tale: and she told it to
her sister from Auchinblae: and *she* told it to her man who told
it to Mutch; and so the whole thing came out. And next time
he rode down by the Peesie's Knapp, the minister, a head shot
out of a hedge behind him, it was wee Wat Strachan, and cried
loud as you like *Any chambers to-day?*

Not that they'd much to shout for that winter themselves, the
Strachans; folk said it was easy to see why Chae was so strong
on Rich and Poor being Equal: he was sore in need of the
sharing out to start ere he went clean broke himself. Maybe old
Sinclair or the wife were tight with the silver that year, but early
as December Chae had to sell his corn, he brought the first
threshing of the season down in Kinraddie. John Guthrie and
Will were off at the keek of dawn when they saw the smoke
rise from the engines, Chris followed an hour later to help
Chae's wife with the dinner and things. And faith! broke he
might be but he wasn't mean, Chae, when the folk came trampling in to eat there was broth and beef and chicken and oat-
cakes, champion cakes they made at the Knapp; and loaf and
jelly and dumpling with sugar and milk; and if any soul were
that gutsy he wanted more he could hold to the turnip-field,
said Chae.

The first three men to come in Chris hardly saw, so busied
she was pouring their broth for them. Syne, setting the plates,
she saw Alec Mutch, his great lugs like red clouts hung out to
dry: and he cried *Ay, Chris!* and began to sup as though he
hadn't seen food for a fortnight. Beside him was Munro of the
Cuddiestoun, he was eating like a collie ta'en off its chain,
Chae's thresh was a spree to the pair of them. Then more
trampling and scraping came from the door, folk came drifting
in two-three at a time, Chris over-busied to notice their faces,
but some watched her and gave a bit smile and Cuddiestoun
cried to father, *Losh, man, she's fair an expert getting, the
daughter. The kitchen's more her style than the College.*

Some folk at the tables laughed out at that, the ill-nature
grinned from the faces of them, and suddenly Chris hated the

lot, the English Chris came back in her skin a minute, she saw
them the yokels and clowns everlasting, dull-brained and crude.
Alec Mutch took up the card from Cuddiestoun then and began
on education and the speak ran round the tables. Most said it
was a coarse thing, learning, just teaching your children a lot
of damned nonsense that put them above themselves, they'd
turn round and give you their lip as soon as look at you. But
Chae was sitting down himself by then and he wouldn't have
that. *Damn't man, you're clean wrong to think that. Education's the thing the working man wants to put him up level
with the Rich.* And Long Rob of the Mill said *I'd have thought
a bit balance in the bank would do that.* But for once he seemed
right in agreement with Chae – *the more education the more of
sense and the less of kirks and ministers.* Cuddiestoun and
Mutch were fair shocked at that, Cuddiestoun cried out *Well,
well, we'll hear nothing coarse of religion,* as though he didn't
want to hear anything more about it and was giving out orders.
But Long Rob wasn't a bit took aback, the long rangy childe,
he just cocked an eye at Cuddiestoun and cried *Well, well,
Munro, we'll turn to the mentally afflicted in general, not just
in particular. How's that foreman of yours getting on, Tony?
Is he still keeping up with his shorthand?* There was a snicker
at that, you may well be sure, and Cuddiestoun closed up quick
enough, here and there folk had another bit laugh and said
Long Rob was an ill hand to counter. And Chris thought of her
clowns and yokels, and was shamed as she thought – Chae and
Long Rob they were, the poorest folk in Kinraddie!

At a quarter past six the mill loosed off again from its bumble-
bee hum, the threshers came trooping down to the tables again.
More dumpling there was, cut up for tea, and bread and butter
and scones and baps from the grocer, and rhubarb and black-
berry jam, and syrup for them that preferred it, some folk liked
to live on dirt out of tins. Most of the mill folk sat down in a
right fine tune, well they might, and loosed out their waistcoats.
Will was near last to come in from the close, a long, dark young
childe came in at his heels, Chris hadn't set eyes on him before,
nor he on her by the way he glowered. The two of them stood
about, lost-like and gowkèd, looking for seats in the crowded

kitchen till Mistress Strachan cried over to Chris *Will you lay them places ben in the room?*

So she did and took them their supper there, Will looked up and cried *Hello, Chris, how have you gotten on?* and Chris said *Fine, how've you?* Will laughed *Well, God, my back would feel a damned sight easier if I'd spent the day in my bed. Eh, Tavendale?* And then he minded his manners. *This is Ewan Tavendale from Upprums, Chris.*

So that was who; Chris felt queer as he raised his head and held out his hand, and she felt the blood come in her face and saw it come dark in his. He looked over-young for the coarse, dour brute folk said he was, like a wild cat, strong and quick, she half-liked his face and half-hated it, it could surely never have been him that did THAT in the larch wood of Upperhill? But then if you could read every childe's nature in the way he wiped his nose, said Long Rob of the Mill, it would be a fine and easy world to go through.

So she paid him no more heed and was out of the Knapp a minute later and ran nearly all the way up to Blawearie to see to the milking there. The wind was still up but the frost was crackling below her feet as she ran, the brae rose cold and uncanny with Blawearie's biggings uncertain shadows high up in the cold mirk there. She felt tingling and blithe from her run, she said to herself if she'd only the time she'd go out every winter night and run up over hills with frost and the night star coming in the sky.

But that night as Blawearie went to its bed Will opened his bedroom door and cried *Father! Chris! See that light down there in the Knapp!*

Chris was over at her window then in a minute, bare-footed she ran and peered by the shadow of the great beech tree. And there was a light right plain enough, more than a light, a lowe that crackled to yellow and red and rose in the wind that had come with the night. Peesie's Knapp would be all in a blaze in a minute, Chris knew; and then father came tearing down the stairs, crying to Will to get on his clothes and follow him, Chris was to bide at home, mind that. They heard him open

the front door and go out and go running right fleetly down
the night of Blawearie hill, Chris cried to Will *Wait for me, I'm
coming as well*, and he cried back *All right, but for Christ's
sake hurry!*

She couldn't find her stockings then, she was trembling and
daft; and when found they were, her corsets were missing,
slipped down the back of the kist they had, Will came knocking
at the door *Come on!—Light a match and come in*, she called
and in he came, knotting his muffler, and lighted a match and
looked at her in her knickers and vest, reaching out for the
new-seen corsets. *Leave the damn things where they are, you're
fine, you should never have been born a quean*. She was into
her skirt by then, and said *I wish I hadn't*, and pulled on her
boots and half-laced them, and ran down the stairs after Will
and put on her coat at the foot. In a minute they were out in
the dimness then, under the starlight, it was rimed with frost,
and running like mad down to the lowe that now rose like a
beacon against the whole of Kinraddie. *God, I hope they've
wakened!* Will panted, for every soul knew the Strachans went
straight to bed at the chap of eight. Running, they could see by
then it was the barn itself that had taken alight, the straw sow
seemed burned to a cinder already, and the barn had caught
and maybe the house. And all over Kinraddie lights were springing up, as they ran Chris lifted her eyes and saw Cuddiestoun's
blink and shine bright down through the dark.

And faith, quick though they were, it was father that saved
Chae Strachan's folk. He was first down at the blazing Knapp,
John Guthrie; and he ran round the biggings and saw the flames
lapping and lowing at the kitchen end of the house, not a soul
about or trying to stop them though the noise was fair awful,
the crackling and burning, and the winter air bright with flying
sticks and straw. He banged at the door and cried *Damn't to
hell do you want to be roasted?* and when he got no answer he
smashed in the window, they heard him then and the bairns
scraiched, there was never such a lot for sleep, folk said, Chae'd
have slept himself out of this world and into hell in his own
firewood if John Guthrie hadn't roused him then. But out he
came stumbling at last, he'd only his breeks on; and he took a

keek at John Guthrie and another at the fire and cried out
Kirsty, we're all to hell! and off he tore to the byre.

But half-way across the close as he ran the barn swithered
and roared and fell, right in front of him, and he'd to run back,
there was no way then of getting at the byre. By then Long Rob
of the Mill came in about, he'd run over the fields, louping
dykes like a hare, and his lungs were panting like bellows, he
was clean winded. He it was that helped Mrs Strachan with the
bairns and such clothes as they could drag out to the road while
Chae and John Guthrie tried to get at the byre from another
angle: but that was no good, the place was already roaring
alight. For a while there was only the snarling of the fire eating
in to the wooden couplings, the rattle of falling slates through
the old charred beams, and then, the first sound that Will and
Chris heard as they came panting down the road, a scream that
was awful, a scream that made them think one of the Strachans
was trapped down there. And at that sound Chae covered his
ears and cried *Oh God, that's old Clytie*, Clytie was his little
horse, his sholtie, and she screamed and screamed, terrible and
terrible, Chris ran back to the house trying not to hear and to
help poor Kirsty Strachan, snivelling and weeping, and the
bairns laughing and dancing about as though they were at a
picnic, and Long Rob of the Mill smoking his pipe as cool as
you please, there was surely enough smell and smoke without
that? But pipe and all he dived in and out of the house and
saved chairs and dishes and baskets of eggs; and Mistress
Strachan cried *Oh, my sampler!* and in Rob tore and rived that
off a blazing wall, a meikle worsted thing in a cracked glass
case that Mistress Strachan had made as a bairn at school.

And then came the clip-clop of a gig, it was Ellison down
from the Mains, him and two of his men, and God! he might
be little more than a windy Irish brute but he'd sense for all
that, the gig was crammed with ropes and pails, Ellison strung
out the folk and took charge, the pails went swinging from
hand to hand over the close from the well to the childe that
stood nearest the fire, and he pelted the fire with water. But
feint the much good that did for a while and then there was an
awful sound from the byre, the lowing of the cattle with the

flames among them, and Long Rob of the Mill cried out *I can't stand it!* and took a pick-axe and ran round the back of the close; and there he found the sow was nothing but a black heap then, hardly burning at all, and he cried back the news and himself louped through the smoke and came at the back wall of the byre and started to smash it in fast as he could. Chae followed and John Guthrie, and the three of them worked like madmen there, Ellison's men splashed water down on the roof above them till suddenly the wall gave way before them and Chae's oldest cow stuck out its head and said *Moo!* right in Chae's face. The three scrambled through into the byre then, that was fell dangerous, the rafters were crumbling and falling all about the stalls, and it was half-dark there in spite of the flames. But they loosed another cow and two stirks before the fire drove them out, the others they had to leave, their lowing was fair demented and the smell of their burning sickening in your throat, it was nearly a quarter of an hour later before the roof fell in and killed the cattle. Long Rob of the Mill sat down by the side of the road and was suddenly as sick as could be, and he said *By God, I never want to smell roasting beef again.*

So that was the burning of the Peesie's Knapp, there was a great throng of folk in about by then, the Netherhill folk and the Upperhill, and Cuddiestoun, and Alec Mutch with his great lugs lit up by the fire, some had come on bicycles and some had run across half Kinraddie and two had brought their gigs. But there was little to do now but stand and glower at the fire and its mischief, Ellison drove off to the Mains with Mistress Strachan and the bairns, there for the night they were bedded. The cattle he'd saved from the byre Chae drove to Netherhill, folk began to put on their jackets again, it was little use waiting for anything else, they'd away home to their beds.

Chris could see nothing of either father or Will, she turned to make for Blawearie then. Outside the radiance of the burning Knapp it was hard and cold, starless but clear, as though the steel of the ground glowed faintly of itself; beyond rose the darkness as a black wall, still and opaque. On the verge of its embrasure it was that she nearly ran into two men tramping back along the road, she hardly saw them till she was on them.

She cried *Oh, I'm sorry*, and one of them laughed and said something to the other, next instant before she knew what was happening that other had her in his arms, rough and strong, and had kissed her, he had a face with a soft, grained skin, it was the first time a man had ever kissed her like that, dark and frightening and terrible in the winter road. The other stood by, Chris, paralysed, heard him breathing and knew he was laughing, and a far crackle rose from the last of the lowe in the burning biggings. Then she came to herself and kicked the man that held her, young he was with his soft, grained face, kicked him hard with her knee and then brought her nails down across his face. As he swore *You bitch!* and let go of her she kicked him again, with her foot this time, and he swore again, but the other said *Hist! Here's somebody coming*, and the two of them began to run, the cowardly tinks, it was father and Will on the road behind them.

And when Chris told Will of what happened, next morning it was that she told him when father wasn't by, he looked at her queerly, half-laughing, half-solemn, and made out he thought nothing of the happening, all ploughmen were like that, aye ready for fun. But it hadn't seemed fun to her, dead earnest rather; and lying that night in her bed between the cold sheets, curled up so that she might rub her white toes to some warmth and ease, it was in her memory like being chased and bitten by a beast, but worse and with something else in it, as though half she'd liked the beast and the biting and the smell of that sleeve around her neck and that soft, unshaven face against her own. Sweet breath he had had anyway, she thought, and laughed to herself, that was some consolation, the tink. And then she fell asleep and dreamed of him, an awful dream that made her blush even while she knew she was dreaming, she was glad when the morning came and was sane and cool and herself again.

But that dream came to her often while the winter wore on through Kinraddie, a winter that brought hardly any snow till New Year's Eve and then brought plenty, darkening the sky with its white cascading. It was funny that darkening the blind

fall and wheep of the snow should bring, like the loosening of
a feather pillow above the hills, night came as early as three in
the afternoon. They redd up the beasts early that evening, father
and Will, feeding them well with turnips and straw and hot
treacle poured on the straw; and then they came in to their
supper and had it and sat close round the fire while Chris made
a fine dumpling for New Year's Day. None of them spoke for
long, listening to that whoom and blatter on the window-panes,
and the clap-clap-clap of some loose slate far up on the roof,
till father whispered and looked at them, his whisper hurt worse
than a shout, *God, I wonder why Jean left us?*

Chris cried then, making no sound, she looked at Will and
saw him with his face red and shamed, all three of them thinking
of mother, her that was by them so kind and friendly and quick
that last New Year, so cold and quiet and forgotten now with
the little dead twins in the kirkyard of Kinraddie, piling black
with the driving of the snow it would be under the rustle and
swing and creak of the yews. And Will stared at father, his face
was blind with pity, once he made to speak, but couldn't, always
they'd hated one the other so much and they'd feel shamed if
they spoke in friendship now.

So father took up his paper again and at ten o'clock Chris
went out to milk the kye and Will went with her over the
close, carrying the lantern, the flame of it leapt and starred and
quivered and hesitated in the drive of the snow. In the light of
it, like a rain of arrows they saw the coming of the storm that
night swept down from the Grampian heuchs, thick and strong
it was in Blawearie, but high in the real hills a smoring, straight
wall must be sweeping the dark, blinding down against the lone
huts of the shepherds and the faces of lost tinks tramping
through it looking for lights the snow'd smothered long before.
Chris was shaking, but not with cold, and inside the byre she
leant on a stall and Will said *God, you look awful, what is't?*
And she shook herself and said *Nothing. Why haven't you gone
to see Mollie to-night?*

He said he was going next day, wasn't that enough, he'd be
a corpse long ere he reached Drumlithie to-night – *listen to the
wind, it'll blow the damn place down on our lugs in a minute!*

And the byre shook, between the lulls it seemed to set its breath to rise and take from the hill-side into the air, there was such straining and creaking. Not that the calves or the stirks paid heed, they slept and snored in their stalls with never a care, there were worse things in the world than being a beast.

Back in the house it seemed to Chris she'd but hardly sieved the milk when the great clock ben in the parlour sent peal after peal out dirling through the place. Will looked at Chris and the two at father, and John Guthrie was just raising up his head from his paper, but if he'd been to wish them a happy New Year or not they were never to know, for right at that minute there came a brisk chap at the door and somebody lifted the sneck and stamped the snow from his feet and banged the door behind him.

And there he was, Long Rob of the Mill, muffled in a great grey cravat and with leggings up to the knees, covered and frosted from head to foot in the snow, he cried *Happy New Year to you all! Am I the first?* And John Guthrie was up on his feet, *Ay, man, you're fairly that, out of that coat of yours!* They stripped off the coat between them, faith! Rob's mouser was nearly frozen, but he said it was fine and laughed, and waited the glass of toddy father brought him and cried *Your health!* And just as it went down his throat there came a new knock, damn't if it wasn't Chae Strachan, he'd had more than a drink already and he cried *Happy New Year, I'm the first foot in am I not?* And he made to kiss Chris, she wouldn't have minded, laughing, but he slithered and couped on the floor, Long Rob peered down at him and cried out, shocked-like, *God Almighty, Chae, you can't sleep there!*

So he was hoisted into a chair and was better in a minute when he'd had another drink; and he began to tell what a hell of a life it was he'd to live in Netherhill now, the old mistress grew worse with the years, she'd near girn the jaws from her face if the Strachan bairns so much as gave a bit howl or had a bit fight – fell unreasoning that, no bairns there were but fought like tinks. And Long Rob said Ay, that was true, as it said in the hymn 'twas dog's delight to bark and bite,[7] and faith! the average human could out-dog any cur that ever was pupped.

Now, horses were different, you'd hardly ever meet a horse that was naturally a quarreller, a coarse horse was a beast they'd broken in badly. He'd once had a horse – a three-four years come Martinmas that would have been, or no! man, it was only two – that he bought up in Auchinblae at the fall of the year, a big roan, coarse as hell, they said, and he'd nearly kicked the guts out of an old man there. Well, Rob had borrowed a bridle and tried to ride home the beast to the Mill, and twice in the first mile the horse threw him off with a snort and stood still, just laughing, as Rob picked himself up from the stour. But Rob just said to himself, *All right, my mannie, we'll see who'll laugh last:* and when he'd got that horse home he tied him up in his stall and gave him such a hammering, by God he nearly kicked down the stable. Every night for a week he was walloped like that, and damn't man! in the shortest while he'd quietened down and turned into a real good worker, near human he was, that horse, he'd turn at the end of a rig as it drew to eleven o'clock and begin to nicker and neigh, he knew the time fine. Ay, a canty beast that, he'd turned, and sold at a profit in a year or so, it just showed you what a handless man did with a horse, for Rob had heard that the beast's new owner had let the horse clean go over him. A sound bit leathering and a pinch of kindness was the only way to cure a coarse horse.

Chae hiccupped and said *Damn't ay, man, maybe you're right. It's a pity old Sinclair never thought of treating his fish-wife like that, she'd deave a door-nail with her whines and plaints, the thrawn old Tory bitch.* And Long Rob said there were worse folk than Tories and Chae said if there were they kept themselves damn close hidden, if he'd his way he'd have all Tories nailed up in barrels full of spikes and rolled down the side of the Grampians; and Long Rob said there would be a gey boom in the barrel trade then, the most of Kinraddie would be inside the barrels; and Chae said *And a damned good riddance of rubbish, too.*

They were both heated up with the toddy then, and raising their voices, but father just said, cool-like, that he was a Liberal himself; and what did they think of this bye-election coming off in the February? Chae said it would make no difference

who got in, one tink robber was bad as another, Tory as
Liberal;[8] damn't if he understood why Blawearie should be
taken in by those Liberals. Long Rob said *Why don't you stand
as the Socialist man yourself, Chae?* and winked at Chris, but
Chae took it real serious and said maybe he'd do that yet once
Peesie's Knapp was builded again. And Long Rob said *Why
wait for that? You're allowing your opinions to eat their heads
off in idleness, like a horse in a stall in winter. Losh, man, but
they're queer beasts, horses. There's my sholtie, Kate—* But
Chae said *Och, away to hell with your horses, Rob. Damn't, if
you want a canty kind of beast there's nothing like a camel*,
and maybe he'd have just begun to tell them about the camel if
he hadn't fallen off his chair then, nearly into the fire he went,
and John Guthrie smiled at him over his beard, as though he'd
really rather cut his throat than smile. And then Will and Long
Rob helped Chae to his feet, Long Rob gave a laugh and said
it was time they went dandering back to their beds, he'd see
Chae far as the Netherhill. The storm had cleared a bit by then,
it was bright starlight Chris saw looking after the figures of the
two from her bedroom window – not very steady, either of
them, with shrouded Kinraddie lying below and a smudge there,
faint and dark, far down in the night, that was the burned-out
steading of Peesie's Knapp.

And there the smudge glimmered through many a week, they
didn't start on Peesie's new steading till well in the February.
But faith! there was clatter enough of tongues round the place
right from the night of the fire onwards. All kinds of folk came
down and poked in the ash with their walking-sticks, the police
and the Cruelty came from Stonehaven; and the factor came,
he was seldom seen unless there was money in question; and
insurance creatures buzzed down from Aberdeen like a swarm
of fleas, their humming and hawing and gabbling were the
speak of all Kinraddie. Soon all kinds of stories flew up and
down the Howe, some said the fire had been lighted by Chae
himself, a Drumlithie billy riding by the Knapp late that night
of the fire had seen Chae with a box of spunks in his hand,
coming from the lighting of the straw sow, sure; for soon as he

saw the billy on the bicycle back Chae had jumped to the lithe
again. Others said the fire had been set by the folk of Netherhill,
their only chance of recovering the silver they'd loaned to Chae.
But that was just a plain lie, like the others, Chris thought,
Chae'd have never cried for his burning sholtie like that if he'd
meant it to burn for insurance.

But stories or no, they couldn't shake Chae, he was paid his
claims up to the hilt, folk said he'd made two-three hundred
pounds on the business, he'd be less keen now for Equality. But
faith! if he'd won queer silver queerly, he'd lost feint the queer
notion in the winning of it. Just as the building of the new bit
Knapp began so did the bye-election, the old member had died
in London of drink, poor brute, folk said when they cut his
corpse open it fair gushed out with whisky. Ah well, he was
dead then, him and his whisky, and though he'd maybe been a
good enough childe to represent the shire, feint the thing had
the shire ever seen of him except at election times. Now there
came a young Tory gent in the field, called Rose he was, an
Englishman with a funny bit squeak of a voice, like a bairn
that's wet its breeks. But the Liberal was an oldish creature
from Glasgow, fell rich he was, folk said, with as many ships
to his name as others had fields. And real Radical he was, with
everybody's money but his own, and he said he'd support the
Insurance and to Hell with the House of Lords,[9] *Vote for the
Scottish Thistle and not for the English Rose.*[10]

But the Tory said the House of Lords had aye been defenders
of the Common People, only he didn't say aye, his English was
a real drawback; and it was at the meeting where he said that,
that Chae Strachan up and asked if it wasn't true that his own
uncle was a lord? And the Tory said *Yes*, and Chae said that
maybe *that* lord would be glad to see him in Parliament but
there was a greater Lord who heard when the Tories took the
name of poor folk in vain. The God of old Scotland there was,
aye fighting on the side of the people since the days of old John
Knox, and He would yet bring to an end the day of wealth and
waster throughout the world, liberty and equality and fraternity
were coming though all the damned lordies in the House of
Lords should pawn their bit coronets and throw their whores

back in the streets and raise private armies to fight the common folk with their savings.

But then the stewards made at Chae, he hadn't near finished, and an awful stamash broke out in the hall; for though most of the folk had been laughing at Chae they weren't to see him mishandled by an English tink and the coarse fisher brutes he'd hired from Gourdon to keep folk from asking him questions. So when the first steward laid hands on Chae, John Guthrie, who was sitting near, cried *Ay, man, who'll you be?* And the fisher swore *You keep quiet as well*, and father rose and took him a belt in the face, and the fisher's nose bled like the Don in spate, and somebody put out a leg and tripped him up and that was the end of his stewarding. And when the other steward made to come to his help Long Rob of the Mill said *Away home to your stinking fish!* and took him by the lug and ran him out of the hall and kicked him into the grass outside.

Then everybody was speaking at once, Mr Gibbon was the Tory lad's chairman and he called out *Can't you give us fair play, Charles Strachan?* But Chae's blood was up, strong for the Kirk though he was in a way he clean forgot who he spoke to – *Come outside a minute, my mannie, and I'll fair-play you!* The minister wasn't such a fool as that, though, he said that the meeting was closed, fair useless it was to go on; and he said that Chae was a demagogue and Chae said that he was a liar, folk cried out *Wheest, wheest!* at that and began to go home. The Tory childe got hantle few votes in the end, Chae boasted it was his help put in the old Liberal stock: and God knows if he thought that fine he was easily pleased, they never saw the creature again in Kinraddie.

But that was the last time father struck a man, striking in cold anger and cold blood as was the way of him. Folk said he was an unchancy childe to set in a rage; but his next rage mischieved himself, not others. For a while up into the New Year, April and the turnip-time, things at Blawearie went fair and smooth, Will saying no more than his say at plate or park, never countering father, hardly he looked at him even; and father maybe thought to rule the roost as he'd done before when Will was no more than a boy that cowered when he heard that sharp voice raised, frightened and beaten and lying through nights with his sore wealed body in the arms of Chris. But Chris, knowing none of his plannings, guessed right well something new it was kept Will quiet, so quiet day on day, yet if you looked at him sudden you'd more likely than not see him smiling to himself, lovely the face that he smiled with, brown and clean, and his eyes were kind and clear and the hair grew down on his head in a bonny mop, Will took after mother with that flame of rusty gold that was hers.

Ah well, he kept to his whistling and his secret smiling, and every night after loosening and suppering was done, off down the road on his old bit bicycle he'd go, you'd hear through the evening stillness nothing but the sound of the old machine whirring down Blawearie road, and the weet-weet of the pee-wits flying twilit over Kinraddie, wheeling and circling there in the dark, daft creatures that made their nests in this rig and that and would come back next day and find them robbed or smoth-ered away. So for hundreds of years they'd done, the peewits, said Long Rob of the Mill, and hadn't learned the sense of the thing even yet; and if you were to take that as a sample of the Divine Intelligence that had allotted a fitting amount of brain to each creature's needs then all you could suppose was that the Divine had more than a spite against the peesie.

Chris heard him say that one day she looked in at the Mill to ask when a sack of bruised corn, left there by Will, would be ready. But there on the bench outside the Mill, in the shade from the hot Spring weather, sat Rob and Chae and Mutch of Bridge End, all guzzling beer from long bottles they were, Rob more bent on bruising their arguments than on bruising Blawearie's corn. Peewits were flying round the Mill fell thick, peewits and crows that nested in the pines above the Mill, and the birds it was had begun the argument. Chris waited for a while, pleased enough with the shade and rest, hearkening to Long Rob make a fool of God. But Alec Mutch wagged his meikle lugs, *No, man, you're fair wrong there. And man, Rob, you'll burn in hell for that, you know*. Chae was half on his side and half wasn't, he said *Damn the fears, that's nothing but an old wife's gabble for fearing the bairns. But Something there IS up there, Rob man, there's no denying that. If I thought there wasn't I'd out and cut my throat this minute.* Then the three of them sighted Chris and Rob got up, the long, rangy childe with the glinting eyes, and cried *Is't about the bruised corn, Chris? Tell Will I'll do it to-night.*

But Will had unyoked and made off to Drumlithie, his usual gait, when Chris got home, and father was up on the moor with his gun, you heard the bang of the shots come now and then. Chris had a great baking to do that night, both father and Will would eat oat-cakes and scones for a wager, bought bread from the vans soon scunnered them sore. Warm work it was when you'd heaped a great fire and the girdle glowed below, you'd nearly to strip in fine weather if you weren't to sweat yourself sick. Chris got out of most things but a vest and a petticoat, she was all alone and could do as she pleased, it was fine and free and she baked with a will.

She was lifting the last cake, browned and good and twice cross cut, when she knew that somebody watched her from the door of the kitchen, and she looked, it was Ewan Tavendale, him she hadn't seen since the day of the thresh at Peesie's Knapp. He was standing against the jamb, long and dark with his glowering eyes, but he reddened when she looked, not half as much as she did herself, she could feel the red warm blushing come through her skin from tip to toe; *such a look he's taking,* she thought, *it's a pity I'm wearing a thing and he can't study the blush to its end.*

But he just said *Hello, is Will about?* and Chris said *No, in Drumlithie I think,* and they stood and glowered like a couple of gowks, Chris saw his eyes queer and soft and shy, the neck of his shirt had fallen apart, below it the skin was white as new milk, frothed white it looked, and a drop of sweat stood there where the brown of his tanning and the white of his real skin met. And then Chris suddenly knew *something* and blushed again, sharp and silly, she couldn't stop, she'd minded the night of the fire at Peesie's Knapp and the man that had kissed her on the homeward road, Ewan Tavendale it had been, no other, shameless and coarse.

He was blushing himself again by then, they looked at each other in a white, queer daze, Chris wondered in a kind of a panic if he knew what she knew at last, half-praying she was he wouldn't speak of it when he began to move off from the door, still red, stepping softly, like father, like a limber, soft-stepping cat. *Well, I was hoping I'd see him in case he should leave us sudden-like.*

She stared at him all awake, that kissing on the winter road forgotten. *Leave? Who said Will was leaving?—Oh, I heard he was trying for a job in Aberdeen, maybe it's a lie. Tell him I called in about. Ta-ta.*

She called *Ta-ta, Ewan,* after him as he crossed the close, he half-turned round and smiled at her, quick and dark like a cat again, *Ta-ta, Chris.* And she stood looking after him a long while, not thinking, smiling, till the smell of a burning cake roused her to run, just like the English creature Alfred.[11]

And next morning she said to Will after breakfast, casual-like, but her heart in her throat, *Ewan Tavendale was down to see you last night, he thought you'd be leaving Blawearie soon.* And Will took it cool and quiet, *Did he? God, they'd haver the breeks from a Highlandman's haunches, the gossipers of Kinraddie. Tavendale down to see me? More likely he was down to take a bit keek at you, Chris lass. So look after yourself, for he's Highland and coarse.*

In July it came to the hay-time, and John Guthrie looked at Will and said he was going to have down the hay with a scythe this year, not spoil the bit stuff with a mower. Fair plain to Chris he expected Will to fly in a rage at that and say he wasn't to chave and sweat in the forking of rig after rig when a mower would clear Blawearie's park in a day or two at the most. But Will just said *All right* and went on with his porridge, and went out to the field in the tail of father, a fork on his shoulder and whistling happy as a lark, so that father turned round and snapped *Hold your damned wheeber, you'll need your breath for the bout.* Even at that Will laughed, as a man at a girning bairn, right off they were worse friends than even the year before. But all that time Will was making his plans and on the morning of the August's last Saturday, Chris aye remembered that morning with its red sun and the singing of the North Sea over the Howe, that morning he said to father *I'm off to Aberdeen to-day.*

Father said never a word, he went on with his porridge and finished it, he mightn't have heard Will speak, he lighted his pipe and stepped out of the house, fleet as ever he went, and began coling the hayfield in front of the house; Will could see him then and be shamed of himself and his idle jaunting. But Will wasn't ashamed, he looked after father with a sneer, *The old fool thinks he can frighten me still,* and said something else Chris didn't catch, syne looked at her suddenly, his eyes bright and his lips moving, *Chris – Lord, I wish you were coming as well!*

She stared at that amazed, pleased as well. *What, up to Aberdeen? I'd like it fine but I can't. Hurry and dress, else you'll miss your train.*

So he went and dressed, fell slow-like he seemed at the business, she thought, the morning and a jaunt in front of him. She went to the foot of the stairs and cried up to ask if he were having a sleep before he set out? And instead of answering her back with a jest and a fleer he laughed a shaky laugh and called out All right, he'd soon be down. And when he came she saw him in his Sunday suit, with his new boots shining, he'd on a new hat that suited him fine. *Well, will I do?* he asked and Chris said *You look fair brave,* and he said *Havers!* and picked up his waterproof, *Well, ta-ta, Chris;* and suddenly turned round to her and she saw his face red and strange and he kissed her, they hadn't kissed since they were children lying in a bed together on a frosty night. She wiped her mouth, feeling shamed and pleased, and pushed him away, he tried to speak, and couldn't, and said *Oh, to hell!* and turned and ran out of the door, she saw him go down the Blawearie road fast as he could walk, looking up at the hills he was with the sun on them and the slow fog rising off the Howe, jerking his head this way and that, fast though he walked, but he didn't once look in father's direction nor father at him. Syne she heard him whistling bonny and clear, *Up in the Morning*[12] it was, they'd used that for a signal in the days when they went the school-road together, and down on the turnpike edge he looked round and stood still, and waved his hand, he knew she was watching. Then a queer kind of pain came into her throat, her eyes smarted and she told herself she was daft, Will was only off for the day, he'd be back at night.

But Will didn't come back that night, he didn't come back the next day, he came back never again to John Guthrie's Kinraddie. For up in Aberdeen he was wed to his Mollie Douglas, he'd altered his birth certificate for that; and the earth might have opened and swallowed them up after that, it seemed not a soul in Aberdeen had seen them go. So when father went into Aberdeen on the track of the two there wasn't a trace to be found, he went to the police and raged at them, but they only laughed – had he lain with the quean himself, maybe, that so mad he was with this son of his?

So father came home, fair bursting with rage, but that didn't help. And ten days went by before they heard of the couple again, it came in a letter Will sent to Chris at Blawearie; and it told that through Mollie's mother, old Mistress Douglas, Will had got him a job in the Argentine, cattleman there on a big Polled Angus ranch, and he and Mollie were sailing from Southampton the day he wrote; and oh! he wished Chris could have seen them married; and remember them kindly, they would write again, and Mrs Douglas at Drumlithie would aye be a friend to her.

So that was Will's going, it was fair the speak of the parish a while, folk laughed at father behind his back and said maybe that would bring down his pride a bit; and they asked Chae Strachan, that well-travelled childe, where was this Argentine, was it a fine place, would you say? And Chae said Och, fine, he'd never been actually there, you might say, but a gey fine place it was, no doubt, a lot of silver was there; and *Damn't man, young Guthrie's no fool to spread his bit wings, I was just the same myself.* But most said it was fair shameful of Will to go off and leave his father like that, black burning shame he might think of himself; it just showed you what the world was coming to, you brought bairns into the world and reared them up and expected some comfort from them in your old age and what did you get? Nothing but a lot of damned impudence, it was all this education and dirt. You might well depend on it, that coarse young Guthrie brute would never thrive, there'd be a judgment on him, you'd see, him and his coarse tink quean.

Judgment or not on Will, it was hardly a week before his own rage struck down John Guthrie. He'd been setting up ricks in the cornyard when Chris heard a frightened squawk break out from the hens. She thought maybe some strange dog was among them and caught up a spurtle and ran out to the close and there saw father lying still in his blood, black blood it looked on his face where he'd fallen and mischieved himself against a stone. She cried out to him in fright and then cooled herself down, and ran for water from the spring and dipped her hanky in it and bathed his face. He opened his eyes then, dazed-like he seemed, and he said *All right, Jean lass*, and tried to rise, and couldn't. And rage came on him again, he put out his hand and gave Chris a push that near threw her down, he tried and tried to rise up, it was sickening to see. He chaved on the ground as though something tied him there, all one of his sides and legs, and the blood veins stood out blue on his face; and he cursed and said *Get into the house, you white-face bitch!* he wouldn't have her looking at him. So she watched from behind the door, near sick she felt, it was as though a great frog were squattering there in the stour, and the hens gathered and squawked about him.

And at last he stood up and staggered to a stone, and Chris didn't look more, going on with her work as well as she could with hands that quivered and quivered. But when he came in for supper he looked much as ever, and grumbled at this and that, and ate his egg as though it would do him ill, syne got his gun and went off to the hill as fleet as ever. He was long up there, Chris went to the window and watched for him, seeing the August late night close in, Cuddiestoun's sheep were baaing high up in the Cuddiestoun moor and a sprig of the honey-suckle that made the Blawearie hedges so bonny through the summer tapped and touched against the window-pane, it was like a slow hand tapping there; and the evening was quiet in the blow of the night-wind, and no sign of father till Chris grew alarmed and nearly went out to look for him. But then she heard his step in the porch, in he came and put down his gun and saw her stand there and cried out *Damn't to hell, is that all you've to do, stand about like a lady?* So you could hardly believe there was much wrong with him then, except ill-nature, he'd plenty of that, you'd no foreseeing that next morning he'd try to get out of bed and lie paralysed.

She wouldn't in a hurry forget the sight of him then, nor the run she had down Blawearie brae till the new Knapp came in sight, brave with its biggings and house. But there at last was Chae Strachan, he was busied letting a strainer into the ground, smoking, the blue smoke of his pipe rose into the air, blue, like a pencil-stroke, a cock was crowing across the Denburn and he didn't hear her cry for a while. But then he did and was quick enough, he ran up to meet her, *What's wrong, Chris lass?* and she told him and he turned and ran down – *Go back to your father and I'll get to the doctor myself and send the wife up to Blawearie.*

And up she came, the fat, fusionless creature, all she could do was to stand and gowk at father, *Mighty me, Mr Guthrie, this is a sore, sore sight, whatever will you do now, eh?* And father mouthed and mowed at her from the bed as though the first thing he'd be keen on doing was braining her, paralysis or not he'd still plenty of rage. For when the doctor came up at last from Bervie and bustled into the room, peering and poking with the sharp, quick face of him, and his bald head shining, and snapped in his curt-like way, *What's this? what's wrong with you now, Blawearie?* father managed to speak out then right enough – *That's for you to find out, what the hell do you think you're paid for?*

So the doctor grinned behind his hand, *One of you women must help me strip him.* And he looked from Kirsty to Chris and said *You, Chris lass*, and that she did while Mrs Strachan went down to the kitchen to make him tea and trail around like a clucking hen, God! what mightn't be happening in Peesie's Knapp without her? Chris lost her temper at last, she lost it seldom enough, this time it went with a bang – *I don't know either what's happening in Peesie's Knapp but if you're in such tune about it you'd better go home and find out.* Mrs Strachan reddened up at that, bubbling like a hubbley-jock, that wasn't the way for a quean to speak to a woman that might well be her mother, she might think shame to curse and swear with her father lying at death's door there. And Chris said she hadn't sworn, but she was over-weary to argue about it, and knew right well that whatever she said now Mistress Strachan would spread a fine story about her.

And sure as death so she did, it was soon all over the Howe that that coarse quean at Blawearie had started to swear at Mistress Strachan while her father was lying near dead in the room above their heads. Only Chae himself didn't believe it, and when he came up to Blawearie next day he whispered to Chris, *Is't true you gave Kirsty a bit of a damning yesterday?* and when she said she hadn't he said it was a pity, it was time that somebody did.

So there father lay and had lain ever since, all those five weeks he'd lain there half-paralysed, with a whistle beside his bed when he wanted attention, and God! that was often enough. Creeping to her bed half-dead at night Chris would find herself thinking a thing that wouldn't bear a rethinking out here in the sun, with the hum of the heather-bees, heather-smell in her face, Lord! could she only lie here a day how she'd sleep and sleep! Fold over her soul and her heart and put them away with their hours of vexing and caring, the ploughing was done, she was set to her drilling, and faith! it was weary work!

She started and sighed and took her hands down from her face and listened again. Far down in Blawearie there rose the blast of an angry-blown whistle.

III

Seed-Time

She'd thought, running, stumbling up through the moor, with that livid flush on her cheek, up through the green of the April day with the bushes misted with cobwebs, *I'll never go back, I'll never go back, I'll drown myself in the loch!* Then she stopped, her heart it seemed near to bursting and terribly below it moved something, heavy and slow it had been when she ran out from Blawearie but now it seemed to move and uncoil. Slow, dreadfully, it moved and changed, like a snake she had once seen up on this hill, and the sweat broke out on her forehead. Had anything happened with it? Oh God, there couldn't be anything! If only she hadn't run so, had kept herself quiet, not struck as she'd done, deaved and angry and mad she had been!

Sobbing, she fell to a slow walk then, her hand at her side, and through the gate into the moorland went with slow steps, the livid flush burning still on her cheek, she felt it was branded there. Tears had come in her eyes at last, but she wouldn't have them, shook them off, wouldn't think; and a pheasant flew up beneath her feet, *whirroo!* as she came to the mere of the loch. She bent over there through the rushes, raising her hands to her hair that had come all undone, and parted it from her face and looked down at her face in the water. It rippled a moment, it was brown with detritus, at first she could see nothing of herself but a tremulous amorphousness in the shadow of the rushes; and then the water cleared, she saw the flush below her cheekbone, her own face, strange to her this last month and stranger now. Below in Kinraddie the carts were rattling up every farmroad, driving out dung to the turnip-planting, somewhere there

was a driller on the go, maybe it was Upperhill's, the clank was
a deafening thing. Nine o'clock in the morning and here up on
the hill she was, she didn't know where to go or where to turn.

There were the Standing Stones, so seldom she'd seen them
this last nine months. Cobwebbed and waiting they stood, she
went and leant her cheek against the meikle one, the monster
that stood and seemed to peer over the water and blue distances
that went up to the Grampians. She leant against it, the bruised
cheek she leaned and it was strange and comforting – stranger
still when you thought that this old stone circle, more and more
as the years went on at Kinraddie, was the only place where
ever she could come and stand back a little from the clamour
of the days. It seemed to her now that she'd had feint the minute
at all to stand and think since that last September day she'd
spent up here, caught and clamped and turning she'd been in
the wheel and grind of the days since father died.

But at the time a thing fine and shining it had been, she hadn't
cared if folk deemed her heartless and godless – fine she thought
it, a prayer prayed and answered, him dead at last with his
glooming and glaring, his whistlings and whisperings. *Chris,
do this*, and *Chris, do that* it went on from morn till night till
but hardly she could drag herself to the foot of the stairs to
heed him.

But a worse thing came as that slow September dragged to
its end, a thing she would never tell to a soul, festering away in
a closet of her mind the memory lay, it would die sometime,
everything died, love and hate; fainter and fainter it had grown
this year till but half she believed it a fancy, those evening
fancies when father lay with the red in his face and his eye on
her, whispering and whispering at her, the harvest in his blood,
whispering her to come to him, they'd done it in Old Testament
times,[1] whispering *You're my flesh and blood, I can do with
you what I will, come to me, Chris, do you hear?*

And she would hear him and stare at him, whispering also, *I
won't*, they never spoke but in whispers those evenings. And
then she'd slip down from his room, frightened and frightened,
quivering below-stairs while her fancies raced, starting at every

creak that went through the harvest stillness of Blawearie house, seeing father somehow struggling from his bed, like a great frog struggling, squattering across the floor, thump, thump on the stairs, coming down on her while she slept, that madness and tenderness there in his eyes.

She took to locking her door because of that wild fear. The morning of the day she woke to find him dead she leaned out from her bedroom window and heard Long Rob of the Mill, far ayont the parks of Peesie's Knapp, out even so early, hard at work with his chaving and singing, singing *Ladies of Spain* with a throat as young and clear as a boy's. She had slept but little that night, because of the fear upon her and the tiredness, but that singing was sweet to hear, sweet and heart-breaking, as though the world outside Blawearie were singing to her, telling her this thing in the dark, still house could never go on, no more than a chance and an accident it was in the wind-loved world of men.

She got into her clothes then, clearer-headed, and slipped down to the kitchen and put on the kettle and milked the kye and then made breakfast. Below the windows the parks stood cut and stooked and trim, Ellison and Chae and Long Rob had done that, good neighbours John Guthrie had, had he never aught else. There came no movement from father's room, he was sleeping long, and setting the tray with porridge and milk she hoped he'd have nothing to say, just glower and eat, she'd slip away then.

So she went up the stair and into his room without knocking, he hated knocking and all such gentry-like notions, she put down the tray and saw he was dead. For a moment she looked and then turned to the curtains and drew them, and took the tray in her hand again, no sense in leaving it there, and went down and ate a good breakfast, slowly and enjoyingly she ate and felt quiet and happy, even though she fell fast asleep in her chair and awoke to find it gone nine. She lay and looked at her outspread arms a while, dimpled and brown, soft-skinned with the play of muscles below them. Sleep? She could sleep as she chose now, often and long.

Then she tidied the kitchen and found a spare sheet and went out to the hedge above the road and spread the sheet there, the sign she'd arranged with Chae should she need him. In an hour or so, out in his parks he saw it and came hurrying up to Blawearie, crying to her half-way up *Chris, lass, what's wrong?* Then only she realised she hadn't yet spoken that day to a soul, wondered if her voice would shake and break, it didn't, was ringing and clear as a bell crying down to Chae, *My father's dead.*

It was fair a speak in Kinraddie, her coolness, she knew that well but she didn't care, she was free at last. And when Mistress Munro, her that came to wash down the corpse, poked out her futret face and said, *A body would hardly think to look at you that your father was new dead,* Chris looked at the dark, coarse creature and saw her so clearly as she'd never done before, she'd never had time to look at a soul through her own eyes before, Chris-come-here and Chris-go-there. Not a pringle of anger she felt, just smiled and said *Wouldn't you, now, Mistress Munro?* and watched her at work and watched her go, not caring a fig what she thought and did. Then she roused herself for a while, free yet she could hardly be for a day or so, and got ready the big room for Auntie Janet and her man to sleep in, medals and all, when they came down to the funeral.

Down the next day they came, the two of them, Auntie as cheery as ever, Uncle as fat, he'd another bit medal stuck on his chain; and when they saw she wasn't sniftering or weeping they put off the long decent faces they'd set for her sight, and told her the news, Dod and Alec did fine and had sent their love. And Auntie said they must sell up the things at Blawearie and Chris come and bide with them in the North, some brave bit farmer would soon marry her there.

And Chris said neither yea nor nay, but smiled at them, biding her time, waiting till she found if a will had been left by father. Chae Strachan and old Sinclair of Netherhill saw to the funeral, old Sinclair moving so slow up the road, you'd half think he'd stop and take root, clean agony it was to watch him, and his face so pitted and old, father had been young by the like of him. And Mr Gibbon came over to see her, he'd been drinking a fell lot of late, folk said, maybe that accounted for the fact that as he crossed the twilit brae he was singing out loud to himself, Auntie heard the singing and ran up and out and hid in the lithe of a stack to try and make out what he sang. But he left off then and left her fair vexed, she said later she could have sworn it was a song they sang in the bothies about the bedding of a lad and a lass.

But Chris didn't care, keeping that secret resolve she'd made warm and clean and unsoiled in her heart, taking it out only alone to look at it, that old-time dream of hers. She'd never looked at herself so often or so long as now she did, the secret shining deep in her eyes, she saw her face thinner and finer than of yore, no yokel face it seemed. So she cared nothing for Mr Gibbon and his singing, the great curly brute and his breath that smelt so bad, he went up with her to father's room where father lay in his coffin, in a fine white shirt and a tie, his beard combed out and decent and jutting up, you'd say in a minute he'd raise those dead eyelids and whisper at you. Down on his knees the minister went, the great curly bull, and began to pray, Chris hesitated a minute and looked at the floor, and then, canny-like, when he wasn't seeing her, dusted a patch and herself knelt down. But she didn't heed a word he was saying, honeysuckle smell was drifting in on the air from the night, up on the hills the dog of some ploughman out poaching was barking and barking itself to a fair hysteria following the white blink of some rabbit's tail, in the closing dark she could see across the brae's shoulder the red light of Kinraddie House shine like a quiet star. So the curly bull prayed and boomed beside her, it was what he was paid for, she neither listened nor cared.

And that brought the funeral, it was raining early in the dawn when they woke, a fine drizzle that seeped and seeped from the sky, so soft and fine you'd think it snow without whiteness; there was no sun at all at first but it came up at last, a red ball, and hung there so till ten o'clock brought up the first of the funeral folk, and that was Chae, and his father-in-law, syne Ellison and Maitland in a gig they loosed in the cornyard, setting the sholtie to graze. And Ellison cried out, but low and decent, *I'll leave him here, me dear, sure he'll be all right, won't he?* and Chris smiled and said *Fine, Mr Ellison,* and he goggled his eyes, Irish as ever, you could never change Erbert Ellison, not even for the worse, folk said. Next there came a whole drove of folk, the factor, the minister, Cuddiestoun with his ill-marled face like a potato-park dug in coarse weather, but a fine white front, new-starched, to cover his working sark, and cuffs that fair chafed his meikle red hands, right decent, and he'd on fine yellow boots on his meikle feet. Rob of the Mill and Alec Mutch came next, you could hear their tongues from the foot of Blawearie brae, folk were affronted and went out and cried *Wheest-wheest!* down to them, and Rob called back *What is't?* and faith! it would have been better if they'd been left alone, what with the wheesting and whispering that rose.

But they were real good, Rob bringing a bottle of whisky, Glenlivet[2] it was, and Alec a half-bottle, they whisked them over to Uncle Tam when nobody looked; or anyway not a body but looked the other way and spoke, canny-like, of the weather. The kitchen was fair crowded, so was the room, like a threshing-day, folk sat and each had a dram, Mr Gibbon said *Spirits? Yes, thank you, I'll have a drop,* there'd have been barely enough to go round but for Rob and Alec. Then they heard another gig come up the hill, it was Gordon's from Upperhill, him and his foreman. Uncle Tam winked at the whisky, *You'll have a dram, Upperhill, you and your man?* but Mr Gordon said, sniffy-like, *I hardly think it shows respect and Ewan's tee-tee as well.*

Long Rob of the Mill sat next the door, he winked at Chris and then at Ewan Tavendale, Ewan turned fair red and said nothing. So he hadn't a dram, he'd have liked one fine, Chris guessed, and felt mean and pleased and shy, and then gave herself a shake inside, what did it matter to her? Then the minister looked at his watch and the undertaker came in about, and then last of all, they hadn't expected the poor old stock, there was Pooty on the doorstep, he'd on a clean collar and shirt and an old hat, green but well-brushed; and when Uncle whispered if he'd have a dram he said *Och, ay, it's the custom, isn't it?* and had two.

The undertaker had gone up by then, Uncle with him, folk followed them one by one and came down, syne Auntie beckoned Chris to the neuk of the stair and said *Would you like to see him before he's screwed down?*

Uncle Tam and Long Rob of the Mill were there and as Chris went in Long Rob said *Well, well, good-bye, Blawearie man*, and shook father's hand, his eyes looked queer when he turned away, he said *He was a fine neighbour* and went out and closed the door. Chris stood and looked at her father, seeing him so plain as never in life she'd seen him, he'd been over-restless for that and quick enough he'd have raged at you had you glowered at his face like this. Still enough now, never-moving there in the coffin, he seemed to have changed already since he died, the face sunk in, it wasn't John Guthrie and yet it was. Uncle whispered behind her, him and the undertaker, and then Auntie was beside her, *They're to screw it down now, kiss your father, Chris.* But she shook her head, she couldn't do that, the room was still as they looked at her, for a moment she felt almost sick again as in those evening hours when *that* in the coffin had lain and whispered that she should lie with it. Then she just said *Good-bye, father*, and turned from him and went down to her own room and put on her coat and hat, it wasn't decent for a quean to go to a funeral, folk said, but in Blawearie's case there was no son or brother to see him into the kirkyard.

Chae and Long Rob and Ellison and Gordon carried the coffin down to the stair-foot, and settled it on their shoulders there, and went slow with it out through the front door then; and the rain held off a little, wind blowing in their faces, though, as they held down the hill. Behind walked the Reverend Gibbon, bare-headed, all the folk were bare-headed but Chris, Long Rob and Chae stepping easily and cannily, Ellison as well, but Gordon quivering at his coffin corner, he'd have done better with a dram to steady him up. But Chris walked free and un-caring, soon as the burial was over she'd be free as never in her life she'd been, she lifted her face to the blow of the wet September wind and the world that was free to her. Then it was that she saw Ewan Tavendale walked beside her, he glanced down just then and straight and fair up into his eyes she looked, she nearly stumbled in the slow walk because of that looking. They came to the turnpike then, there Ewan took Gordon's corner and Alec Mutch Ellison's, and these two fell back beside the minister, but Chae and Long Rob shook their heads when others offered to change with them, they'd manage fine.

The rain still held off, presently the wind soughing down the Howe died away and a little peek of sun came through, not down the Denburn it came but high up in the hill peaks, the lost, coarse ground where never a soul lived or passed but some shepherd or gillie, you could see them far off, lone and lonesome there on a still, clear day. Maybe so the dead walked in a still clear, deserted land, the coarse lands of death where only the chance wanderer showed his face, Chris thought, and the dead lapwings wheeled and cried against another sun. Then she ceased from that, startled out a moment from the calm that had come to her with her father's dying – daft to dream these things now, when she planned so much. Step, step, steadily and cannily went Long Rob and Chae, Chae getting bald and sandy in the crown, but Rob still with the corn hair clustered thick and the great moustaches swinging from his cheeks as they turned up the road that led to the kirkyard.

Then the sun went again, it was eleven o'clock perhaps, and Chris raised her eyes and saw through the trees the blinded windows of the Mains, the curtains were all drawn, decent-like, in respect for the funeral; and she felt a queer, sick thrill just below her left breast, not ill or sick, but just like a starting of the blood there, as though she'd leant on that place too long, and it had grown numb. It was dark under the yews, they dripped on the coffin and Long Rob, then there came a pattering as they passed by slow beneath, and Chris saw the long, oval leaves suddenly begin to quiver, it was as though a hand shook them, and through the leaves was the sky, it had blackened over and the rain was coming driving in a sheet down the brae from the Grampian haughs. It came and whipped the wet skirts about her legs, she saw Long Rob and Chae and Ewan stagger and then stand leaning against the drift, and then go on, not a soul put on his hat, there'd be bad colds by night and ill-tunes over this funeral yet.

That wasn't decent to think, but what did it matter to her? She wished she were back in Blawearie, and hoped the minister would not be over long-winded when he said his say. There was the grave-digger, a man from the Mains, a big scrawny childe who lived ill with his wife, folk said, he had his coat collar up and came out below the eaves of the kirk and motioned them along a path. And ben it they went, then Chris saw the grave, red clay and bright it was, not as she'd expected his grave somehow to be, they weren't burying him in mother's grave. For that land was over-crowded, folk said that every time the grave-digger stuck his bit spade in the ground some bone or another from the dead of olden time would came spattering out, fair scunnering you. But this was an old enough bit as well, right opposite rose the stone with the cross-bones, maybe all the dead bodies had long mouldered away into red clay here, clay themselves, and folk were glad they left the earth free for newcomers.

Uncle had come to her elbow then and he stood with her, the others stood back, it was strange and silent but for the soft patter of the rain on the yews and the Reverend Gibbon shielding his Bible away from the wet drive of it, beginning to read. And Chris listened, her head bent against the rain's whisper, to the words that promised Resurrection and Life through Jesus Christ our Lord, who had died long syne in Palestine and had risen on the third day and would take from that thing that had been John Guthrie quick, and was now John Guthrie dead, the quickness and give it habitation again. And Chris thought of her dream looking up at the coarse lands of the hills and thinking of the lands of death, was that where Christ would meet with father? Unco and strange to think, standing here in the rain and listening to that voice, that father himself was there in that dark box heaped with the little flowers that folk had sent, father whom they were to leave here happed in red clay, alone in darkness and earth when the night came down. Surely he'd be back waiting her up in Blawearie, she'd hear his sharp, vexed voice and see him come fleetly out of the house, that red beard of his cocked as ever at the world he'd fought so dourly and well—

Somebody chaved at her hand then, it was the grave-digger, he was gentle and strangely kind, and she looked down and couldn't see, for now she was crying, she hadn't thought she would ever cry for father, but she hadn't known, she hadn't known this thing that was happening to him! She found herself praying then, blind with tears in the rain, lowering the cord with the hand of the grave-digger over hers, the coffin dirling below the spears of the rain. *Father, father, I didn't know! Oh father, I didn't KNOW!* She hadn't known, she'd been dazed and daft with her planning, her days could never be aught without father; and she minded then, wildly, in a long, broken flash of remembrance, all the fine things of him that the years had hidden from their sight, the fleetness of him and his justice, and the fight unwearying he'd fought with the land and its masters to have them all clad and fed and respectable, he'd never rested working and chaving for them, only God had beaten him in the end. And she minded the long roads he'd tramped to the kirk with her when she was young, how he'd smiled at her and called her his lass in days before the world's fight and the fight of his own flesh grew over-bitter, and poisoned his love to hate. *Oh father, I didn't know!* she prayed again, and then that was over, she was in the drive of the rain, hard and tearless, the grave-digger was pointing to the ground and she picked up a handful of soft, wet earth, and heard the Reverend Gibbon's voice drone out *Dust to dust, ashes to ashes,*[3] and leant over the grave and dropped the wet earth; and then the grave-digger was throwing in the turf, the coffin rang as though it were hollow, she stared at it till Uncle had her by the elbow, speaking to her, and so was the Reverend Gibbon but she couldn't hear them at first; and folk were to say she must have been real fond of her father after all, the best of a coarse bit family in the end.

And then she was walking back through the kirkyard and the folk at the gate were stopping to shake her hand, Long Rob and Chae to say they'd aye help her, and Ellison, kind and solemn and Irish, and old Sinclair dripping in the rain, he should never have been out in a day like this. The last was Ewan Tavendale, he said *Ta-ta, Chris,* his hand was wet meeting hers as her own hand was, but he put up his left hand as well as his right and held both of hers a minute; and he didn't look ashamed and shy any more, but as though he was so sorry he'd help her in any way, not only the ways he could.

That was the last of them she saw and the end of father's funeral. Back in Blawearie Auntie Janet made her strip from her clothes and get into bed, *God be here, it's you that'll be next in your grave!* she cried. And Chris slept throughout the remainder of that day, undreaming, she didn't wake till late in the night, Blawearie listening and hearkening about her. And then she was afraid, awfully afraid, sitting up in bed and hearkening to that Something that walked the house with sharp, quick footsteps, running so fleetly up the stairs, impatient and unresting, a shadow with footfalls that were shadows; and into the night and far towards the dawn it roamed the house of Blawearie till the cocks were crowing and Uncle and Auntie moving, and Chris didn't feel afraid at all by then, only lay and wept softly for the father she'd never helped and forgot to love.

And the next forenoon the lawyer man came down from Stonehaven, it was Peter Semple, folk called him Simple Simon but swore that he was a swick. Father had trusted him, though, and faith! you'd be fell straight in your gait ere John Guthrie trusted you. Not that he'd listened to advice, father, he'd directed a will be made and the things to be set in that will; and when Mr Semple had said he was being fell sore on some of his family father had told him to mind his own business, and that was a clerk's. So Mr Semple drew up the will, it had been just after Will went off to the Argentine, and father had signed it; and now the Blawearie folk sat down in the parlour, with whisky and biscuits for Mr Semple, to hear it read. It was short and plain as you please, Chris watched the face of her uncle as the lawyer read and saw it go white in the gills, he'd expected something far different from that. And the will told that John Guthrie left all his possessions, in silver and belongings, to his daughter Christine, to be hers without let or condition, Mr Semple her guardian in such law matters as needed one, but Chris to control the goods and gear as she pleased. And folk were to say, soon as Kinraddie heard of the will, and faith! they seemed to have heard it all before it was well out of the envelope, that it was an unco will, old Guthrie had been fair spiteful to his sons, maybe Will would dispute his sister's tocher.

The money was over three hundred pounds in the bank, it was hard to believe that father could have saved all that. But he had; and Chris sat and stared at the lawyer, hearing him explain and explain this, that, and the next, in the way of lawyers: they presume you're a fool and double their fees. Three hundred pounds! And now she could do as she'd planned, she'd go up to the College again and pass her exams and go on to Aberdeen and get her degrees, come out as a teacher and finish with the filthy soss of a farm. She'd sell up the gear of Blawearie, the lease was dead, it had died with father, oh! she was free and free to do as she liked and dream as she liked at last!

And it was pity now that she'd all she wanted she felt no longer that fine thrill that had been with her while she made her secret plans. It was as though she'd lost it down in Kinraddie kirkyard; and she sat and stared so still and white at the lawyer man that he closed up his case with a snap. *So think it well over, Christine*, he said and she roused and said *Oh, I'll do that;* and off he went, Uncle Tam drew a long, deep breath, as though fair near choked he'd been *Not a word of his two poor, motherless boys!*

It seemed he'd expected Alec and Dod would be left their share, maybe that was why he'd been so eager to adopt them the year before. But Auntie cried *For shame, Tam, how are they motherless now that I've got them? And you'll come up and live with us when you've sold Blawearie's furnishings, Chris?* And her voice was kind but her eyes were keen, Chris looked at her with her own eyes hard, *Ay, maybe* and got up and slipped from the room, *I'll go down and bring home the kye.*

And out she went, though it wasn't near kye-time yet, and wandered away over the fields; it was a cold and louring day, the sound of the sea came plain to her, as though heard in a shell, Kinraddie wilted under the greyness. In the ley field old Bob stood with his tail to the wind, his hair ruffled up by the wind, his head bent away from the smore of it. He heard her pass and gave a bit neigh, but he didn't try to follow her, poor brute, he'd soon be over-old for work. The wet fields squelched below her feet, oozing up their smell of red clay from under the sodden grasses, and up in the hills she saw the trail of the mist, great sailing shapes of it, going south on the wind into Forfar, past Laurencekirk they would sail, down the wide Howe with its sheltered glens and its late, drenched harvests, past Brechin smoking against its hill, with its ancient tower[4] that the Pictish folk had reared, out of the Mearns, sailing and passing, sailing and passing, she minded Greek words of forgotten lessons, Παντα ρει, *Nothing endures.*[5] And then a queer thought came to her there in the drookèd fields, that nothing endured at all, nothing but the land she passed across, tossed and turned and perpetually changed below the hands of the crofter folk since the oldest of them had set the Standing Stones by the loch of Blawearie and climbed there on their holy days and saw their terraced crops ride brave in the wind and sun. Sea and sky and the folk who wrote and fought and were learned, teaching and saying and praying, they lasted but as a breath, a mist of fog in the hills, but the land was forever, it moved and changed below you, but was forever, you were close to it and it to you, not at a bleak remove it held you and hurted you. And she had thought to leave it all!

She walked weeping then, stricken and frightened because of that knowledge that had come on her, she could never leave it, this life of toiling days and the needs of beasts and the smoke of wood fires and the air that stung your throat so acrid, Autumn and Spring, she was bound and held as though they had prisoned her here. And her fine bit plannings! – they'd been just the dreamings of a child over toys it lacked, toys that would never content it when it heard the smore of a storm or the cry of sheep on the moors or smelt the pringling smell of a new-ploughed park under the drive of a coulter. She could no more teach a school than fly, night and day she'd want to be back, for all the fine clothes and gear she might get and hold, the books and the light and learning.

The kye were in sight then, they stood in the lithe of the free-stone dyke that ebbed and flowed over the shoulder of the long ley field, and they hugged to it close from the drive of the wind, not heeding her as she came among them, the smell of their bodies foul in her face – foul and known and enduring as the land itself. Oh, she hated and loved in a breath! Even her love might hardly endure, but beside it the hate was no more than the whimpering and fear of a child that cowered from the wind in the lithe of its mother's skirts.

And again that night she hardly slept, thinking and thinking till her head ached, the house quiet enough now without fairlies treading the stairs, she felt cool and calm, if only she could sleep. But by morning she knew she couldn't go on with Uncle and Auntie beside her, they smothered her over with their years and their canny supposings. Quick after breakfast she dressed and came down and Auntie cried out, real sharp-like, *Mighty be here, Chris, where are you going?* as though she owned Blawearie stick and stone, hoof and hide. And Chris looked at her coolly, *I'm away to Stonehaven to see Mr Semple, can I bring you anything?* Uncle Tam rose up from the table then, goggling, with his medals clinking, *Away to Stonehive? What are you jaunting there for? I'll transact any business you have.* Their faces reddened up with rage, she saw plain as daylight how near it lay, dependence on them, she felt herself go white as she looked at them. *I'll transact my own business fine*, she said hardly, and called *Ta-ta* from the door and heard no answer and held down the Blawearie road and ran over the parks to the station, and caught the early scholars' train that went in to Stonehaven Academy.

It was crowded fell close, there were three-four scholars in the carriage she got in to, she didn't know any, they were learning French verbs. And she'd wanted to go back to things as silly!

They were past Drumlithie and the Carmont[6] then, you could smell the woods of Dunnottar and look out at them from the window, girdling Stonehaven down to its bay, shining and white, the sun was out on the woods and the train like a weasel slipped through the wet smell of them. And there was Stonehaven itself, the home of the poverty toffs, folk said, where you might live in sin as much as you pleased but were damned to hell if you hadn't a white sark. She'd heard Chae Strachan say that, but it wasn't all true, there were fell poor folk in Stonehaven as well as the come-ups; and douce folk that were neither poor nor proud and had never a say when Stonehaven boomed of its braveness. And that it did fair often, the Mearns' capital, awful proud of its sarks but not of its slums; and it thought itself real genteel, and a fine seafront it had that the English came to in summer – daft, as usual, folk said, hadn't they a sea in England?

Because it was early in the day and the lawyer's office still shut Chris loitered on the road in the tail of the hasting scholars, the little things they were, all legs and long boots, funny how they tried to speak English one to the other, looking sideways as they cried the words to see if folk thought them gentry. Had Marget and she been daft as that?

But the sun was out now on the long Stonehaven streets and Chris went past the Academy down to the market, still at that hour with just a stray cat or so on the sniff around, genteel and toff-like, Stonehaven cats. Down through a lane she caught a glimmer of the North Sea then, or maybe it was the sunlight against the sky, but the smell of the sea came up. And she still had plenty of time.

So she went down to the shore, the tide was out, thundering among the rocks, not a soul on the beach but herself, gulls flying and crying, the sun strong and warm. She sat on a seat in the glow of it and shut her eyes and was happy. Below her feet the ground drummed and trembled with reverberations from that far-off siege of the rocks that the sea was making out there by the point of the bay, it was strange to feel it and be of it, maybe folk there were who felt for the sea as last night she had felt in the rain-drenched fields of Kinraddie. But to her it seemed restless, awaiting and abiding nowhither, not fine like the glens that nestled and listened high up the coarse country, or the parks sun-heavy with clover that waited your feet at evening.

She fell asleep then, she slept there two hours in the sun and woke feeling fresher than she'd done since father's funeral. So hungry also she felt she couldn't wait the ending of the business

she'd come on but went into a tea-house up in the square, two
women kept it, old bodies they were that moved backward and
forward the room, slow and rheumatic. One looked like the
cats she'd seen in the square that morning, sleeked and stroked,
the other was thin as a lathe, their tea-room looked scrubbed
and clean and their tea had a taste to match. They were sharp
and stroked and genteel, Chris thought for the first time then
in her life how awful it would be to grow old like them, old
maids without men, without ever having lain with a man, or
had him kiss you and hold you, and be with you, and have
children of his, or the arm of a man when you needed it, kind
and steadfast and strong. If she'd lived her plan to train as a
teacher she'd have grown like them.

She might grow so still! she thought, and daft-like suddenly
felt quite feared, she paid for her tea in a hurry and went out
to the square again, thinking of herself as an old maid, it
wouldn't bear thinking about. So she hurried to the office of
Simple Simon and a little clerk asked her business, perky-like,
and she looked at him coolly and said her business was Mr
Semple's. And then she minded the old maids, was she herself
one by nature? And in a cold fear she smiled at the clerk,
desperately, with her lips and eyes, it was fine, the boy smiled
also and blushed and thawed, and said *Sit down, this is fine
and comfortable;* and pulled out a padded chair for her; and
down she sat, light-hearted again. Then the clerk came back
and led her through a passage to Semple's room, he looked
busy enough, with a telephone beside him and heaps of papers,
and rows of little black boxes round the shelves. Then he rose
and shook hands, *Well, well, it's Miss Guthrie come up; you've
been thinking of the will, no doubt?*

She told him, *Yes, just that;* and she was going to live on at
Blawearie a while, not roup the gear out at once, could he see
to that with the factor?

He stared at her with his mouth fallen open, *But you can't
live there alone!*

She told him she'd no such intention, couldn't he get her
some woman come live with her, some old bit body who'd be
glad of a home?

He said *Oh, God, there are plenty of them!* and began to chew at his mouser.

She told him it mightn't be for more than a month or so, till she'd made up her mind, just.

He said absent-like, *Just? Hell, a woman's mind just!* and then pulled himself up right sudden as she looked at him hardly and cool. Then he argued a bit, but Chris hardly listened, father's will had said she could do what she liked.

And presently, seeing she cared not a fig for him, Semple gave in and said he'd settle up with the factor, and he knew an old widow body, Melon, he'd send down to Blawearie the morn.

So Chris said *Thank you, good-bye*, and went out from the office, cool as she'd come, the sun was a fell blaze then and the streets chock-a-block with sheep, great droves of them, driven in to the weekly mart. Collies were running hither and yon, silent and cocked of ear, clean and quick as you'd wish, paying heed to none but shepherd and sheep. Drovers and beasts, they took a good look at Chris both, as she stood in her black clothes watching them; and just as she wondered what she'd do next, walk down to the sea and sit on a bench till it neared to dinner-time in the hotels, or go up to the station and take the 11.00, a gig going by slowed down of a sudden, a man jumped down and cried back to the driver.

The man that had jumped was the foreman at Upperhill, Ewan Tavendale, the driver old Gordon himself, he looked in a rage about something. And he cried *Mind the time then!* and gave Chris a sore glower and drove spanking away.

And then Ewan had crossed the pavement and was standing in front of her, he lifted his cap and said, shy-like, *Hello!* Chris said *Hello*, and they looked at each other, he was blushing, she minded the last time, she didn't like him half as she'd done at the funeral. He said *Are you in for the day?* and she mocked him, not knowing why she did that, it wasn't decent and father new dead, *Och ay, just that.* He blushed some more, she felt cool and queerly giddy in a breath, looking at the fool of a lad, folk were glowering at them both they were later to learn, not Gordon only but Ellison: and back the two of them went to Kinraddie and told every soul it was a sore shame there wasn't

somebody about to heed to the Guthrie girl from the hands of
that coarse tink brute, Ewan Tavendale.

But they hadn't known that and mightn't have cared, suddenly Chris felt herself hungry again, happy as well, not caring
about Ewan himself but not wanting either he should leave her
and go on to the mart. She said *I'm going up to the Inn for
dinner*, and he looked at her, still shy, but with a kind of
smoulder in the shyness, his eyes like the smoulder of a burning
whin – *Maybe we can eat together?* And she said, as he turned
by her side, *Oh, maybe. But what will Mr Gordon do?* And
Ewan said he could dance a jig on the head of the mart with
sheer rage, for all he cared.

So in they went to old Mother White's, not that they saw the
old body herself; and there was a fine room to eat in, with white
cloths set, and a canary that sang above them, the windows fast
closed to the dust and dirt. And they'd broth, it was good, and
the oat-cakes better; and then boiled beef and potatoes and
turnip; and then rice pudding with prunes; and then some tea,
Ewan found his tongue as they drank the tea and said to-day
was his holiday, for he'd worked all the last Sunday on a job
libbing lambs. And Chris said, it was out of her mouth before
she thought, *So you're in no hurry to be back?* and Ewan leaned
across the table, the smoulder near kindled to a fire, *Not unless
you should be? What train are you taking up to Kinraddie?*

And then how it all came about, their planning to spend the
day together and their walk to Dunnottar, Chris never knew,
maybe neither did Ewan. But half an hour later, Stonehaven a
blinding white glimmer behind, Dunnottar in front, they were
climbing down the path that led to the island. The air was blind
with the splash of the incoming tide, above you the rock rose
sheer as the path wound downwards sheer; and high up,
crowning the rock were the ruins of the castle walls, splashed
with sunlight and the droppings of sea-birds. Gulls there were
everywhere, Chris was deafened in the clamour of the brutes,
but quiet enough in the castle it proved, not a soul seemed
visiting there but themselves.

They paid their shillings and the old man came with them

from room to room, a scunner to Ewan, Chris guessed, for his
eyes kept wandering, wearied, to her from this ruin and that.
In walls little slits rose up, through these it was that in olden
times the garrisons had shot their arrows at besiegers; and down
below, in the dungeons, were the mouldering clefts where a
prisoner's hands were nailed while they put him to torment.
There the Covenanting folk had screamed and died[7] while the
gentry dined and danced in their lithe, warm halls, Chris stared
at the places, sick and angry and sad for those folk she could
never help now, that hatred of rulers and gentry a flame in her
heart, John Guthrie's hate. Her folk and his they had been,
those whose names stand graved in tragedy:

HERE : LYES : IOHN : STOT : IAMES : ATCHI
SON : IAMES : RUSSELL : & WILLIAM : BRO
UN : AND : ONE : WHOSE : NAME : WEE : HAVE :
NOT: GOTTEN : AND : TWO : WOMEN : WHOSE :
NAMES : ALSO : WEE: KNOW : NOT : AND : TWO :
WHO: PERISHD.:COMEING:DOUNE:THE: ROCK
ONE : WHOSE : NAME : WAS : IAMES : WATSON
THE : OTHER : NOT : KNOWN : WHO : ALL : DIED
PRISONERS   :   IN   :   DUNNOTTAR   :   CASTLE
ANNO : 1685 : FOR : THEIR : ADHERENCE :
TO : THE : WORD : OF : GOD : AND : SCOTLANDS
COVENANTED   :   WORK   :   OF   :   REFORMA
TION :   REV : XI CH : 12 VERSE[8]

But Ewan whispered, *Oh, let's get out of this*, though it was
he himself that had planned they come to Dunnottar. So out in
the sun, at the shelving entrance, they stood awhile in the cry
of the gulls; and then Ewan said *Come down to the sea: I know
a nook*.

And they climbed down and then up again, along the cliff-
edge, it made you dizzy to look over and down at the incoming
wash of froth, and sometimes, far under their feet, there rose a
loud *boom!* like a gun going off. Ewan said that the rocks were
sometimes hollow and the water ran far below the fields, so
that ploughmen ploughed above the sea and in stormy weather

they'd sometimes see their furrows quiver from that storm that raged under their feet. So they came to a crumbling path, it seemed to fall sheer away, a seagull sailed up to meet them, and Ewan with his feet already out of sight turned back and asked, *You'll not be dizzy?* And Chris shook her head and followed him, it seemed to her between sea and sky, down and down, and then Ewan was gripping her ankle, she swung almost loose for a moment, looking down in his face, it was white and strained, then her foot and hand caught again, Ewan called that it wasn't much further; and they got to the bottom and sat and looked at each other on a ledge of sand.

The sun poured in there, the tide whispered and splashed and threw out its hands at them on the sand, but it didn't come further up. And Chris saw that the place was closed in, you couldn't see a thing of the coast but the rocks overhanging, and only a segment of the sea itself, a mile or so out a boat had tacked, it flashed its wings like a wheeling gull; and Ewan was sitting beside her, peeling an orange.

They ate it together and Chris took off her hat, she felt hot and uncouth in her sad black clothes. And suddenly, for no reason, she thought of a time, years before, when she'd been trampling blankets for mother a fine summer day in May, and had taken off her skirts and her mother had come out and laughed at her, *You'd make a fine lad!* It was as though she heard mother speak, she looked up and around, daftly, dazed-like a moment, but there was not a soul near but Ewan Tavendale lying on an elbow, looking at the sea, the sun in his face, young and smooth with its smouldering eyes. And she found she didn't mislike him any longer, she felt queer and strange to him, not feared, but as though he was to say something in a moment that she knew she couldn't answer. And then he said it, blushing, but his smouldering eyes didn't waver, *Chris, do you like me a bit?*

Can't thole you at all, that's why we're out lazing in this place together.

But a nervousness came on her, not that she feared him, she'd known all along she was safe with Ewan as Mollie with Will in those long-gone days of the court at Drumlithie. Only, it was

as though her blood ran so clear and with such a fine, sweet
song in her veins she must hold her breath and heark to it; and
for the first time she knew the strange thing her hand was, held
there dripping sand, it seemed as though all her body sat a little
apart from herself, and she looked at it, wondering. So it was
that she knew she liked him, loved him as they said in the soppy
English books, you were shamed and a fool to say that in
Scotland. Ewan Tavendale – that it should be him! And then
she minded something, it didn't matter at all, but she wanted
to know for all that. *Ewan, was it true that story they told
about you and old Sarah Sinclair?*

It was as though she had belted him in the face. He went
white then, funnily white leaving brown the red tan in the little
creases of his face that the coarse field weather had made; and
he sat up, angrily, and glowered at her, the great black cat, so
sleekèd and quick to anger. And the feeling she'd had for him,
that dizziness that made earth and sea and her heart so light,
quite went from her. She said *Oh, I don't want to know*, and
began to hum to herself; and then Ewan reached out his hand
and gripped her arm, it hurt, he said *Damn well listen now that
you've asked me*. And it was awful, awful and terrible, she
didn't want to listen to him, covering her face with her hands,
he went on and on and then stopped at last – *Now you're
frightened, frightened that a woman should feel like that, maybe
some day you'll feel it yourself.*

She jumped to her feet then, angry as him, forgetting to feel
shamed. *Maybe I will, but when I do I'll get a better man than
you to serve me!* And before he could answer that she had
caught up her hat and was up the cliff path so quick she didn't
know how she did it, her fingers and feet were nimble and sure,
she heard Ewan cry below her and paid no heed. He was barely
half-way up when she reached the top and looked down, and
then the rage quite went from her, she leaned over the edge
instead, holding down her hand, and he caught it and smiled,
and they stood and panted and smiled one at the other, fools
again as they'd been in the market-square of Stonehaven.

But suddenly Ewan whipped out his watch, *God, it must be
getting fell late*, and as he said it the sunshine went. Chris raised

her head and saw why, they'd been sitting down there in the last of it, the gloaming was down on the countryside and the noise of the gulls rising up through the mirk. Ewan caught her hand and they ran by the cliff-edge of the gloaming-stilled parks, there were great dappled kye that stopped their grazing to look; and up in front, dark and uncanny, they saw Dunnottar rise on its rock. And then they reached the main road and slowed down, but she still left her hand in Ewan's.

And in Stonehaven they caught by the skin of the teeth the six o'clock train, the mart was long over and folk gone home. In the carriage were only themselves all the way to Kinraddie, Ewan sat on the opposite seat, she liked him sit there, liked him not wanting to hold her hand, she'd have hated him touch her now. And they didn't say a word till they neared Kinraddie, and then he said *Chrissie! Tired?* and she said *Losh, no, and my name's Chris, Ewan.* Then she saw him blush again in the flicker of the gaslight; and a strange, sweet surge of pity came on her, she leant over and patted his knee, he was only a boy in spite of his Sarah Sinclair.

But she thought of Sarah all the same that night, lying listening in bed to the coming of the rain again, a wet winter it promised the Howe. So women were like that when they didn't have the men they wanted? – many of them maybe like that, hiding it away even from themselves till a summer of heat drove one here and there to such acts as affronted Kinraddie. But she didn't feel affronted, it was maybe because she was over-young, had read over-many of the books, had been the English Chris as well as this one that lay thinking of Ewan; and the old ways of sinning and winning, having your own pleasure and standing affronted at other folk having theirs, seemed often daft to her. Sarah Sinclair might well have obliged her and met with some other lad than Ewan that August night; but then she wasn't to know Chris Guthrie would ever lie and think of him in her bed, hearing the batter of the rain against her window and the swish of the great Blawearie trees.

It was then, in a lull of the swishing, she heard the great crack of thunder that opened the worst storm that had struck the

Howe in years. It was far up, she thought, and yet so close Blawearie's stones seemed falling about her ears, she half-scrambled erect. Outside the night flashed, flashed and flashed, she saw Kinraddie lighted up and fearful, then it was dark again, but not quiet. In the sky outside a great beast moved and purred and scrabbled, and then suddenly it opened its mouth again and again there was the roar and the flash of its claws, tearing at the earth, it seemed neither house nor hall could escape. The rain had died away, it was listening – quiet in the next lull, and then Chris heard her Auntie crying to her *Are you all right, Chrissie?* and cried back she was fine. Funny Uncle Tam had cried never a word, maybe he was still in the sulks, he'd plumped head-first in when he'd heard of the old woman that Semple was sending to help keep house in Blawearie. They were off to Auchterless the morn, and oh! she'd be glad to see them go, she'd enough to do and to think without fighting relations.

The thunder clamoured again, and then she suddenly sat shivering, remembering something – Clyde and old Bob and Bess, all three of them were out in the ley field there, they weren't taken in till late in the year. Round the ley field was barbed wire, almost new, that father had put up in the Spring, folk said it was awful for drawing the lightning, maybe it had drawn it already.

She was out of bed in the next flash, it was a ground flash, it hung and it seemed to wait, sizzling, outside the window as she pulled on stockings and vest and knickers and ran to the door and cried up *Uncle Tam, Uncle Tam, we must take in the horses!* He didn't hear, she waited, the house shook and dirled in another great flash, then Auntie was crying something, Chris stood as if she couldn't believe her own ears. Uncle Tam was feared at the lightning, he wouldn't go out, she herself had best go back to her bed and wait for the morning.

She didn't wait to hear more than that, but ran to the kitchen and groped about for the box of matches and lighted the little lamp, it with the glass bowl, and then found the littlest lantern and lighted that, though her fingers shook and she almost dropped the funnel. Then she found old shoes and a raincoat,

it had been father's and came near to her ankles, and she caught
up the lamp and opened the kitchen door and closed it quick
behind her just as the sky banged again and a flare of sheet
lightning came flowing down the hill-side, frothing like the
incoming tide at Dunnottar. It dried up, leaving her blinded,
her eyes ached and she almost dropped the lantern again.

In the byre the kye were lowing fit to raise the roof, even the
stirks were up and stamping about in their stalls. But they were
safe enough unless the biggings were struck, it was the horses
she'd to think of.

Right athwart her vision the haystacks shone up like great
pointed pyramids a blinding moment, vanished, darkness complete and heavy flowed back on her again, the lantern-light
seeking to pierce it like the bore of a drill. Still the rain held off
as she stumbled and cried down the sodden fields. Then she
saw that the barbed wire was alive, the lightning ran and glowed
along it, a living thing, a tremulous, vibrant serpent that spat
and glowed and hid its head and quivered again to sight. If the
horses stood anywhere near to that they were finished, she cried
to them again and stopped and listened, it was deathly still in
the night between the bursts of the thunder, so still that she
heard the grass she had pressed underfoot crawl and quiver
erect again a step behind her. Then, as the thunder moved away
– it seemed to break and roar down the rightward hill, above
the Manse and Kinraddie Mains – something tripped her, she
fell and the lantern-flame flared up and seemed almost to vanish;
but she righted it, almost sick though she was because of the
wet, warm thing that her body and face lay upon.

It was old Bob, he lay dead, his tongue hanging out, his legs
doubled under him queerly, poor brute, and she shook at his
halter a minute before she realised it was useless and there were
still Bess and Clyde to see to. And then she heard the thunder
and clop of their hooves coming across the grass to her, they
loomed suddenly into the light of the lamp, nearly running her
down, they stood beside her and whinnied, frightened and
quivering so that her hand on Bess's neck dirled as on the floor
of a threshing-machine. Then the lightning smote down again,
quite near, though the thunder had seemed to move off, it

played a great zig-zag over the field where she stood with the horses, and they pressed so near her she was almost crushed between them; and the lantern was pressed from her hand at last, it fell and went out with a crash and a crinkle of breaking glass. She caught Bess's bridle with one hand, Clyde's with another, and the lightning went and they began to move forward in the darkness, she thought she was in the right direction but she couldn't be sure. The next flash showed a field she didn't know, close at hand, with a high, staked dyke, and then she knew she had gone utterly wrong, it was the dyke on the turnpike.

The thunder growled satisfiedly and Clyde whinnied and whinnied, she saw then the reason for that, right ahead was the waving of a lantern, it must be Uncle come out to look for her at last, she cried *I'm here!* and a voice cried *Where?* She cried again and the lantern came in her direction, it was two men climbing the dyke. The horses started and whinnied and dragged her forward and then she found herself with Chae Strachan and Ewan, they had seen to their own horses on Upperhill and the Knapp, and had met and had minded hers on Blawearie; and up they had come to look for them. In the moment as they recognised one the other the lightning flared, a last sizzling glow, and then the rain came again, they heard it coming far up in the moors, it whistled and moaned and then was a great driving swish. Chae thrust his lantern upon Ewan, *Damn't man, take that and the lass and run for the house! I'll see to the horse!*

Ewan caught Chris under the arm, he swung the lantern in his other hand, they ran for a gate that led to the turnpike, the horses galloped behind them, Chae dragging at their halters and cursing them; and the rain overtook them as they gained the road, it was a battering wet hand that beat at them, Chris was soaked to the skin in a moment.

But in another they'd gained the new biggings of Peesie's Knapp, there shone a light in the kitchen, Ewan opened the door and pushed Chris in, *Bide here and I'll off and help Chae!* He disappeared into the blackness, the door closed behind him, Chris went forward into the kitchen and the glow of the fire.

She felt daft and deaf in the sudden silence and out of the rain, in the stillness of the new kitchen with its meikle clock wagging against the wall, and its calendars and pictures all spaced about, it looked calm and fine. Then she realised how wetted she was and took off the raincoat, it rained a puddle on the kitchen floor, she was dressed below only in knickers and vest, she'd not remembered that!

There came a rattle and clatter outside in the close as the men ran to the house, Chris slipped on the coat again and was tugging at the buttons as the two came stamping in. Chae cried, *Damn't, Chris, get out of that coat, you must fair be soaked. Here, I'll stir up the fire, the old wife's in bed, she'd sleep through a hundred storms.*

He bent over the fire then, poking it up, Chris found Ewan beside her, his hair black with the rain, the great cat, to help her off with her coat. She whispered, *I can't, Ewan, I've nothing on below!* and he blushed as red as a girl himself, and dropped his hands, and looked like a foolish boy so that she lost her own shyness at once, and told the same thing to Chae when he turned him round. He laughed at her with his twinkling eyes, *What, nothing at all?—Well, not very much, Chae.—Then come ben and I'll get you a coat of the wife's, you can slip into that.*

The rain was pelting on the roof as she followed him through to Mistress Strachan's new parlour, it sounded loud enough to wake the dead let alone her that had been Kirsty Sinclair. Chae opened the wardrobe and brought out a fine coat, Mistress Strachan's best for the Sunday, lined and fine and smelling of moth-balls; and then a pair of her slippers. *Get out of your things, Chris lass, and bring them to dry. I'll have something warm for you and Ewan to drink.*

Left alone with the candle she wished she'd asked for a towel; Chae was kind but a man had no sense. But she managed without, though stripping from vest and knickers and stockings felt like parting wetly from her own skin, almost, so soaked she had been. Then she put on the coat and slippers and gathered up the wet under-things and went through with them to the kitchen; and there was Chae one side of the fire with a bottle of whisky at his elbow, making toddy, and Ewan at the other, with his coat off, warming his hands and looking at the door for her to come ben. They didn't look at her over-close, either of them, Chae pulled in one chair for her to sit on and another for her things to dry on, and when she'd spread them out he stopped in his toddy-making and said *Damn't, Chris, was that ALL you'd on?* And she nodded and he said *You'll have your death of cold, sit closer.*

And that was fine, sitting next to Ewan, close to the blaze of the meikle larch logs that Chae had put on, they were swack with resin. Syne Chae had the toddy made and he handed a glass to Ewan first, as was right with a man, and another to Chris, with three spoonfuls of sugar in it, Mistress Strachan might have had something to say about that if she'd seen such wastry. But she was fast asleep up in Chae's bed and knew nothing of it all till the morning, she made up for it then, folk said she accused both Chae and Ewan of cuddling and sossing with the Guthrie quean all the hours of the night.

So that was the ongoing there was that night of lightning, nor was it the only one in Kinraddie, for the lightning, and maybe it was the big flash Chris had seen as she gained the brae leading down to the horses, drove a great hole through the Manse spare bedroom, and let in the rain and fair ruined the place. Folk said that when the Reverend Gibbon heard the bolt strike the house, he'd been awake and listening, he dived like a rabbit below the blankets and cried *Oh, Christ, keep it away from me!* Which wasn't the kind of conduct you'd have expected from a minister, but there was a fair flock of folk the lightning scared that night in one place or another, Jock Gordon at Upperhill ran to his mother's bedroom and wept all over the counterpane there like a bairn. And Alec Mutch of Bridge End went out about midnight to look for his sheep, but he was half-drunk when he went and got drunker every minute as he chaved about, not seeing a thing. And at last he came to a big stook out in the corn-parks and crawled into that, it was a stook that stood near the turnpike, and feint the thing else was seen of him till late the next morning when the postman was going by and the sun was shining fine, and out Alec's face and meikle lugs were stuck from the stook and gave the postman such a turn in the wame he was nearly sick on the spot.

But of all that Chris knew nothing, she'd plenty to think of with her own bit ploys. For after the rain cleared and her under-things dried she went through to the parlour and got in them again, and into the raincoat of father's, and Chae lighted a lantern, fair yawning with sleep was Chae, and Ewan was to guide home to Blawearie both Chris and the horses. So out to the night again, the rain had cleared and freshened it, there was a wind from off the sea blowing in the stars, and clouds like the drifting of great women's veils, fisher-wives' veils, across the sad faces of the coarse high hills. Then the horses champed in the courtyard, Ewan had their halter-ropes in his hand, Chris was beside him swinging the lantern, they cried *Ta-ta!* to Chae and Chae nearly uncovered the back of his gums, so sleepy he was, poor stock; and he started to cry something to Chris about coming up the morn and seeing to old Bob whom the lightning had killed, they'd be able to sell him to the knacker in Brechin. But a yawn put an end to whatever he'd to say, it hardly mattered, it was morn already, you could see far down by Bervie a band of greyness stroke the horizon, as though an idle finger stroked it there on a window-pane.

Tramp, tramp, with a nicker now and then and long snortings through their nostrils, the horses, glad to be roaded up to Blawearie, Ewan big by the side of Chris, she hadn't realised before how big he was. He said nothing at all, except shy-like, once *Are you warm enough?* and she laughed and said *Fine*, she'd never again be shy with Ewan Tavendale. And it seemed to her even then it would be long before she forgot this walk through the night that was hardly night at all, an hour poised on the edge of the morning, like a penny on its rim, the flutter of the wind in their faces and the wet country sleeping about them, it smelt like Spring, not a morning in fore-winter. Then she was yawning, stopping from that, it was still a bit way to the house, she wondered if Uncle or Auntie had known she went out to the horses in the lightning. But she needn't have worried, not a thing they'd guessed and didn't till the morning came, Blawearie was black as the inside of a lum-hat when they climbed to it, the kye quietened down, it hardly seemed home at all she had come to, a strange place this, with Ewan beside her. She opened the stable door for him, he led in the horses and made a shake-down, and came out and closed and barred up the door, she held him the lantern to see to that. And then he turned round, they were standing there in the close, his arms went round her, below her arms, and she said *Oh, don't!* and turned away her face; and he did nothing and she turned up her face to him again, peeping to see what he did.

Dark still it was but she saw his teeth, laughing at her, and then she put down the lantern and somehow resistance went from her, she hadn't wanted to resist, he was holding her close to him, kissing her, her cheeks and the tip of her nose because he couldn't see well in the darkness. And then he waited a moment and his lips came to hers and they were trembling as her own were, she wanted to cry and she wanted to laugh in a breath, and have him hold her forever, so, in the close, and his trembling lips that came into hers, sweet and terrible those lips in hers. There was a great power of honeysuckle that year, the smell of it drenched all the close in wet, still weather, it per-fumed the night and that kiss, she wouldn't ever forget them both though she lived unkissed again till she died. And then she knew they were near to other things, both of them, Ewan's breath was quicker than it should [be], he'd stopped from kissing her that kiss in the lips, his lips were urgent on her neck and breast; and she let him, she pulled aside the coat for him, standing so still, it was warm and sweet, she was his, he hers, for all things and everything, she never wanted better than that.

And then, in that ultimate moment, close at hand Chris heard the Blue Wyandotte,[9] already so cocky that he was, stir on his ree, he gave a bit squawk before he stirred and peeked for the day he would crow so lustily. Somehow that stirring brought Chris to her senses, she wasn't afraid, only this could wait for another night's coming, it was sweet and she wanted it to live and last, not snatch it and fumble it blindly and stupidly. And she caught Ewan's hand and kissed him, he stopped with that kiss of hers on his cheek, his cheek with the soft brown skin; and she whispered *Wait, Ewan!*

He let her go at once, shamed of himself, he had little need to be that, she saw him troubled and uncertain in the dim light and put her arms about him and kissed him again and whispered *Come down and see me to-morrow evening*, and he said *Chris, when'll you marry me?* and she quivered strangely and sweetly as he said that, his hands holding her again, but gently. And then something happened, and the happening was a yawn, she yawned as though her head would fall off, she couldn't stop yawning; and a laugh came in the middle of it and that only made it worse. And Ewan let go of her again, maybe he was nearly in a rage at first, and then he yawned himself, they stood like two daft geese, yawning, and then they were laughing together, holding hands, not laughing too loud in case they'd be heard. And five minutes after that Ewan was far on his way to the steading of Upperhill and Chris lying in her bed, she'd hardly touched it when she thought of Ewan, she wanted to think of him long and long, only next minute she was fast asleep.

It didn't seem that minute had passed when she heard Uncle Tam come chapping at her door, fair testy, *Come away, come away, now; there's a fire to light and your Auntie wants her tea.* She sat up in bed, still sleepy and dazed, *All right, Uncle Tam*, and yawned and didn't move for a minute, remembering the things of the night and day she'd forgotten in sleep. And then she threw off the blankets and got out from the bed, and stretched till each muscle was taut and quivering, she felt light and free and fine, not at all Chris Guthrie with the grave brown face and heavy hair, light and free as a feather; and without a stitch on she did a little dance at her window in the splash of early sun that came there – what a speak for Kinraddie were she seen! And she was singing to herself as she dressed and went slipping downstairs, Uncle was kneeling at the kitchen fire, like a cow with colic, and fair sour in the face. *You're in fine tune this morning*, he glowered, and she said *Ay, Uncle, I'm that, give the sticks to me*, and had them out of his hand and the fire snapping into them all in a minute.

Uncle went out to the close then, to look over the fields for the horses, and came back at a run, his little quoit medals swinging and clashing from his meikle belly, *Mighty, Chris, there's no sign of a horse!* She didn't turn round, just said *You could hardly have looked in the stable*, and heard him stop and breathe a great breath, and then go out again. And not a word more he said at the breakfast, he went up to their room to pack; but Auntie asked how the horses came to be in and was told Chris had done it herself, with Chae Strachan and Ewan to help. She seemed fair shamed to hear that, Auntie Janet, but angry as well, she whisked round the house like a wasp, *Ah well, it's plain you've no use for your relatives here, I only pray you don't come to disaster*. And Chris said *That's awfully fine of you, Auntie*, and that made her madder than ever, but Chris didn't care, she didn't care though all the world, all Kinraddie and the Howe, went mad and choked itself with its bootlaces over the things that had been between her and Ewan.

If it wasn't in a rage it was fair in a stir of scandal by post-man time, Kinraddie. Not a thing but it knew of her day in Stonehaven with that coarse tink brute, Ewan Tavendale, they'd been seen to go wandering out to Dunnottar together, they'd hidden away down in a hole by the sea – what did they that for if they'd nothing to hide? The postie told this to Auntie while Chris meated the chickens, Auntie fair grew worked up and forgot to rage, near crying she was as she told the story to Chris. How funny were folk! Chris thought, standing and fronting that trembling face. You knew them, saw through them, tied them up in little packets stowed away in your mind, labelled COARSE or TINKS or FINE; and they came tumbling from the packets at the very first shake, mixed and up-jumbled, she'd never known a soul bide neat and sure in his packet yet. For here was Auntie near crying because she thought her niece had been raped by Ewan Tavendale overnight, ashamed for her, sorry for her, fair set to carry her off to Aberdeen and cover her shame. But Chris said *There's nothing to cry about yet, Auntie Janet, Ewan and I haven't lain together. We'll wait till we're married*, and laughed at her Auntie's face, it was funny and pitiful both at once. And Auntie said *He's to marry you then?* and Chris said she hoped so, but you never knew, and

Auntie fell in a fearsome stew again, it wasn't fair to torment her like that, but that was the mood of Chris that morning.

Then Chae Strachan came up from the Knapp and looked at old Bob lying dead in his park. He shook his head over him, he doubted if the knacker would pay more than a pound – the closest muckers in Scotland, knackers, and *that* was fair saying a lot. Syne he promised to drive Auntie and her man to the station, and went back to the Knapp for his gig and was up and waiting before you could blink. And Chris helped her relatives up in the gig, and sent them her love to her brothers, and off the gig spanked, they looked over their shoulders and saw her stand laughing, she didn't care a button, coarse quean that she was.

And fair a relief was the riddance, the place to herself again; and then as she watched the gig whip round the corner into the turnpike it came on her that it wasn't *again*, it was just the first time! Blawearie was hers, there wasn't a soul in the place but herself, nobody had a right to come near it but if she allowed. The honeysuckle was blinding sweet in the sun, wet still, and she stood beside it and buried her face in it, laughed into it, blushed in it, remembering herself of the night before. And Ewan would be up to see her soon, to see her . . . and she wouldn't think of more! she had hundreds of things to do.

By noon she had dinner set for the old wife sent from Stonehaven. And then she heard Chae's gig come driving up to Blawearie and there was Chae and an old bit body, fair tottery she seemed as she got from the gig, with a black mutch on and a string bag gripped in her hand. But when she'd reached the ground she was none so tottery, she said that the heights aye feared her legs; and she looked Chris all over as though to make sure of her, living or dead, and asked *Where'll I put my box, Mem?* And Chris blushed for shame that any old soul should *Mem* at her, *Maybe Chae will carry it up for us?* And Chae said *Och, fine that*, and hoisted the old tin thing on his shoulder, and went swaggering into the house, and Mrs Melon followed after and Chris turned to Chae's gig.

By the time Chae came down she had nearly unyoked it, Chae cried *Damn't, Chris, what's on?* and she told him *Dinner, you're to stay for that.* So he was fell pleased, though he hummed and hawed a minute about rousting back to the Knapp. But she smiled at him, that way she'd done to the boy in Semple's office, and Chae stared at her and wound up his waxed mouser and twinkled his eyes and gave her shoulder a slap, *Lord, Chris, they'll right soon be after you, the lads, with your eyes like that!* And he gave a bit sigh as though, other times, other ways, he'd have headed the band himself.

So into the kitchen he came and sat himself down with old Mistress Melon, and Chris dished up the rabbit stew and they ate a great dinner, Mistress Melon was a funny old wife as soon as she saw you put on no airs. She'd a great red face as though she'd just unbended from a day's hard baking, and pale blue eyes like a summer sky, and faded hair that had once been brown, and Chris soon saw she was maybe the biggest gossip that had ever come into Kinraddie, and faith! that meant the challenging of many a champion. But her stories of Stonehaven had a lilt and a laugh, and the best was the one of the Provost that had lost his stud in his tumbler when speaking to a teetotal gathering. And Chae said that was a fine one, *Damn't, mistress, when I was in Africa . . .* and he told them a story of a man he knew, a black he'd been, real brave, and he found a diamond, on his own ground too, but as soon as the British heard of it they sent to arrest him for't. And what had that black childe done? Swallowed the damned thing and nothing of him could the British make, and they couldn't arrest him, and the black got his diamond back in a day or so in the course of nature, they were awful constipated folk, the blacks.

All the time he was telling the story Chae had been tearing into his rabbit and oat-cake; and soon's he'd finished one plate he took a look over the pot and cried *God, that was right fine, Chris quean. Is there more on the go?* Chris liked that, it was fine to have somebody that was hungry and liked his meat and didn't make out he was gentry or polite, there was less politeness about Chae than about a potato fork. Mistress Melon was eating right heartily too, and syne Chae told them another story, about a lion that he and the black head childe had hunted, they'd been awful chief together . . . And Mistress Melon asked

What, you and the lion? and winked at Chris, but Chae wasn't a bit put out, he just said *Damn't no, mistress, me and the head man*, and went on with the story again, it was plain Mistress Melon thought he was a bit of a liar till suddenly, casual-like, Chae opened the front of his sark and finished up *And that was the bit memento the damned beast left on me*. Syne they saw the marks on his chest, the marks of great raking claws they were they had torn fair deep and sure, and Chae's dark body-hair didn't grow in them. So Mistress Melon was fair stammy-gastered at that, and said so to Chris when Chae was gone.

Soon as that was Chris set to arranging with the Melon wife how the two of them would partition the work, Mistress Melon could do the cooking and cleaning, Chris preferred the outside, she'd milk and see to the kine; and they'd get on bravely, no doubt. Mistress Melon was a fell good worker in spite of her awful tongue, she'd cleared up the dinner things and washed them and put them away ere Chris was well out of the house. Then down on her knees she went and was scrubbing the kitchen floor, Chris was glad enough to see her at that, she hated scrubbing herself. If only she'd been born a boy she'd never had such hatings vexing her, she'd have ploughed up parks and seen to their draining, lived and lived, gone up to the hills a shepherd and never had to scunner herself with the making of beds or the scouring of pots. But neither would she ever have had Ewan hold her as last night he had.

And then she blushed and went on in silence with the cleaning of the byre, thinking of his coming and what she would say to him and the thing it was they'd arrange. Before she knew it the new plan came shaping up bravely in her mind, neat and trim and trig, and when she looked out and saw the gloaming near and went over the close and down through the parks for the kye, she had everything fixed, it didn't matter a fig what folk might say.

So when Ewan came in by at last she waited him ben in the parlour, with a great fire kindled there and the two big leather chairs drawn close. It was Mistress Melon that brought him through, her meikle red face fair shaking with ill-fashionce, agog to know what was toward. But Chris just said *Thank you, Mistress Melon*, and ticed Ewan over to his chair, and took his cap from him and made him sit down and fair closed the door in the old wife's face. It was bright and warm in the room, she turned round and saw her lad sit so; and then she raised her head and saw herself in the long, old mirror of the parlour wall, and thought how she'd changed, it crept on you and you hardly noted, in ways you were still as young as the quean with the plaits that had run by Marget to catch the scholars' train. But she saw herself then in her long green skirt, long under the knee, and her hair wound in its great fair plaits about her head, and her high cheek-bones that caught the light and her mouth that was well enough, her figure was better still; and she knew for one wild passing moment herself both frightened and sorry she should be a woman, she'd never dream things again, she'd live them, the days of dreaming were by; and maybe they had been the best; and there was Ewan waiting her, the great quiet cat, reddening and turning his head up with its smouldering eyes.

She went to him then and put her hand on his shoulder and before she knew it they were close together and so stayed long after they had finished with kissing, just quiet, in the firelight, his arms about her, her head on his shoulder, watching the fire. And when at last they began to speak she put her hands over his lips, whispering to him to whisper in case Mistress Melon should be listening out by. Maybe she wasn't but in the shortest while they heard her go stamping about the kitchen, singing a hymn fell loud, and that was a bit suspicious.

But they ceased from heeding her soon enough, they'd a hundred things to plan and discuss, there in the fireglow, they lit no lamp, Chris listened with her head down-bent as he told her he couldn't marry, he'd no more than a hundred pounds saved up, they'd have to wait. And she told him *she* had three hundred pounds, no credit to her, it was father's saving, but if she and Ewan married fair soon he could take over Blawearie's lease, they could stay where they were, *and that would be fine, no need for you any day then to go back through the parks to Upperhill.* He kissed her again at that, hurting her lips, but she didn't heed, it was fine to be hurt like that; but she wouldn't kiss back till he'd put him his Highland pride in his pouch and muttered *All right*.

They'd planned to be married in December and as they'd planned so the thing worked out without any hitch at all. In November Ewan found and fee'd a substitute foreman for Upperhill, a quiet-like childe James Leslie; and though old Gordon was none so pleased he couldn't well afford to fall out with so near a neighbour as the new Blawearie. Chris went into Stonehaven again with Ewan and saw the man Semple, he was fair suspicious, at first, but she argued him soon from that, and he got the lease changed to Ewan's name, and well-feathered his own nest in the changing, no doubt.

By then the news was no news, Kinraddie knew all, and when they came from the station that night they met in with Ellison down from the Mains, he'd been waiting them there to go by and he wouldn't have it but that they go up to the house and drink their own healths in a dram. Mistress Ellison was gentry and nice, more gentry than nice, poor thing, she was still no more than a servant quean and fleered and arched to make Chris and Ewan blush, she managed with Ewan. But Chris kept cool as ice, and nearly as friendly, she didn't see that a joke was less dirty if a neighbour spoke it. She and Ewan fair quarrelled over that when they left the Mains, it was their first quarrel and she wouldn't let him touch her, she said *If you like foul stories, I don't*, and he said, prigging at her, *Oh, don't be a fool, Chris quean*, and she said *There's no need for you marry a fool, then*, and the Highland temper quite went with him then, he flared up like a whin with a match at it, *Don't be feared, I've no such intention!* and off he went, up over the hill through the evening parks. Chris walked on prim and cold and quick, it was near to sunset, she turned her head, she couldn't but help it, to see if he wasn't looking back, he wasn't; and that was too much, she stopped and cried *Ewan!* and he wheeled like a shot and came running to her, she was crying in earnest by then, she cried up against his coat while he held her and panted and swore at himself, *Oh Chris, I didn't mean to hurt you!* And she sniffed *You didn't, it was myself*; and they made it all up again.

She walked home subdued-like that night, it wouldn't be always plain sailing, they'd awful tempers, both of them. Then she saw the light of Blawearie shine steadfast across the parks and her heart kindled to a queer, quiet warmth at that.

They'd arranged to be married on New Year's Eve, most folk would be free to come that day. For three evenings they sat in Blawearie parlour and wrote their invitations to folk they knew and some they didn't, nearly every soul in Kinraddie was asked, they couldn't well miss out one of them. And to Auntie and Uncle and Dod and Alec they wrote, and to Ewan's friend McIvor, a Highlandman out of Ross.[10] He hadn't any near relatives, Ewan, and faith! they were feint the loss.

Chris knew that some would be sore affronted she should marry so close to her father's death, and with all the stir they intended, too. But Ewan said *Damn it, you're only married once as a general rule, and it won't hurt the old man in Kinraddie kirkyard.* So when Uncle wrote down from Auchterless that he'd think black, burning shame to attend such a marriage, Ewan said he could blacken and burn till he was more like a cinder heap than a man, for all they need care.

Chris was sorry they wouldn't let her brothers come, but it couldn't be helped, she wasn't to weep for that. So they planned out a wedding they'd mind on when they grew old, ordering food enough to feed the French,[11] as the saying went, Mistress Melon near burst her meikle face with amaze as the packages came pouring in; and she spread the story of Chris's extravagance out through the Howe, she'd soon see the end of old Guthrie's silver. Folk shook their heads when they heard of that, it was plain that the quean wouldn't store the kin long.[12]

When Ewan went over to see to the banns the Reverend Gibbon tried to read him a lecture about such a display so close to John Guthrie's death. But he gave it up quick enough when Ewan began to spit like a cat and say the service he wanted was a wedding, not a sermon. Syne it grew plain they couldn't meet so often, Ewan would have to bide at the Upperhill all the day before the marriage. Chris kissed him good-bye that evening and told him to look after himself, and herself looked after him, troubled, knowing the kind of coarse things they might try him with in the bothy. And try they did, but Ewan couped one of them into the midden and threw young Gordon into the horse-trough when that brute was trying the same on Ewan himself; so they let him be, dour devils to handle, those Highlandmen.

And down in Blawearie next day, what with cooking and chaving and tending to beasts, and wrestling with the worry of the barn, it wasn't half spruced for the dance, Chris might well have gone off her head if Chae and Long Rob of the Mill hadn't come dandering up the road in the afternoon, shy-like, bringing their presents. And Rob's was fine, two great biscuit-barrels in oak and silver; and Chae's was from him and Kirsty, sheets and pillows, kind of Mistress Strachan, that, when you minded how the two of you'd fallen out over father ill. And when they heard of the barn they cast off their coats, *Leave it to us, Chris lass, just tell's what you want*; and they set to with ladders and tow and fancy frills and worked till near it was dark, redding up the place, it looked fine as a fairy-palace in a picture-book when they finished. Chae said *And who's your musician?* Chris nearly dropped through the floor with shock, she and Ewan had fair forgot about music. But Chae said it didn't matter, he'd bring his melodeon and Long Rob his fiddle; and faith! if that didn't content the folk they were looking for a church parade of the Gordons, not a wedding.

Syne they bade good night to Chris, and they laughed at her, kind-like, and said *This time the morn you'll be a married woman, Chris, not a quean. Sleep sound to-night!* And she laughed back and said *Oh, fine that;* but she blushed when Long Rob began to glint his grey eyes at her, he'd have to think of getting married himself, he said, fine it must be to sleep with a slim bit the like of herself those coldrife winter nights. And Chae said *Away, Rob, feint the much sleep you'd give her!*

And then they cried their good nights again and went off, leaving Chris with such lonesome feeling as she'd seldom had, all had been done that could be done, she wanted to sleep but couldn't sleep; and she wandered from room to room till Mistress Melon was fair upset and cried *For God's sake gang to your bed, lass, I'll tend to the rest; if you don't lie down you'll look more like a bull for the butcher's than a bride the morn.* And Chris laughed, she heard her laugh funny and faint-like, and said she supposed so, and went off to her room, but not to bed. She sat by the window, it was a night that was rimed with a frost of stars, rime in the sky and rime on the earth, the Milky Way shone clear and hard and the black trees of Blawearie waved their leafless boughs up against the window, sparkling white with the hoar; and far across the countryside for hours she watched the winking of the paraffin-lights in the farmhouses, till they sank and went out, and she was left in a world that might well have been dead but that she lived. Strange and eerie it was, sitting there, she couldn't move from the frozen flow of thoughts that came to her then, daft things she'd no need to think on her marriage eve . . . that this marriage of hers was nothing, that it would pass on and forward into days that had long forgotten it, her life and Ewan's, and they pass also, and the face of the land change and change again in the coming of the seasons and centuries till the last lights sank away from it and the sea came flooding up the Howe, all her love and tears for Ewan not even a ripple on that flood of water far in the times to be. And then she found herself cold as an icicle and got to her feet and at last began to get from her clothes – strange to think that to-morrow and all the to-morrows Ewan would share her room and her bed with her.

She thought that cool and unwarmed, still in the grip of the strange white dreaming that had been hers, looking down at herself naked as though she looked at some other than herself, a statue like that of the folk of olden time that they set in the picture galleries. And she saw the light white on the satin of her smooth skin then, and the long, smooth lines that lay from waist to thigh, thigh to knee, and was glad her legs were long from the knee to the ankle, that made legs seem stumbling and stumpy, shortness there. And still impersonally she bent to see if that dimple still hid there under her left breast, it did, it was deep as ever. Then she straightened and took down her hair and brushed it, standing so, silly to stand without her night-gown, but that was the mood she was in, somehow it seemed that never again would she be herself, have this body that was hers and her own, those fine lines that curved from thigh to knee hers, that dimple she'd loved when a child – oh, years before!

And then a clock began to strike, it struck two, and suddenly she was in a panic to be bedded and snug and herself again; and was in between the sheets in an instant, cuddling herself to some warmth and counting how many hours it would be till morning. And oh! it was still so long!

It came in snow that morning; she looked out from her window and saw it sheeting across the countryside, all silent; but still the daft peewits wheeped and wheeled against the hills, looking for the nests they'd lost in the harvest and couldn't forget. In the race and whip of the great broad flakes the leafless trees stood shivering; but down below Mistress Melon was already at work, Chris heard the clatter of the breakfast things, it was time she herself was into her clothes, there were hundreds of things to do.

Then she took out of the chest of drawers her under-things, there was no need to wait to change them, and looked at them, the silken vest, awful price it had been, and knickers and petticoat, vest, knickers and petticoat all of a shade, blue, with white ribbon; and they looked lovely and they smelt fine, she buried her face in them, so lovely they were and the queer feeling they brought her. And she changed her mind, she couldn't wear anything now she'd be wearing when she was married, she put on her old things and her old skirt and went down the stairs; and there was Mistress Melon smiling at her, *How do you feel on your marriage-morn, Chris?*

And Chris said *Fine*, and Mistress Melon said that was a good job, too, she'd known creatures of queans come down fair hysterical, others that just shook with fright, still others that spoke so undecent you knew fine a man's bed was no unco place for *them*. She hoped Chris would be awful happy, no fear of that, and soon have a two-three bairns keep her out of longer. And Chris said *You never know*, and she ate her porridge and Mistress Melon hers, and they cleared the table and scrubbed the kitchen and then Chris went out and tended the beasts, the very horses seemed to guess there was an unco thing on the go,

Bess nozzled up against her shoulder; and there in the barn
when she peeked in it, right in the middle of the floor were two
great rats, sitting up on their tails, sniffing at each other's
mouths, maybe kissing, and that was so funny, she tried not to
laugh, but gave a choked gurgle and flirt! the rats were out of
sight and into their holes.

In the cornyard the hens came tearing about her, mad with
hunger, she gave them meat hot from the pot and then a bushel
of corn, they liked that fine. But first the little bit Wyandotte
got up on the cart-shaft and gave a great crow that might have
been heard in the Upperhill; and he cocked a bright eye on her,
first one eye and then the other, and Chris laughed again.

She didn't feel hurried after that, then the postman came, fell
dry, they gave him a dram and he licked his lips and said *Here's
to you, Chris!* as blithe to drink to her health as to blacken her
character. He'd brought him two parcels, one was a lovely bed-
spread from Mistress Gibbon of the Manse, nice of the quiet-
voiced English thing, and the other from the Gordons of
Upperhill, a canteen of cutlery, full enough of knives and forks
and things to keep you cleaning them a week on end and not
be finished, said Mistress Melon.

Then up the road came the wife of the grave-digger,
Garthmore, him that had buried father. Sore made as always
she was, poor thing, they'd asked her to come and lend them a
hand more out of pity than anything else; and when the three
sat down to dinner she said *Eh, me! it's fine to be young and
be married, and maybe he'll treat you all right, but mine, my
first man, him that's now dead, God! he was a fair bull of a
man and not only the first night, either. He was aye at it, near
deaved me to death he would if he hadn't fallen over the edge
of a quarry on the road from the feeing-market some nine-ten
years come Martinmas.* But Mistress Melon said, *Havers, are
you trying to frighten the lass? She'll be fine, her lad's both
blithe and kind;* and Chris loved her for that, she'd never seemed
to see and know Mistress Melon before, thinking her just a
hard-working, hard-gossiping old body, now she saw the kind-
liness of her shine out, her gossiping no more than the dreams
she aye dreamt and must tell to others. And then Mistress

Melon cried *Away and get into your dress now, Chris, before the folk come up.*

It had left off snowing, Chris, dressing, saw from her window, a sunless day; and a great patching of clouds was upon the sky, the light below bright and sharp, flung by the snow itself; and the smoke rose straight in the air. Far over the braes by Upperhill where Ewan would be getting set in his clothes – unless he'd done that long before in the morning – the sheep were baaing in their winter buchts. Then Chris took off her clothes, and stood white again, and put on the wedding things, mother'd have liked to see them, mother lying dead and forgotten in Kinraddie kirkyard with the twins beside her. She found herself weep then, slowly, hardly, lost and desolate a moment without mother on her marriage-day. And than she shook her head, *Oh, don't be a fool, do you want to look a fright before Ewan and the folk?*

She peered at her face in the glass, then, fine! her eyes were bright, the crying had helped them. Pretty in a way, not only good-looking, she saw herself, dour cheek-bones softened for the hour in their chilled bronze setting. And she combed out her hair, it came far past her middle, thick and soft and sweet-smelling and rusty and tarnished gold. Then last was her dress, blue also, but darker than her under-clothes because so short was the time since father had died, she threaded the neck with a narrow black ribbon but round her own neck put nothing, her skin was the guerdon there.

So, ready, she turned herself round a minute, and held back the skirt from her ankles and liked them, they were neat and round, she had comely bones, her feet looked long and lithe in the black silk stockings and shoes. She found herself a hanky, last, and sprinkled some scent in that, only a little; and hid it away in her breast and went down the stairs just as she heard the first gig drive up.

That was the Strachans from Peesie's Knapp, Mistress Strachan fell long in the face at first. But Chae soon kindled her up with a dram, he whispered to Chris that he'd look after the drink; and Mistress Melon said it was aye best to have a man body at that end of the stir. And before they could say much more there came a fair stream of traffic up from the turnpike, all Kinraddie seemed on the move to Blawearie: except the old folk from Netherhill, and they sent their kind wishes and two clucking hens for Chris's nests. The hens broke the ice, you might say, for they got themselves loose from the gig of the Netherhill folk and started a wild flutter and chirawk everywhere, anywhere out of Blawearie. Long Rob of the Mill was coming up the road at that minute, in his Sunday best, and he met the first hen and heard the cry-out that followed her, and he cried himself, *Shoo, you bitch!* The hen dodged into the ditch, but Rob was after her, grabbing her, she squawked fair piercing as he carried her up to the house, his fine Sunday coat was lathered with snow; and he said that such-like work would have been nothing to Chae, who had chased the bit ostriches out in the Transvaal, but he'd had no training himself. Syne he took up the dram that Chae had poured him and cried *Here's to the bonniest maid Kinraddie will mind for many a year!*

That was kind of him, Chris had been cool and quiet enough until then, but she blushed at that, seeing Rob stand like a Viking out of the picture-books with the iron-grey glint in his eyes. Mistress Munro, though, was right sore jealous as usual, she poked her nose in the air and said, and not over-low, *The great fool might wait for the tea before he starts his speechifying;* she was maybe mad that nobody had ever said *she* was bonny; or if anybody ever had, he was an uncommon liar.

Then the Bridge End folk came up, then Ellison and his wife and their daughter, and then the Gordons, and then the minister, riding on his bicycle, it looked as though he'd had a fall or two and he wasn't in the best of temper, he wouldn't have a dram, *No, thank you, Chae*, he said, real stiff-like. And when Rob gave him a sly bit look, *You've been communing with Mother Earth, I see, Mr Gibbon*, he just turned his back and made out he didn't hear, and folk looked fair uncomfortable, all except Long Rob himself and Chae, they winked one at the other and then at Chris.

She thought the minister a fusionless fool, and went to the door to see who else was coming; and there, would you believe it, was poor old Pooty toiling up through the drifts with a great parcel under his oxter, his old face was white with snow and he shivered and hoasted as he came in, peeking out below his old, worn brows for Chris. *Where's the bit lllllass?* he cried, and then saw her and put the parcel in her hands, and she opened it then, as the custom was, and in it lay a fine pair of shoes he had made for her, shoes of glistening leather with gay green soles, and a pair of slippers, soft-lined with wool, there wouldn't be a grander pair in Kinraddie. And she said *Oh, thank you*, and she knew that wasn't enough, he stood peering up at her like an old hen peers, she didn't know why she did it but she put her arms round him and kissed him, folk laughed at that, all but the two of them, Pooty blinked and stuttered till Long Rob reached out a hand and pulled him into a chair and cried *Wet your whistle with this, Pooty man, you've hardly a minute ere the wedding begins.*

And he was right, for up the road came walking the last two, Ewan and his best man, the Highlander McIvor, near six feet six, red-headed, red-faced, a red Highlandman that bowed so low to Chris that she felt a fool; and presented his present, and it was a ram's horn shod with silver, real bonny and unco, like all Highland things. But Ewan took never a look at Chris, they made out they didn't see one the other, and Mistress Melon whispered to her to go tidy her hair, and when she came down again all the place was quiet, there was hardly a murmur. She stopped at the foot of the stairs with the heart beating so against her skin it was like to burst from her breast; and there was Chae Strachan waiting her, he held out his arm and patted her hand when she laid it on his arm, and he whispered *Ready then, Chris?*

Then he opened the parlour door, the place was crowded, there were all the folk sitting in chairs, solemn as a kirk congregation, and over by the window stood the Reverend Gibbon, very stern and more like a curly bull than ever; and in front of him waited Ewan and his best man, McIvor. Chris had for bridesmaids the little Ellison girl and Maggie Jean Gordon, they joined with her, she couldn't see clear for a minute then, or maybe too clear, she didn't seem to be seeing with her own eyes at all. And then Chae had loosed her hand from his arm and she and Ewan stood side by side, he was wearing a new suit, tweed it was, and smelt lovely, his dark face was solemn and frightened and white, he stood close to her, she knew him more frightened than she was herself. Something of her own fear went from her then, she stood listening to the Reverend Gibbon and the words he was reading, words that she'd never heard before, this was the first marriage she'd ever been at.

And then she heard Chae whisper behind her and listened more carefully still, and heard Ewan say *I will*, in a desperate kind of a voice, and then said it herself, her voice was as happy and clear as well you'd have wished, she smiled up at Ewan, the white went from his face and the red came in spate. The Red Highlander behind slipped something forward, she saw it was the ring, and then Ewan fitted it over her finger, his fingers were hot and unsteady, and Mr Gibbon closed his eyes and said, *Let us pray*.

And Chris held on to Ewan's hand and bent her head and listened to him, the minister; and he asked God to bless their union, to give them courage and strength for the difficulties that the years might bring to them, to make fruitful their marriage and their love as pure and enduring in its fulfilment as in its conception. They were lovely words, words like the marching of a bronze-leafed beech on the lips of a summer sky. So Chris thought, her head down-bent and her hand in Ewan's, then she lost the thread that the words were strung on, because of that hand of Ewan's that still held hers; and she curved her little finger into his palm, it was hard and rough there and she tickled the skin, secretly, and his hand quivered and she took the littlest keek at his face. There was that smile of his, flitting like a startled cat; and then his hand closed firm and warm and sure on hers, and hers lay quiet in his, and the minister had finished and was shaking their hands.

He hesitated a minute and then bent to kiss Chris; close to hers she saw his face older far than when he came to Kinraddie, there were pouches under his eyes, and a weary look in his eyes, and his kiss she didn't like. Ewan's was a peck, but Chae's was fine, it was hearty and kind though he reeked of the awful tobacco he smoked, and then Long Rob's, it was clean and sweet and dry, like a whiff from the Mill itself; and then it seemed every soul in Kinraddie was kissing her, except only Tony, the daftie, he'd been left at home. Everybody was speaking and laughing and slapping Ewan on the back and coming to kiss her, those that knew her well and some that didn't. And last it was Mistress Melon, her eyes were over-bright but careful still, she nearly smothered Chris and then whispered *Up to your room and tidy yourself, they've messed your hair*.

She escaped them then, the folk trooped out to the kitchen where the fire was roaring, Chae passed round the drams again, there was port for the women if they wanted it and raspberry drinks for the children. Soon's the parlour was clear Mistress Melon and Mistress Garthmore had the chairs whisked aside, the tables put forward and the cloths spread; and there came a loud tinkling as they spread the supper, barely past three though it was. But Chris knew it fell likely that few had eaten much at their dinners in Kinraddie that day, there wouldn't have been much sense with a marriage in prospect: and as soon as they'd something solid in their bellies to foundation the drink, as a man might say, the better it would be. In her room that wouldn't be her room for long Chris brushed her hair and settled her dress and looked at her flushed, fair face, it was nearly the same, hard to believe though you thought it. And then something felt queer about her, the ring on her hand it was, she stood and stared at the thing till a soft bit whispering drew her eyes to the window, the snow had come on again, a scurry and a blinding drive from down the hills; and below in the house they were crying *The bride, where is she?*

So down she went, folk had trooped back in the parlour by then and were sitting them round the tables, the minister at the head of one, Long Rob at the head of another, in the centre one the wedding cake stood tall on its stand with the Highland dirk beside it that Ewan had gotten from McIvor to do the cutting. The wind had risen storming without as Chris stood to cut, there in her blue frock with the long, loose sleeves, there came a great whoom in the chimney and some looked out at the window and said that the drifts would be a fell feet deep by the morn. And then the cake was cut and Chris sat down, Ewan

beside her, and found she wasn't hungry at all, about the only
soul in the place that wasn't, everybody else was taking a fair
hearty meal.

The minister had thawed away by then, he was laughing real
friendly-like in his bull-like boom of a voice, telling of other
weddings he'd made in his time, they'd all been gey funny and
queer-like weddings, things that you laughed at, not fine like
this. And Chris listened and glowed with pride that everything
at hers was just and right; and then again as so often that qualm
of doubt came down on her, separating her away from these
kindly folk of the farms – kind, and aye ready to believe the
worst of others they heard, unbelieving that others could think
the same of themselves. So maybe the minister no more than
buttered her, she looked at him with the dark, cool doubt in
her face, next instant forgot him in a glow of remembrance that
blinded all else: she was married to Ewan!

Beside her: He whispered *Oh, eat something, Chris, you'll
fair go famished*, and she tried some ham and a bit of the
dumpling, sugared and fine, that Mistress Melon had made.
And everybody praised it, as well they might, and cried for
more helpings, and more cups of tea, and there were scones
and pancakes and soda-cakes and cakes made with honey that
everybody ate; and little Wat Strachan stopped eating of a
sudden and cried *Mother, I'm not right in the belly!* everybody
laughed at that but Kirsty, she jumped to her feet and hurried
him out, and came back with him with his face real frightened.
But faith! it didn't put a stop to the bairn, he started in again
as hungry as ever, and Chae cried out *Well, well, let him be,
maybe it tasted as fine coming up as it did going down!*

Some laughed at that, others reddened up and looked real
affronted, Chris herself didn't care. Cuddiestoun and his wife
sat opposite her, it was like watching a meikle collie and a futret
at meat, him gulping down everything that came his way and a
lot that didn't, he would rax for that; and his ugly face, poor
stock, fair shone and glimmered with the exercise. But Mistress
Munro snapped down at her plate with sharp, quick teeth, her
head never still a minute, just like a futret with a dog nearby.
They were saying hardly anything, so busied they were, but

Ellison next to them had plenty to say, he'd taken a dram over-much already and was crying things across the table to Chris, Mistress Tavendale he called her at every turn; and he said that she and Mistress Ellison must get better acquaint. Maybe he'd regret that the morn, if he minded his promise: and that wasn't likely. Next to him was Kirsty and the boys and next to that the minister's table with Alec Mutch and his folk and young Gordon; a real minister's man was Alec, awful chief-like the two of them were, but Mistress Mutch sat lazy as ever, now and then she cast a bit look at Chris out of the lazy, gley eyes of her, maybe there was a funniness in the look that hadn't to do with the squint.

Up at Rob's table an argument rose, Chris hoped that it wasn't religion, she saw Mr Gordon's wee face pecked up to counter Rob. But Rob was just saying what a shame it was that folk should be shamed nowadays to speak Scotch – or they called it Scots if they did, the split-tongued sourocks! Every damned little narrow-dowped rat that you met put on the English if he thought he'd impress you – as though Scotch wasn't good enough now, it had words in it that the thin bit scraichs of the English could never come at. And Rob said *You can tell me, man, what's the English for sotter, or greip, or smore, or pleiter, gloaming or glunching or well-kenspeckled? And if you said gloaming was sunset you'd fair be a liar; and you're hardly that, Mr Gordon.*

But Gordon was real decent and reasonable, *You can't help it, Rob. If folk are to get on in the world nowadays, away from the ploughshafts and out of the pleiter, they must use the English, orra though it be.* And Chae cried out that was right enough, and God! who could you blame? And a fair bit breeze got up about it all, every soul in the parlour seemed speaking at once; and as aye when they spoke of the thing they agreed that the land was a coarse, coarse life, you'd do better at almost anything else, folks that could send their lads to learn a trade were right wise, no doubt of that, there was nothing on the land but work, work, work, and chave, chave, chave, from the blink of day till the fall of night, no thanks from the soss and sotter, and hardly a living to be made.

Syne Cuddiestoun said that he'd heard of a childe up Laurencekirk way, a banker's son from the town he was, and he'd come to do farming in a scientific way. So he'd said at first, had the childe, but God! by now you could hardly get into the place for the clutter of machines that lay in the yard; and *he* wouldn't store the kin long. But Chae wouldn't have that, he swore *Damn't, no, the machine's the best friend of man, or it would be so in a socialist state. It's coming and the chaving'll end, you'll see, the machine'll do all the dirty work.* And Long Rob called out that he'd like right well to see the damned machine that would muck you a pigsty even though they all turned socialist to-morrow. And they all took a bit laugh at that, Chris and Ewan were fair forgotten for a while, they looked at each other and smiled, Ewan reached down and squeezed her hand and Chris wished every soul but themselves a hundred miles from Blawearie.

But then Chae cried *Fill up your glasses, folk, the best man has a toast.* And the red Highlander, McIvor, got up to his feet and bowed his red head to Chris, and began to speak; he spoke fine, though funny with that Highland twist, he said he'd never seen a sweeter quean than the bride or known a better friend than the groom; and he wished them long and lovely days, a marriage in the winter had the best of it. For was not the Spring to come and the seed-time springing of their love, and the bonny days of the summer, flowering it, and autumn with the harvest of their days? And when they passed to that other winter together they would know that was not the end of it, it was but a sleep that in another life would burgeon fresh from another earth. He could never believe but that two so young and fair as his friend and his friend's wife, once made one flesh would be one in the spirit as well; and have their days built of happiness and their nights of the music of the stars. And he lifted his glass and cried *The bride!* looking at Chris with his queer, bright eyes, the daft Highland poet, they were all like that, the red Highlanders. And everybody cried *Good luck to her!* and they all drank up and Chris felt herself blush from head to foot under all the blue things she wore.

And then Long Rob of the Mill was making a speech, differ-

ent from McIvor's as well it might be. He said he'd never
married himself because he'd over-much respect for those kittle
folk, women; but if he'd been ten years younger he was damned
if his respect would have kept him from having a try for Chris
Guthrie, and beating that Highland childe, Ewan, at his own
fell game. That was just Ewan's luck, he thought, not his judgment, and Chris was clean thrown away on her husband, as
she'd have been on any husband at all: but himself. Ah well, no
doubt she'd train him up well, and he advised Ewan now, from
the little that he knew of marriage, never to counter his wife;
not that he thought she wasn't well able to look after herself,
but just that Ewan mightn't find himself worsted though he
thought himself winner. Marriage, he took it, was like yoking
together two two-year-olds, they were kittle and brisk on the
first bit rig – unless they'd fallen out as soon as they were yoked
and near kicked themselves and their harness to bits – but the
second rig was the testing-time, it was then you knew when one
was pulling and one held back, the one that had sheer sweirty
– and that was a word for Mr Gordon to put into English – in
its bones, and the one with a stout bit heart and a good guts.
Well, he wouldn't say more about horses, though faith! it was
a fascinating topic, he'd just come back to marriage and say
they all wished the best to Chris, so sweet and trig, and to
Ewan, the Highland cateran, and long might they live and grow
healthy, wealthy, and well content.

Then they all drank up again, and God knows who mightn't
have made the next speech if Chae then hadn't stood up and
cried *The night's near on us. Who's game for a daylight dance
at Chris's wedding?*

So out they all went to the kitchen, it was cold enough there
from the heat of the room, but nothing to the coldrife air of the
barn when the first of them had crossed the close and stood in
the door. But Mistress Melon had kindled a brazier with coal,
it crackled fine, well away from the straw, Rob tuned up his
fiddle, Chae squeaked on his melodeon, it began to feel brisk
and warm even while you stood and near shivered your sark off.
Chris was there with the men, of course, and the children and
Mistress Gordon and Mistress Mutch and Mistress Strachan

were there, Mistress Munro had stayed behind to help clear the tables, she said, and some whispered it was more than likely she'd clear most of the clearings down her own throat, by God she couldn't have eaten a mouthful since Candlemas.

But then Chae cried *Strip the Willow*, and they all lined up, and the melodeon played bonnily in Chae's hands, and Long Rob's fiddle-bow was darting and glimmering, and in two minutes, in the whirl and go of *Strip the Willow*, there wasn't a cold soul in Blawearie barn, or a cold sole either. Then here, soon's they'd finished, was Mistress Melon with a great jar of hot toddy to drink, she set it on a bench between Chae and Long Rob. And whoever wanted to drink had just to go there, few were bashful in the going, too; and another dance started, it was a schottische, and Chris found herself in the arms of the minister, he could dance like a daft young lad. And as he swung her round and around he opened his mouth and cried *Hooch!* and so did the red Highlander, McIvor, *Hooch!* careering by with fat Kirsty Strachan, real scared-like she looked, clipped round the waist.

Then Chae and Long Rob hardly gave them a breather, they were at it dance on dance; and every time they stopped for a panting second Chae would dip in the jar and give Rob a wink and cry *Here's to you, man!* and Rob would dip, solemn-like as well, and say *Same to you!* and off the fiddle and melodeon would go again, faster than ever. Ewan danced the schottische with prim Mistress Gordon, but for waltzing he found a quean from the Mains, a red-faced, daft-like limmer, she screamed with excitement and everybody laughed, Chris laughed as well. Some were watching to see if she did, she knew, and she heard a whisper she'd have all her work cut out looking after him, coarse among the queans he was, Ewan Tavendale. But she didn't care, she knew it a lie, Ewan was hers and hers only; but she wished he would dance with her for a change. And here at the *Petronella* he was, he anyway hadn't been drinking, in the noise of the dance as they swayed up and down the barn he whispered *Well, Chris?* and she whispered back *Fine*, and he said *You're the bonniest thing ever seen in Kinraddie, Long Rob was right*. And she said she liked him to think so and he pulled her back in the darkness away from the dancers, and kissed her quickly and slowly, she didn't hurry either, it was blithe and glad to stand there kissing, each strained to hear when they'd be discovered.

And then they were, Chae crying *Where's the bride and the groom? Damn't, they're lost!* and out they'd to come. Chae cried was there anyone else could play the melodeon? and young Jock Gordon cried back to him *Ay, fine that*, and came stitering across the floor and sat himself down by the toddy-jar, and played loud and clear and fine. Then Chae caught Chris, he said to Ewan *Away, you greedy brute, wait a while till she's yours forever and aye*, and he danced right neatly, you didn't expect it from Chae, with his grey eyes laughing down at you. And as he danced he said suddenly, grave-like, *Never doubt your Ewan, Chris, or never let him know that you do. That's the hell of a married life. Praise him up and tell him he's fine, that there's not a soul in the Howe can stand beside him, and he'll want to cuddle you till the day he dies; and he'll blush at the sight of you fifty years on as much as he does the day*. She said *I'll try*, and *Thank you, Chae*, and he said *Och, it must be the whisky speaking*, and surrendered her up to Ellison, and took the melodeon from Gordon again, but staggered and leant back against the sack that hung as a draught-shield behind the musician's place. Down came the sack and there among the hay was the minister and the maid from the Mains that had scraiched so loud, she'd her arms round him and the big curly bull was kissing the quean like a dog lapping up its porridge.

Chris's heart near stopped, but Chae snatched up the sack, hooked it back on its hook again, nobody saw the sight except himself and Chris and maybe Long Rob. But you couldn't be sure about Rob, he looked as solemn as five owls all in one, and was playing as though, said Chae, he was paid by piece-work and not by time.[13]

Between eight and nine Mistress Melon came out to the barn and cried them to supper, the storm had left off, all but a flake that sailed down now and then like a sailing gull in the beam from the barn door. On the ground the snow crinkled under their feet, frost had set in, the folk stood and breathed in the open air, and laughed, and cried one to the other, *Man, I'll have aching joints the morn!* The women ran first to the house, to tidy their hair, Ewan saw everybody in, except Munro of the Cuddiestoun, he was nowhere to be seen.

And then Ewan heard a funny bit breathing as he passed by the stable; and he stopped and opened the door and struck a match, and there was Munro, all in his Sunday best, lying in the stall beside Clyde the horse, and his arms were round the beast's neck, and faith! the beast looked real disgusted. Ewan shook him and cried *Munro, you can't sleep here*, but Munro just blinked the eyes in his face, daft-like, and grumbled *Why not?* Syne Alec Mutch turned back from the house to see what all the stir was about, and both he and Ewan had another go at the prostrate Munro, but damn the move would he make, Alec cried *To hell with him, leave him there with the mare, she's maybe a damned sight kinder a bed-mate than ever was that futret of a wife of his.*

So they closed the door of the stable and went into their supper, everybody ate near as well as at tea-time, fair starved they were with the dancing and drink. Chris had thought she herself was tired till she ate some supper, and then she felt fresh as ever, and backed up Long Rob, who looked twice as sober as any of the men and had drunk about twice as much as any three of them, when he cried *Who's for a dance again?* Mistress Melon had the toddy-jar filled fresh full and they carried that out, everybody came to the barn this time except Mistress Munro, *No, no, I'll clear the table.*

And young Elsie Ellison, wondering for why the creature should stay behind, stayed herself and took a bit keek round the corner of the door: and there was Mistress Munro, with a paper bag in her hand, stuffing it with scones and biscuits and cake, and twisting her head this side and that, like the head of a futret. So Elsie, fair scared, ran off to the barn and caught at her father's tails and cried *The Cuddiestoun wife's away home with all the pieces*, and Ellison, he was whiskied up to high tune by then, cried *Let her run to hell and be damned to her.*

Syne he started a tale about how once she'd insulted him, the dirty Scotch bitch. But Long Rob and Chae were striking up a

dance again and Chris heard no more of the Ellison story,
dancing a waltz with young Jock Gordon, it was like flying,
Jock's face was white with excitement. The fourth dance Alec
Mutch, the fool, began to stiter the floor, backwards and forwards, he was a real nuisance till he passed Long Rob and then
Rob cried *Hoots, Alec, man, your feet are all wrong!* and thrust
out a foot among Alec's and couped him down and Chae shoved
him aside to the straw with a foot and a hand, and played on
with the other foot and hand, or maybe with a foot and his
teeth, a skilly man, Chae.

Mistress Mutch said nothing, just standing and laughing and
smoking at her cigarette. There were more men than women in
the barn, though, even when the men made do with a little
quean, and soon Chris found herself dancing with Mistress
Mutch, the great, easy-going slummock, she spoke slow and
easy as though she'd just wakened up from her sleep. Chris
couldn't tell what way she looked with that gleying eye, but
what she spoke was *Take things easy in married life, Chris, but
not over-easy, that's been MY ruin. Though God knows it'll
make not a difference in a hundred years time and we're dead.
Don't let Ewan saddle you with a birn of bairns, Chris, it kills
you and eats your heart away, forbye the unease and the dirt
of it. Don't let him, Chris, they're all the same, men; and you
won't well steer clear of the first or second. But you belong to
yourself, mind that.*

Chris went hot and cold and then wanted to ask something
of Mistress Mutch and looked at her and found she couldn't,
she'd just have to find the thing out for herself. Long Rob came
down to dance with her next, he'd left the fiddle to old Gordon,
and he asked what that meikle slummock had been saying to
her? And Chris said *Oh, just stite*, and Rob said *Mind, don't
let any of those damned women fear you, Chris; it's been the
curse of the human race, listening to advice.* And Chris said *But
I'm listening to yours, Rob, now, amn't I?* He nodded to her,
solemn, and said, *Oh, you've your head screwed on and you'll
manage fine. But mind, if there's ever a thing you want with a
friend, not to speak it abroad all over Kinraddie, I'll aye be
there at the Mill to help you.* Chris thought that a daft-like

speak for Rob, kind maybe he meant it, but she'd have Ewan, who else could she want?

And then the fun slackened off, the barn was warm, folk sat or lay on the benches or straw, Chris looked round and saw nothing of the minister then, maybe he'd gone. She whispered to Chae about that, but he said *Damn the fears, he's out to be sick, can't you hear him like a cat with a fish-bone in its throat?* And hear him they could, but Chris had been right after all, he didn't come back. Maybe he was shamed and maybe he just lost his way, for next noon there were folk who swore they'd seen the marks of great feet that walked round and round in a circle, circle after circle, all across the parks from Blawearie to the Manse; and if these weren't the minister's feet they must have been the devil's, you could choose whichever you liked.

No sooner was the dancing done than there were cries *Rob, what about a song now, man?* And Rob said *Och, ay, I'll manage that fine*, and he off with his coat and loosened his collar and sang them *Ladies of Spain;* and then he turned round to where Chris stood beside her Ewan and sang *The Lass that Made the Bed to Me:*

> Her hair was like the link o' gowd,
>   Her teeth were like the ivorie,
> Her cheeks like lilies dipt in wine,
>   The lass that made the bed to me.

> Her bosom was the driven snaw,
>   Two drifted heaps sae fair to see,
> Her limbs, the polished marble stane,
>   The lass that made the bed to me.

> I kissed her owre and owre again,
>   And aye she wist na what to say,
> I laid her between me and the wa',
>   The lassie thought na long till day.

Folk stared and nodded at Chris while Rob was singing, and Ewan looked at first as though he'd like to brain him; and then he blushed; but Chris just listened and didn't care, she thought the song fine and the lass lovely, she hoped she herself would seem as lovely this night – or as much of it as their dancing would leave. So she clapped Rob and syne it was Ellison's turn, he stood up with his meikle belly a-wag and sang them a song they didn't know:

> Roses and lilies her cheeks disclose,
> But her red lips are sweeter than those,
> Kiss her, caress her,
> With blisses her kisses,
> Dissolve us in pleasure and soft repose.

and then another, an English one and awful sad, about a young childe called Villikins and a quean called Dinah, and it finished:

> For a cup of cold pizen lay there on the ground
> .   .   .   .   .
> With a tooril-i-ooril-i-ooril-i-ay.

Chae cried that was hardly the kind of thing that they wanted, woeful as that; and they'd better give Chris a rest about her roses and lips and limbs, she had them all in safe-keeping and would know how to use them; and what about a seasonable song? And he sang so that all joined in, seasonable enough, for the snow had come on again in spite of the frost:

> Up in the morning's no for me,
> Up in the morning early,
> When a' the hills are covered wi' snaw
> I'm sure it's winter fairly!

Then Mistress Mutch sang, that was hardly expected, and folk tittered a bit; but she had as good a voice as most and better than some, she sang *The Bonnie House o' Airlie*, and then the *Auld Robin Gray*[14] that aye brought Chris near to weeping, and did now, and not her alone, with Rob's fiddle whispering it out, the sadness and the soreness of it, though it was long, long syne:

> When the sheep are in the fauld, and the kye are a' at hame,
> And a' the weary world to its rest has gane,
> The tears o' my sorrow fa' in shooers frae my e'e
> And Auld Robin Gray he lies sound by me.

and all the tale of young Jamie who went to sea and was thought to be drowned in an awful storm; and his lass married Auld Robin Gray; and syne Jamie came back but couldn't win his lass away from the old man, though near heart-broken she was:

> I gang like a ghaist, and I carena' to spin,
> I daurna' think o' Jamie, for that wad be a sin,
> But I'll try aye my best a guid wife to be,
> For Auld Robin Gray he is kind to me.

Old Pooty was sleeping in a corner; he woke up then, fell keen to recite his TIMROUS BEASTIE; but they pulled him down and cried on the bride herself for a song. And all she could think of was that south country woman crying in the night by the side of her good man, the world asleep and grey without; and she whispered the song to Rob and he tuned his fiddle and she sang, facing them, young and earnest, and she saw Ewan looking at her, solemn and proud, *The Flowers of the Forest*:

> I've heard them lilting at our ewe-milking,
>   Lasses a' lilting before dawn o' day;
> But now they are moaning on ilka green loaning,
>   The Flooers o' the Forest are a' wede away.

> Dool and wae for the order sent oor lads tae the Border!
>   The English for ance, by guile wan the day,
> The Flooers o' the Forest, that fought aye the foremost,
>   The pride o' oor land lie cauld in the clay.

Chae jumped up when she finished, he said *Damn't,*[15] *folk, we'll all have the whimsies if we listen to any more woesome songs! Have none of you a cheerful one?* And the folk in the barn laughed at him and shook their heads, it came on Chris how strange was the sadness of Scotland's singing, made for the sadness of the land and sky in dark autumn evenings, the crying of men and women of the land who had seen their lives and loves sink away in the years, things wept for beside the sheep-buchts, remembered at night and in twilight. The gladness and kindness had passed, lived and forgotten, it was Scotland of the mist and rain and the crying sea that made the songs – And Chae cried *Let's have another dance, then, it's nearly a quarter to twelve, we must all be off soon as midnight chaps.*

And they all minded what midnight would bring, and Chae and Rob had the melodeon and fiddle in hand again, and struck up an eightsome, and everybody grabbed him a partner, it didn't matter who was who, McIvor had Chris and danced with her as though he would like to squeeze her to death, he danced light as thistle-down, the great red Highlander; and no sooner was one dance finished than Rob and Chae swept forward into another, they played like mad and the lights whipped and jumped as the couples spun round and round; and the music went out across the snowing night; and then Chae pulled out his great silver watch, and laid it beside him, playing on.

And suddenly it was the New Year, the dancing stopped and folk all shook hands, coming to shake Chris's and Ewan's; and Long Rob struck up the sugary surge of *Auld Lang Syne*[16] and they all joined hands and stood in a circle to sing it, and Chris thought of Will far over the seas in Argentine, under the hot night there. Then the singing finished, they all found themselves tired, somebody began to take down the barn lights, there was half an hour's scramble of folk getting themselves into coats and getting their shivering sholts from out the empty stalls in the byre. Then Chris and Ewan were hand-shook again, Chris's arm began to ache, and then the last woof-woof of wheels on snow thick-carpeted came up the Blawearie road to them, it was fell uncanny that silence in the place after all the noise and fun of the long, lit hours. And there was Mistress

Melon in the kitchen door, yawning fit to swallow a horse, she whispered to Chris *I'm taking your room now, don't forget*, and cried them *Good night, and a sound sleep, both!* and was up the stairs and left them alone.

He hardly seemed tired even then, though, Ewan, prowling locking the doors like a great quiet cat till Chris called to him softly *Oh, sit by me!* So he came to the chair she sat in and picked her out of it, so strong he was, and himself sat down, still holding her. They watched the fire a long time and then Chris's head drooped down, she didn't know she had been asleep till she woke to find Ewan shaking her, *Chris, Chris, you're fair done, come on to bed.* The fire was dying then and the paraffin had run low in the lamp, the flame swithered and went out with a plop! as Ewan blew on it; and then they were in the dark, going up the stairs together, past the room that had been Chris's and where Mistress Melon slept for a night ere she went back to Stonehaven.

And to Chris going up that stair holding the hand of her man there came a memory of one with awful eyes and jutting beard, lying in that room they came to, lying there and whispering and cursing her. But she put the memory away, it had never happened, sad and daft to remember that, she was tired. Then, with her hand on the door, Ewan kissed her there in the dark, sweet and wild his kiss, she had not thought he could kiss her like that, not as though he wanted her as a man might do in that hour and place, but as though he minded the song he had heard her sing. She put up her face to the kiss, forgetting tiredness, suddenly she was wakeful as never she had been, the sleep went out of her head and body and the chill with it, Ewan's hand came over hers and opened the door.

A fire burned bright in the fireplace, they had thought the place would be black and cold, but Mistress Melon had seen to that. And there was the bridal bed, pulled out from the wall, all in white it was, with sheet and blanket turned back, the window curtains were drawn, and in the moment they stood breathing from their climb of the stairs Chris heard the sound of the snow that stroked the window, with quiet, soft fingers, as though writing there.

Then she forgot it, standing by the fire getting out of her blue
things, one by one. She found it sweet to do that, so slowly,
and to have Ewan kiss her at last when there was no bar to his
kisses, lying with him then, with the light put out and the
radiance of the fire on the walls and ceiling. And she turned
towards him at last, whispering and tender for him, *We're daft,
we'll catch cold without anything on!* and then she saw his face
beside her, solemn and strange, yet not strange at all. And he
put his left hand below her neck, and he took her close to him,
and they were one flesh, one and together; and far into the
morning she woke, and was not cold at all, him holding her so,
and then she heard again the hand of winter write on the
window, and listened a moment, happy, happy, and fell fast
asleep till morning brought Mistress Melon and two great cups
of tea to waken Ewan and herself.

So that was her marriage, not like wakening from a dream was
marrying, but like going into one, rather, she wasn't sure, not
for days, what things they had dreamt and what actually done
– she and this farmer of Blawearie who would stir of a morning
at the jangle of the clock and creep from bed, the great cat, and
be down the stairs to light the fire and put on the kettle. She'd
never be far behind him, though, she loved even the bitterness
of those frozen mornings, and a bitter winter it was, every crack
and joist of the old house played a spray of cold wind across
the rooms. He'd be gone to the byre and stable as she came
down and sought out the porridge meal and put it to boil,
Blawearie's own meal, fine rounded stuff that Ewan so liked.
She'd leave it to hotter there on the fire and then bring the pails
from the dairy and open the kitchen door on the close and gasp
in the bite of the wind, seeing a grey world on the edge of
morning, the bare stubble of the ley riding quick on the close,
peering between the shapes of the stacks, the lights of the
lanterns shining in byre and stable and barn as Ewan feeded
and mucked and tended horses and kye.

And the byre would hang heavy with the breaths of the kye,
they'd have finished their turnips as she came in, and Ewan
would come swinging after her with a great armful of straw to

spread them in front, he'd tickle her neck as she sat to milk and she'd cry *Your hand's freezing!* and he'd say *Away, woman, you're still asleep. Up in the morning's the thing!* and go whistling out to the stable, Clyde and Bess stamping there, getting fell cornfilled and frolicsome, they more than wanted exercise. She would carry the milk back herself most mornings, and make the breakfast, but sometimes Ewan would come with her, so young and daft they were, folk would have laughed to see them at that, both making breakfast and sitting them close to eat it. Then Ewan would light his pipe when he'd done and sit and smoke while she finished more slowly; and then he'd say that he'd meat the hens, and she'd tell him not to haver, she'd do that herself, and he'd argue, maybe sulk, till she kissed him back to his senses again. Then he'd laugh and get up and get down John Guthrie's gun, and be out and up in the moors till eleven, sometimes he'd bring a great bag and Chris would sell the spare rabbits to the grocer that came on Tuesdays.

There was little to be done, such weather on Blawearie. Ewan tidied the barn they'd danced in, it seemed years ago since that night, and got ready plough and sock and coulter for the time when the weather would break. And then he found the bruised corn running low in the great kist there, that was his first outgoing from the place since his marriage, Chris watched him go, sitting in the front of the box-cart, Clyde in the shafts, the cart loaded down with corn for the Mill, and Ewan turning to wave to her from the foot of Blawearie brae. And all that afternoon he was away she fretted from room to room, oh! she was a fool, there was nothing could happen to him! And when at last he came back she ran out to him, fair scared he was at the way she looked, and thought her ill, and when she cried she had missed him so he went white and then blushed, just a boy still, and forgot to unyoke Clyde left in the cold, he was kissing Chris instead. And faith! for the bairns of farmers both they might well have had more sense.

But, and it crept into her mind that night and came often in the morning and days that followed, somehow that going of Ewan's to the Mill had ended the foolishness that shut them in fast from Kinraddie and all the world, they two alone, with all

the gladness that was theirs alone and her kisses the most that
Ewan'd ever seek and his kisses ending days and nights, and
almost life itself for her. Kinraddie came in again, something of
her own cool reliance came back, the winter wore on to its
close, and mid-February brought the sun, weather that might
well have come out of a May. Looking out from her window
as every morning still she did, Chris saw the steam of the lands
below the house, it was as though the earth had swung round
the fields of Kinraddie into the maw of the sun, a great furnace,
and left them there to dry. The hills marched their great banners
of steam into the face of each sunrise and through the whisper
and wakening and shrouding of the morning came presently
the moan of the fog-horn at Todhead,[17] a dreadful bellow, like
a sore-sick calf, it went on and on, long after the mist had
cleared, it rose and faded into the sun-dazzle overhead as great
clouds of gulls came wheeling in from the sea. They knew what
was toward on Kinraddie's land, Chris heard the call of them
as she went about the day's work, and looked out on the ley
field then, there was Ewan with the horses, ploughing his first
rig, bent over the shafts, one foot in the drill, one the rig
side, the ploughshare, sharp and crude and new, cleaving the
red-black clay. The earth wound back like a ribbon and curved
and lay; and the cloud of gulls cawed and screamed and pecked
on the rig and followed at Ewan's heels again.

All over Kinraddie there were horse-pairs out, though none
so early as Ewan's, it seemed, folk had stayed undecided about
the weather, they'd other things to do, they'd say, than just
wait about to show off like that young Blawearie. But, when
the day rose and at nine Chris set her a jug of tea in a basket,
and set by it scones well buttered and jammed, and carried
out the basket to Ewan *wisshing* up the face of the rig, Chae
Strachan, far away and below, was a-bend above his ploughshafts at the tail of his team, Upperhill had two pairs in the
great park that loitered up to the larch wood, and there was
Cuddiestoun's pair, you guessed it him and his horses, though
they never came full in sight, their heads and backs just skimmed
the verge of the wood and hill.

Spring had come and was singing and rilling all over the

fields, you listened and heard, it was like listening to the land
new wake, to the burst and flow of a dozen burns in this ditch
and that; and when you turned out the cattle for their first
spring dander, in case they went off the legs, they near went off
the face of the earth instead, daft and delighted, they ran and
scampered and slid, Chris was feared that the kye would break
their legs. She tried driving them down to the old hayfield, but
the steers broke loose and held down the road, and Ewan saw
them and left his plough and chased them across the parks,
swearing blue murder at them as he ran; and faith! if it hadn't
been for the postman meeting them and turning them at the
end of the road they might well have been running still.

Chris had known then mazes of things to do in that bright
coming of the weather, the house was all wrong, it was foul
and feckless, Ewan unyoking at midday would come in and
make hardly his way through the kitchen, heaped high with the
gear of some room, Chris saw her long hands grow sore and
red with the scrubbing she did on the sour old walls. Ewan said
she was daft, the place was fine, what more did she want? And
she said *Less dirt;* and that maybe he liked dirt, she didn't; and
he laughed *Well, maybe I do, I like you right well!* and put his
arm round her shoulders and they stood and kissed in the mid
of the heaped and littered kitchen – awful to be like that, said
Chris, they could hardly be sane.

In March the weather broke, the rain came down in plashing
pelts, you could hardly see a hand's-length in front of your face
if you ran through the close. Ewan sat in the barn, winnowing
corn or tying ropes, or just smoking and swearing out at the
rain. Chae Strachan came up for a talk on the second day, all
in oilskins he came; and he sat in the barn with Ewan and said
he'd seen it rain like this in Alaska, and the mountains move
when the snows were melting. And Ewan said he didn't care a
damn though Alaska moved under the sea the morn, when
would it clear on Blawearie? Munro came next, then Mutch of
Bridge End, they'd nothing on their hands but watch the rain
and shake their heads and swear they were all fair ruined.

But at last it went, the unending rain of a fortnight went, and that morning they woke and found it fine, Ewan took him a look at the land from the bedroom window and prompt lay back in the bed again. *Damn Blawearie and all that's on't, let's have a holiday the day, Chris quean.* She said *I can't, I'm cleaning the garret,* and Ewan got angered, she'd never seen him angry like that before, Highland and foreign then, spitting like a cat. *Are you to spend all your days cleaning damned rooms? You'll be old and wizened and a second Mistress Munro before you're well twenty. Off on a holiday we're going to-day.*

And, secretly glad, she lay back, lying with her hands under her head, lazy, and looking at him, thinking how different he was from that lad she'd tramped to Dunnottar with, so close she knew him now, the way he thought and the things he liked and his kindness and slowness to take offence, and the bitter offence, how it rankled in him, once it was there! Like and not like what she'd thought and wanted in those days before they had married. Spite of their closest moments together, Ewan could still blush at a look or a touch of hers; she touched him then to make sure, and he did! He said *Hold off! you're a shameless limmer, for sure, and not nineteen yet. Come on, let's get out and get off.*

So they raced through the morning's work and by nine were down at the Peesie's Knapp, and borrowed Chae's gig and heard Chae promise to milk and take in Blawearie's kye. Then out they drove and swung left through Kinraddie, into the Laurencekirk road, the sun shining and the peewits calling, there were snipe in a loch they passed, the North Sea was gloom-away by Bervie as the sholtie trotted south. You could see then as the land rose higher the low parks that sloped to the woods and steeple of Drumlithie, beyond that the hills of Barras, the Reisk in its hollow among its larch woods. West of that rose Arbuthnott, a fair jumble of bent and brae, Fordoun came marching up the horizon in front of them then, and they were soon going through it. Ewan said if he bided in Fordoun he'd lay his neck on the railway line and invite the Flying Scotsman[18] to run over it, so tired he'd be of biding in a place that looked like a barn painted by a man with nothing but thumbs and a squint in both eyes.

But Chris liked the little place, she'd never seen it before and the farms that lay about it, big and rich, with fine black loam for soil, different from the clay of bleak Blawearie. Ewan said *To hell with them and their fine land too, they're not farmers, them, only lazy muckers that sit and make silver out of their cotters;* and he said he'd rather bide in a town and wear a damned apron than work in this countryside. And then they were near Laurencekirk, the best of weather the day held still, Laurencekirk looked brave in the forenoon stir, with its cattle mart and its printing office where they printed weekly the *Kincardineshire Observer*, folk called it *The Squeaker* for short. It had aye had a hate for Stonehaven, Laurencekirk, and some said that it should be the county capital, but others said God help the capital that was entrusted to it; and would speak a bit verse that Thomas the Rhymour[19] had made, how ere Rome—

> became a great imperial city,
> 'Twas peopled first, as we are told,
> By pirates, robbers, thieves, banditti:
> Quoth Tammas: 'Then the day may come
> When Laurencekirk shall equal Rome.'

And when Laurencekirk folk heard that they would laugh, not nearly cry as they did in Drumlithie when you mocked at their steeple, or smile sick and genteel as they did in Stonehaven when you spoke of the poverty toffs. Ewan said it was a fine town, he liked Laurencekirk, and they'd stop and have dinner there.

So they did, it was fine to eat food that another had cooked. Then they looked at the day and saw how it wore and planned to drive over to Edzell Castle[20] – *There's nothing to see there but a rickle of stones*, said Ewan, *but you'll like them fine, no doubt.*

So they did as they'd planned, the afternoon flew, it was golden and green. Under Drumtochty Hill they passed, Ewan told that in summer it came deeper with the purple of heather than any other hill in Scotland; but it hung dark and asleep like a great cloud scraping the earth as they trotted past. There was never a soul at the castle but themselves, they climbed and clambered about in the ruins, stone on stone they were crumbling away, there were little dark chambers in the angle walls that had sheltered the bowmen long syne. Ewan said they must fair have been fusionless folk, the bowmen, to live in places like that; and Chris laughed and looked at him, queer and sorry, and glimpsed the remoteness that her books had made.

She was glad to be out in the sun again, though clouds were racing it up from the North and Ewan said they'd not need to loiter long. In the garden of the castle they wandered from wall to wall, looking at the pictures crumbling there, balls and roses and rings and callipers, and wild heraldic beasts without number, Ewan said he was glad that they'd all been killed. But Chris didn't laugh at him, she knew right well that such beasts had never been, but she felt fey that day, even out here she grew chill where the long grasses stood in the sun, the dead garden about them with its dead stone beasts of an ill-stomached fancy. Folk rich and brave, and blithe and young as themselves, had once walked and talked and taken their pleasure here, and their play was done and they were gone, they had no name or remembered place, even in the lands of death they were maybe forgotten, for maybe the dead died once again and again, and went on. And, daft-like, she tried to tell Ewan that whimsy, and he stared at her, pushing his cap from his brow, and looked puzzled and said *Ay*, half-heartedly; he didn't know what she blithered about. She laughed then and turned away from him, angry at herself and her daftness; but once she'd thought there wouldn't be a thing they wouldn't understand together. . . .

And the rain that had held away all the day came down at last and caught them on their way back home, overtaking them near to Laurencekirk, in a blinding surge that they watched come hissing across the fields, the sholtie bent its head to the storm and trotted on cannily, it grew dark all of a moment and Ewan found there was never a lamp on Chae's bit gig. He swore at Chae and then drove in silence, and the wind began to rise as they came on the long, bare road past Fordoun, near lifting the sholt from off its feet; and out in the darkness they heard the fog-horn moaning by Todhead lighthouse. They were a pair

of drookèd rats when they turned the gig into the close at
Peesie's Knapp, and Chae cried to them to come in and dry,
but they wouldn't, they ran all the way to Blawearie and the
wet trees were creaking in the wind as they reached to their
door.

Now that was the last wet day of the Spring and to Chris the
weeks began to slip by like posts you glimpse from the fleeing
window of a railway train in a day of summer – light and shade
and marled wood, light and shade and the whoom of the train,
life itself seemed to fly like that up through the Spring, Ewan
had the corn land all ploughed and sown himself almost early
as was the Mains; only in the yavil did Chris go out and carry
the corn for him.

And that she liked fine, not a chave and a weariness as it was
with father, Ewan brisk and cheerful with the smoulder gone
from his eyes, they had settled to a clear, slow shining it seemed
to Chris, now he had his own home and wife. Then in the days
of the harrowing Chris drove the harrows while he carted
manure to the turnip-land, she was glad that she hadn't that
work, glad to tramp behind the horses instead, with kilted
skirts, a switch in her hand and the reins there and the horses
plod-plodding steadily, they knew her fine, and she spoiled
them with bits of loaf and jam so that Ewan, coming to drive
them himself, cried vexedly, *Hold up your head from my
pockets, Clyde! What the hell are you sniff-sniff-sniffing for?*

Then he went down to Stonehaven and bought a new sower
and sowed the turnips; and the night he finished and unloosed
and came back to the biggings for his supper, he couldn't find
Chris though he called and called. She heard him calling and
didn't answer, herself lying out in the garden under the beeches,
brave and green and rustling their new Spring leaves, whispering without cease over her head that was buried in the grass
while she lay and thought. A little insect ran over her hand and
she hated it, but it mightn't disturb her for this time at the least,
nothing might do that, she lay so certain and still because of
this thing that had come to her. She felt neither gladness nor
pain, only dazed, as though running in the fields with Ewan she

had struck against a great stone, body and legs and arms, and
lay stunned and bruised, the running and the fine crying in the
sweet air still on about her, Ewan running free and careless still,
not knowing or heeding the things she had met. The days of
love and holidaying and the foolishness of kisses – they might
be for him yet but never the same for her again, dreams were
fulfilled and their days put by, the hills climbed still to sunset
but her heart might climb with them never again and long for
to-morrow, the night still her own. No night would she ever be
her own again, in her body the seed of that pleasure she had sown
with Ewan burgeoning and growing, dark, in the warmth below
her heart. And Chris Guthrie crept out from the place below the
beech trees where Chris Tavendale lay and went wandering off
into the waiting quiet of the afternoon,[21] Chris Tavendale heard
her go, and she came back to Blawearie never again.

But she did not tell Ewan, not that night nor the week that
followed, nor the weeks after that, watching her own body with
a secret care and fluttering eyes for the marks and stigmata of
this thing that had come to her. And she saw her breast nipples
change and harden and grow soft again, the breasts that Ewan
had kissed and thought the wonder of God, a maid's breasts a
maid's no longer, changing in slow rhythm of purpose with the
sway and measure of each note in the rhythm, her belly rounding to plumpness below the navel, she looked in the glass and
saw also her eyes changed, deeper and most strange, with red
lights and veinings set in them. And in the silences of the night,
when the whit-owl had quieted out by the barn, once something
moved there under her heart, moved and stirred drowsily, a
sleeper from dreams; and she gasped and cried and then lay
still, not wakening Ewan, for this was her rig and furrow, she
had brought him the unsown field and the tending and reaping
was hers, even as with herself when she lay in her own mother's
body. And she thought of that, queer it seemed then how
unclearly she had thought of that aforetime, shamed, indecent
and coarse for a quean to think of such things – that her mother
had once carried her as seed and fruit and dark movingness of
flesh hid away within her.

And she wakened more fully at that, lying thinking while

Ewan slept at her side, turned away from him, thinking of mother, not as her mother at all, just as Jean Murdoch, another woman who had faced this terror-daze in the night. They went sleepless in the long, dark hours for the fruitage of love that the sower slept all unaware, they were the plants that stood dark and quiet in the night, unmoving, immobile, the bee hummed home and away, drowsy with treasure, and another to-morrow for the hunting his. So was the way of things, there was the wall and the prison that you couldn't break down, there was nothing to be done – nothing, though your heart stirred from its daze and suddenly the frozenness melted from you and still you might not sleep . . . But now it was because of that babble of words that went round and around in your mind, soundless and scared of your lips, a babble of hours in the hills and loitering by lochs and the splendour of books and sleeping secure – babble of a world that still marched and cried beyond the prison walls, fair and unutterable its loveliness still outside the doors of Blawearie house, mocked by its ghost, a crying in the night for things that were lost and foregone and ended.

It quietened away then, morning came tapping at the window, she turned and slept, sleeping exhausted, rising with white face and slow steps so that she was long in the kitchen. And Ewan came hasting in, hurried that morning, the first of the turnips were pushing their thin, sweet blades of grass above the drills, he wanted to be out to them. *Damn't, Chris, are you still asleep?* he cried, half-laughing, half-angry, and Chris said nothing, going back to the dairy, Ewan stared and then moved uneasily and followed her with hesitant feet, *What's wrong? What's up?*

Turning to look at him, suddenly Chris knew that she hated him, standing there with the health in his face, clear of eyes – every day they grew clearer here in the parks he loved and thought of noon, morning and night; that, and the tending to beasts and the grooming of horses, herself to warm him at night and set him his meat by day. *What are you glowering for?* he asked, and she spoke then at last, calmly and thinly, *For God's sake don't deave me. Must you aye be an old wife and come trailing after me wherever I go?*

He flinched like a horse with the lash on its back, his eyes
kindled their smoky glow, but he swung round and away from
her. *You're out of bed the wrong side this morning,* and out he
went. She was sorry then, wanted to cry to him, dropped the
pails to run after him, when he spoilt it all, crying from the
middle of the close: *And I'd like my breakfast before the night
comes down.*

It was as though she were dry whin and his speech a fire set
to it, she ran out and overtook him there in the close, catching
his shoulder and whirling him round, so surprised he was that
he almost fell. *Speak to me like that?* she cried, *Do you think
I'm your servant? You're mine, mind that, living off my meal
and my milk, you Highland pauper!* ... More than that she
said, so she knew, no memory of the words abided with her, it
was a blur of rage out of which she came with Ewan holding
her shoulders and shaking her: *You damned bitch, you'd say
that to me? To me?* ... he was glaring like a beast, then he
seemed to crumple, his hands fell from her. *Och, you're ill, you
should be in your bed!*

He left her in the close then, striding to the barn, she stood
like a fool with the tears of rage and remorse blinding her eyes.
And as she went back to the kitchen and came out with the
pails Ewan went striding away over the fields, his hoe on his
shoulder, it was barely yet light, he was going to the parks
without his breakfast. Milking the kye she hurried, her anger
dying away, hurrying to be finished and have the breakfast
ready, for he'd sure to be back again soon.

So she planned; but Ewan didn't come back. The porridge
hottered to a thick, tough mess, beyond the raised blind the
day broke thick and evilly red, hot like a pouring of steam
across the hills; the tea grew cold. Herself half-desperate with
hunger she waited, couldn't sit, wandering from fire to door
and door to table; and then she caught sight on the dresser of
the whistle that had lain by father while he lay in paralysis in
bed, and snatched it down, and all in a moment had run over
the close to the lithe of the corn ricks.

Shading her eyes she saw Ewan then, down in the turnip-
park, swinging steady and quick in lunge and recovery,

Kinraddie's best hoer. Then she whistled to him loud and clear
down through the morning, half Kinraddie must have heard
the blast, but he took no notice. Then she went desperate in a
way, she stopped from whistling and screamed to him, *Ewan,
Ewan!* and at her first scream he looked up and dropped his
hoe – he'd heard her whistling all right, the thrawn swine! She
screamed again, he was running by then over the parks to the
close; him not ten yards away she screamed a third time, hurting
her throat, but she did it calmly, anger boiled in her, yet in a
way she was cool enough.

And Ewan cried *God, Chris, have you gone clean daft? What
are you screaming for, what do you want?* He towered up
above her, angry, amazed, it was then that she knew for sure,
she gathered up all the force in her voice and body for the reply
that sprang to her lips and the thing that followed it. *That!* she
said, and struck him across the face with her arm's full force,
her fingers cried agony and then went numb, on Ewan's face a
great red mark sprang up, the clap of the blow went echoing
around the Blawearie biggings.

So she saw and heard, only a moment, next minute he was
at her himself like a cat, her head rang and dirled as he struck
her twice, she tried to keep her footing and failed and fell back,
against the rick-side, clutching at the thing, staring feared at
Ewan, the madness on his face, his fists coming again. *Get up,
get up!* he cried, *Damn you, get up!* and she knew he would
strike her again, and rising shielded her face with her arm,
trying to cram back the sobs in her throat, too late for that.
Dizzy, she saw him in front of her swaying and moving, she
couldn't see him but she cried *No, no!* and turned then and ran
stumbling up through the close, up the hill to the moor. Twice
he called as she ran, the second time so that nearly she stopped,
Chris, Chris, come back! in a voice that was breaking as her
own had been. But she couldn't stop running, a hare that the
snare had whipped, *Never again, never again, the loch, the
loch!* she sobbed as she ran and panted, the Standing Stones
wheeling up from the whins to peer with quiet faces then in
her face.

*

A quarter of an hour, half an hour, how long had she lain and dozed? Still morning in the air, she was soaked with dew. She turned and half-rose, heard the whistling of the broom and sank down again.

It was Ewan by the moor-gate, searching, he'd stopped to stare at the loch, thinking the thing she had thought, not seeing her yet. She sighed. She felt tired as though she had worked a great day in the sweat of the land, but Ewan would see to her, Ewan would take heed.

So she raised her voice and called to him and he came.

IV

Harvest

It seemed to her that but hardly could she have left the place since that May-day more than six years ago when Ewan had come seeking her through the red, evil weather. She closed her eyes and put out a hand against the greatest of the Standing Stones, the coarse texture of the stone leapt cold to her hand, for a shivering wind blew down the hills. She started at thought of another thing then, opening her eyes to look round; but there he was, still and safe as he stood and looked at her. She cried *Stay by me, Ewan!* and he came running to her side; and she caught his hand and closed her eyes again, praying in a wild compassion of pity for that Ewan whose hand lay far from hers.

Six years: Spring rains and seeding, harvests and winters and springs again since that day that Ewan had come seeking her here with his white, chill face that kindled to warmth and well-being when she called him at last. She'd cried in his arms then, tired and tired, as he carried her down the hill; and the rage was quite gone from him, he bore her into the house and up to their bed, and patted her hand, and said *Bide you quiet!* and went off down the hill at a run.

So she learned he had run, and to Peesie's Knapp, but she didn't know then, she sank and sank away into sleep, and awakened long after with Ewan and still another man come in the room, it was Meldrum from Bervie, the doctor. He peeled off his gloves from his long white hands, and peered at her like a hen with his gley, sharp eye. *What's this you've been doing, Chris Guthrie?*

He didn't wait a reply but caught up her hand and wrist and

listened, still like a hen, head on one side while Ewan stared at
him greyly. Then he said *Well, well, that's fine, let's see a bit
more of you, young Mistress Tavendale.*

While he listened with the funny things at his ears and the
end of it on her chest, she closed her eyes, ill no longer though
drowsy still, and peeked sideways at Ewan, smiling at him. And
then the doctor moved his stethoscope further down, it tickled
her bared skin there and she knew he knew, and he straightened
up *And you tell me you didn't know what the thing was, Chris
Tavendale?*

She said *Oh, yes,* and he said *But not Ewan?* and she shook
her head and they both laughed at Ewan standing there staring
from one to the other, black hair unbrushed, she had gone near
to killing him that morning. And then Dr Meldrum shook him
by the arm, *You're going to be a father, Blawearie man, what
think you of that? Away and make me a cup of tea while Chris
and I go into more intimate details – you needn't bide, she's
safe enough with an old man, bonny though she be.*

All that he said as canny as ordering a jug of milk, Ewan
gasped, and made to speak, and couldn't, but his face was blithe
as he turned and ran down the stairs. They heard him singing
below and old Meldrum cocked his head to the side and
listened, *Damned easy for him to sing, eh, Chris? But you'll
sing yourself when this bairn of yours comes into the world.
Let's see if everything's right.*

It was. He put his hand on her shoulder when he finished
and gave her a shake. *A body as fine and natural and comely
as a cow or a rose, Chris Guthrie. You'll have no trouble and
you needn't fret. But look after yourself, eat vegetables, and be
still as kind to Ewan as the wear of the months will let you be.
Good for him and good for you.* She nodded to that, understanding, and he gave her another shake and went down to
Ewan, and drank the tea that Ewan had made, if tea it was,
which you doubted later when you smelt the cups.

Ewan knowing, Meldrum knowing, it was as though a bank
had gone down behind which she had dreamt a torrent and a
storm would burst and blind and whelm her. But there was
nothing there but the corn growing and the peewits calling,

summer coming, marching up each morning with unbraided
hair, the dew rising in whorling mists from the urgent corn that
carpeted Ewan's trim fields. Nothing to fear and much to do,
most of all to tell Ewan not to fret, she wasn't a doll, she'd be
safe as a cow though she hoped to God she didn't quite look
like one. And Ewan said *You look fine, bonnier than ever*,
saying it solemnly, meaning it, and she was glad, peeking at
herself in the long mirror when she was alone, seeing gradually
that smooth rounding of belly and hips below her frock – lucky,
she had never that ugliness that some poor folk have to bear,
awful for them. She took pleasure in being herself, in being as
before, not making a difference, cooking and baking and running to the parks with the early morning piece for Ewan, he'd
cry *Don't run!* and she'd cry *Don't blether!* and reach beside
him, and sink down beside him midway the long potato rows
he was hoeing, growing low and broad and well-branched, the
shaws, it was set a fine year for potatoes. And as he sat and ate
she'd gather his coat below her head for a pillow, and lean back
with her arms outspread in the sun, and make of that few
minutes her resting-time, listening to Ewan on the crops and
the weather that was so good folk didn't believe it could last,
there must soon be a break of the fine interplay of the last two
months.

That was late in June he said that, and all the dour Howe
watched the sky darkly, certain some trick was on *up there*. For
the rain that was needed came in the night, just enough, not
more, as though cannily sprinkled, and the day would be fine
with sun, you couldn't want better; but it wasn't in the nature
of things it would last. And Chris said, dreamily, *Maybe things
are changing for the better all round*, and Ewan said *Damn the
fears!* his gaze far off and dark and intent, the crops and the
earth in his bones and blood, and she'd look in his face and
find content, not jealous or curious or caring though she herself
found in his eyes a place with the crops and land. And she'd
close her eyes in the sun-dazzle then, in the smell, green, pungent, strong and fine, of the coming potato shaws, and sometimes she'd doze and waken sun-weary, Ewan working a little
bit off, not clattering his hoe lest she wake.

She made up her mind she'd have the baby born in the room that had once been her own. So she rubbed it and scrubbed it till it shone again and brought out the bed mattress and hung it to air, in the garden, between the beeches, all in leaf they were, so thick. You could hardly see the sky looking up in that malachite, whispering dome; and by as she looked came Long Rob of the Mill to settle his bills with Ewan, he saw Chris then and came to lean on the hedge, hatless, and long as ever, with the great moustaches and the iron-blue eyes.

And he picked a sprig of the honeysuckle and bit it between his teeth. *This'll be for the son, eh, Chris? And when are you having him born?* She said *Late September or early October, I think*, and Rob shook his head, it wasn't the best time for bairns, though feint the fear for hers. And he laughed as he leaned there, minding something, and he told Chris of the thing, his own mother it was, the wife of a crofter down in the Reisk. She'd had her twelve children in sixteen years, nine of them died, Rob was the oldest and only a lad and he'd seen the youngest of his brothers born. *Seen? I helped, think of that, Chris quean!* And think she did and she shivered, and Rob said *That was daft, the telling of that. But things are fair right with you, then, Chris?*

So maybe, going home, he told of Blawearie's news; soon Kinraddie knew more than did Chris herself. Folk began to trail in about in the quiet of an evening, out of ill-fashionce, and nothing much more, they'd gley sidewise at Chris as they'd argue with Ewan, syne home they would go and tell it was true, *Ay, there'll soon be a family Blawearie way, Chris must fair have taken at the first bit sett.* But others knew better, Mutch and Munro, and the speak went round that the taking was well ere the marriage, Ewan had married the quean when she threatened him with law. Kinraddie mouthed that over, it was toothsome and tasty, and the speak came creeping up to Blawearie, Chris never knew how she heard it. But she did, Ewan did, and he swore to go out and kick the backsides of Mutch and Munro till they'd dream of sitting as a pleasure and a passion. And off he'd have set in the rage of the moment but Chris caught him and held him, that would only be daft, folk would think it the truer, the scandal; and if it made them the happier to think as they did, let them think!

And then it seemed to Chris that her world up Blawearie brae began to draw in, in and about her and the life she carried, that moved now often and often, turning slow under her heart in the early days, but jerking with suddenness, a moment at a stretch now, sometimes, so that she would sit and gasp with closed eyes. In, nearer and nearer round herself and the house, the days seemed to creep, Will in Argentine was somebody she'd met in a dream of the night, Aberdeenshire far away, nothing living or moving but shadows in sunlight or night outside the circle of the hills and woods she saw from Blawearie's biggings. Then fancies came on her and passed, but were daft and straining and strange while they lasted, she couldn't break herself of the things, they'd to wear and fade at their own bit gait.

One night it was that she couldn't touch kye, Ewan had to do the milking himself, sore puzzled and handless he was but she couldn't help that, though next morning she laughed at herself, what was there to fear in the milking of kye? Then came the day when they drove Chae Strachan's sheep to the buchts and the libbing of the lambs went on till it nearly drove her mad, the thin young baaing that rose an unending plaint, the folk with their pipes and knives and the blood that ran in the sunlight. All in a picture it rose to her on the sound of that baaing, and she hid in the dairy at last, the only place that shut out the sound.

But another fad, and the one that lasted the longest, was fear that all sounds would go, fear of the night when it might be so nearly still, Ewan sleeping with his head in his arm as he sometimes did, soundless, till she'd think him dead and shake him to a sleepy wakefulness; and he'd ask *What's wrong? Have I been stealing the blankets from you?* and she'd say *Yes*, ashamed to let him know of that fear of hers.

So she found the days blithe enough then, the scraich and scratch of hens in the close, the sound of the mower that Ewan drove up and down the rigs of the hay, the mooing of the calves wild-plagued with flies, Clyde's neighing to a passing stallion.

Only night was the time to be feared, if she woke and there was that stillness; but even the quietest night if she listened hard she'd hear the wisp-wisp of the beech leaves near to the window, quietening her, comforting her, she never knew why, as though the sap that swelled in branch and twig were one with the blood that swelled the new life below her navel, that coming day in the months to be a thing she'd share with that whisperer out in the darkness.

And oh! but the time was long! She could almost have wished that she and Ewan had bedded unblessed as Mutch said they had, the baby would have been here by now and not still to come, still waiting harvest and stooking and the gathering of stooks. But it lay with her, warm and shielded, and saw with her the growth and ripening of that autumn's corn, yellow and great, and the harvest moons that came so soon in that year, red moons a-slant and a-tilt on the rim of the earth they saw as they went to bed, you felt it another land and another world that hung there in the quietness of the sky.

One night, the mid-days of August as they sat at meat, the door burst open and in strode Chae Strachan, a paper in his hand, and was fell excited, Chris listened and didn't, a war was on, Britain was to war with Germany.[1] But Chris didn't care and Ewan didn't either, he was thinking of his coles that the weather might ruin; so Chae took himself off with his paper again, and after that, though she minded it sometimes, Chris paid no heed to the war, there were aye daft devils fighting about something or other, as Ewan had said; and God! they could fight till they were black and blue for all that he cared if only the ley field would come on a bit faster, it was near fit for cutting but the straw so short it fair broke your heart. And out he'd go in the evening light, down to the ley park and poke about there, rig to rig, as though coaxing the straw to grow and grow in the night for his delight in the morning. A bairn with a toy, Chris thought, laughing as she watched him then; and then came that movement in her body as she watched Ewan still – a mother with his child he was, the corn his as this seed of his hers, burgeoning and ripening, growing to harvest.

The corn was first. Up and down the rigs on his brave new

binder, Clyde and Bess each aside the pole, rode Ewan; and the corn bent and was smitten on the flyboard, and gathered up on the forking teeth and wound and bound and ejected. Up and down went the whirling arms, and fine harvest weather came then in Kinraddie, though it rained in Dee, folk said, and down in Forfar[2] the year was wet. Park by park Ewan rode it down, Chris still could carry him a piece as he worked, but she walked slow now, careful and slow, and he'd jump from the binder and come running and meet her, and down he would sit her in the lithe of a stook while he stood and ate, his gaze as ever on the fields and sky, there was still the harvest to finish.

But finished it was, September's end, and there came a blatter of rain next day, Chris saw the coming of the rain and the bright summer went as the stooks stood laden and tall in the fields. And Chris found herself sick, a great pain came and gripped at her breast, at her thighs, she cried *Ewan!* and nearly fell and he ran to her. They stared in each other's faces, hearing the rain, and then again the pain drove through and through Chris like a heated sword, and she set her teeth and shook Ewan free, she knew the things she'd to do. *It'll maybe be a long time yet, but get Chae to drive for the doctor and nurse. He'll bring the nurse back from Bervie, Chae.*

Ewan stood and stared and his face was working, she smiled at him then though the pain of the sword was as nothing now, iron hooks were tearing in her body instead, rusty and dragging and blunt. She held up her face to be kissed and kept her teeth fast and said *Hurry, though I'm fine!* and syne watched him run down the road to the Knapp. Then, white, in a daze of pain, she began to walk backwards and forwards on the kitchen floor, as she knew she must do to bring on the birth quick, everything else was ready and waiting in the room upstairs. And after a while the pain waned and went, but she knew it would soon be back. So she filled her a hot-water bottle and almost ran up the stairs to put it in the bed, almost running lest the pain come midway and catch her unaware. But it held off still, she smoothed out the sheets, brought out the rubber one she'd had bought, and tied that down, firm and strong, and set the great basin on the rug by the window and wondered what else there might be. Then she saw her face in the glass, it was flushed and bright and her eyes all hot; and suddenly she thought how strange it would be if she died, like the many women who died in childbed, she felt well and strong, they had felt the same, strange to think that her face might be dead and still in another day, that face that she looked at now, it couldn't be hers, it was still the face of a quean.

From the window she saw Ewan running back and as she reached to the foot of the stairs to meet him the pain came on her again, she had to sit down. But that was daft, it would make it last longer, she struggled to her feet and walked in the kitchen again, Ewan was in the doorway, a white blur of a face and nothing else unless she looked at him hard and hard. He kept saying *Chris, go and lie down!* and she opened her mouth and gasped and meant to tell him she was fine; and instead found herself swearing and swearing, terrible words she hadn't known she knew, they were wrung from her lips as she went stumbling to and fro, better than screaming, women screamed, but she wouldn't.

And then came relief again, the kitchen straightened and she sat down, Ewan emerged from his blur and made her tea. Something kept worrying her – what was he to have for his dinner? She couldn't remember the thing she'd intended, and gave it up, her tormentors were nearby again. *Boil yourself an egg, Ewan!* she gasped, and he didn't understand, he thought it something she wanted – *Boil what?* And at that a frenzy of irritation came on her, *Oh, boil your head if you like!* and she dragged herself to her feet, the clock on the mantelshelf was expanding and contracting, its dial blurred and brightened as she stood. And then she was sure, she cried *Ewan, help me up to the room*, for she knew that her time had come.

What happened then she didn't know, there came a clear patch and she found herself nude, all but a stocking, it wouldn't come off, she sat on the bedside and tried, Ewan tried, it was so funny she giggled in spite of the pain. And then she saw Ewan's face, it had grown to the face of an old man, now, she must lie and get him out of the room. She cried *Mind the fire, Ewan, there's no wood there, run and hack some*, and when he was out of the room she could heed to herself and her agony at last; and she bit the sheets, she rolled herself tight in a ball, the pain seemed to go for a moment, maybe she had smothered the baby, she didn't care, she couldn't abide it, not through hours and hours and days and days, for weeks it had gone on now, she had seen the room darken and lighten and night come, tormented by Ewan and father her body, and Will was dead, they had tortured him first.

She cried *Will!* then and opened her eyes from an hour-long sleep. In the room was the doctor and the nurse from Bervie, he came over to her side, old Meldrum, *Well, Chris lass, how do you feel? Fine to send for us in such a stour, and here we coming tearing up to find you sleeping like a lamb! This is Mrs Ogilvie, you've heard of her.*

Chris tried to speak, and managed, her body was a furnace, but she managed to speak, she didn't get it clear and she tried again. And Mrs Ogilvie patted her and said *Don't bother with that. Do you feel you're getting on fine?* Dr Meldrum came back then, *Well, let's see;* and Chris poised herself on the rim of a glistening cup of pain while they looked at and felt at and straightened something alien and white, it was her own body she remembered. Meldrum said *Fine, fine, it shouldn't be long, I'll wait down below,* and went out and closed the door, he hated confinements. Mrs Ogilvie sat down and next minute jumped to her feet again, *Don't do that, Mrs Tavendale, don't grip yourself up! Slacken and it's easy, wish it to come, there's a brave girl!*

Chris tried: it was torment: the beast moved away from her breasts, scrabbled and tore and returned again, it wasn't a beast, red-hot pincers were riving her apart. Riven and riven she bit at her lips, the blood on her tongue, she couldn't bite more, she heard herself scream then, twice. And then there were feet on the stairs, the room rose and fell, hands on her everywhere, holding her, tormenting her, she cried out again, ringingly, deep, a cry that ebbed to a sigh, the cry and the sigh with which young Ewan Tavendale came into the world in the farmhouse of Blawearie.

*

So quick as all that, she was lucky, folk said, bringing a birth in a forenoon, just; it was twelve when Ewan was born. Some folk, Mrs Ogilvie told, had to thresh from dawn to dusk and through another night to another day, and Chris lay and nodded and said *Yes, I know*, and fell fast asleep, she didn't dream at all. And, waking, she found herself washed and dried, a new night-gown put on her and Mrs Ogilvie knitting by the side of the bed, nothing else, oh! she couldn't have dreamt and not known it. She whispered, scared, *My baby?* and Mrs Ogilvie whispered *Beside you, don't crush him*, and Chris turned round her head and saw then beside her a face as small as though carved from an apple, near, perfect and small, with a fluff of black hair and a blue tinge on long eyelids, and a mouth that was Ewan's and a nose her own, and she nearly cried out *Oh, my baby!*

So she lay and wondered, near cried again, and put out her hand, it felt strong and quick, only heavy, and her fingers passed up and along, under its swathings, a body as small and warm as a cat's, with a heart that beat steady and assured. And the baby opened his eyes and fluttered them at her and yawned and she saw a tongue like a little red fish in the little red mouth; and the blue-shaded eyelids went down again and young Ewan Tavendale slept.

Sweet to lie beside him in the hours that went by, sleeping herself now and then and wakening to watch him, not ugly as she'd thought he'd be, lovely and perfect. And then he moved and whimpered, unrestful, and was picked from the bed in Mrs Ogilvie's hands, and fluttered his eyelids at her, Chris saw, and opened his mouth and weeked like a kitten. And Mrs Ogilvie said *He's hungry now*, Chris found him in her arms at last, and hugged him, just once, and held him to her breast. The blind little mouth came kissing and lapping, he wailed his disappointment, his little hands clawing at her. Then his lips found her nipple, it hurt and it didn't, it was as though he were draining the life from her body, there was nothing better than to die that way, he was hers close and closer than his father had been, closer than again could any child be. And she wondered above him and kissed his black hair, damp still from the travail of birth; and looked at the eyes that stared so unwinkingly as the hungry lips clung to her breast. So at last he was finished, then Ewan came up, he'd come while she slept before and he bent and kissed her and she cried *Mind the baby!* and he said *By God, am I like to forget?* And he wiped his forehead, poor Ewan!

In a week Mrs Ogilvie was gone and Chris felt so well she was up and about, it was daft to lie wearied and feckless when she felt so fine. So down to the kitchen and the shining of the October sun she came, she and her baby, into the whisper and murmur of that war that had so excited Chae Strachan.

For it was on, not a haver only, every soul that came up to look at young Ewan began to speak of it sooner or later. Chae came and looked at young Ewan and tickled his toes and said *Ay, man!* And he told them they'd brought out a fine bit bairn between them, every man might yet have to fight for bairn and wife ere this war was over; and he said that the Germans had broken loose, fair devils, and were raping women and braining bairns all over Belgium,[3] it was hell let loose. And Ewan said *Who'll win, then?* and Chae said if the Germans did there'd be an end of both peace and progress forever, there wouldn't be safety in the world again till the Prussians – and they were a kind of German, with meikle spiked helmets, awful brutes, and the very worst – were beaten back to the hell they came from. But Ewan just yawned and said *Oh, to hell with them and their hell both, Chae! Are you going to the mart the morn?*

For he didn't care, Ewan; but the mart was as bad, nobody spoke of anything but war, Munro of the Cuddiestoun was there, and Mutch, they'd a fair drink in their bellies, both, and swore they'd 'list the morn were they younger, by God. That was just the drink speaking, no doubt, but the very next day the Upperhill foreman, James Leslie he was that had taken Ewan's place, went into Aberdeen and joined in the Gordons,[4] he was the first man to go from Kinraddie and was killed fell early. But folk thought him fair daft, showing off and looking for a holiday, just, there was no use coming to such stir as that when the war would so soon be over. For the papers all said that it would, right fierce they were, *Man, some of those editors are right rough creatures, God pity the Germans if they'd their hands on them!* And folk shook their heads, and agreed that the newspaper billies were ill to run counter.

But the Germans didn't care – maybe they didn't read the papers, said Long Rob of the Mill; they just went on with their raping of women and their gutting of bairns, till Chae Strachan came up to Blawearie one night with a paper in his hand and a blaze on his face, and he cried that he for one was off to enlist, old Sinclair could heed to the Knapp and to Kirsty. And Ewan cried after him, *You're havering, man, you don't mean it!* but Chae cried back *Damn't ay, that I do!* And sure as death he did and went off, by Saturday a letter came to Peesie's Knapp that told he had joined the North Highlanders and been sent to Perth.[5]

So there was such speak and stir as Kinraddie hadn't known for long, sugar was awful up in price and Chris got as much as she could from the grocer and stored it away in the barn. Then Ewan heard funny things about the sermon that the Reverend Gibbon had preached the Sunday before, and though he couldn't bear with a kirk he broke his habit and put on his best suit and went down to the service next Sabbath. There was a fell crowd there, more than Ewan had heard of the last week's sermon, and the place was all on edge to hear what the Reverend Gibbon would say. He looked bigger and more like a bull than ever, Ewan thought, as he mounted the pulpit, there was nothing unusual as he gave out the hymn and the prayer. But then he took a text, Ewan couldn't mind which, about Babylon's corruptions,[6] they'd been right coarse there. And he said that God was sending the Germans for a curse and a plague on the world because of its sins, it had grown wicked and lustful, God's anger was loosed as in the days of Attila.[7] How long it would rage, to what deeps of pain their punishments would go, only God and His Anger might know. But from the chastisement by blood and fire the nations might rise anew, Scotland not the least in its ancient health and humility, to tread again the path to grace.

And just as he got there, up rose old Sinclair of the Netherhill,

all the kirk watched him, and he put on his hat and he turned
his back and went step-stepping slow down the aisle, he
wouldn't listen to this brute defending the German tinks and
some friend that he called Attila. Hardly had he risen when
Mutch rose too, syne Cuddiestoun, and they too clapped on
their hats; and Ellison half made to rise but his wife pulled him
down, he looked daft as a half-throttled turkey then, Ella White
wasn't to have him make himself a fool for any damned war
they waged. But the minister turned red and then white and he
stuttered when he saw folk leaving; and his sermon quietened
down, he finished off early and rattled off the blessing as though
it was a cursing. Outside in the kirkyard some young folk
gathered to clout him in the lug as he came from the kirk, but the
elders were there and they edged them away, and Mr Gibbon
threaded the throngs like a futret with kittle, and made for the
Manse, and padlocked the gate.

But Ewan didn't care one way or the other, as he told to Chris.
The minister might be right or be wrong with his Babylons
and whores and might slobber Attila every night of the week,
Blawearie had its crop all in and that was what mattered.
And Chris said *Yes, what a blither about a war, isn't it,
Ewan?* and tickled young Ewan as he lay on her lap. And he
laughed and kicked and his father sat down and looked at him,
solemn, and said it was fair wonderful, *Did you see him look
up at me then, Chris quean?*

So they were douce and safe and blithe in Blawearie though
Kinraddie was unco with Chae Strachan gone. Kirsty came up
on a visit and cried when she sat in the kitchen beside the crib,
Chris made her tea but she wouldn't take comfort. She said she
knew well enough Chae'd never come back, he was in such a
rage with the Germans he'd just run forward in his bit of the
front and kill and kill till he'd fair lost himself. Chris said *And
they're maybe not such bad folk as the papers make out*, and
at that Kirsty Strachan jumped up *So, you're another damned
pro-German as well, are you? There's over-many of your kind in
Kinraddie*. Chris stared clean amazed, but out Kirsty Strachan
went running, still crying, and that was the last they saw of her
in many a week, maybe she was ashamed of her outburst.

Whether or not *she* was, there could be never a doubt about the Reverend Gibbon. For the next Sabbath day, when another great crowd came down to the kirk to hear him preach, they got all the patriotism they could wish, the minister said that the Kaiser was the Antichrist,[8] and that until this foul evil had been swept from the earth there could be neither peace nor progress again. And he gave out a hymn then, *Onward, Christian Soldiers*[9] it was, and his own great bull's voice led the singing, he had fair become a patriot and it seemed likely he thought the Germans real bad. But Long Rob of the Mill, when he heard the story, said it was a sight more likely that he thought the chance of losing his kirk and collections a damned sight worse than any German that was ever yet clecked.

For, and it grew a fair scandal all through the Howe, you could hardly believe it, it was funny enough, Long Rob of the Mill didn't hold with the war. He said it was a lot of damned nonsense, those that wanted to fight, the M.P.s and bankers and editors and muckers, should all be locked up in a pleiter of a park and made to gut each other with graips: there'd be no great loss to the world and a fine bit sight it would make for decent folk to look on at. But for folk with sense to take part in the soss and yammer about King and country was just plain hysteria; and as for Belgium invaded, it got what it needed, what about the Congo and your Belgians[10] there? Not that the Germans weren't as bad, they were all tarred with the same black brush.

But, though folk weren't patriots as daft as Chae Strachan, that didn't look when he was being laughed at, they knew right well that Long Rob couldn't lie like that, the long, rangy childe, without being pro-German, as the papers called it. For all the papers were full of pro-Germans then, British folk that thought that the German rascals were right; and in England folk went and smashed in their windows, such a rage they were in with the pro-Germans for being so coarse. There was little danger that they'd smash Rob's windows, there were few that cared to tackle the childe except Chae Strachan that was training in Perth. So the whole stour might well have blown over, Rob was a well-liked billy and you needn't heed his blithers, if the

Reverend Gibbon hadn't taken to the business and preached a sermon about tinks and traitors, and a lot he preached about a jade called Jael,[11] fell unchancy she'd been, right holy, though, and she'd killed a childe Sisera that she couldn't thole, because he was coarse to the Jews. And the Reverend Gibbon boomed out she was fine, a patriot and a light unto Israel she'd been, and we in like manner must act the same, right here in our midst were traitors that sided with the Antichrist, shame on Kinraddie that it should be so!

Folk listened to the sermon and fair got excited, and after dinner that Sabbath a horde of billies, some came from Kinraddie though most did not, but Upperhill's new foreman was there, and an awful patriot childe just like Gordon himself, they went down to the Mill, and there was Long Rob sitting out by his door, smoking at his pipe and reading in a book, coarse stite about God and God knows what. And the Upperhill foreman cried out *Here's the Kaiser's crony, let's duck the mucker!* and the lot made a run at Rob and got him gripped in their hands, Rob thought it some joke and he laughed at them, setting by his bit book. But they soon let him know they were serious enough, they were clean worked up about the sermon and Long Rob the Antichrist's friend, and they started to haul Rob over to the mill-course then, where the water was sparkling and raging from a good bit spate in the hills.

Syne at last Rob knew they meant what they said, folk told that he gave a great cry that wasn't a curse and wasn't a shout, it was both together; and as they dragged him he lifted his foot, real coarse-like, and he kicked the foreman at the Upperhill right in the private parts then, and the foreman at the Upperhill he screamed like a fell stuck pig; and God! folk laughed right well when they heard about that. Well, the next thing that happened was that Rob got a hand free then, and he took a childe near him, a meikle man from the Mains, a clout in the ear that stretched him flat; and then Rob was free and he ran, all the rest at his heels, for the house. But he could run right well, could Rob, and fair outdistanced the pack, and he leapt inside and he barred the door.

So they threw some stones and rammed at the door with

their shoulders, half-shamed by then at the stour they were raising, and maybe they knew they'd feel fools by Monday; and they might have gone home in another bit minute if it hadn't been that the meikle Mains man, him that Rob had couped on the ground with a clout in the ear, crawled up to his feet and picked up a great stone; and crack! through the kitchen window it went with a bang and a splinter inside!

Next minute the door flung open, they turned and looked and there was Long Rob, a gun in his hand and his face fair grey with rage. Some cried *Take care, man, now, put down that gun!* but they edged away back for all that. And Rob cried out *Smash in my window you would, then, would you, you scum?* and he swung the gun at the nearest billy and let drive at him. The pellets sang past the billy's head and he'd had enough of the war, he turned and ran like a rabbit; and the others scattered and ran as well, and Long Rob ran after them, and his gun went bang! again and again, you could hear it all over Kinraddie. Folk ran to their doors, they thought the Germans had landed and were looting the Mearns; Chris, who had run across the Blawearie cornyard, shaded her eyes and looked over the country and at last she saw them, the running figures, like beetles in the distance, they fanned out and ran from the Mill as focus. And behind ran another that stopped now and then, and a puff of smoke went up at each stopping, and there came the bang of the gun. Mist was coming down and it blinded the battlefield, and through it the attacking army ran in an awful rout, Chris saw them vanish into its coming and Long Rob, still shooting, go scudding in chase.

So that was the result of the Reverend Gibbon's sermon, Kinraddie fair seethed with the news next day, all about the attack on the Mill and how Rob had chased the childes that came up against him, some could hardly sit down for a week after that, so full were their backsides with pellets. And some said that Long Rob was a coarse tink brute, if he was willing to fight like that at the Mill it was him that should go out to France and fight; but others, though they weren't so many, Chris and Ewan were among them, liked Long Rob and sided with him, and said it was a damn poor show for Scotland if her

patriots aye ran as they had at the Mill. That had been the
Sunday, but on Wednesday was another happening, and God
knows what mightn't have come of *it* but for the interfering of
the daftie Tony, him that bided at Cuddiestoun.

He'd been stitering along the Denburn road, had Tony, when
he rounded a bend and there, on the road outside the Mill, was
the Reverend Gibbon, his bicycle was lying in the stour and
Long Rob had him gripped by the collar, and if he wasn't in
danger of a bash in the face appearances were sore deceptive.
For Long Rob had seen the minister come riding in the distance
and knew his black coat and stopped the Mill and ran down to
the road to ask what the hell the Reverend had meant by saying
he was friends with the Antichrist. And the Reverend Gibbon
turned red with rage and cried *Stand out of my way there, Rob*,
and Rob cried *Stand still you first, my man, for we've a bit
bone to pick!* and as the minister tried to ride him down Rob
caught the handles and twisted them sore, and off the minister
came, like a sack of corn, right flump in Rob's hands.

And Rob gave him a bit shake and asked *Who's pro-German?*
and the minister swore himself blue and made at Rob, and Rob
shook him like a futret a rabbit, and syne stood back and
looked close at his face, and made up his mind that he'd smash
in the minister's bit nose right then, he'd seen that kind of thing
done before and it fair sossed up a pretty man, you just struck
and struck till the bone gave way. So Rob was just starting to
mash up the minister childe when round the bend with a funny
bit screech came the daftie Tony, he scraiched like a hen with
a seed in its throat and ran and caught at Rob's arm. *He's only
a half-witted cleric, Rob, you'll dirty your hands on him*, he
cried, and both Rob and minister, sore astounded, stopped
from their fighting and stared at the creature, the impudence of
him with his wee red beard, and him only a daftie, like. But he
nodded to the minister *Get while the going's good and your
hide's still intact*, he said: and if you'd believe it the minister
louped on his bicycle without a word, and off he rode; and
Long Rob turned and asked the daftie where he'd hidden his
sense all the time they'd known him, but Tony stood still like
a stock of rags, a daft-like look on his face. And when Rob

spoke to him again he just smiled like a gowk, and went shuffling away through the stour.

Some said that if all things were true that wouldn't be a lie, but Rob swore to it, he wasn't boasting what he'd done to the minister, he said, he was just so astonished at Tony he'd to tell them the story to make Tony's part plain. Cuddiestoun swore 'twas a lie from beginning to end, the thing you'd expect from a damned pro-German, like; but he didn't say that to Long Rob, he was over coarse in the feet, Munro, to run as fleet as the other billies had when Rob got in action. But he stopped his trade with Long Rob and he carted his corn for crushing and bruising over to the mill at Mondynes, syne Mutch of Bridge End did the same. Ah well, they might do that if they liked, folk as a rule were hardly so daft as leave the best miller for miles around just because of his saying that all the Germans could hardly be tinks. Maybe, you know, there was something in what the man said, coarse devils though most of the Germans were.

But Chris didn't care, sitting there at Blawearie with young Ewan at her breast, her man beside her, Blawearie theirs and the grain a fine price, forbye that the stirks sold well in the marts. Maybe there was war and bloodshed and that was awful, but far off also, you'd hear it like the North Sea cry in a morning, a crying and a thunder that became unending as the weeks went by, part of life's plan, fringing the horizon of your days with its pelt and uproar. So the new year came in and Chris watched young Ewan change and grow there at her breast, he was quick of temper like his father, good like his mother, she told Ewan; and Ewan laughed *God, maybe you're right! You could hardly be wrong in a thing after bringing a bairn like that in the world.* And she laughed at him *But you helped a little!* and he blushed as red as he always did, they seemed daft as ever in their love as the days wore on. It was still as strange and as kind to lie with him, live with him, watch the sweat on his forehead when he came from tramping a day in the parks at the heels of his horses; still miracle to hear beside her his soundless breathing in the dark of the night when their pleasure was past and he slept so soon. But she didn't herself, those nights as the Winter wore to March, into Spring: she'd lie and listen to that hushed breathing of his one side of her, the boy's quicker breath in his cradle out by – content, content, what more could she have or want than the two of them, body and blood and breath? And morning would bring her out of her bed to tend young Ewan and make the breakfast and clean out the byre and the stable, singing; she worked never knowing she tired and Long Rob of the Mill came on her one morning as she cleaned the manure from the stable and he cried *The Spring of life, eh, Chris quean? Sing it and cherish it, 'twill never come again!*

Different from the old Rob he looked, she thought, but thought that carelessly, hurried to be in to young Ewan. But she stopped and watched him swing down the rigs to Ewan by the side of his horses, Ewan with his horses halted on the side of the brae and the breath of them rising up like a steam. And she heard Ewan call *Ay, man, Rob*, and Rob call *Ay, man, Ewan*, and they called the truth, they seemed fine men both against the horizon of Spring, their feet deep laired in the wet clay ground, brown and great, with their feet on the earth and the sky that waited behind. And Chris looked at them over-long, they glimmered to her eyes as though they had ceased to be there, mirages of men dreamt by a land grown desolate against its changing sky. And the Chris that had ruled those other two selves of herself, content, unquestioning these many months now, shook her head and called herself daft.

That year's harvest fell sharp away, but the price of corn made up for it, other prices might rise but farming folk did well. So it went in the winter and into the next year too, Ewan took in a drove of Irish steers to eat up the lush green grass of nineteen-sixteen. They grew fat and round in the shortest while, Chris proud to see them, so many beasts had Blawearie. You'd hardly believe 'twas here father had chaved and fought for a living the way he did; but that was before the War.

For it still went on, rumbling its rumours like the thunder of summer beyond the hills. But nobody knew now when it would finish, not even Chae Strachan come home, a soldier all the way

from the front, as they called it; in the orra-looking khaki he
came, with two stripes sewn on his arm, he said they had made
him a corporal. He came up to Blawearie the night he got home
and scraped his feet on the scraper outside and came dandering
into the kitchen as aye he had done, not knocking but crying
through the door *Ay, folk, are you in?*

So there was Chae, Chris gave a loud gasp to see him, Chae
himself, so altered you'd hardly believe it, Chae himself, thin,
his fine eyes queered and strained somehow. Even his laugh
seemed different, hearty as it was, and he cried *God, Chris, I'm
not a ghost yet!* and syne Chris and Ewan were shaking his
hands and sitting him down and pouring him a dram and
another after that. And young Ewan came running to see and
cried *soldier!* and Chae caught him and swung him up from the
floor and cried *Chris's bairn – God, it can't be, I mind the day
he was born, just yesterday it was!*

Young Ewan took little to strangers, most, not frightened but
keep-your-distance he was, but he made no try to keep distant
from Chae, he sat on his knee as Chris spread them supper and
Chae spoke up about things in the War, it wasn't so bad if it
wasn't the lice. He said they were awful, but Chris needn't be
feared, he'd been made to stand out in the close by Kirsty and
strip off everything he had on, and fling the clothes in a tub and
syne get into another himself. So he was fell clean, and God! he
found it a change not trying to reach up his shoulders to get at
some devil fair sucking and sucking the life from his skin.

And he gave a great laugh when he told them that, his old
laugh queerly crippled it was. And Ewan asked what he thought
of the Germans, were they truly coarse? And Chae said he was
damned if he knew, he'd hardly seen one alive, though a body
or so you saw now and then, gey green and *feuch! there's a
supper on the table!* Well, out there you hardly did fighting at
all, you just lay about in those damned bit trenches and had a
keek at the soil they were made of. And man, it was funny land,
clay and a kind of black marl, but the French were no good as
farmers at all, they just pleitered and pottered in little bit parks
that you'd hardly use as a hanky to wipe your neb. Chae didn't
like the French at all, he said they were damned poor folk you'd

to fight for, them, meaner than dirt and not half so sweet. And Ewan listened and said *So you don't think that I should join up, Chae?* and Chris stared at him, Chae stared at him, young Ewan stared, and they all three stared till Chae snorted *There are fools enough in the fighting as it is.* Chris felt something holding her throat, she'd to cough and cough, trying to speak, and couldn't, and Ewan looked at her shamed-like and blushed and said *Och, I was asking, only.*

Chae went round all Kinraddie on his leave that time and found changes enough to open his eyes, maybe he was fell wearied with the front, folk thought, there was nothing on there but their pleitering and fighting. And the first change he saw the first morning, did Chae, lying down in his bed for the pleasure of it and Kirsty at the making of his breakfast. And Chae sat up in his bed to reach for his pipe when he looked from the window and he gave a great roar; and he louped from his bed in his sark so that Kirsty came running and crying *What is't? Is't a wound?* But she found Chae standing by the window then, cursing himself black in the face he was, and he asked how long had *this* been going? So Mistress Strachan looked out the way he looked and she saw it was only the long bit wood that ran by the Peesie's Knapp that vexed him, it was nearly down the whole stretch of it, now. It made a gey difference to the look-out faith! but fine for Kinraddie the woodmen had been, they'd lodged at the Knapp and paid high for their board. But Chae cried out *To hell with their board, the bastards, they're ruining my land, do you hear!* And he pulled on his trousers and boots and would fair have run over the park and been at them; but Kirsty caught at his sark and held him back and cried *Have you fair gone mad with the killing of Germans?*

And he asked her hadn't she got eyes in her head, the fool, not telling him before that the wood was cut? It would lay the whole Knapp open to the north-east now, and was fair the end of a living here. And Mistress Strachan answered up that she wasn't a fool, and they'd be no worse than the other folk, would they? all the woods in Kinraddie were due to come down. Chae shouted *What, others?* and went out to look; and when he came back he didn't shout at all, he said he'd often minded of them out there in France, the woods, so bonny they were, and thick and brave, fine shelter and lithe for the cattle. Nor more than that would he say, it seemed then to Kirsty that he quietened down, and was quiet and queer all his leave, it was daft to let a bit wood go vex him like that.

But the last night of his leave he climbed to Blawearie and he said there was nothing but the woods and their fate that could draw his eyes. For over by the Mains he'd come on the wood-men, teams and teams of them hard at work on the long bit forest that ran up the high brae, sparing nothing they were but the yews of the Manse. And up above Upperhill they had cut down the larch, and the wood was down that lay back of old Pooty's. Folk had told him the trustees had sold it well, they got awful high prices, the trustees did, it was wanted for aero-planes and such-like things. And over at the office he had found the factor and the creature had peeked at Chae through his horn-rimmed glasses and said that the Government would replant all the trees when the War was won. And Chae had said that would console him a bloody lot, sure, if he'd the chance of living two hundred years and seeing the woods grow up as some shelter for beast and man: but he doubted he'd not last so long. Then the factor said thay must all do their bit at a sacrifice, and Chae asked *And what sacrifices have you made, tell me, you scrawny wee mucker?*

That wasn't fair to the factor, maybe, who was a decent childe and not fit to fight, but Chae was so mad he hardly knew what he said, and didn't much care. So when he fell in with old Ellison things were no better. For Ellison'd grown fair big in the mind and the pouch, folk said he was making silver like a dung-heap sourocks; and he'd bought him a car and another piano; and he said *Ow, it's you, Charles lad! Are you home for long?* and he said *And I'll bet you want back to the front line, eh?* And Chae said that he'd be wrong in the betting, faith ay! *Did you ever hear tell of a body of a woman that wanted a new bairn put back in her womb?* And Ellison gowked and said *No.* And Chae said *And neither have I, you gowk-eyed gomeril,* and left him at that; and it was hardly a kindly remark, you would say.

But it seemed the same wherever he went in Kinraddie, except

at the Mill and his father-in-law's: every soul made money and
didn't care a damn though the War outlasted their lives; they
didn't care though the land was shaved of its timber till the
whole bit place would soon be a waste with the wind a-blow
over heath and heather where once the corn came green. At
Cuddiestoun he came on the Munro pair, they were rearing up
hundreds of chickens that year and they sold them at great bit
prices to the Aberdeen hospitals. So busy they were with their
incubators they'd but hardly time to take notice of him, Mistress
Munro snapped and tweeted at him, still like a futret, and the
creature wrinkled its long thin neb: *Ah well, we'll have to get
on with our work. Fine being you and a soldier, Chae, with
your holidays and all. But poor folk aye have to work.* Munro
himself looked shamed at that and coloured all over his ugly
face, poor stock, but he'd hardly time to give Chae a dram, so
anxious he was with a new brood of hens. So Chae left him fell
quick, the place got on his stomach, and syne as he held through
the parks he came bang on Tony, standing right mid-way the
turnip-field. And his eyes were fixed on the ground and God!
he might well have stood there for days by the look of him.
Chae cried out to him *Ay, then, Tony man,* not expecting any
reply, but Tony looked up and aside *Ay, Chae, so the mills of
God still grind?*[12]

And Chae went on, and he thought of that, a real daft-like
speak he thought it at first, but further up the brae as he held
by Upprums, he scratched his head, was the thing so daft? He
stopped and looked back, and there, far below, was the Tony
childe standing, glued to the ground. And Chae shivered in a
way, and went on.

So Chae wandered his round of Kinraddie, a strange place
and desolate with its crash of trees and its missing faces. And
not that alone, for the folk seemed different, into their bones
the War had eaten, they were money-mad or mad with grief for
somebody killed or somebody wounded – like Mistress Gordon
of the Upperhill, all her pride gone now because of the Jock she
had loved and aye called John. But it was Jock she called him
when Chae sat with her in the parlour then, and she told him
the news of her blinded son in the hospital in England. He

wouldn't ever see again, it wasn't just a nervous trouble or anything like that, he'd drawn back the bandages when she went to see him and shown her the great red holes in his head; and syne he'd laughed at her, demented like, and cried: *What think you of your son now, old wife? – the son you wanted to make a name for you with his bravery in Kinraddie? Be proud, be proud, I'll be home right soon to crawl round the parks and I'll show these holes to every bitch in the Mearns that's looking for a hero.* He'd fair screamed the words at his mother and a nurse had come running and soothed him down, she said he didn't know what he said, but Mistress Gordon had never a doubt about that. And she told Chae about it and wept uncovered, her braveness and her Englishness all fair gone; and when Gordon came into the room he looked different too, shrivelled up he was, he'd taken to drink, folk said.

So Chae went out across the parks to the Bridge End then and half-wished that he'd missed the Upperhill. But across the nethermost park below the larch wood he ran into young Maggie Jean, her that Andy the daftie had near mischieved, grown a gey lass, and he hardly knew her. But she knew him fine and smiled at him, blithe and open. *It's Chae Strachan! You look fine as a soldier, Chae! And please can I have a button?* So he cut off a button from his tunic for her and they smiled at each other, and he went out across the fields with a lighter heart then, she was sweet as a sprig of Blawearie 'suckle.

Bridge End he found with Alec away, he'd gone selling sheep in Stonehaven. But Mistress Mutch was there and she sat and smoked at a cigarette and told him that Alec was still a fell patriot, he'd enrolled in the volunteers of Glenbervie and every other night went down to Drumlithie for drill, a sight for sore eyes, the gowks, prancing about like dogs with diarrhœa, that's what they minded her of. And she asked Chae when the War was to end, and Chae said *God only knows* and she asked *And you still believe in Him?* And Chae was real shocked, a man might have doubts and his disbelief, you expected a woman to be different, they needed more support in the world. But now that he thought of God for himself he just couldn't say, there was more of his Enemy over in France, that minded him now

he must give the Reverend Gibbon a look up at the Manse. But
Mistress Mutch said *Haven't you heard, then? Mr Gibbon's
gone, he's a colonel-chaplain in Edinburgh now, or something
like that; and he wears a right brave uniform with a black
hanky across the neck of it. His father's come down to take his
place, an old bit stock that drinks German blood by the gill
with his porridge, by the way he preaches.*

At Pooty's Chae knocked and knocked and got feint the
answer. And folk were to tell him that wasn't surprising, old
Pooty had taken to locking himself in nowadays, he got queerer
and queerer, he said every night he heard men tramping the
roads in the dark, chill hours, and they crept off the roads and
slithered and slipped by the hedges and fields, and he knew
who they were, they were Germans, the German dead from out
of the earth that had come to work ill on Scotland. And even
in the daytime if you but looked quick, right sharp and sudden
between the bending of a bough or the bar of a gate, you'd see
a white German face, distorted still in the last red pain, haunt-
ing the Scottish fields. And that was queer fancying well you
might say.

But Chae knew nothing of the business, he near knocked in
the door of the little house ere he gave it up and went ben the
road to Long Rob's. And Rob saw him coming and turned off
the Mill and ran to meet him; and they sat and argued the rest
of the day, Rob brought out his bottle and they had a bit dram;
and then Rob made them their supper and they'd another long
dram, and they argued far to the wee, small hours. And Chae
swore that he still believed the War would bring a good thing
to the world, it would end the armies and fighting forever, the
day of socialism at last would dawn, the common folk had seen
what their guns could do[13] and right soon they'd use them when
once they came back.

And Rob said *Havers, havers. The common folk when they
aren't sheep are swine, Chae man; you're an exception, being a
goat.*

Well, it was fine enough that long arguing with Rob, but out
in the dark by the side of Chae as they walked along the road
together Rob cried *Oh man, I'd go back with you the morn if*

only – and the words fair seemed to stick in his throat. And Chae asked *If only what, man?* and Rob said *If only I wanted to be easy – easy and a liar. But I've never gone that gait yet and I'm damned if I'll begin for any bit war!*

And what he meant by that Chae didn't know, he left him then and held over the moor land towards the Knapp under the rising moon. And it was there that a strange thing happened to him, maybe he'd drunk over-much of Long Rob's whisky, though his head was steady enough as a rule for thrice the amount he'd drunk. Ah well, the thing was this, that as he went over an open space of the vanished Standing Stones he saw right in front of him a halted cart; and a man had got out of the cart and knelt by the axle and looked at it. And Chae thought it some carter billy from the Netherhill taking the near-cut through the moor, and steered out to go by and cried *Good night, then!* But there wasn't an answer, so he looked again, and no cart was there, the shingly stones shone white and deserted under the light of the moon, the peewits were crying away in the distance. And Chae's hackles fair stood up on end, for it came on him that it was no cart of the countryside he had seen, it was a thing of light wood or basket-work, battered and bent, low behind, with a pole and two ponies yoked to it; and the childe that knelt by the axle had been in strange gear, hardly clad at all, and something had flashed on his head, like a helmet maybe. And Chae stood and swore, his blood running cold, and near jumping from his skin when a pheasant started under his feet with a screech and a whirr and shot away into the dimness. And maybe it was one of the men of old time that he saw there, a Calgacus' man from the Graupius battle when they fought the Romans up from the south; or maybe it had only been the power of Long Rob's Glenlivet.

So that was Chae's round of the countryside, in a blink his leave was gone and Chae had gone with it, folk said he was still the same old Chae, he blithered still about Rich and Poor, you'd have thought the Army would have taught him better. But Chris stuck up for him, Chae was fine, not that she herself cared for the Rich and Poor, she was neither one nor the other herself.

That year the crops came so thick Ewan said they must hire some help, and that they did, an oldish stock from Bervie he was, gey handless at first, John Brigson his name. But he soon got into the set of Blawearie, sleeping in the room that had once been Chris's, and making rare friends with young Ewan, it was lucky they had him. And the harvest came fine and Chris thought it near time that another baby should come to Blawearie. They'd been careful as blithe in the thing so far, but now it was different, Ewan'd love to have another.

And one night went on and then another and she whispered to herself *In the Spring I'll tell him;* and the New Year went by; and then news came up to Blawearie in a wave of gossip from all over the Howe. For the Parliament had passed the Conscription Act,[14] that meant you'd to go out and fight whatever you said, they'd shoot you down if you didn't. And sure as death Ewan soon had his papers sent to him, he'd to go up to Aberdeen and be there examined, he'd been excused before as a farmer childe. Long Rob got his papers on the very same day and he laughed and said *Fine, I'll like a bit jaunt.*

And into Aberdeen they all went, a fair crowd of them then, all in one carriage; and the ploughmen all swore that they didn't care a button were they taken or not; and Ewan knew right well that they wouldn't take him, they didn't take folk that farmed their own land; and Long Rob said nothing, just sat and smoked. So they came to Aberdeen and went to the place and sat in a long, bare room. And a soldier stood near the door of the room and cried out their names one after the other; and Long Rob sat still and smoked his pipe. So they finished at last with the ploughmen childes, the whole jing-bang were passed as soldiers. And they called Long Rob, but he just sat still and smoked his pipe, he wouldn't stir out of his jacket, even. So there was a great bit stir at that, they danced around him and swore at him, but he blew his smoke up in their faces, calm, like a man unvexed by midges met on a summer day.

They gave up the try, they did nothing to him then, he came back to the Howe and sat down at the Mill. But next he was called to appear at Stonehaven, the Exemption Board sat there for the cases;[15] and Rob rode down on his bicycle, smoking his pipe. So they called out his name and in he went and the chairman, a wee grocer man that worked night and day to send other folk out to fight the Germans, he asked Long Rob how he liked the idea that folk called him a coward? And Long Rob said *Fine, man, fine. I'd rather any day be a coward than a corpse.* And they told him he couldn't have exemption and Long Rob lit up his pipe and said that was sad.

Home to the Mill he came again, and that night folk saw him on the round of his parks, standing and smoking and looking at his land and sky, the long rangy childe. Ewan went by fell late that evening and saw him and cried *Ay, Rob!* but the miller said never a word, Ewan went home to Blawearie vexed about that. But Chris said it was just that Long Rob was thinking of the morn, he'd been ordered to report to the Aberdeen barracks.

And the next day passed and all Kinraddie watched from its steadings the ingoings and outgoings of Rob at the Mill; and damn the move all the day long did he make to set out as they'd ordered him. The next day came, the policeman came with it, he rode up to the Mill on his bicycle and bided at the Mill a good two hours and syne rode out again. And folk told later that he'd spent all that time arguing and prigging at Rob to set out. But Rob said *If you want me, carry me!* and faith! the policeman couldn't very well do that, angered though he was, it would look fair daft wheeling Rob along the roads on his bicycle tail. So the policeman went off to Stonehaven and out from it late in the evening there drove a gig, the policeman again, and two home-time soldiers, it needed all three to take Rob of the Mill away to the War. He wouldn't move even then, though he made no struggle, he just sat still and smoked at his pipe, and they'd to carry him out and put him in the gig. And off they drove, that was how Long Rob went off to the War, and what happened to him next there rose this rumour and that, some said he was in jail, some said he'd given in, some said he'd escaped and was hiding in the hills; but nobody knew for sure.

And to Chris it seemed then, Chae gone, Rob gone, that their best friends were out of Kinraddie now, friends close and fine, but they had themselves, Ewan and her and young Ewan. And she held close to them both, working for them, tending them, seeing young Ewan grow straight and strong, with that slim white body of his, like his father's, just; and it made a strange, sweet dizziness go singing in her heart as she bathed him, he stood so strong and white, she would mind that agony that had been hers at the birth of this body, it had been worth it and more. And now she wanted another bairn, Spring was coming, fast and fast, the land smelt of it, the caller sea winds came fresh with the tang that only in Spring they brought, it was nineteen-seventeen. And Chris said in her heart that in April their baby would be conceived.

So she planned and went singing those days about the kitchen of Blawearie toun, busy with this plot, she planned fresh linen and fresh clothes for herself, she grew young and wayward as before she married, and she looked at Ewan with secret eyes. And old John Brigson would cry *Faith, mistress, you're light of heart!*

But Ewan said nothing, strange enough that. She knew then that something troubled him, maybe he was ill and would say nothing about it, sitting so silent at meat and after, it grew worse as the days went on. And when he looked at her no longer was the old look there, but a blank, dark one, and he'd turn his face from her slowly. She was vexed and then frightened and out in the close one morning, over the stillness of the hens' chirawk, she heard his voice raised in cursing at Brigson, it was shameful for him to do that and not like Ewan at all to do it. Then he came back from the steading with quick stepping feet, as he passed through the kitchen Chris cried *What's wrong?* He muttered back *Nothing*, and went up the stairs, and he took no notice of young Ewan that ran after him, bairn-like, to show him some picture in a book he had.

Chris heard him rummage in their room, and then he came down, he was fully dressed, his dark face heavy and stranger than ever, Chris stared at him *Where are you going?* and he snapped *To Aberdeen, if you'd like to know*, and off he went. He had never spoken to her like that – he was EWAN, hers! ... She stood at the window, dazed, looking after him, so strange she must then have looked that little Ewan ran to her, *Mother, mother!* and she picked him up and soothed him and the two of them stood and watched Ewan Tavendale out of sight on the bright Spring road.

It seemed to Chris he had hated her that minute when he looked at her in the kitchen, she went through the day with a twist of sickness about her heart. To old Brigson, shamed for her man, she said that Ewan had been worried with this business and that, he'd been out of his temper that morning and had gone to Aberdeen for the day. And John Brigson said cheerily *Never heed, mistress. He'll be right as rain when he's back the night*, and he helped her wash up the supper things, and they had a fine long talk. Syne off he went to tend to the beasts, and Chris grew anxious, looking at the clock, till she minded that there was a later train still, the ten o'clock train. So she bedded young Ewan and milked the kye, and came back to the kitchen, and waited. John Brigson had gone to his bed, Blawearie was quiet, she went out and walked down to the road to meet Ewan in the fresh-fallen dew of the night – so young the year and so sweet, she'd make it this night, the night with Ewan that she'd planned!

By Peesie's Knapp a snipe was sounding, she stood and listened to the bird, and saw in the starlight the skeleton timbers of the great wood that once fronted the north wind there. A hare scuttled over the road, the ditches were running and trilling, hidden, filled with the waters of Spring, she smelt the turned grass of the ploughlands and shivered in the blow of the wind, Ewan was long on the road. At the turnpike bend she stopped and listened for the sound of his feet, and minded a thing out of childhood then, if you put your ear to the ground you'd hear far off steps long ere you'd hear them when standing and upright. And she laughed to herself, remembering that, and knelt on the ground, agile and fleet, as the Guthries were, and put close her ear to the road, it was cold and crumbly with little stones. She heard a flock of little sounds going home to their buchts, far and near, each sound went home, but never the sound of a footstep.

And then, Stonehaven way, a great car came flashing down

through the night, its headlights leaping from brae to brae, Chris stood back and aside and she saw it go by, there were soldiers in it, one bent on the wheel, she saw the floating ends of his Glengarry bonnet,[16] the car whirled past and was gone in the night. She stared after it, dazed and dreaming, and shivered again. Ewan must have held over the hills and was already at Blawearie, it was daft to be here, he'd be anxious about her and go out seeking *her!*

So she ran back to Blawearie and she got there panting. But her heart was light, she'd play a trick on Ewan, creep in on him quiet as quiet, come up behind him sudden in the kitchen and make him jump. And she padded softly across the close to the kitchen door and looked in, and the lamp stood lit on the table, and the place was quiet in its glow. She went up the stairs to their room, there was no sign of Ewan, young Ewan lay sleeping with his face in the pillow, she righted him away from that and went down to the kitchen again. She sat in a chair there, waiting, and her heart froze and froze with the fears that came up in it, she saw Ewan run over by a car in the streets, and why hadn't they sent her a telegram? But maybe she was wrong, maybe he'd missed the last train and taken one out to Stonehaven instead and was tramping from there in the darkness now. She piled new logs on the fire and sat and waited, and the night went on, she fell fast asleep and waking found the lamp gone out, in the sky between bar and blind was a sharp, dead whiteness like the hand of a corpse. And as she stretched herself, chilled and queer, up in John Brigson's room the alarum clock went. It was half-past five, the night had gone, and still Ewan had not come back.

Nor came he back that day, nor many a day beyond that. For the postman at noon brought Chris a letter, it was from Ewan and she sat in the kitchen and read it, and didn't understand, and her lip hurt, and she put up the back of her hand to wipe it and looked at the hand and saw blood on it. Young Ewan came playing about her, he took the letter out of her hand and ran off with it, screaming with laughter in his young, shrill voice, she sat and did not look after him and he came back and laughed in her face, surprised that she did not play.

And she took him in her arms and asked for the letter again, and again she tried to read it. And what Ewan wrote was he'd grown sick of it all, folk laughing and sneering at him for a coward, Mutch and Munro aye girding at him. He was off to the War, he had joined the North Highlanders that day, he would let her know where they sent him, she wasn't to worry; and *I am yours truly Ewan*.

When John Brigson came in at dinner-time he found Chris looking white as a ghost, but she wasn't dazed any longer, it just couldn't be helped, Ewan was gone but maybe the War would be over before he had finished with his training. And John Brigson said *Of course it will, I see the Germans are retreating on all the fronts, they're fair scared white, they say, when our men take to the bayonet.* Little Ewan wanted to know what a bayonet was and why the Germans were scared at them, and John Brigson told him and Chris was sick, she'd to run out to be sick, for if you've ever gutted a rabbit or a hen you can guess what is inside a man, and she'd seen a bayonet going into Ewan there. And John Brigson was awful sorry, he said he hadn't thought, and she wasn't to worry, Ewan would be fine.

Oh, but that Spring was long! Out in the parks in the daytime she'd go to help John Brigson and ease her weariness, she took little Ewan with her then and a plaid to wrap him in for sleep, under the lithe of a hedge or a whin, when he grew over-tired. And the fields were a comfort, the crumble of the fine earth under your feet, swinging a graip as you walked, breaking dung, the larks above, the horses plodding by with snorting breath, old Brigson a-bend above the shafts. He made fair poor drills, they were better than none, and he aye was pleasant and canty, a fine old stock, he did lots of the things that Ewan had done and asked no more pay for the doing of them. That was as well, he wouldn't have got it, the weather was bitter, corn spoiled in the planting.

Early in the year, about May that was, the rain came down and it seemed it never would end, there was nothing to be done out of doors, the rain came down from the north-east across Kinraddie and Chris wasn't the only one that noted its difference from other years. In Peesie's Knapp there was Mistress Strachan vexing herself in trying to make out the change; and then she minded what Chae had said would happen when the woods came down; once the place had been sheltered and lithe, it poised now up on the brae in whatever storm might come. The woodmen had all finished by then, they'd left a country that looked as though it had been shelled by a German army. Looking out on those storms that May Chris could hardly believe that this was the place she and Will had watched from the window that first morning they came to Blawearie.

And then the very next day as she made the butter, young Ewan was up the stairs with his blocks and books, John Brigson had gone to Mondynes with a load of corn, Chris heard a step in the close, somebody running in a hurry from the rain. Then the door burst open and a soldier came in, panting, in the queerest uniform, a hat with gold lacing and red breeches and leggings, Chris stared at the hat and then at the face. And the soldier cried *Oh, Chris, I believe you don't know me!* and she cried then *Will!* and her arms went round him, they cuddled one the other like children, Chris crying, Will near to crying himself, patting her shoulder and saying *Oh, Chris!*

Then she pushed him away and looked at him and they cuddled each other again and Will danced her all round the kitchen, and little Ewan up the stairs heard the stir and came tearing down and when he saw a strange man holding his mother in his arms he made at Will and whacked his legs and cried, *Away, man!* Will cried *God Almighty, what's this you've got, Chris?* and swung Ewan high and stared in his face and shook his head *You're a fine lad, ay, but you've over-much of your father in you ever to be as bonny as your mother!*

That wasn't true but fine to hear, Chris could hardly get any work done or a meal made ready, so many the things they'd to take through hand, Will sat and smoked and every now and then they'd look one at the other and Will would give a great laugh *Oh Chris, mind this . . . mind that . . . !* And his laughter had tears in it, they were daft, the pair of them. And when old John Brigson came home, they heard the noise of the wheels in the close and Will went out to lend him a hand, the old stock jumped off the cart and made for a fork that was lying to hand, he thought Will a German in that strange bit uniform. But he laughed right heartily when Will said who he was, and the two of them came in for dinner and Will sat at the table's head, in Ewan's place. And as he ate he told them how he came in the uniform, and all the chances and wanderings that were his and Mollie's when they went from Scotland.

And faith! he'd had more than enough of both, for in Argentine, as he'd told Chris already by letter, he'd left his first work after a while, he and Mollie had both learned up the Spanish, and he took a job with a Frenchman then, an awful fine stock. He liked Will well and Will liked him, and he gave Will half of his house to bide in, it was a great ranch out in the parks of that meikle country. So there they had lived and were happy and blithe till the Frenchman had to go to the War. Will had thought of going himself more than once but the Frenchman had told him he'd be a fair fool, he might well be glad there wasn't British conscription; besides, some body or other had to look to the ranch. But in less than two years the Frenchman came back, sore wounded he'd been, and soon as he came Will told him it was *his* turn now, he'd see some of this War for himself. And the Frenchman told him he was fair a fool, but he'd get him a job with the French. So he did, after cables and cables to Paris, and Will said good-bye to Mollie and the Frenchman and the Frenchman's wife, and sailed from Buenos Ayres to Cherbourg; and in Paris they knew all about him, he found himself listed as a sergeant-major in the French Foreign Legion,[17] an interpreter he was, for he knew three languages fine. Then they'd given him a fortnight's leave and here he was.

And when he was alone with Chris that evening and she told him about Ewan down training in Lanark,[18] he said Ewan was either soft or daft or both. *Why did you marry the dour devil, Chris? Did he make you or were you going to have a bairn?* And Chris didn't feel affronted, it was Will that asked, he'd treat her just the same if she owned up to a fatherless bairn once a year, or twice, if it came to that. So she shook her head, *It was just because he was to me as Mollie to you*, and Will nodded to that, *Ah well, we can't help when it gets that way.*

Mind when you wanted to know ... ? And they stood and laughed in the evening, remembering that, and they walked arm in arm up and down the road and Chris forgot her Ewan, forgot young Ewan, forgot all her worries remembering the days when she and Will were bairns together, and the dourness and the loveliness then, and Will asked *Do you mind when we slept together – that last time we did it when the old man had near killed me up in the barn?* And his face grew dark, he still couldn't forgive, he said that folk who ill-treated their children deserved to be shot, father had tormented and spoiled him out of sheer cruelty when he was young. But Chris said nothing to that, remembering the day of father's funeral and how she had wept by his grave in Kinraddie kirkyard.

But she knew she could never tell Will of that, he'd never understand, and they spoke of other things, Will of the Argentine and the life out there, and the smell of the sun and the warm weather and the fruit and flowers and flame of life below the Southern Cross.[19] Chris said *But you'll come back, you and Mollie, to bide in Scotland again?* and Will laughed, he seemed still a mere lad in spite of his foreign French uniform, *Havers, who'd want to come back to this country? It's dead or it's dying – and a damned good job!*

And, daftly, Chris felt a sudden thrust of anger through her heart at that; and then she looked round Kinraddie in the evening light, seeing it so quiet and secure and still, thinking of the seeds that pushed up their shoots from a thousand earthy mouths. Daft of Will to say that: Scotland lived, she could never die, the land would outlast them all, their wars and their Argentines, and the winds come sailing over the Grampians still with their storms and rain and the dew that ripened the crops – long and long after all their little vexings in the evening light were dead and done. And her thoughts went back to the kirkyard, she asked Will would he like to come to the kirk next day, she hadn't been there herself for a year.

He looked surprised and then laughed *You're not getting religious, are you?* as though she had taken to drink. And Chris said *No*, and then thought about that, time to think for once in the pother of the days with Blawearie so quiet above them,

young Ewan and old Brigson asleep. And she said *I don't
believe they were ever religious, the Scots folk, Will – not really
religious like Irish or French or all the rest in the history books.
They've never BELIEVED. It's just been a place to collect and
argue, the kirk, and criticise God*. And Will yawned, he said
maybe, he didn't care one way or the other himself, Mollie in
the Argentine had taken up with the Catholics, and faith! she
was welcome if she got any fun.

So next day they set out for the kirk, the weather had cleared,
blowing wet and sunny in a blink, there were teeth of rainbows
out over Kinraddie, Chris said it was Will's uniform that messed
up the sky. But she was proud of him for all that, how folk
stared as the two of them went down the aisle! Chris was in
her blue, with her new short skirt and long boots, and Will in
his blue and red trousers and leggings, and his jacket with the
gold lace on it and the high collar and the soft fine hat with
the shiny peak. Old Gibbon, him that preached for his son,
near fell down the stairs of the pulpit at sight of Will. But he
recovered fell soon and preached them one of the sermons that
had made such stir throughout the Howe a year or so back, he
told how the German beasts now boiled the corpses of their
own dead men and fed the leavings to pigs. And he ground his
teeth at the Germans, they were so coarse; and he said that
GUD would assuredly smite them.

But folk had grown sick of him and his ragings, there was
only a small attendance to hear him and when they came out
in the end Will said *It's good to be out of that creature's stink!*
Syne Ellison recognised Will and came swaggering over, redder
than ever and fatter than ever, and he cried *If it ain't Will
Guthrie! How are you?* and Will said *Fine*. Most of the folk
seemed pleased to see him, even Mutch and Munro, excepting
the Munro wife herself, she snapped, *And what would you be,
then, Will? They've a man at the picture palace in Stonehaven
that wears breeks just like that*. And Will said *Faith, Mistress
Munro, you're an authority on breeks. I hear you still wear
them at the Cuddiestoun*. Folk standing around gave a snicker
at that, real fine for the futret, she'd met her match.

And Will's leave went by like a shot, he was all over the

Howe in the first few days, up in Fordoun and down in Drumlithie, and everywhere folk made much of him. But after that
he bided nearly all the time by Chris, he helped her or Brigson
in old clothes of Ewan's she'd raked out for him. He went
shooting with father's gun fell often, up in the moor it was
blithe to hear him and his singing, young Ewan would go
wandering up to meet him. And when it came to the end and
the last day, young Ewan in bed and they sat by the fire and the
June night came softly down without, Chris didn't fear at all
for Will, he was clean and happy and quick, things went well
with him. And next morning only young Ewan cried at the
parting, and off he went, it seemed then at Blawearie that more
than Will had gone out of their lives, it was a happy voice that
had sung for itself a chamber in their hearts those weeks he had
been with them.

But the hills flowed up and down, day after day, in their dark
and sunshine, and even those weeks were covered and laid past,
and Chris saw the harvest near, so near, a good harvest again
in spite of the weather; and still the War went on. Sometimes
she'd a note or postcard from Ewan in Lanark, sometimes she
wouldn't hear for week on week till she grew fair alarmed. But
he just said it was that he never could write, he didn't know
how, they were awfully busy and she wasn't to worry.

And then through Kinraddie a motor came driving one day,
it turned at the cross-roads and drove down by the Denburn.
It stopped at the Mill and folk ran to their doors and wondered
who it could be, the place was locked up and deserted-like. And
when the motor stopped a man got out, and another came after,
slow, and he took the arm of the first one, and they went
step-stepping at snail's pace up to the Mill-house and folk could
see no more. But soon the story of it was known all over the
place, it was Long Rob himself come back, he had never given
in, they had put him in prison and ill-used him awful; but he
wouldn't give in whatever they did, he laughed in their faces,
Fine, man, fine. Last he went on the hunger-strike, that was
when you just starved to death to spite them, and grew weaker
and weaker. So they took him from prison to a doctor childe

and the doctor said it was useless to keep him, he'd never be of use to his King and country.

So home at last he had come, folk told he was fairly a wreck, he could hardly stand up and walk or make his own meat, God knows how he ever got into his clothes. And Mutch and Munro wouldn't go near him, neither would Gordon, they said that it served him right, the coarse pro-German. And when Chris heard that there came a stinging pain in her eyes, and she called old John Brigson to yoke a cart and put corn in it, as though taking it to Rob for bruising; and Chris got into the cart as well and took young Ewan on her knee, and off they set from Blawearie. Outside the Mill-house Chris cried on Brigson to stop, and found the basket she'd laid on the bottom of the cart and ran through the close to the kitchen door. It stood half-open, the place was dark with hardly a glimmer from the fire. But she saw someone sitting, she stopped and stared, an old man it seemed with a white, drawn face, his hands fumbling at the lighting of a pipe.

She called *Rob!* and he looked up and she saw his eyes, they were filled with awful things, he cried *Chris! God, is't Chris Guthrie?* She was shaking his hand and his shoulder then, minding things about him, not looking at him, minding the fine neighbour he'd been to her and Ewan in the days they married. And she asked *What are you sitting here for? You should be in your bed*, and Rob said *I'm damned if I should, I've had over-much of bed. I was waiting about for the grocer childe, but he didn't stop, though he knows I'm home. I suppose he's still an ill-will at pro-Germans, like.*

Chris told him never to mind the grocer, and she spoke to him roughly, in case she should weep at the sight of him; and she told him to go out and see John Brigson. Then, soon as he'd hirpled out with his stick she looked round the place and started to clean it, and made a fine fire and a meal with fresh eggs and butter, and oat-cakes and scones and jam, she'd brought the lot from Blawearie. So when Rob came in from his speak with Brigson, there it was waiting him on the table, he blinked and sat down and said in a whisper, *You shouldn't have done this, Chris quean.* But Chris said nothing, just sat him down at the

table and sat there herself and saw that he ate; and when young
Ewan came in with old Brigson she fed them as well; and syne
Brigson set off for the farm at Auchinblae where Rob's horse
and sholtie were housed.

When he'd gone Chris set to work on the place and opened
the windows to the air and cleaned out the rooms and dragged
off the dirty linen from the bed and made it up in a bundle
to take back with her. Syne she baked oat-cakes for Rob and
told him that each day he'd get him a pail of milk from the
Netherhill, till time came when he'd kye of his own again, she'd
arranged for that. And when John Brigson came back in the
evening with horse and sholtie Long Rob was fast asleep in his
chair, they didn't rouse him but spread him his supper, and set
him his breakfast as well, and left a lamp low-burning and clear
beside him, and a hot-water bottle in his bed. Syne they left him
and rode them back to Blawearie, all three were tired, young
Ewan asleep in the arms of Chris, dear to hold him so with his
dark head sleeping against her breast and old Brigson's shoulder
seen as a dark quiet bulking against the night.

Next morning they looked out from Blawearie and saw Rob's
horse and sholtie at graze in a park of the Mill, and Long Rob
himself, a dot in the sunlight, making slow way to the moor
land he'd wrought at so long. And as they looked they heard,
thin and remote, the sound of a song Kinraddie had missed for
many a day. It was *Ladies of Spain*.

Soon maybe the War would end, Chris had dreamt as she
listened to that singing, and they all be back in Kinraddie as
once they had been, Chae and Long Rob and her dark lad,
Ewan himself. So she'd dreamt that morning, she'd never grow
out from long dreamings in autumn dawns like those. And
fruition of dream came soon enough, it was a telegram boy that
came riding his bicycle up to Blawearie. Chris read the telegram,
it was Ewan that had sent it, *Home on leave to-night before
going to France*. She stared at it and the lad that had brought
it, and he asked *Any reply?* and she said *Any what?* and he
asked her again, and she said *No*, and ran into the kitchen and
stared at the writing in the telegram. He was going to France.

It lingered at the back of her mind, dark, like a black cat creeping at the back of a hedge, she saw the fluff of its fur or the peek of its eyes, a wild and sinister thing in the sunlight; but you would not look often or see those eyes, how they glared at you. He was going out there, where the sky was a troubled nightmare and the earth shook night and day, into the lands of the coarse French folk, her Ewan, her lad with his dark, dear face and that quick, blithe blush. And suddenly she was filled with a weeping pity in her heart for him, a pity that brought no tears to her eyes, he must never see her shed tears all the time he was with her, he'd go out to the dark, far land with memories of her and Blawearie that were shining and brave and kind.

So all that forenoon she fled and bustled from room to room, brightening the place, she brought out fresh sheets and pillows for the bed she had found so lonely, she sent out young Ewan to gather roses and honeysuckle to set in a jar on the ledge above the bed. And she hung new curtains there and brought out Ewan's clothes and brushed them, he'd want to get out of his uniform, they were sick of the khaki the men that came back. Then she made a great baking against his coming, so much that she'd hardly time to make dinner for young Ewan and Brigson, but they didn't care, they were both excited as herself. She knew the train he would come by, the half-past five, and she swept and dusted the kitchen and set his tea, and punched a great cushion ready for his chair, and dressed herself in the blue he liked and young Ewan in his brave brown cords. John Brigson cried *This is hardly the place for me with your man come home, I'll away to Bervie then for the night.*

Off he set, Chris waved to the old, kind childe as he bicycled down Blawearie brae. And then she ran back, ben to the parlour to look at herself in the mirror again, in the long glass her figure seemed blithe and slim even still, she'd be fine to sleep with yet, she supposed – oh, Ewan! Her face hadn't changed, it was flushed and fair, the eyes maybe older, but shining and bright. And she finished with that looking and went over the close to stand by the side of young Ewan, looking down the hill for his father coming up. The sun flung the long shadows of Blawearie and the beeches far in the east, and across the Den, high in the fields of Upperhill, a lost sheep baaed in the whins.

She had hardly been able to believe it him, lying awake after he slept, he slept with a snoring breath and fuddled mumblings, bulging out against her so that she had but little of the bed and less of the blankets. She closed her eyes and pressed her knuckles against her teeth that the pain might waken her, that she might know Ewan hadn't come home, was still the same Ewan she'd dreamt of in the silence of the night and her own lonely bed. But he moved, flinging out an arm that struck her across the face, she lay still below it, then it wabbled away. She took her knuckles from her mouth and lay quiet then, no need for her to hurt herself now.

Drunk he had come from the station and more than two hours late. Standing at last in the kitchen in his kilts he'd looked round and sneered *Hell, Chris, what a bloody place!* as she ran to him. And he'd flung his pack one way and his hat the other and kissed her as though she were a tink, his hands on her as quickly as that, hot and questing and wise as his hands had never been. She saw the hot smoulder fire in his eyes then, but no blush on his face, it was red with other things. But she smothered her horror and laughed, and kissed him and struggled from him, and cried *Ewan, who's this?*

Young Ewan held back, shy-like, staring, and just said *It's father*. At that the strange, swaying figure in the tartan kilts laughed, coarse-like, *Well, we'll hope so, eh Chris? Any supper left – unless you're too bloody stand-offish even to have that?*

She couldn't believe her own ears. *Stand-offish? Oh, Ewan!* and ran to him again, but he shook her away, *Och, all right, I'm wearied. For Christ's sake let a man sit down.* He staggered to the chair she'd made ready for him, a picture-book of young Ewan's lay there, he picked the thing up and flung it to the other side of the room, and slumped down into the chair. *Hell, what a blasted climb to a blasted place. Here, give us some tea.*

She sat beside him to serve him, she knew her face had gone white. But she poured the tea and spread the fine supper she'd been proud to make, it might hardly have been there for the notice he paid it, drinking cup after cup of the tea like a beast at a trough. She saw him clearer then, the coarse hair that sprang like short bristles all over his head, the neck with its red and angry circle about the collar of the khaki jacket, a great half-healed scar across the back of his hand glinted putrescent blue. Suddenly his eyes came on her, *Well, damn't, is that all you've to say to me now I've come home? I'd have done better to spend the night with a tart in the town.*

She didn't say anything, she couldn't, the tears were choking in her throat and smarting and biting at her eyelids, pressing to come, the tears that she'd sworn she'd never shed all the time he was home on leave. And she didn't dare look at him lest he should see, but he saw and pushed back his chair and got up in a rage, *God Almighty, what are you snivelling about now? You always were snivelling, I mind.* And out he went, young Ewan ran to her side and flung his arms round her, *Mother, don't cry, I don't like him, he's a tink, that soldier!* She'd pressed back the tears then, *Whist, Ewan, never say that again;* and got up and cleared off the supper things and went out to the close and cried gently *Ewan!*

He cried back *All right, all right!* still angrily; and at that some anger kindled within herself, she didn't wait for him to come back but turned and took young Ewan in her arms and climbed the stairs and put him to bed, he was vexed and troubled about her, kissing her as he lay there. *Sleep with me to-night, mother.* She laughed at him, she was sleeping with his father to-night, he must be good and sleep himself, quick and quick, there'd be such fun with father the morn. He said *I'll try,* and closed his eyes and she went down the stairs, it was dark there, getting on for eight. She thought Ewan was still outside but as she made for the lamp something stirred in the chair, she thought it a cat, it was Ewan. He caught her and pulled her on to his knees and said *Be stand-offish now if you can, what the devil do you think I've come home for?*

It had been like struggling with someone deep in a nightmare, when the blankets are over your head and you can barely breathe, awful she should come to think that of Ewan. But it wasn't Ewan, her Ewan, someone coarse and strange and strong

had come back in his body to torment her. He laughed as he
fought her there in the chair and held her tight and began to
tell stories – oh, he was drunk and didn't know what he said,
terrible and sickening things, he'd had women when he pleased
in Lanark, he said. And he whispered of them to her, his breath
was hot on her face, she saw the gleam of his teeth, he told her
how he'd lain with them and the things he'd done. Sickened
and shamed she had felt and then worse than that, stopping
from struggling, a shameful, searing desire come on her. And
he knew, he knew at once, he said *Well, now that you know
you can get!*

She had picked herself up from the floor and in a dream went
out to milk the kye, leaving him there. When she came back he
had gone from the kitchen, she was slow to finish sieving and
skimming the milk and go up to the room she'd made ready
that morning, singing she had made it ready. And up there he
waited her, lying in the bed, he'd carried up a lamp from the
kitchen, they who'd always gone to bed in the darkness and
thought it fine to lie in each other's arms in the night-glimmer
from the window. But now he grumbled *For God's sake hurry
up!* and when she made to put out the light – *I'll do that, come
on!* And she lay beside him and he took her.

She remembered that now, lying in the darkness the while he
slept, why he had left the lamp alight; and at memory of that
foulness something cold and vile turned and turned like a wheeling mirror inside her brain. For it had been other things than
his beast-like mauling that had made her whisper in agony, *Oh
Ewan, put out the light!* The horror of his eyes upon her she
would never forget, they burned and danced on that mirror
that wheeled and wheeled in her brain.[20]

So that was Ewan's homecoming on leave and the days that
went by were the same as that first night foreshadowed. He had
gone away Ewan Tavendale, he came back a man so coarse and
cruel that in place of love hate came singing in the heart of
Chris – hate that never found speech, that but slowly found
lodgement secure and unshaken. For often it seemed to her that
a tortured, tormented thing looked out from Ewan's eyes while

he told them his foulest tale, ill-used old Brigson and jeered at him, came drunken back to Blawearie night after night – that tortured thing that was the lost lad she had married. But the fancy wilted and vanished as the days went by. He stayed five days, had his breakfast in bed, and never got up till dinner-time; he never looked at the parks or stock or took notice of young Ewan; he dressed in his khaki and kilts alone, and to Chris's suggestion that he wear a suit – *What, me dress up like [a] bloody conchy? I'll leave that to your friend, Rob Duncan.*

Every day he went swaggering down the road and was off to Drumlithie or Stonehaven or Fordoun, drinking there. Before he went he'd ask for money, Chris gave him all that he asked, not saying a word, but he'd fancy a reluctance and sneer at her. Wasn't he entitled to what was his own? Did she think him still the young fool he had been, content to slave and slave at Blawearie – *without as much as a dram to savour the soss, or a quean or so at night to waken your blood – nothing but a wife you hardly dared touch in case you put her in the family way, eh Chris?*

He would say this at dinner-time, sneering and boasting, old Brigson would colour and look down at his plate and young Ewan stare and stare at his father till Ewan would say *God, what a damned glower! Eyes like your mother and a nature the same;* and he'd swear at the bairn, it was shameful to hear that. He'd made friends with Mutch, him that once he could hardly abide, and with him he went driving each night on their drunken sprees. As he went to bed John Brigson would look at Chris with trouble in his kind old eyes, but she didn't dare say a thing to him, he'd go stamping slow up above her head the while she sat down to await Ewan's return and have the hirpling note of the clock stamp each second in her heart, hating him home, wanting him home.

For after that first night he had ceased to touch her, she would lie beside him, quivering and waiting. And he'd lie quiet, she knew him awake and knew that he knew what she waited; and it was as though he were a cat that played with a mouse, he would laugh out after a while and then go to sleep, she herself to lie tortured in the hours thereafter. The last night she refused the torment, she got up near three o'clock and kindled a fire and made herself tea and watched the morning come down the hill passes – a fine summer morning, yellow and grey and lovely with its chirping of birds in the beeches. And suddenly then, as always these changes took her, she was calm and secure, putting Ewan from her heart, locking it up that he never could vex her again, she was finished with him, either loving or hating. And at that release she rose and went slow about her work, a great load had gone from her then, John Brigson coming down in the morning heard her sing and was cheery himself, cheery with relief, but she sang her release.

At nine o'clock Ewan cried down from his room *When the hell are you bringing some breakfast?* She took no notice of that, but she sent young Ewan out to play and then went on with her work. And at last she heard a clatter on the stairs, and there he stood at the kitchen entrance, glaring at her *Have you gone clean deaf?* She answered him then, raising her head and looking at him, *If you're in need of a breakfast – get it.*

He said *You bitch!* and he made to strike her. But she caught up a knife from the table, she had it waiting there nearby, he swore and drew back. She nodded and smiled at that, calm, and put the knife down and went on with her work.

So he made his own tea, grumbling and swearing, a fine send-off this for a man that was going to France to do his bit. And Chris listened to the catch-phrase, contempt in her heart, she looked at him with a curling lip, and he saw her look and swore at her, but was frightened for all that, always now she knew she had known him the frightened one. And a queer, cold curiosity came on her then that so she should have slaved to tend him and love him and give him the best, body and mind and soul she had given, for a gift to the body of a drunken lout from the plough-stilts.

And now that body she saw with a cold repulsion him wash and shave and dress, she could hardly bear to look at him and went out and worked in the close, cleaning pots there in the shining weather, young Ewan played douce and content with his toys, it was hay-time all down the Howe and the hens came pecking around her. She heard Ewan stamp about in the kitchen, he wanted that she should look, go running and fetch him his things. And she smiled again, cold and secure and serene, and heard him come out and bang the door; and without raising her head she saw him then. He was all in his gear, the Glengarry on his head, his pack on his shoulder, his kilts a-swing, and he went past her jauntily, but she knew he expected her to stop him, to run after him and throw her arms about him: she saw in his eyes as he went by the fear that she'd pay no heed.

And none she paid, she did not speak, she did not unbend, young Ewan stopped from his playing and looked after his father incuriously, as at a strange alien that went from the place. At the gate of the close, as he banged it behind him, Ewan stooped to sort up his garters, red in the face, not looking at her still. And she paid him no heed.

He swung the pack on his shoulders then and went slow down the road to the turnpike bend, she saw that from the kitchen window, knew he believed she would cry to him at the last. And she smiled, cold and sure, that she knew him so, every action and thought, and why he stood there at last, not trying to look back. He fumbled for matches and lighted his pipe as she watched; and a cloud came over the sun and went on with Ewan, the two of them went down the turnpike then together, out of her sight in the shadow and flame of the bright sun weather, it was strange and impossibly strange. She stood long staring down at that point where he'd vanished, sharp under her breast, tearing her body, her heart was breaking, and she did not care! She was outside and away from its travail and agony, he had done all to her that he ever could now, he who had tramped down the road in that shadow that fled from the sun.

And then it was she found no salvation at all may endure forever, or beyond the pitch that the heart may bear it, she was weeping and weeping, her arms flung over the kitchen table, weeping for that Ewan who had never come back, for the shamed, tormented boy with the swagger airs she had let go from Blawearie without a kiss or a parting word. *Ewan, Ewan!* her heart cried then, breaking and breaking, *Oh Ewan, I didn't mean it!* Ewan – he was hers, hers still in spite of all he had done and said, he had lived more close in her body than the heart that broke now, young Ewan was his, Oh God, she had never let him go like that! And in her desolation of weeping she began to pray, she had known it useless, but she prayed and prayed for him to come back, to kiss her and hold her in kindness just once before he went down that road. She ran wild-eyed and weeping to the close and there was John Brigson, he stared dumbfounded as she cried *Oh, don't let him go, run after him, John!*

And syne he said he didn't understand, if she meant her man, it was more than an hour since Ewan had gone down the road, he'd heard long syne the whistle of his train out across the hills.

It was a month before she heard from him, and then only a scrape and a score on a thing they called a field postcard, written somewhere in France; and it said no more than that he was well. No more than a whisper out of the dark cave of days into which he had gone, it yet salved her mind from the searing agony that tormented the early weeks. They would never be the same again, but some day he would come back to her, their madness forgotten, back to her and young Ewan and Blawearie when the War was done, they'd forget and forget, busy themselves in new hours and seasons, there would never be fire and gladness between them again but still undying the labour of the fields in which she now buried her days.

For she sank herself in that, the way to forget, she was hardly indoors from dawn to dusk in all the range of the harvest weather, running down the bouts behind the binder that John Brigson drove, little Ewan running and laughing beside her. He thought it a fun and a play she made, stooking and stooking so quickly then, her hands became as machines, tireless and quick and ceaseless through the long hours, she stooked so quickly that with an extra hour each evening, old Brigson helping her, she was close to the uncut rigs again. Corn and the shining hollow stalks of the straw, they wove a pattern about her life, her nights and days, she would creep to bed and dream of the endless rigs and her hands in the night would waken her, all

pins and needles they would be. Once she went ben to the
parlour to look in the glass and saw then why pity came often
in old Brigson's eyes, she was thinner than ever she'd been, her
face was thin, it seemed to her some gloss had gone from her
hair, her eyes grown dull and patient and pupil-less; like the
eyes of a cow.

So, hurt and dazed, she turned to the land, close to it and the
smell of it, kind and kind it was, it didn't rise up and torment
your heart, you could keep at peace with the land if you gave
it your heart and hands, tended it and slaved for it, it was
wild and a tyrant, but it was not cruel. And often, in the
night-stooking with old John Brigson near, a ghost of gladness
would come to her then, working under the coming of the
moon before the evening dew came pringling over Kinraddie,
night-birds whistling over the fields, so quiet, so quiet, stilling
away the pain in her body, the pain in her heart that this reaping
and harvesting had brought.

And then Long Rob of the Mill came up to Blawearie. He
came one morning as they started the yavil, he came through
the close and into the kitchen, long and as rangy as ever he was,
his face filled out and his eyes the same, and he cried *How's
Chris? Bonny as ever!* And he caught young Ewan up on his
shoulder and Ewan looked down at him, dark and grave, and
smiled, and thought him fine.

Rob had come over to help, he'd no cutting to do; and when
Chris said nay, he mustn't leave the Mill, he twinkled his eyes
and shook his head. And Chris knew he'd have little loss, folk
changed and were changing again, not a soul had driven his
corn cart to the Mill since Long Rob came back. He'd had
nothing to do but pleiter about from park to park and look out
on the road for the custom that never came; and if any came
now it could damn well wait, he'd come up to stook Blawearie.

So the two went down to the park, young Ewan went with
them, and they stooked it together, the best of the crop, Rob
cheery as ever it seemed to Chris. But sometimes his eyes would
wander up to the hills, like a man seeking a thing he had never
desired, and into the iron-blue eyes a shadow like a dark,
quiet question would creep. Maybe he minded the jail and its

torments then, he spoke never of that, and never a word of the War, nor Chris, all the stooking of the yavil park. Strange she had hardly known him before, Long Rob of the Mill, unco and atheist; he'd been only the miller with the twinkling eyes, his singings by morn and his whistlings by night, his stories of horses till your head fair reeled. Now it seemed she had known him always, closely and queerly, she felt queer, as though shy, when she sat by his side at the supper table and he spoke to old Brigson that night. The pallor of the jail came out in the lamp-light, under the brown that the sun had brought, and she saw his hand by the side of her hand, thin and strong, the miller's horse-taming hand.

He bedded young Ewan that night, for a play, and sung him to sleep, Chris and old Brigson heard the singing as they sat in the kitchen below, *Ladies of Spain* and *There was a Young Farmer* and *A' the Blue Bonnets are Over the Border*. Hardly anybody left in Kinraddie sang these songs, it was full of other tunes from the bothy windows now, *Tipperary* and squawling English things, like the squeak of a rat that is bedded in syrup, the *Long, Long Trail*[21] and the like. It was queer and eerie, listening to Rob, like listening to an echo from far in the years at the mouth of a long lost glen.

And she never knew when and how in the days that followed, it came on her silently, secretly, out of the earth itself, maybe, the knowledge she was Rob's to do with as he willed, she willed. She wanted more than the clap of his hand on her shoulder as they finished the bout at evening and up through the shadows took their slow way, by parkside and dyke, to the close that hung drenched with honeysuckle smell. She wanted more than his iron-blue eye turned on her, warm and clean and kind though she felt her skin colour below that gaze, she wanted those things that now all her life she came to know she had never known – a man to love her, not such a boy as the Ewan that had been or the poor demented beast he'd become.

And if old John Brigson guessed of those things that whispered so shamelessly there in her heart he gave never a sign, wise and canny and kind. And no sign that he knew did Rob give either, swinging by her side in the harvest that drew to its end. And in Chris as she bent and straightened and stooked the last day was a prayer to the earth and fields, a praying that this harvest might never end, that she and Long Rob would tramp it forever. But the binder flashed its blades at the head of the last, long bout, and Long Rob had his hand on her shoulder, *He's finished, Chris quean, and it's clyak!*

That evening she went out with him to the gate of the close, and he swung his coat on his shoulder, *Well, well, Chris lass, I've liked this fine.* And then, not looking at her, he added *I'm away to Aberdeen to enlist the morn.*

For a moment she was stupefied and stared at him silently, but she had no place in his thoughts, he was staring across Kinraddie's stooked fields. And then he began to tell her, he'd resolved on this days before, he couldn't stay out of it longer, all the world had gone daft and well he might go with the rest, there was neither trade nor trust for him here, or rest ever again till this War was over, if it ever ended at all. *So I'm giving in at last, I suppose they'll say. And this is ta-ta, Chris; mind on me kindly some times.*

She held to his hand in the gloaming light and so he looked down at last, she was biting her lips to keep down the tears, but he saw them shine brimming then in her eyes. And his own changed, changed and were kind and then something else, he cried *Why, lass!* and his hand on her shoulder drew her close, she was close and against him, held tight so that she felt the slow beat of his heart, she wanted to rest there, safe and safe in these corded arms. And then she minded that to-morrow he'd be gone, it cried through the evening in every cry of the lapwings, *So near, so near!* So this also ended as everything else, every thing she had ever loved and desired went out to the madness beyond the hills on that ill road that flung its evil white ribbon down the dusk. And it was her arms then that went round his neck, drawing down his head and kissing him, queer and awful to kiss a man so, kissing him till she heard his breath come quick, and he gripped her, pleading with her, *We're daft, Chris quean, we mustn't!* But she knew then she had won, she wound her arms about him, she whispered *The haystacks!* and he carried her there, the smell of the clover rose crushed and pungent and sweet from under her head; and lying so in the dark, held to him, kissing him, she sought with lips and limbs and blood to die with him then.

But that dark, hot cloud went by, she found herself still lying there, Rob was there, and she drew his head to her breast, lying so with him, seeing out below the rounded breasts of the haystacks the dusky red of the harvest night, this harvest gathered to herself at last, reaped and garnered and hers in her heart and body. So they were for hours, John Brigson never called out to them; and then she stood beside Rob at the head of the road again, drowsy and quiet and content. They made no promises, kissing for last, she knew already he was growing remote from her, his eyes already remote to that madness that beckoned beyond the hills. So it was that he went from her next, she heard him go step-stepping slow with that swinging stride of his down through the darkness, and she never saw him again, was never to see him again.

It had burned up as a fire in a whin-bush, that thing in her life, and it burned out again and was finished. She went about the Blawearie biggings next day singing under breath to herself, quiet and unvexed, tending to hens and kye, seeing to young Ewan's sleep in the day and the setting of old Brigson's supper ere he came at night. She felt shamed not at all, all the vexing fears had gone from her, she made no try to turn from the eyes in the glass that looked out at her, wakened and living again. She was glad she'd gone out with Long Rob, glad and content, they were one and the same now, Ewan and her.

So the telegram boy that came riding to Blawearie found her singing there in the close, mending young Ewan's clothes. She heard the click of the gate and he took the telegram out of his wallet and gave it to her and she stared at him and then at her hands. They were quivering like the leaves of the beech in the forecoming of rain, they quivered in a little mist below her eyes. Then she opened the envelope and read the words and she said there was no reply, the boy swung on his bicycle again and rode out, riding and leaning he clicked the gate behind him; and laughed back at her for the cleverness of that.

She stood up then, she put down her work on the hackstock and read again in the telegram, and began to speak to herself till that frightened her and she stopped. But she forgot to be frightened, in a minute she was speaking again, the chirawking hens in the close stopped and came near and turned up bright eyes to her loud and toneless whispering, *What do I do – oh, what do I do?*

She was vexed and startled by that – what was it she did? Did she go out to France and up to the front line, maybe, into a room where they'd show her Ewan lying dead, quiet and dead, white and bloodless, sweat on his hair, killed in action? She went out to the front door and waved to the harvesters, Brigson, young Ewan, and a tink they'd hired, they saw her and stared till she waved again and then John Brigson abandoned the half-loaded cart and came waddling up the park, so slow he was, *Did you cry me, Chris?*

Sweat on his hair as sweat on Ewan's. She stared at that and held out the telegram, he wiped slow hands and took it and read it, while she clung to the door-post and whispered and whispered *What is it I do now, John? Have I to go out to France?* And at last he looked up, his face was grizzled and hot and old, he wiped the sweat from it, slow. *God, mistress, this is sore news, but he's died like a man out there, your Ewan's died fine.*

But she wouldn't listen to that, wanting to know the thing she must do; and not till he told her that she did nothing, they could never take all the widows to France and Ewan must already be buried, did she stop from that twisting of her hands and ceaseless whisper. Then anger came, *Why didn't you tell me before? Oh, damn you, you liked tormenting me!* and she turned from him into the house and ran up the stairs to the bed, the bed that was hers and Ewan's, and lay on it, and put her hands over her ears trying not to hear a cry of agony in a lost French field, not to think that the body that had lain by hers, frank and free and kind and young, was torn and dead and unmoving flesh, blood twisted upon it, not Ewan at all, riven and terrible, still and dead when the harvest stood out in Blawearie's land and the snipe were calling up on the loch and the beech trees whispered and rustled. And SHE KNEW THAT IT WAS A LIE!

He wasn't dead, he could never have died or been killed for nothing at all, far away from her over the sea, what matter to him their War and their fighting, their King and their country? Kinraddie was his land, Blawearie his, he was never dead for those things of no concern, he'd the crops to put in and the loch to drain and her to come back to. It had nothing to do with Ewan this telegram. They were only tormenting her, cowards and liars and bloody men, the English generals and their like down there in London. But she wouldn't bear it, she'd have the law on them, cowards and liars as she knew them to be!

It was only then that she knew she was moaning, dreadful to hear; and they heard it outside, John Brigson heard it and nearly went daft, he caught up young Ewan and ran with him into the kitchen and then to the foot of the stairs; and told him to go up to his mother, she wanted him. And young Ewan came, it was his hand tugging at her skirts that brought her out of that moaning coma, and he wasn't crying, fearsome the sounds though she made, his face was white and resolute, *Mother, mother!* She picked him up then and held him close, rocking in an agony of despair because of that look on his face, that lost look and the smouldering eyes he had. *Oh Ewan, your father's dead!* she told him the lie that the world believed. And she wept at last, blindly, freeingly, for a little, old Brigson was to say it was the boy that had saved her from going mad.

But throughout Kinraddie the news went underbreath that mad she'd gone, the death of her man had fair unhinged her. For still she swore it was a lie, that Ewan wasn't dead, he could never have died for nothing. Kirsty Strachan and Mistress Munro came up to see her, they shook their heads and said he'd died fine, for his country and his King he'd died, young Ewan would grow up to be proud of his father. They said that sitting at tea, with long faces on them, and then Chris laughed, they quivered away from her at that laugh.

Country and King?[22] *You're havering, havering! What have they to do with my Ewan, what was the King to him, what*

their damned country? Blawearie's his land, it's not his wight
that others fight wars!

She went fair daft with rage then, seeing the pity in their
faces. And also it was then, and then only, staring through an
angry haze at them, that she knew at last she was living a dream
in a world gone mad. Ewan was dead, they knew it and she
knew it herself; and he'd died for nothing, for nothing, hurt
and murdered and crying for her, maybe, killed for nothing:
and those bitches sat and spoke of their King and country. . . .

They ran out of the house and down the brae, and, panting,
she stood and screamed after them. It was fair the speak of
Kinraddie next day the way she'd behaved, and nobody else
came up to see her. But she'd finished with screaming, she went
quiet and cold. Mornings came up, and she saw them come,
she minded that morning she'd sent him away and she might
not cry him back. Noons with their sun and rain came over the
Howe and she saw the cruelty and pain of life as crimson
rainbows that spanned the horizons of the wheeling hours.
Nights came soft and grey and quiet across Kinraddie's fields,
they brought neither terror nor hope to her now. Behind the
walls of a sanity cold and high, locked in from the lie of life,
she would live, from the world that had murdered her man for
nothing, for a madman's gibberish heard in the night behind
the hills.

And then Chae Strachan came home at last on leave, he came
home and came swift to Blawearie. She met him out by the
kitchen door, a sergeant by then, grown thinner and taller, and
he stopped and looked in her frozen face. Then, as her hand
dropped down from his, he went past her with swinging kilts,
into the kitchen, and sat him down and took off his bonnet.
Chris, I've come to tell you of Ewan.

She stared at him, waking, a hope like a fluttering bird in her
breast. *Ewan? Chae – Chae, he's not living?* And then, as he
shook his head, the frozen wall came down on her heart again.
Ewan's dead, don't vex yourself hoping else. They can't hurt
him more, even this can't hurt him, though I swore I'd tell you
nothing about it. But I know right well you should know it,

Chris. Ewan was shot as a coward and deserter out there in France.

        *   *   *   *

Chae had lain in a camp near by and had heard of the thing by chance, he'd read Ewan's name in some list of papers that was posted up. And he'd gone the night before Ewan was shot, and they'd let him see Ewan, and he'd heard it all, the story he was telling her now – *better always to know what truth's in a thing, for lies come creeping home to roost on unco rees, Chris quean. You're young yet, you've hardly begun to live, and I swore to myself that I'd tell you it all, that you'd never be vexed with some twisted bit in the years to come. Ewan was shot as a deserter, it was fair enough, he'd deserted from the front line trenches.*

He had deserted in a blink of fine weather between the rains that splashed the glutted rat-runs of the front. He had done it quickly and easily, he told to Chae, he had just turned and walked back. And other soldiers that met him had thought him a messenger, or wounded, or maybe on leave, none had questioned him, he'd set out at ten o'clock in the morning and by afternoon, taking to the fields, was ten miles or more from the front. Then the military policemen came on him and took him, he was marched back and court-martialled and found to be guilty.

And Chae said to him, they sat together in the hut where he waited the coming of the morning, *But why did you do it, Ewan? You might well have known you'd never get free.* And Ewan looked at him and shook his head, *It was that wind that came with the sun, I minded Blawearie, I seemed to waken up smelling that smell. And I couldn't believe it was me that stood in the trench, it was just daft to be there. So I turned and got out of it.*

In a flash it had come on him, he had wakened up, he was daft and a fool to be there; and, like somebody minding things done in a coarse wild dream there had flashed on him memory of Chris at Blawearie and his last days there, mad and mad he had been, he had treated her as a devil might, he had tried to hurt her and maul her, trying in the nightmare to waken, to make her waken him up; and now in the blink of sun he saw her face as last he'd seen it while she quivered away from his taunts. He knew he had lost her, she'd never be his again, he'd known it in that moment he clambered back from the trenches; but he knew that he'd be a coward if he didn't try though all hope was past.

So out he had gone for that, remembering Chris, wanting to reach her, knowing as he tramped mile on mile that he never would. But he'd made her that promise that he'd never fail her, long syne he had made it that night when he'd held her so bonny and sweet and a quean in his arms, young and desirous and kind. So mile on mile on the laired French roads: she was lost to him, but that didn't help, he'd to try to win to her side again, to see her again, to tell her nothing he'd said was his saying, it was the foulness dripping from the dream that devoured him. And young Ewan came into his thoughts, he'd so much to tell her of him, so much he'd to say and do if only he might win to Blawearie. . . .

Then the military policemen had taken him and he'd listened to them and others in the days that followed, listening and not listening at all, wearied and quiet. *Oh, wearied and wakened at last, Chae, and I haven't cared, they can take me out fine and shoot me to-morrow, I'll be glad for the rest of it, Chris lost to me through my own coarse daftness. She didn't even come to give me a kiss at good-bye, Chae, we never said good-bye; but I mind the bonny head of her down-bent there in the close. She'll never know, my dear quean, and that's best – they tell lies about folk they shoot and she'll think I just died like the rest; you're not to tell her.*

Then he'd been silent long, and Chae'd had nothing to say, he knew it was useless to make try for reprieve, he was only a sergeant and had no business even in the hut with the prisoner. And then Ewan said, sudden-like, it clean took Chae by surprise, *Mind the smell of dung in the parks on an April morning, Chae? And the peewits over the rigs? Bonny they're flying this night in Kinraddie, and Chris sleeping there, and all the Howe happèd in mist.* Chae said that he mustn't mind about that, he was feared that the dawn was close; and Ewan should be thinking of other things now, had he seen a minister? And Ewan said that an old bit billy had come and blethered, an officer creature, but he'd paid no heed, it had nothing to do with him. Even as he spoke there rose a great clamour of guns far up in the front, it was four miles off, not more; and Chae thought of the hurried watches climbing to their posts and the blash and flare of the Verey lights,[23] the machine-gun crackle from pits in the mud, things he himself mightn't hear for long: Ewan'd never hear it at all beyond this night.

And not feared at all he looked, Chae saw, he sat there in his kilt and shirt-sleeves, and he looked no more than a young lad still, his head between his hands, he didn't seem to be thinking at all of the morning so close. For he started to speak of Blawearie then and the parks that he would have drained, though he thought the land would go fair to hell without the woods to shelter it. And Chae said that he thought the same, there were sore changes waiting them when they went back; and then he minded that Ewan would never go back, and could near have bitten his tongue in half, but Ewan hadn't noticed, he'd been speaking of the horses he'd had, Clyde and old Bess, fine beasts, fine beasts – did Chae mind that night of lightning when they found Chris wandering the fields with those two horses? That was the night he had known she liked him well – *nothing more than that, so quick and fierce she was, Chae man, she guarded herself like a queen in a palace, there was nothing between her and me till the night we married. Mind that – and the singing there was, Chae? What was it that Chris sang then?*

And neither could remember that, it had vexed Ewan a while, and then he forgot it, sitting quiet in that hut on the edge of morning. Then at last he'd stood up and gone to the window and said *There's bare a quarter of an hour now, Chae, you'll need to be getting back*.

And they'd shaken hands, the sentry opened the door for Chae, and he tried to say all he could for comfort, the foreshadowing of the morning in Ewan's young eyes was strange and terrible, he couldn't take out his hand from that grip. And all that Ewan said was *Oh man, mind me when next you hear*

*the peewits over Blawearie – look at my lass for me when you
see her again, close and close, for that kiss that I'll never give
her.* So he'd turned back into the hut, he wasn't feared or crying,
he went quiet and calm; and Chae went down through the hut
lines grouped about that place, a farm-place it had been, he'd
got to the lorry that waited him, he was cursing and weeping
then and the driver thought him daft, he hadn't known himself
how he'd been. So they'd driven off, the wet morning had come
crawling across the laired fields, and Chae had never seen Ewan
again, they killed him that morning.[24]

*   *   *   *

This was the story Chae told to Chris, sitting the two of them
in the kitchen of Blawearie. Then he moved and got up and she
did the same, and like one coming from a far, dark country,
she saw his face now, he'd been all that time but a voice in the
dark. And at last she found speech herself *Never vex for me or
the telling me this, it was best, it was best!*

She crept up the stairs to their room when he'd gone, she
opened the press where Ewan's clothes were, and kissed them
and held them close, those clothes that had once been his near
as ever he'd come to her now. And she whispered then in the
stillness, with only the beech for a listener, *Oh, Ewan, Ewan,
sleep quiet and sound now, lad, I understand! You did it for
me, and I'm proud and proud, for me and Blawearie, my dear,
my dear – sleep quiet and brave, for I've understood!*

The beech listened and whispered, whispered and listened,
on and on. And a strange impulse and urge came on Chris
Tavendale as she too listened. She ran down the stairs and
found young Ewan and kissed him, *Let's go a jaunt up to the
hill.*

Below them, Kinraddie; above, the hill; the loch shimmering
and sleeping in the autumn sun; young Ewan at her feet; the
peewits crying down the Howe.

She gave a long sigh and withdrew her hand from the face of
the Standing Stone. The mist of memories fell away and the
aching urge came back – for what, for what? Sun and sky and

the loneliness of the hills, they had cried her up here – for what?

And then something made her raise her eyes,[25] she stood awful and rigid, fronting him, coming up the path through the broom. Laired with glaur was his uniform, his face was white and the great hole sagged and opened, sagged and opened, red-glazed and black, at every upwards step he took. Up through the broom: she saw the grass wave with no press below his feet, her lad, the light in his eyes that aye she could bring.

The snipe stilled their calling, a cloud came over the sun. He was close to her now and she held out her hands to him, blind with tears and bright her eyes, the bright weather in their faces, her voice shaping a question that she heard him answer in the rustle of the loch-side rushes as closer his soundless feet carried him to her lips and hands.

Oh lassie, I've come home! he said, and went into the heart that was his forever.

THE EPILUDE

EPILUDE[1]
The Unfurrowed Field

Folk said that winter that the War had done feint the much good to Mutch of Bridge End. In spite of his blowing and boasting, his silver he might as well have flung into a midden as poured in his belly, though faith! there wasn't much difference in destination. He'd gone in for the Irish cattle, had Mutch, quick you bought them and quick you sold and reaped a fine profit with prices so brave. More especially you did that if you crammed the beasts up with hay and water the morning before they were driven to the mart, they'd fairly seem to bulge with beef. But sometimes old Aitken of Bervie, a sly old brute, would give a bit stirk a wallop in the wame and it would belch like a bellows, and Aitken would say, *Ay, Mutch, the wind still bloweth as it listeth,*[2] *I see,* he was aye quoting his bits of poetry, Aitken.

But he'd made silver for all that, Mutch, and many an awful feed had his great red lugs overhung, there in the Bridge End while the War went on. For that was how it struck him and his family, they'd gorge from morn till night, the grocer would stop three times a week and out to him Alec and his mistress would come, the bairns racing at the heels of them, and they'd buy up ham and biscuits and cheese and sausage, and tins of this and tins of that, enough to feed the German army, folk told – it that was said to be so hungry it was eating up its own bit corpses, feuch!

Though faith! it was little more than eating their own corpses they did at Bridge End. And what little they left uneaten they turned to drink, by the end of the War he'd got him a car, had Alec, it was only a Ford but it clattered up and down the road to Drumlithie every day of the week, and back it would bump to the Bridge End place with beer in crates and whisky in bottles

wagging drunken-like over the hinder end. But Alec would blow
and boast as much as ever, he'd say the Bridge End was a fine
bit place and could easily stand him a dram – *it's the knack of
farming you want, that's all.*

Mutch had just got up and come out blear-eyed that day
when the postman handed him the letter from Kinraddie House.
So he had one read of it and then another, syne he cried to
his wife *Nine hundred pounds – have YOU got nine hundred
pounds, you?* And she answered him back, canty and cool, *No,
I've seen neither silver nor sense since I married you. Why do you
need nine hundred pounds?* So Alec showed her the letter, 'twas
long and dreich and went on and on; but the gist of it was the
Trustees were to sell up Kinraddie at last; and the farmers that
wanted them could buy their own places; and if Mutch of Bridge
End still wanted his the price was nine hundred pounds.

So that was how the Mutches left Kinraddie, they said never
a word about buying the place, Alec sold off his stock fell
quietly and they did a moonlight flit; some said they heard the
Ford that night go rattling up by Laurencekirk, others swore
that Mutch had gone north to Aberdeen and had got him a fine
bit job in a public house there. North or south, feint the thing
more folk saw of him; and before the New Year was out old
Gordon of Upperhill had bought up the Bridge End forbye his
own place, he said he would farm the fields with a tractor. But
damn the tractor ever appeared, he put sheep on the place
instead, and sometimes the shepherd would wander into the
kitchen where that gley-eyed wife of Mutch had sat to smoke
her bit cigarettes; and he said that the smell of the damned
things lingered there still, they'd been as unco at changing their
shirts, the Mutches, as ever old Pooty had been.

What with his Germans and ghosts and dirt, he'd fair been in
a way, had old Pooty. Long ere the War had finished he'd have
nothing to do with the mending of boots, he wouldn't let the
grocer up to the door, but would scraich at him to leave the messages out by the road. And at last he clean went over the gate, as
a man might say, he took in his cuddy to live with him there in
the kitchen, and the farmer lads going by on their bicycles of a
Saturday night would hear the two of them speaking together,

old Pooty they'd hear, thinking himself back at some concert or other in the olden days, reciting his TIMROUS BEASTIE, stuttering and stammering at the head of his voice. And then he'd be heard to give the donkey a bit clout, and *Damn you! Clap, you creature!* he'd cry; and it was a fair entertainment.

But at last it grew over-much to bear, that was just about the month when the letters went out from the Trustee childes, and folk said that fell awful sounds were heard coming from the Pooty place, the creature was clean demented. Not a body would do a thing till at last old Gordon did, he roaded off with his foreman, they went in old Gordon's car, it was night, and the nearer they came to Pooty's the more awful came the sounds. The cuddy was braying and braying in an awful stamash, they tried to look through the window, but there was a thick leather blind there and feint the thing could they see. So the foreman tried the door and it wouldn't budge, but the braying of the cuddy grew worse and worse; and the foreman was a big bit childe and he took a great run at the door and open it flew and the sight he saw would have scunnered a sow from its supper, the coarse old creature was tormenting the donkey this way and that with a red-hot poker, he scraiched the beast was a German, and they had to tie him up.

So the foreman went back for his gun and to send a message to bring the police; and when the police came down next day the donkey was shot, and some said old Pooty should have been instead. But they took the old creature away to the madhouse, fair a good riddance to Kinraddie it was. For a while after that there was speak of the Upperhill's foreman biding at Pooty's, he wanted to marry and it would be fine and close for his work. And the foreman said the place was fine if you thought of breeding a family of swine: but he was neither a boar himself nor was his quean a bit sow.

So the place began to moulder away, soon the roof went all agley and half fell in, it was fit for neither man nor beast, the thistles and weeds were all over the close, right they'd have pleased old Pooty's cuddy if he'd lived to see them. It looked a dreich, cold place as you rode by at night, near as lonesome as the old Mill was, and not near so handy. For the Mill was a place you could take your quean to, you'd lean your bicycles up by the wall and take a peek through the kitchen window; syne off you'd go, your two selves, and sit inside the old Mill itself; and your quean would say *Don't!* and smooth her short skirts; and she'd tell you you *would* be lucky if you got two dances at the Fordoun ball, John Edwards was to take her there in his side-car, mind.

For Long Rob had never come back to the Mill. It had fair been a wonder him joining the soldiers and going off to the War the way he did – after swearing black was blue that he'd never fight, that the one was as bad as the other, Scotch or German. Some said it was just plain daft he had gone, with no need for him to enlist; but when Munro of the Cuddiestoun told that to Chris Tavendale up at Blawearie she said there had been more sweetness and sense in Rob's little finger than in all the Munro carcases clecked since the Flood. Ill to say that to a man of an age with your father, it showed you the kind of creature Chris Tavendale was, folk shook their heads, minding how she'd gone near mad when her man was killed; as if he'd been the only one! And there was her brother, Will was his name, that had come from the War in a queer bit uniform, French he had said that it was; but them that were fine acquainted with uniforms weren't so sure, the Uhlans[3] had worn uniforms just like that.

They had been the German horse-billies away back at the War's beginning, you minded, and syne shook your head over that, and turned to thinking of Long Rob again, him that was killed in the April of the last year's fighting. He'd been one of the soldiers they'd rushed to France in such hurry when it seemed that the German childes were fair over us, and he'd never come back to Kinraddie again, just notice of his death came through and syne a bit in the paper about him. You could hardly believe your eyes when you read it, him such a fell pacifist, too, he'd been killed in a bit retreat that they made, him and two-three more billies had stood up to the Germans right well and held them back while the Scots retreated; they'd held on long after the others had gone, and Rob had been given a medal for that. Not that he got it, faith! he was dead, they came on his corpse long after, the British, but just as a mark of respect.

And you minded Long Rob right well, the long rangy childe, with his twinkling eyes and his great bit mouser and those stories of his that he'd deave you with, horses and horses, damn't! he had horses on the brain. There'd been his coarse speak about religion, too, fair a scandal once in the Howe, but for all that he'd been a fine stock, had Rob, you minded him singing out there in the morning, he'd sung— And you couldn't mind what the song had been till maybe a bairn would up and tell you, they'd heard it often on the way to school, and Ay, it was *Ladies of Spain*. You heard feint the meikle of those old songs now, they were daft and old-fashioned, there were fine new ones in their places, right from America, folk said, and all about the queer blue babies that were born there,[4] they were clever brutes, the Americans.

Well, that was the Mill, all its trade was gone, old Gordon bought up its land for a two-three pounds, and joined the lot on to Upperhill. Jock Gordon came blinded back from the War, they said he'd been near demented at first when he lost the use of his eyes. But old Gordon was making silver like dirt, he coddled up Jock like a pig with a tit, and he'd settled down fell content, as well the creature might be, with all he could smoke or drink at his elbow, and his mother near ready to lick his boots. Fell gentry and all they were now, the Gordons, you couldn't get within a mile of the Upperhill without you'd hear a blast of the English, so fine and genteel; and the ploughmen grew fair mad when they dropped in for a dram at Drumlithie Hotel and some billy would up and ask, *Is't true they dish you out white dickies at Upperhill now and you've all to go to the Academy?*

He was one of the folk that broke up the ploughmen's Union, old Gordon, right proud he was of it, too; and faith, the man was but right, whoever heard tell of such nonsense, a Union for ploughmen? But he didn't get off scot-free, faith, no! For what should happen in the General Election but that the secretary of the Farm Servants' Union put up as a candidate for the Mearns; and from far and near over Scotland a drove of those socialist creatures came riding to help him, dressed up in specs and baggy breeks and stockings with meikle checks. Now, one of them was a doctor childe and up to the Upperhill he came on a canvass, like, when old Gordon and the wife had driven off to lend help to the Coalition.⁵ The door was opened by Maggie Jean, she'd grown up bonny as a flower in spring, a fine quean, sweet and kind, with no English airs. And damn't if they didn't take up, the doctor and her, all in a minute, the doctor forgot about the bothy he'd come to canvass and Maggie Jean had him in to tea, and they spoke on politics for hours and hours, the servant quean told, she said it was nothing but politics; and there have been greater miracles.

Well, the next thing was that old Gordon found his men being harried to vote for the Labour man, harried by his own lass Maggie Jean, it sent him fair wild and the blind son too. But Maggie Jean didn't care a fig, the doctor childe had turned her head; and when the election was over and the Labour man beaten she told her father she wasn't going on to the college any longer, she was set on marrying her Labour doctor. Gordon said he'd soon put his foot on that, she wasn't of age and he'd stop the marriage. But Maggie Jean put her arms round his neck, *I know, but you wouldn't like people to point at you and say 'Have you heard of old Gordon's illegitimate grandchild?'* And at that they say old Gordon fair caved in, *Oh, my lass, my Maggie Jean, you haven't done that!* For answer Maggie Jean just stood and laughed, shaky-like, though, till ben came Mistress Gordon herself and heard the news, and started in on the lass. Syne Maggie Jean grew cool as ice, *Very well, then, mother, I hear there's a good bed in Stonehaven Workhouse where women can have their babies.*

So she won in the end, you may well be sure, the Gordons fair rushed the marriage, and every now and then the doctor and Maggie Jean would take a bit look at each other and laugh out loud, they weren't a bit ashamed or decent. And when the wedding was over Mistress Gordon said *It's glad I am that you're off from Kinraddie to Edinburgh, where the shame of your half-named bairn won't aye be cast in my face.* And Maggie Jean said *What bairn, mother? I'm not to have a baby yet, you know, unless George and I get over-enthusiastic to-night.* Fair dumbfoundered was Mistress Gordon, she gasped, *But you said that you were with a bairn!* and Maggie Jean just shook her head and laughed, *Oh, no, I just asked father if he'd like to grandfather one. And I don't suppose that he would. I won't have time for babies for years yet, mother, I'm to help ORGANISING THE FARM SERVANTS!*

Ah well, folk said there was damned little chance of Nellie, the other bit daughter, ever having anything legitimate or illegitimate, she was growing up as sour and wizened as an old potato, for all her English she'd sleep cold and unhandled, an old maid all her days. But faith! you're sure of nothing in this world, or whoever would have guessed that Sarah Sinclair, the daft old skate, would go marrying? It all came through the War and the stir at the Netherhill when old Sinclair bought up the Knapp and his own bit place all at one whip. Soon's she heard of that Sarah went to him and said *You did plenty for Kirsty and she'll not be needing the Knapp any more, you can bravely settle me there!*

Old Sinclair, he was nearly ninety and blind, he stared at her like a stirk at a water-jump, and then cried for his wife. And Sarah told them she meant what she said, Dave Brown, the Gourdon childe, would marry her the morn if they'd Peesie's Knapp to sit down in.

And she got her way, but she didn't get the land, old Sinclair pastured his sheep on it, and Dave stayed on as a Netherhill ploughman. So Sarah was married off at last and taken to bed in the house that had been her sister's. She soon had her man well in hand, had Sarah, folk said she'd to take him to bed by the lug the first night, but there are aye coarse brutes to say things like that. And damn it, if before a twelvemonth was up she didn't have a bairn, a peely-wally girl, but a bairn for all that. It wasn't much, but still it was something, and when old Sinclair heard the news he got it all mixed, he was in bed by then and sinking fast, he thought it was Kirsty's first bairn that they told of, and all the time he kept whispering *Chae!* he wanted his good-son, Chae, that had married Kirsty long syne.

But Chae had been gone long ere that, he was killed in the first fighting of Armistice Day,[6] an hour before the guns grew quiet. You minded him well and the arguings he'd have with

Long Rob of the Mill; he'd have been keen for the Labour
candidate, for Rich and Poor were as far off being Equal as
ever they'd been, poor Chae. Ay, it struck you strange that he'd
gone, fine childe he had been though a bit of a fool that you
laughed at behind his back. In his last bit leave folk said he'd
been awful quiet, maybe he knew right well he would never
come back, he tramped the parks most of the time, muttering
of the woods they'd cut and the land that would never get over
it. And when he said good-bye to Kirsty it wasn't just the usual
slap on the shoulder and *Well, I'm away!* He held her and
kissed her, folk saw it at the station, and he said *Be good to the
bairns, lass.* And Kirsty, the meikle sumph, had stood there
crying as the train went out, you'd have thought she'd have had
more sense with all the folk glowering at her. And that was
the last of Chae, you'd say, except that in the November of
nineteen-eighteen they sent home his pocket-book and hankies
and things; and they'd been well washed, but blood lay still in
a pouch of the pocket-book, cold and black, and when Kirsty
saw it she screamed and fainted away.

Women had little guts, except one or two, said Munro of the
Cuddiestoun, as though he himself had been killing a German
for breakfast every day of the War. And maybe that's what he'd
liked to think as he chased the hens and thrawed their necks for
the hospital trade, or swore at the daftie, Tony, over this or that.
Feint the much heed paid Tony, though, he'd just stand about the
same as ever, staring at the ground and driving Mistress Munro
fair out of her senses when she'd sent him to lower the heat in
one incubator or raise it up in another. For it was more than
likely the creature would do clean the opposite of what he'd
been told, and syne stand and glower at the ground a whole
afternoon till somebody came out to look for him and would
find every damned egg hard-boiled or stone cold, as the case
might be. Some said he wasn't so daft, he did it for spite, but
you'd hardly believe that a daftie would have the sense for that.

But nobody could deny the Munros had got on, they'd clean
stopped from farming every park except one to grow their
potatoes in, all the rest were covered with runs and rees for the
hens, they'd made a fair fortune with their poultry and all.

You'd never hear such a scraich in your life as when night-time came and they closed up the Cuddiestoun rees, it was then that Mistress Munro would nip out a cockerel here and an old hen there and thraw the creature's neck as quick as you'd blink and syne sit up half the night in the plucking of the birds. They'd hardly ever a well-cooked meal in the house themselves, but if their stomachs had little in them their bank books knew no lack, maybe one more than consoled for the other. But Ellison said that they made him sick, the only mean Scotch he'd ever met, and be damned if they didn't make up for all the free ones.

Though that was only the kind of speak you'd expect from an Irish creature, he still spoke like one, fell fat he'd grown, his belly wabbled down right near to his knees and his breeks were meikle in girth. When the Trustees sent out their notice to buy, folk wondered what he'd do, there'd be an end to Ellison now, they said. But sore mistaken they found themselves, he bought up the Mains, stock and all, he bought up the ruins of Kinraddie House, and he bought Blawearie when there were no bids, he got it for less than two hundred pounds. And where had he got all that money except that he stole it?

Fair Kinraddie's big man he thought himself, faith! folk laughed at him and called him the waiter-laird, Cospatric that killed the gryphon would have looked at him sore surprised. He spoke fell big about tractors for ploughing, but then the slump came down and his blowing with it, he bought up sheep for Blawearie instead. And that was the way things went in the end on the old bit place up there on the brae, sheep baaed and scrunched where once the parks flowed thick with corn, no corn would come at all, they said, since the woods went down. And the new minister when he preached his incoming sermon cried *They have made a desert and they call it peace;*[7] and some had no liking of the creature for that, but God! there was truth in his speak.

For the Gibbons had gone clean out of Kinraddie, there'd be far more room and far less smell, folk said, Stuart Gibbon had never come back from the War to stand in the pulpit his father had held. Not that he'd been killed, no, no, you might well depend that the great, curled steer had more sense in him than that. But the gentry liked him in Edinburgh right well in his chaplain's uniform, and syne he fell in with some American creatures that controlled a kirk in New York. And they asked him if he'd like to have that kirk, all the well-off Scots went to it; and he took the offer like a shot and was off to America before you could wink, him and that thin bit English wife of his and their young bit daughter. Well, well, he'd done well for himself, it was plain to see; no doubt the Americans would like him fine, they could stand near anything out in America, their stomachs were awful tough with all the coarse things that they ate out of tins.

As for the father, the old man that had had such an ill-will for the Germans, he'd grown over-frail to preach and had to retire; and faith! if the British armies had killed half the Germans with their guns that he did with his mouth it would have been a clean deserted Germany long ere the end of the War. But off he went at last and only two ministers made try for the pulpit, both of them young, the one just a bit student from Aberdeen, the other new out of the Army. There seemed little to choose between the pair, they'd no pulpit voices, either of them, but folk thought it only fair to give the soldier billy the chance.

And it was only after he headed the leet, Colquohoun was his name, that the story went round he was son to that old minister from Banff that made try for Kinraddie before the War and was fair out-preached by the Reverend Gibbon. You minded him, surely? – he'd preached about beasts and the Golden Age, that the dragons still lived but sometime they'd die and the Golden Age come back. Feuch ay! no sermon at all, you might say. Well, that was him and this was the son, thin and tall, with a clean-shaved face, and he lectured on this and he wrote on that and he made himself fair objectionable before he'd been there a month. For he chummed up with ploughmen, he drove his own coal, he never wore a collar that fastened at the back, and when folk called him the Reverend he pulled them up sharp – *reverent, I am, no more, my friend*. And he whistled when he went on a Sunday walk and he stormed at farmers for the pay they paid and he helped the ploughmen's Union; and he'd preach just rank sedition about it, and speak as though Christ had meant Kinraddie,[8] and folk would grow fair uncomfortable.

You couldn't well call him pro-German, like, for he'd been a plain soldier all through the War. Folk felt clean lost without a bit name to hit at him with, till Ellison said that he was a Bolshevik, one of those awful creatures, coarse tinks, that had made such a spleiter in Russia. They'd shot their king-creature, the Tsar they called him, and they bedded all over the place, folk said, a man would go home and find his wife commandeered any bit night and Lenin and Trotsky[9] lying with her. And Ellison said that the same would come in Kinraddie if Mr Colquohoun had his way; maybe he was feared for his mistress, was Ellison, though God knows there'd be little danger of *her* being commandeered, even Lenin and Trotsky would fair be desperate before they would go to that length.

Well, that was your new minister, then; and next there came scandalous stories that he'd taken up with young Chris Tavendale. Nearly every evening of the week he'd ride up to Blawearie, and bide there all the hours of the night, or so folk said. And what could he want with a common bit quean like the Tavendale widow? Ministers took up with ladies if they meant no jookery-packery. But when Munro said that to old Brigson the creature fair flew into a rage; and he said that many a decent thing had gone out of Kinraddie with the War but that only one had come in, and that was the new minister. Well, well, it might be so and it mightn't; but one night Dave Brown climbed up the hill from the Knapp, to see old Brigson about buying a horse, and he heard folk speaking inside the kitchen and he took a bit keek round the door. And there near the fire stood Chris herself, and the Reverend Colquohoun was before her, she was looking up into the minister's face and he'd both her hands in his. And *Oh, my dear, maybe the second Chris, maybe the third, but Ewan has the first forever!* she was saying, whatever she meant by that; and syne as Dave Brown still looked the minister bent down and kissed her, the fool.

Folk said that fair proved the stories were true, but the very next Sunday the minister stood up in the pulpit, and, calm as ever, read out the banns of Upperhill's foreman and his quean from Fordoun, and syne the banns of *Robert Colquohoun,*

*bachelor of this parish, and Christine Tavendale, widow, also
of this same parish.* You could near have heard a pin drop then,
so quiet it was in the kirk, folk sat fair stunned. And there'd
never been such a claik in Kinraddie as when the service was
over and the congregation got out – ay, Chris Tavendale had
feathered her nest right well, the sleekèd creature, who'd have
thought it of her?

And that made the minister no more well-liked with Kinraddie's new gentry, you may well be sure. But worse than that
came: he'd been handed the money, the minister, to raise a
memorial for Kinraddie's bit men that the War had killed. Folk
thought he'd have a fine stone angel, with a night-gown on,
raised up at Kinraddie cross-roads. But he sent for a mason
instead and had the old stone circle by Blawearie loch raised
up and cleaned and set all in place, real heathen-like, and a
paling put round it. And after reading out his banns on that
Sunday the minister read that next Saturday the Kinraddie
Memorial would be unveiled on Blawearie brae, and that he
expected a fine attendance, whatever the weather – *they'd to
attend in ill weather, the folk that fell.*

Fine weather for January that Saturday brought, sunny, yet
caller, you could see the clouds come sailing down from the
north and over the sun and off again. But there was rain not
far, the seagulls had come sooming inland; for once the snipe
were still. Nearly every soul in Kinraddie seemed climbing
Blawearie brae as the afternoon wore on, a fair bit stir there
was in the close, the place was empty of horses and stock, Chris
would be leaving there at the term. Soon she'd be down at the
Manse instead, and a proud-like creature no doubt she'd be.

Well, up on the brae through the road in the broom there
drew a fell concourse of folk, Ellison was there, and his mistress,
and the Gordons and gentry generally, forbye a reischle of
ploughmen and queans, lying round on the grass and sniggering. There was the old circle of the Standing Stones, the
middle one draped with a clout, you wondered what could be
under it and how much the mason had charged. It was high,
there, you saw as you sat on the grass and looked round, you

could see all Kinraddie and near half the Howe shine under your feet in the sun, *Out of the World and into Blawearie* as the old speak went. And faith! the land looked unco and woe with its woods all gone, even in the thin sun-glimmer there came a cold shiver up over the parks of the Knapp and Blawearie, folk said that the land had gone cold and wet right up to the very Mains.

Snow was shining in the Grampians, far in the coarse hills there, and it wouldn't be long ere the dark came. Syne at last the minister was seen coming up, he'd on the bit robes that he hardly ever wore, Chris Tavendale walked by the side of him and behind was a third childe that nobody knew, a Highlander in kilts and with pipes on his shoulder, great and red-headed, who could he be? And then Ellison minded, he said the man had been friend to young Ewan Tavendale, he'd been the best man at Ewan's marriage, McIvor his name was.

The minister held open the gate for Chris and through it she came, all clad in her black, young Ewan's hand held fast in hers, he'd grown fair like his father, the bairn, dark-like and solemn he was. Chris's face was white and solemn as well except when she looked at the minister as he held the gate open, it was hardly decent the look that she gave him, they might keep their courting till the two were alone. Folk cried *Ay, minister!* and he cried back cheerily and went striding to the midst of the old stone circle, John Brigson was standing there with his hands on the strings that held the bit clout.

The minister said, *Let us pray*, and folk took off their hats, it smote cold on your pow. The sun was fleering up in the clouds, it was quiet on the hill, you saw young Chris stand looking down on Kinraddie with her bairn's hand in hers. And then the Lord's Prayer was finished, the minister was speaking just ordinary, he said they had come to honour the folk whom the War had taken, and that the clearing of this ancient site was maybe the memory that best they'd have liked. And he gave a nod to old Brigson and the strings were pulled and off came the clout and there on the Standing Stone the words shone out in their dark grey lettering, plain and short:

FOR : THE : MEMORY : OF : CHA
RLES : STRACHAN : JAMES :
LESLIE : ROBERT : DUNCAN :
EWAN : TAVENDALE : WHO :
WERE : OF : THIS : LAND : AND :
FELL : IN : THE : GREAT : WAR :
IN : FRANCE : REVELATION :
II CH : 28 VERSE[10]

And then, with the night waiting out by on Blawearie brae, and the sun just verging the coarse hills, the minister began to speak again, his short hair blowing in the wind that had come, his voice not decent and a kirk-like bumble, but ringing out over the loch:

FOR I WILL GIVE YOU THE MORNING STAR.

In the sunset of an age and an epoch we may write that for epitaph of the men who were of it. They went quiet and brave from the lands they loved, though seldom of that love might they speak, it was not in them to tell in words of the earth that moved and lived and abided, their life and enduring love. And who knows at the last what memories of it were with them, the springs and the winters of this land and all the sounds and scents of it that had once been theirs, deep, and a passion of their blood and spirit, those four who died in France? With them we may say there died a thing older than themselves, these were the Last of the Peasants, the last of the Old Scots folk. A new generation comes up that will know them not, except as a memory in a song, they pass with the things that seemed good to them, with loves and desires that grow dim and alien in the days to be. It was the old Scotland that perished then, and we may believe that never again will the old speech and the old songs, the old curses and the old benedictions, rise but with alien effort to our lips. The last of the peasants, those four that you knew, took that with them to the darkness and the quietness of the places where they sleep. And the land changes, their

parks and their steadings are a desolation where the sheep are
pastured, we are told that great machines come soon to till the
land, and the great herds come to feed on it, the crofter is gone,
the man with the house and the steading of his own and the
land closer to his heart than the flesh of his body. Nothing, it
has been said, is true but change, nothing abides, and here in
Kinraddie where we watch the building of those little prides
and those little fortunes on the ruins of the little farms we must
give heed that these also do not abide, that a new spirit shall
come to the land with the greater herd and the great machines.
For greed of place and possession and great estate those four
had little heed, the kindness of friends and the warmth of toil
and the peace of rest – they asked no more from God or man,
and no less would they endure. So, lest we shame them, let us
believe that the new oppressions and foolish greeds are no more
than mists that pass. They died for a world that is past, these
men, but they did not die for this that we seem to inherit.
Beyond it and us there shines a greater hope and a newer world,
undreamt when these four died. But need we doubt which side
the battle they would range themselves did they live to-day,[11]
need we doubt the answer they cry to us even now, the four of
them, from the places of the sunset?

And then, as folk stood dumbfounded, this was just sheer
politics, plain what he meant, the Highlandman McIvor tuned
up his pipes and began to step slow round the stone circle by
Blawearie Loch, slow and quiet, and folk watched him, the
dark was near, it lifted your hair and was eerie and uncanny,
the *Flowers of the Forest* as he played it:

It rose and rose and wept and cried, that crying for the men that fell in battle, and there was Kirsty Strachan weeping quietly and others with her, and the young ploughmen they stood with glum, white faces, they'd no understanding or caring, it was something that vexed and tore at them, it belonged to times they had no knowing of.

He fair could play, the piper, he tore at your heart marching there with the tune leaping up the moor and echoing across the loch, folk said that Chris Tavendale alone shed never a tear, she stood quiet, holding her boy by the hand, looking down on Blawearie's fields till the playing was over. And syne folk saw that the dark had come and began to stream down the hill, leaving her there, some were uncertain and looked them back. But they saw the minister was standing behind her, waiting for her, they'd the last of the light with them up there, and maybe they didn't need it or heed it, you can do without the day if you've a lamp quiet-lighted and kind in your heart.

THE END

Maps

The maps of Kinraddie and of The Mearns (and *A Scots Quair*) are based upon the Jarrolds end-papers for the first editions of *Sunset Song* and *Grey Granite* respectively. Additional detail has been added to the Kinraddie map from Gibbon's original pencil draft for his publishers, subsequently passed to his friend Dorothy E. Tweed, a copy of which is contained in the archive of his papers at the Grassic Gibbon Centre. The second, small scale, map has drawn upon Gibbon's original annotated map by John Bartholomew, from James Crabb Watt's *The Mearns of Old* (see The Prelude, note 1). The specific geography of the Mearns has been extended northwards in order to include place names from Donside and beyond, as referred to principally in the early chapters of the novel.

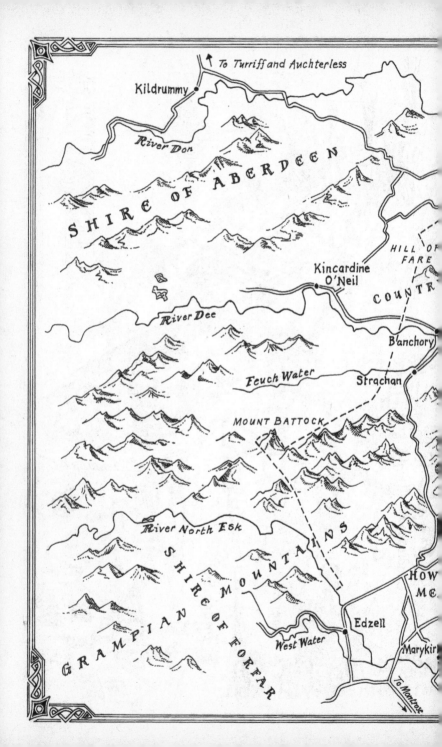

Notes

All Bible quotations are from the Authorised Version. References to *Scottish Scene* (see A Note, note 1 below) are cited as they appear in the contemporary selection *Smeddum: A Lewis Grassic Gibbon Anthology*, ed. Valentina Bold (Edinburgh: Canongate, 2001). For Scots and other unfamiliar words, see the Glossary.

DEDICATION

1. *TO* JEAN BAXTER: Jean Baxter (1886–1968), fellow Scot, originally from Aberdeenshire, with her husband Harold enjoyed a close friendship with the Mitchells in the south of England from 1929. Her keen interest in Scottish culture and language is evident in her Scots vernacular poems, *A' AE 'OO'* (Aberdeen, 1928).

A NOTE

1. *He might import into his pages . . . mould in some fashion his German*: In 'Literary Lights' (Hugh MacDiarmid and Lewis Grassic Gibbon, *Scottish Scene, or The Intelligent Man's Guide to Albyn* (1934), in *Smeddum*, p. 135), Gibbon describes the theory behind his unique linguistic compromise: 'to mould the English language into the rhythms and cadences of Scots spoken speech, and to inject into the English vocabulary such minimum number of words from Braid Scots as that remodelling requires'.

    His reference to a parallel situation existing in Dutch and German literature reflects his enduring interest in, and influence by, European writing. Specifically, Gibbon owned a copy of F. S.

Delmer's 1905 translation of *Jörn Uhl* (Berlin, 1901), Gustav
Frenssen's novel of *Heimatkunst*, or regionalism, which appears
a likely candidate for his Germanic reference (see Douglas F.
Young, *Beyond the Sunset* (Aberdeen: Impulse Books, 1973),
pp. 146–53).

Gibbon's literary (and political) parameters always extended
beyond his native Scotland. Even at his most patriotic, at the
very height of the inter-war period known as the Scottish Literary
Renaissance, Gibbon represented himself as only passively
engaged with the resurgence of interest in things Scottish, casting
himself as, 'non-Nationalist, and yet interested in this new revival
of cultural and political Nationalism' ('News of Battle: Queries
for Mr Whyte', *Free Man*, 3 (17 March 1934), p. 9).

THE PRELUDE
The Unfurrowed Field

1. *Kinraddie lands*: Gibbon's central place name is fictitious,
    although its orthographic resemblance to Kincardine, historical
    name of his home county in the Mearns in North-east Scotland,
    is clear. His pastiche of traditional aristocratically skewed history
    drew upon James Crabb Watt's *The Mearns of Old: A History
    of Kincardine from the Earliest Times to the Seventeenth Century*
    (Edinburgh & Glasgow, 1914), augmented by the anonymous
    Geography of the County of Kincardine (Glasgow, 1875). Gib-
    bon's sketchy satire, very much politically orientated, marries
    historical fact, apocrypha and imaginative fabrication, designed
    to highlight the inadequacy of conventional prefaces, in concen-
    trating upon a relatively small proportion of the population, the
    'gentry' and their acolytes.

    Kinraddie is located four miles due north of Gibbon's native
    Arbuthnott. The map of Kincardineshire by John Bartholomew
    removed from Crabb Watt's volume (now with Gibbon's papers
    in Edinburgh University Library) has Gibbon's insertions of the
    three fictional locales for *A Scots Quair*: Kinraddie, Segget and
    Dundon (later Duncairn – see Ploughing, note 20).

    Gibbon uses real places from the Mearns, such as his own
    country parish of Arbuthnott and the local market villages of
    Drumlithie, Auchenblae ('Auchinblae') and Laurencekirk, as well
    as the county capital of Stonehaven, 16 miles south of Aberdeen.

He also indulges in teasing compounds: Peesie's Knapp is redolent of Birdie Knapp, at Catterline; Upperhill and Netherhill are compressed from Upper Craighill and Nether Craighill, in Arbuthnott.

Gibbon's unpropitious family croft of Bloomfield, high up on the Reisk road in Arbuthnott, provided the real-life setting for Blawearie, although the fictional house (pp. 20–21) has been expanded from the modest family cottage.

2. *Cospatric de Gondeshil . . . when gryphons*: The exotic-sounding first name for the founder of the Kinraddie dynasty is actually a French, Celtic and Latin derivation meaning 'boy of Patrick' and came from local history. Hugh de Swinton, regarded as the true founder of the Arbuthnotts at the end of the twelfth century, reputedly was related to Cospatrick de Swinton, Earl of Northumberland, opponent of William the Conqueror (?1027–87) and later friend to Malcolm Canmore, King of Scots (c. 1031–93). (Hugh de Swinton's son and grandson were also named Cospatric.) William the Lyon, named after the figure on his shield, is William I of Scotland (b. 1143), who ruled as King of Scotland 1165–1214 (see also note 8). The most colourful legend associated with Hugh le Blond, fourth Laird of Arbuthnott (c. 1260–c. 1300), is his heroic slaying with a two-handed sword of a dragon at the Den of Pitcarles (see also note 20). (See Christy Bing, *The Lairds of Arbuthnott*, rev. edn. (Edzell, 1999), p. 10.)

Gibbon embellishes the legend by setting Cospatric's triumph under cover of darkness, in a remote part of Kinraddie and over a gryphon.

3. *Aberlemno's Meikle Stane*: A carved sandstone standing stone in Aberlemno Churchyard in Angus, 30 miles south of Arbuthnott. The most impressive of the five local stones, it most probably commemorates a victory in the Battle of Nechtansmere in 685 AD by the Picts, led by Brude mac Bili, over the invading Northumbrians under King Ecgfrid. For 'meikle', see Glossary.

4. *Grampians*: The sprawling series of mountain ranges, extending south-west to north-east and lying north of the Highland Boundary Fault and south of Strathspey, achieves a height of 4,296 feet (1,309 metres) at Ben Macdui in the Cairngorm Mountains.

The Howe (later in the paragraph) of the Mearns is the popular name for the portion of the valley of Strathmore found in Kincardineshire, lying roughly midway between Aberdeen and Dundee. Gibbon's Mearns setting is bounded by Stonehaven and Laurencekirk in the north and south, with Inverbervie (see

Ploughing, note 1) demarcating east and the Grampian Mountains west.

5.   *the battle that was fought at Mondynes*: Duncan II (b. *c.* 1060),
     son of Malcolm Canmore, died on the losing side in the battle
     fought near Drumlithie in the Mearns in 1094 against Donald
     Bane, his uncle, and Edmund, his brother, who subsequently
     reigned jointly until 1097.

6.   *great-grandson ... the cateran Wallace*: Sir William Wallace
     (*c.* 1270–1305), second son of Sir Malcolm Wallace of Enderslie,
     Renfrewshire, led the resistance against the English in the Scottish
     War of Independence. Following his audacious victory in 1297
     at the Battle of Stirling Bridge, he was knighted and appointed
     Guardian of Scotland. Wallace was defeated by Edward I at the
     Battle of Falkirk in 1298 and disappeared, but was captured in
     1305 (see p. 83); his brutal execution and ritualistic disem-
     bowelling in London vouchsafed his status as a national martyr.

     Gibbon played down the chauvinistic image attached to Wal-
     lace, perceiving him as a proletarian hero and paying unre-
     strained tribute to him as 'a great republican with the first of the
     great republican titles' ('The Antique Scene', in *Smeddum*, p. 13).
     One of Gibbon's unfinished projects was a radical political novel,
     'Knight of Scotland', based upon Wallace.

     Allying himself with the English forces, Cospatric's great-
     grandson is, from a populist Scottish point of view, tantamount
     to committing treason. See also p. 43 and Ploughing, note 12.

7.   *Dunnottar Castle that stands out in the sea beyond Kinneff*: This
     impressive ruined castle, mentioned in the seventh century and
     built substantially before 1394, is set on an ancient fortified site,
     on a rocky outcrop of the coast, just south of Stonehaven, historic
     county town of Kincardineshire, and 6 miles north of Kinneff, a
     small coastal hamlet (p. 49). Dunnottar featured regularly in
     Scottish history, up until its dismantling in the early eighteenth
     century. See also Seed-Time, note 7.

8.   *the Abbey of Aberbrothock*: Arbroath Abbey in Angus was
     founded by William the Lyon in 1178 in tribute to St Thomas
     Beckett.

9.   *when the First Reformation came ... some cried The King*: The
     Reformation reached Scotland in the middle of the sixteenth
     century, led by George Wishart (*c.* 1513–46) and the stern
     religious reformer John Knox (*c.* 1512–72), giving rise to civil
     strife between the Catholic Mary, Queen of Scots (1542–87), and
     her Protestant lords. This conflict led to landmarks in Calvinist

history, principally the signing of the National Covenant in Edinburgh in 1638 to formalise opposition to changes in worship introduced by King Charles I. In 'The Antique Scene', Gibbon registers his staunch opposition to organised religion in a Scottish historical context (*Smeddum*, p. 16).

The quasi-political 'Whiggam!' attained the status of a Protestant war cry countering the dual Catholic invocations ('Rome' and 'The King'), and was probably an abbreviation of 'Whiggamore', ostensibly one of the Scottish Covenanters who in 1648 engaged in the Whiggamore Raid on Edinburgh on the side of the Presbyterian cause. (It was subsequently truncated to the political term 'Whig'.)

10. *then Dutch William came . . . all for the Covenant*: William III of England (1650–1702), also known as William of Orange, was asked to assume the crowns of both Scotland and England in 1688 to oust James II, who was becoming the focus of the Catholics. After the National Covenant, the Covenanters had to defend their religious belief against the Stuart dynasty, who were supported by prominent Scottish nobles.

The heroic dissent of the Covenanters, popularly termed 'the Killing Time', has proved a beguiling subject in Scottish fiction, from Sir Walter Scott's *Old Mortality* (1816) to Fionn MacColla's *Move Up, John* (1994). Gibbon intended to explore it in his projected fictional trilogy, with the working title of 'Men of the Mearns'.

11. *Johnson and James Boswell*: James Boswell (1740–95) was the biographer of Samuel Johnson (1709–84), eminent man of English letters and author of *A Dictionary of the English Language*. Boswell's racy journal from 1776 (first published in a limited edition in 1931), includes an entry covering his encounter with Peggy Dundas, a prostitute, in Edinburgh. The Greek (plus English) means: 'Peggi Dundas was fat in the buttocks and I did lie with her.'

12. *called himself a Jacobin . . . for liberty and equality and fraternity*: The radical supporters of the French Revolution (1789–93) were named after the building in Paris where they convened, which was owned by the Dominican, or Jacobin, Order. Kenneth echoes the popular mantra of the revolution: 'liberté, égalité, fraternité, ou la mort!' ('freedom, equality, brotherhood, or death!').

13. *the crofters dour folk of the old Pict stock*: Gibbon draws a stark contrast between the Picts, cast as the ancient Scottish proletariat, and the Celts, represented as an imperialist, alien aristocracy. In

'The Antique Scene', he condemns the archetypal Celt as 'a typical aristocrat' who enslaved the indigenous Picts (*Smeddum*, p. 10).

14. *died the same day as the Old Queen*: Victoria (b. 1837) died on 22 January 1901.

15. *they flitted off to Canada and Dundee*: Gibbon is historically accurate about the steady drip of Scottish depopulation through emigration to the New World, encouraged by hostile landlords as much as by the promise of self-improvement, and to Dundee, the industrial city, 40 miles south of Arbuthnott.

16. *the estate was mortgaged to the hilt*: The Arbuthnott estate in 1917 that met the incoming thirteenth Viscount was derelict and heavily mortgaged. (See Bing, *The Lairds of Arbuthnott*, pp. 105–6.)

17. *the Auchinblae School ... Stonehaven Academy*: Gibbon's jibe at the expense of the Academy recalls his own unhappy experience at Mackie Academy in Stonehaven in 1916–17. This followed his sound elementary education at Arbuthnott Primary School, with its enlightened headmaster, Alexander Gray.

18. *You're awful like the Turra Coo*: A notorious episode in twentieth-century North-east farming politics, when a farmer named Paterson from Turriff, Aberdeenshire, challenged the 1911 legislation to pay weekly insurance stamps for his workers (see also Drilling, note 9). The authorities impounded one of his cows, which subsequently was bought back on his behalf and returned garlanded, with lavish ceremony, by his friends. (See Alexander Fenton, *The Turra Coo: Legal Episode in the Popular Culture of North East Scotland* (Aberdeen: Aberdeen University Press, 1989).

19. *kirk and manse*: Gibbon's recreation of The Kirk of St Ternan at Arbuthnott is accurate in every detail.

20. *effigy-thing ... Bonny Prince Charlie*: Arbuthnott Kirk's stone effigy in the Arbuthnott Aisle is popularly identified with Hugh le Blond (see note 2). The ancient two-handed sword in the Arbuthnotts' possession is reputed to be the weapon he wielded, but its style places it much later. (See Bing, *The Lairds of Arbuthnott*, p. 23.) Bonnie Prince Charlie refers to the failed Jacobite rising led by Prince Charles Edward Stuart, 'The Young Pretender' (1720–88), from 1745, which ended in bloody defeat at the Battle of Culloden near Inverness on 16 April 1746.

21. *was fee'd his last fee*: Feeing represented a formal transaction, generally conducted at a regular feeing-market, in which farm

workers fixed their contract of work and habitation, with land-
owners or farmers. The main term-times at Arbuthnott were
28 May, for most married men, and 28 November. David Kerr
Cameron gives vivid insight to the structure of North-east farming society in *The Ballad and the Plough: A Portrait of Life
in the Old Scottish Farmtouns* (London: Gollancz, 1978), and
subsequent volumes. Background to the Arbuthnott parish can
be found in *The Annals of Arbuthnott*, 2 vols. (Laurencekirk:
Arbuthnott Community Association, 2001).

22. *in Alaska, looking for gold ... fought against Boers*: The first
    Alaskan gold strikes occurred in the 1870s; the Gold Rush was
    in the 1890s. The Boers was the Afrikaans name in the eighteenth
    and nineteenth century (now Afrikaner), for white South African
    settlers of Dutch, German and French Huguenot origins. The Boer
    Wars (1880–81, 1899–1902) were fought between the British
    Empire and the two independent Boer republics, the Orange Free
    State and the South African Republic.

23. *being a socialist creature*: Chae's vague political label covers
    supporters of systems of social organisation in which the means
    of producing and distributing goods is owned collectively. His
    self-definition was challengingly modern and radical.

24. *the German Kaiser*: Wilhelm II (1859–1941), Queen Victoria's
    grandson and the Commander in Chief of the German armed
    forces (see Harvest, note 8).

25. *Druid stones*: Aberdeenshire and Kincardineshire have many
    standing stones and stone circles, most of which preceded the
    arrival of the Celts with the Druids (see Humphrey Welfare,
    'Standing Stones in Kinraddie: The Archaeology of *A Scots
    Quair*', *Northern Archaeology*, 17/18 (1999), pp. 187–190). The
    Blawearie standing stones are fictional, and are used to introduce
    Gibbon's personal beliefs. (For a full discussion of his philosophy,
    see William Malcolm, *A Blasphemer & Reformer* (Aberdeen:
    Aberdeen University Press, 1984), Chapter Two.)

26. *once been a scholar ... his brain fair softened*: The first in a
    series of running jokes directed at books and reading made in
    response to the vilification that Gibbon received from his unsym-
    pathetic parents and locals (cf. the 'two Chrisses' (pp. 41–2)).

27. *The People's Journal*: The ubiquitous Scottish weekly newspaper
    from the late nineteenth century was characterised by its popular
    tone. In 1933 Gibbon recalled wryly his boyhood debt to one of
    its pseudo-Kailyard (see note 35) historical romances:

Years ago, when I was a schoolboy, I came upon a serial, 'Red Fox'
by J. MacFarlane. It ran for weeks in a Dundee paper, and I ran
with it, devouring it with insatiable zest. The claymores on a wintry
morn! the speeches! the Lennox hills! the battle between the clans!
I loved it and dreamt upon it, and awaited impatiently its re-
appearance each Friday. ('In Oor Kailyaird', *Free Man*, 2 (7 October
1933), p. 9)

The paper included small ads for tenant farms available for lease
(p. 46).

28. *Calgacus . . . battle of Mons Graupius*: The first Scottish freedom-
fighter, Calgacus was the legendary chieftain of the Caledonian
tribes which were actually defeated by Agricola's Roman forces
in the battle in 84 AD, as commemorated by the historian Tacitus
(55–117 AD) in *The Agricola*. (See Gordon S. Maxwell, *A Battle
Lost: Romans and Caledonians at Mons Graupius* (Edinburgh:
Edinburgh University Press, 1990).) See also Epilude, note 7.

29. *of Gourdon stock*: Gibbon appropriates a small coastal fishing
village situated just south of Inverbervie (see Ploughing, note 1),
and exploits the traditional rivalry between farmers and
fisherfolk.

30. *Ingersoll that made watches and didn't believe in God*: Rob's
critics conflate Robert Green Ingersoll (1833–99), noted American lawyer and author of agnostic tracts, and Robert Hawley
Ingersoll (1859–1928), American entrepreneur behind the popular Waterbury dollar watch introduced in 1892. See also pp. 27,
64.

31. *Ladies of Spain . . . made the bed to me*: Rob's signature tune of
'Ladies of Spain' (better known as 'Spanish Ladies'), a shanty
first recorded in print in 1796, and 'There was a young maiden'
are traditional English folk songs, suggesting his worldli-
ness. 'The Lass That Made the Bed to Me' (1795) is one of the
more ribald songs by Scotland's national bard, Robert Burns
(1759–96).

32. *Not very meikle*: Nellie's response has been partially anglified
from Gibbon's typescript: 'Nae very meikle'.

33. *Weeeee . . . TIMROUS BEASTIE*: Burns's sentimental lyric 'To
a Mouse' (1785), l. 1.

34. *a tink*: See Drilling, note 2

35. *fathered between a kailyard and a bonny brier bush . . . house
with green shutters*: Gibbon embraces the polar opposites of his
antecedents in Scottish rural fiction here. In 'The Land', Gibbon

denounced the genteelly romanticised Kailyard ('kitchen garden') tradition in Scottish fiction, dating predominantly from Victorian times, as 'the scum of Kailyard romance' (*Smeddum*, p. 85). Its flagship text was *Beside the Bonnie Brier Bush* (1894) by 'Ian Maclaren' (Revd John Watson (1850–1907)), with its epigraph: 'There grows a bonnie brier bush in our kail-yard, / And white are the blossoms on't in our kail-yard.' In *The House with the Green Shutters* (1901), George Douglas Brown (1869–1902) adopted a caustically realistic approach to Scottish life and character as a direct antidote. Gibbon's typescript omitted the second reference to the colour of the shutters in the final sentence ('a house with shutters'); this was most probably a careless slip, but, if it was intended, it would add force to the folk narrator's dismissal of the minister while softening the impact of the author's renunciation of his literary forebears. See also p. 92. (See Ian Campbell, *Kailyard: A New Assessment* (Edinburgh: Ramsay Head Press, 1981).)

THE SONG

1 *Ploughing*

1. *Bervie*: Inverbervie, coastal town 3 miles south-east of Arbuthnott, would have been the principal social centre.
2. *Gladstone*: William Ewart Gladstone (1809–98), four times Liberal Prime Minister of Great Britain, was much reviled despite his enlightened domestic policies.
3. *Aberdeen . . . Dee*: The city, where Gibbon spent 1917–19 as a journalist, is located between the river mouths of the Dee and the Don. Aberdeen is, confusingly, also used as an abbreviation for Aberdeenshire, e.g. 'a fine land for rain, Aberdeen' (p. 37).
4. *the Prince of Wales*: Edward (1894–1972), son of George V, the future Edward VIII, was to abdicate in 1936. The concern with minor royal health complaints is indicative of the inherent conservatism of the church and the community.
5. *Echt . . . Hill of Fare*: Gibbon spent occasional holidays with Alexander Gray, his old headmaster, in the small village of Echt in Aberdeenshire, 10 miles west of Aberdeen. The Barmekin is an 800-foot hill, with an ancient Iron Age hill fort encircling the summit, while the Hill of Fare is a more substantial hill range 4 miles to the north of Banchory, rising to 1,545 feet (470 metres).

6. *Kildrummie*: Gibbon's maternal ancestors came from this rural parish in Donside, Aberdeenshire.

7. *Pittodrie*: The rural area in Chapel of Garioch, Aberdeenshire, 15 miles north-west of Aberdeen.

8. *Jehovah*: The God of the Israelites in the Old Testament, whose name was not to be spoken (or written).

9. *her Latin Grammar*: Chris's pursuit of Latin, and of Greek and French, signifies her academic prowess, as only fast-tracking pupils received a diet of languages. The arid way in which the subject is taught, however, using doggerel conjugation learned by rote, such as '*Amo, amas, I love a lass*' (p. 42), mnemonic for the verb *amare*, to love, is signalled later.

10. *Too-long and Too-loose*: Common classroom pun on French towns Toulon and Toulouse.

11. *Alice in Wonderland ... The Humours of Scottish Life*: *Alice in Wonderland* (1865), by Lewis Carroll (Charles Lutwidge Dodgson (1832–98)), provides an imaginative escape for Chris, as do *What Katy did at School* (1873), the second volume in the popular, if sanitised, series by Susan Coolidge (1835–1905); and *Rienzi* (1835), a ponderous historical reconstruction by Sir Edward Bulwer-Lytton (1803–73). *The Humours of Scottish Life* (1904), couthy but humourless anecdotes mainly concerning the clergy, was collected by Revd John Gillespie from Dumfries.

12. *captured Wallace ... The Flowers of the Forest*: Gibbon's attitude towards Robert de Bruce (1274–1329), architect of the Scottish victory over Edward II at the Battle of Bannockburn in 1314, was diametrically opposed to Chris's: in 'The Antique Scene', he condemns Bruce as one of 'the various shoddy noble adventurers who now raised the standard against the English', having assumed power 'by intrigue, assassination and some strategical skill' (*Smeddum*, p. 14).

    The Battle of Flodden in 1513 witnessed the bloody defeat of James IV's forces by those of Henry VIII. Gibbon curtly describes the battle as 'the dark end to the greatest raid of the Scots into England' ('The Antique Scene', *Smeddum*, p. 15), although Chris's allegation of English treachery reflects her emotional patriotism. 'The Flowers of the Forest' is a poignant lament with lyrics attributed to Jean Elliot (1727–1805), commemorating the battle. This musical motif has a firm historical basis: it was played on the bagpipe at the first Armistice Day service held in Arbuthnott Church at the end of the First World War.

13. *Mrs Hemans*: Felicia Dorothea Hemans (1793–1835) earned

fame for 'Casabianca' (1826) ('The boy stood on the burning deck'); she was a popular poet in the Victorian era, but her reputation had begun to slide in Gibbon's time.

14. *the twins were born ... haunted Chris*: Gibbon's fixation with the horrors of childbirth runs graphically throughout his writing, from early stories such as 'Gift of the River' and 'Daybreak' (both from 1930) and his first novel *Stained Radiance* (1930). His wife nearly died in childbirth in January 1926, and the baby was stillborn. The ordeal is traced in Gibbon's raw emotional outpouring in letters to his wife (NLS MS26063).

15. *Banchory ... the large-like farm*: The compact Aberdeenshire town on Royal Deeside is 15 miles west of Aberdeen. The large farms are an early warning of the movement towards large-scale capitalist farming.

16. *the Slug road ... into the Mearns*: This twisty and exposed 12-mile road through the hills, which reaches 757 feet (231 metres), connects Banchory with Stonehaven. Gibbon takes liberties with the geography as Portlethen, a coastal town just south of Aberdeen, lies substantially out of the Guthries' route.

17. *Polled Angus and Shorthorns and half-bred Highland stirks*: Traditional breeds of beef cattle; Shorthorns originated in north-east England and Highland in the far north of Scotland and the Western Isles, while the Polled, or hornless, Angus have been bred in North-east Scotland for over four centuries (now known as Aberdeen Angus).

18. *in the Greek The ships of Pytheas*: Refers to the fleeting visit to Scotland of the Greek explorer Pytheas, who circumnavigated the British Isles in the fourth century BC.

19. *a veteran of the '45*: Rob's reference to the Jacobite rising in 1745 satirises the appearance of John Guthrie's gun, and alludes to the fact that members of the defeated army kept weapons afterwards in defiance of the strict measures enforced by the occupying English forces.

20. *Duncairn*: Gibbon originally named his fictional Mearns city Dundon but changed it to prevent erroneous identification with Aberdeen and Dundee. His annotated map places it 1 mile north of Kinneff on the coast (see The Prelude, note 1).

21. *Canaille ... May swee*: Dog-pack ... But yes ('Mais oui') (French).

22. *Caesar's coming in Gaul*: Presumably Chris is reading extracts from *De Bello Gallico* (58–52 BC), Caesar's detailed account of his conquest of ancient Gaul in the first century BC.

23. *a bit walk to Fordoun*: Just under 3 miles from Kinraddie, not considered a particularly taxing walk then.

24. *Bonny wee thing . . . should tyne*: This version of the Burns song 'The Bonie Wee Thing' (1791) has been lightly changed for effect. In addition to minor spelling changes, Burns has 'Canie' not 'Canty', 'wear' not 'clasp', and 'it' for 'I'.

25. *Latter-Day Doubt in the Kirk of Scotland*: The first candidate denounces modern theological deviation from the strictly literal interpretation of Holy Scripture.

26. *his sermon . . . she thought it fine*: The sermon summarises Gibbon's belief in the Diffusionist view of evolution, representing civilisation as a freak degeneration from a natural norm rather than a smooth progression from primitive barbarity. This is also represented later in Chris's enlightened view of her father's corruption by religion (p. 123). (For the influence of Diffusionism on Gibbon, see Young, *Beyond the Sunset*. See also Gibbon's evangelical essay, as J. Leslie Mitchell, 'The Diffusionist Heresy', *Twentieth Century*, 1 (1931), pp. 14–18.)

27. *the cosmic light far off in Palestine*: Palestine signified Israel in biblical times, so the minister is referring to Jesus Christ's life (d. c. AD 33) as providing light for Jews (and all humanity): he is portraying Jesus as a model rather than as a saviour.

28. *forgiven his sins . . . those that trespassed against him*: While The Lord's Prayer (from Matthew 6: 9–13), has the term 'debts' in the Authorised Version used by the Presbyterian Church of Scotland, the 1662 translation used for the Anglican Book of Common Prayer (from 1549) has 'trespasses', as does the Roman Catholic version (ecumenical versions often use 'sins').

29. *Song of Solomon*: Christians interpret Chapter 4 as representing their church allegorically, in sensual terms of female beauty.

30. *esses like effs*: The ancient gravestones follow early printers' practice in using the long s internally (it was very similar to an 'f').

31. *Religio Medici*: An erudite tome (c. 1642), mainly on religious matters, by Sir Thomas Browne (?1605–82).

32. *Mucker*: Gibbon's typescript generally has the stronger expletive 'bugger' for 'mucker', which he toned down in the published text to fit with the less astringent voice employed throughout. See also Seed-Time, note 15.

33. *Colquohoun's*: In a prefatory Note to *Cloud Howe*, Gibbon gives the pronunciation as 'Ca-hoon'.

34. *into Aberdeen University, getting her B.A.*: The first degree is actually the M.A. (Master of Arts).

II *Drilling*

1. *Auchterless*: Gibbon was born at Hillhead of Seggat, in the parish of Auchterless near Turriff in Aberdeenshire, and spent his first six years here.

2. *a tink climbed up the Blawearie road*: The tinkers, now called travelling people, provided a seasonal boost to the agricultural workforce when farming was largely reliant on manual labour. The characters' attitude to this group, and indeed employing the term 'tink' as a general synonym for anti-social misfits, is realistic (and ironic).

3. *Ben Nevis*: The mountain near Fort William is the United Kingdom's highest, at 4,400 feet (1,344 metres).

4. *up on Drumtochty hills*: Gibbon's fondness for the lush Glen of Drumtochty', beginning a few miles west of Arbuthnott, is vividly captured in his nostalgic account of a cycling expedition in 'The Land' (*Smeddum*, pp. 89–92).

5. *Nebuchadnezzar ... to grass*: The king who captured Babylon but subsequently was ritually humiliated by being expelled, and in a deluded state he grazed like the oxen (Daniel 4:33).

6. *For unto us a child is born*: From Isaiah 9:6: 'For unto us a child is born, unto us a son is given: and the government shall be upon his shoulder: and his name shall be called Wonderful, Counsellor, The mighty God, The everlasting Father, The Prince of Peace.'

7. *'twas dog's delight to bark and bite*: Allusion to the opening line of the children's hymn in *Divine Songs* (1715) by theologian Isaac Watts (1674–1748), directed against quarrelling and fighting, which begins:

    > Let dogs delight to bark and bite,
    > For God hath made them so:
    > Let bears and lions growl and fight,
    > For 'tis their nature, too.

8. *one tink robber was as bad as another, Tory as Liberal*: The two major British political parties in the nineteenth and early twentieth centuries, the Conservatives (Tory) and the Liberals, were both seen as compromised.

9. *support the Insurance and to Hell with the House of Lords*: Topical political issues: the Liberal government of David Lloyd George (1863–1945) wanted to tax the rich more in order to

finance medical care for children and old-age pensions; the National Insurance Act of 1911 established workers' rights to health and unemployment benefits; and the powers of the House of Lords to reject legislation (i.e. the 'People's Budget' of 1909) approved by the Commons led to the Parliament Act of 1911 which placed restrictions upon the Lords.

10. *Scottish Thistle . . . English Rose*: The question of national identity was very much a live political issue in Scotland and in Britain in the 1920s and 1930s. Gibbon uses familiar heraldic terms: the thistle having symbolised Scotland from the thirteenth century and the rose England from the Wars of the Roses (1455–85).

11. *burning cake . . . just like the English creature Alfred*: Anecdote associated with King Alfred (849–99), legendary King of Wessex (871–99), reputed to have burned the cakes made by the swineherd's wife when he was in exile in their hut.

12. *Up in the Morning*: Another Burns song, *Up in the Morning Early* (1788). See also p. 169.

III   *Seed-Time*

1. *Old Testament times*: In Genesis 19:30–38, the daughters of Lot seduced their father and gave birth to sons. John Guthrie's incestuous lust and Andy's rampage through Kinraddie (pp. 57–62) were omitted from the American edition.

2. *Glenlivet*: Rob's full bottle of the very best malt whisky reveals his practical nous as well as his innate generosity.

3. *Dust . . . ashes to ashes*: The traditional invocation (based upon Genesis 3:19), from the funeral service in the Book of Common Prayer.

4. *past Brechin . . . with its ancient tower*: Substantial manufacturing town in Forfarshire, 20 miles south of Arbuthnott, which dates from just before the battle of Aberlemno (AD 685), and boasts a cathedral founded around 1150 by David I with an impressive ancient tower. Brechin is in many ways the model for Segget, the mill town in *Cloud Howe*.

5. *she minded Greek words . . . Nothing endures*: Ancient Greek aphorism of Heraclitus of Ephesus from 500 BC: 'Everything flows on.' Chris's philosophy is heavily influenced by Heraclitus' key text *On Nature*, which constructs a proto-materialist vision of a universe that exists in a constant state of flux.

6. *past Drumlithie and the Carmont*: Presumably Chris caught the

train at Fordoun, 4 miles south of Drumlithie on the main Northern Dundee to Aberdeen line, opened in 1849. The Carmont
junction lies just over 2 miles to the north of Drumlithie.

7.   *There the Covenanting folk had screamed and died*: The victims
     of the darkest episode in the castle's history are commemorated
     at Dunnottar (see The Prelude, note 7). In 1685, 122 male and
     45 female Covenanting prisoners were incarcerated without food
     or sanitation in the 'Whigs' Vault', the claustrophobic dungeon,
     for over two months for refusing to acknowledge the king's
     supremacy in spiritual matters. Twenty prisoners attempted to
     escape, 15 of whom were recaptured and tortured, while the
     remainder were transported to the West Indies.

8.   *REV: XI CH: 12 VERSE*: The reference is more apposite if the
     Roman numerals for the chapter are read as Arabic, Revelation
     11:12 (rather than II, as in the first edition), echoing the trium-
     phant cry of the Covenanters in their martyrdom: 'And they
     heard a great voice from heaven saying unto them, Come up
     hither. And they ascended up to heaven in a cloud; and their
     enemies beheld them.' (Revelation 2:12 reads: 'And to the angel
     of the church in Pergamos write; These things saith he which
     hath the sharp sword with two edges.') (For a discussion of
     the biblical inscriptions in the novel, see W. R. Aitken, 'The
     Inscriptions in *Sunset Song*', *Bibliotheck*, 8 (1976), pp. 1–6.)

9.   *the Blue Wyandotte*: A breed imported from America, and there-
     fore wholly credible as the alpha male in Chris's chicken coop.

10. *a Highlandman out of Ross*: Gibbon makes McIvor a northern
     Highlander, by placing his origins in Ross-shire, in the northern-
     most part of mainland Scotland. His lyrical speech is imbued
     with the Gaelic mysticism attributed to the 'Celtic Twilight' from
     the second half of the nineteenth century, appropriate for this
     'daft Highland poet' (p. 162).

11. *ordering food enough to feed the French*: The local maxim draws
     upon the stereotypical reputation of the French as hedonistic
     gourmands.

12. *wouldn't store the kin long*: Gibbon or the typesetter is remiss
     here, and on p. 162, in transcribing 'kiln' (an oven) for 'kin'
     (relations), in the local North-east expression 'to store the kin',
     meaning to keep the human race going, or generally, to endure.
     The word has been corrected in this edition.

13. *paid by piece-work and not by time*: That is, a worker paid a
     single flat fee for his shift – irrespective of the quality of his
     performance – resulting in him going through the motions, rather

than one who is contracted to an hourly payment, which means
that he has to earn the right to continue.

14. *The Lass ... Auld Robin Gray*: Rob's Burns rendition, from
'The Lass that Made the Bed to Me' (1795) is sharply topical,
with its sensual imagery being heavily reminiscent of the Song of
Solomon. Ellison's first turn, taken from Air XXI of *The Beggar's
Opera* (1728) by John Gay (1685–1732), has the semblance of
gentility, and his second, the traditional folk song 'Villikins and
His Dinah', rehashes the popular Victorian music-hall scenario
of suicidal lovers. Chae's reprise of Burns's 'Up in the Morning
Early' revives the Scots theme, intensified by Mistress Mutch's
selections of the traditional Scottish ballad, first published
around 1790, telling the gory tale of 'The Bonnie House o' Airlie'
and of Lady Anne Barnard's eighteenth-century weepy, the waltz
'Auld Robin Gray' (1771).

15. *Damn't*: Gibbon's typescript has the speaker saying '*Bugger't*'
here and p. 197, and pp. 178, 199, 200 (for 'muckers'). See also
Ploughing, note 32.

16. *Auld Lang Syne*: Popular anthem, based on earlier ballads, tran-
scribed and published by Burns in 1788.

17. *the fog-horn at Todhead*: The lighthouse near Kinneff would
have been well within hearing distance from Gibbon's Arbuthnott, 3 miles distant.

18. *the Flying Scotsman*: Locomotive named after the principal rail
line, introduced in June 1862, between London Kings Cross and
Edinburgh Waverley. If Gibbon means the locomotive, he is
guilty of an anachronism, as it only went into service in 1923.

19. *Thomas the Rhymour*: Thomas of Erceldoune, or Earlston, near
Melrose in the Scottish Borders, was a semi-legendary seer and
poet from the thirteenth century whose life gave rise to many
colourful tales, including the eponymous ballad relating his
seven-year kidnapping at the hands of the 'Queen of Fair Elfland'.

20. *Edzell Castle*: The sixteenth-century ruin in Edzell, 15 miles
south-west of Arbuthnott.

21. *waiting quiet of the afternoon*: The original typescript reading
'quiet waitingness' has been revised to a more felicitous phrasing.

IV   *Harvest*

1. *Britain was to war with Germany*: Britain officially declared war
on 4 August 1914, due to its moral obligation to defend France,

which had formally found itself at war the previous day, but in reality due more to its commitment by treaty to the defence of neutral Belgium.

2. *down in Forfar*: Substantial county town just south of the Mearns, 25 miles south-west of Arbuthnott.

3. *the Germans ... braining bairns all over Belgium*: Germany invaded Belgium on 4 August 1914, causing the King of Belgium, Albert I (1875–1934), to appeal, successfully, to Britain for assistance amid rumours of atrocities, including, later, cannibalism by the starving troops (pp. 221, 247), reflecting the jingoistic hysteria whipped up by both sides.

4. *and joined in the Gordons*: The Gordon Highlanders, the home regiment of North-east Scotland, were one of the British army's most celebrated regiments, founded in 1794 for service in the Napoleonic Wars, and recruiting predominantly from Banffshire, Aberdeenshire and Kincardineshire. In the First World War, all the full-time battalions saw active service on the Somme, with more than half of the 50,000 troops being killed or wounded.

5. *joined the North Highlanders and been sent to Perth*: A fabricated regiment, but several battalions of the Black Watch were formed at Perth, 20 miles south of Dundee, during the early stages of the war. This would be the likeliest destination for recruits from the Mearns at that time, when recruitment was predominantly conducted on a regional basis.

6. *Babylon's corruptions*: Frequently cited as a very wicked place, Babylon drew the Old Testament God's wrath on itself (as Europe has with its 'corruptions').

7. *in the days of Attila*: A comparison in barbarism between the Germans and the Hun army led by their notorious king and general, dubbed the Scourge of God by the Romans, that swept through Europe in the fifth century.

8. *Antichrist*: Comparison of the Kaiser with the Christian eschatological synonym for evil, traditionally reputed to be both opposed to truth and disguised as good.

9. *Onward, Christian Soldiers*: The stirring hymn, written by Sabine Baring-Gould (1834–1924), is commonly used in wartime.

10. *the Congo and your Belgians*: While the Belgian rule over the African state (1908–60), now known as the Democratic Republic of the Congo, was presented as paternalistic colonialism, it was more often characterised by negligence and authoritarianism, with a repressive attitude towards the indigenous culture.

11. *a jade called Jael*: See Judges 4:17–22.

12. *mills of God still grind*: The proverb can be traced to the Greek sceptic Sextus Empiricus (late second – early third century AD): 'The mills of the gods grind slowly, but they grind small.'

13. *the common folk had seen what their guns could do*: Chae's socialist idealism is not entirely misplaced, as the First World War witnessed the Easter Rising in Ireland in 1916 and the Bolshevik Revolution in Russia in 1917 (see p. 257 and Epilude, note 9), subsequently fomenting the social unrest that led to the 'Bloody Friday' revolt in Glasgow on 31 January 1919 – which Gibbon himself probably witnessed – as well as the Spartacist uprising in Germany in 1919.

14. *the Conscription Act*: The first Military Service Act passed in January 1916 was known as the 'Bachelors' Bill', as it only applied to unmarried men. The second Act of May 1916 introduced universal conscription.

15. *the Exemption Board sat there for the cases*: Rob's experience of the Exemption Tribunal is made more farcical by its local provenance, a feature satirised by popular North-east poet Charles Murray (1864–1941) in 'Dockens Afore His Peers' in *A Sough of War* (1917).

16. *his Glengarry bonnet*: The distinctive soft-ribboned military cap invented by Colonel Alasdair Ranaldson MacDonell of Glengarry (1771–1828) was adopted by several Scottish regiments, and for a short period in the nineteenth century, worn by all British soldiers.

17. *French Foreign Legion*: Legendary unit within the French army founded in 1831 for foreign volunteers. It was actively involved in both World Wars.

18. *Ewan down training in Lanark*: While Gibbon leaves the details of Ewan's enlistment unspecified, his training at the base in Lanark in the south of Scotland associates him with the Highland Light Infantry.

19. *below the Southern Cross*: A small, bright constellation in the Southern hemisphere in the Milky Way near Centaurus, the four most prominent stars of which form the shape of a cross.

20. *She had hardly been able to believe it him ... wheeled in her brain*: Drawing upon his own unhappy term in the Royal Army Service Corps (1919–1923), Gibbon responded strongly to criticism that Ewan's change was too radical, writing to his friend Helen Cruickshank (1886–1975): 'Quite right about the closing portion being run at too great a rate – it is. But Ewan & the

War-change is factually the truth, if not artistically . . .' (Letter, undated [August 1932], Edinburgh University Library).

21. *There was a Young Farmer . . . Long, Long Trail*: The popular folk song 'There was a Young Farmer' and the 'national' song 'A' the Blue Bonnets are Over the Border', from Sir Walter Scott's *The Monastery* (1820), were replaced by 'Tipperary' (1912) and the 'Long, Long Trail' (1917), which came to be associated with the war, but had been popular music-hall songs.

22. *Country and King*: The treatment by Erich Maria Remarque (1898–1970) in *All Quiet on the Western Front* (1928) of the farmer Detering's defection from the front line is strongly echoed in Ewan's desertion and death. Chris's denunciation of the political powers that she holds responsible for the war is heavily reminiscent of Remarque's anti-authoritarian stance.

23. *the Verey lights*: More accurately designated the Very light, a flare fired from a special pistol for signalling or illumination, named after the U.S. Naval Ordinance Officer Edward W. Very (1852–1910).

24. *they killed him that morning*: Controversy still surrounds the harsh treatment meted out to British deserters. Courts martial for perceived breaches of discipline such as desertion, mutiny and cowardice (even if caused by shell shock or other mental afflictions) resulted in a total of 346 executions (Germany by contrast carried out only 48). In *Goodbye to All That* (1929), Robert Graves testifies angrily to the official secrecy about the trials in France in 1915.

25. *And then something made her raise her eyes*: Chris's vision betrays a possible literary influence, as it has something of the grotesque evanescence of 'Strange Meeting' (1918), the vividly surreal vision of agonised spiritual rebirth in the trenches written by Wilfred Owen (1893–1918), which became a metaphor for the horror of the First World War.

THE EPILUDE
The Unfurrowed Field

1. *EPILUDE*: In a letter to fellow Scottish writer Sir Compton Mackenzie (1883–1972), Gibbon debated the niceties of classical grammar concerning this title:

Afraid I must plead guilty to having used it [Epilude] quite deliber-
ately. 'Postlude' is, of course, correct, but also it seems to me a
curiously dull, fat, frumpish word – the after-song of a singer with
a girth and a leer and a house in Putney, if you get what I mean.
Whereas 'Epilude' is suave and dark (probably because it's a
mulatto) and somehow appropriate to a darkening theme – (Letter,
19 September 1932, Harry Ransom Research Center, University of
Texas at Austin)

Gibbon gave way in the American edition to 'Postlude'.

2. *the wind still bloweth as it listeth*: From John 3:8: 'The wind
   bloweth where it listeth, and thou hearest the sound thereof, but
   canst not tell whence it cometh, and whither it goeth: so is every
   one that is born of the Spirit.'

3. *the Uhlans*: Originally Polish cavalry regiments armed with the
   lance and boasting colourful uniforms, the Uhlans later were
   absorbed into the Prussian army.

4. *queer blue babies that were born there*: Perhaps confusing idioms
   culled from the contemporary blues boom and from a term used
   for infants with congenital heart problems in the United States.

5. *the Coalition*: The 1918 General Election was won by a coalition
   of the Conservatives led by Andrew Bonar Law (1858–1923)
   and the Liberals under Lloyd George (see Drilling, note 9), who
   continued as Prime Minister, as well as a handful of Labour and
   independent MPs.

6. *Armistice Day*: The Armistice – formally meaning a cessation of
   hostilities pending peace negotiations – was signed at 5 a.m. on
   11 November 1918, and came into effect six hours later.

7. *They have made . . . peace*: In *The Agricola*, Tacitus attributes
   these defiant words to Calgacus at Mons Graupius: 'Ubi solitudi-
   nem faciunt, pacem appellant' (see Prelude, note 28).

8. *and speak as though Christ had meant Kinraddie*: Gibbon had
   an abiding interest in Christ as a revolutionary political figure, as
   opposed to divine Son of God, from his first novel *Stained Radiance* (1930), to his modernist story 'Forsaken' (*Scottish Scene*).

9. *Bolshevik . . . Lenin and Trotsky*: The Bolshevik Revolution, the
   second phase of the Marxist Communist uprising in Russia in
   October 1917, witnessed the overthrow of the imperial government and execution on 16 July 1918 of the abdicated monarch
   Tsar Nicholas II (b. 1868), with the subsequent assumption of
   power by Lenin (Vladimir Ilyich Ulyanov, 1870–1924) and Leon
   Trotsky (1879–1940). (Gibbon was a founding member of the

Soviet established in Aberdeen in the wake of the October Revolution.)

10. *REVELATION: II CH: 28 VERSE*: Reads: 'And I will give him the morning star.' The two preceding verses are more combative: 'And he that overcometh, and keepeth my works unto the end, to him will I give power over the nations: And he shall rule them with a rod of iron; as the vessels of a potter shall they be broken to shivers: even as I received of my Father.'

The Arbuthnott War memorial records the names of fourteen men.

11. *they would range themselves did they live to-day*: Colquohoun's sermon here departs from the original typescript: 'they would have ranged themselves had they lived to-day'. The revision gives the climax greater impact.

Glossary

As Gibbon points out in the prefatory note to his Glossary, his literary language is an eclectic hybrid reflecting his innate love of words. While his style has the character of North-east Scots, in actuality the proportion of traditional Scots idioms, mixed in with conventional English vocabulary, is minimal. His list was added to the first American edition and was prefaced by the strict caveat:

> As implied in the note at the beginning of this book,[1] most of the Scots words are untranslatable except in their context setting. Otherwise there would have been little point in using them: English would have served, as elsewhere. So the following 'translations' are very faulty – the English a mere approximation to the Scots.
>
> When various constructions compete for translation, the verb-form only is given and translated.
>
> L. G. G.

This Glossary expands upon Gibbon's modest list of just over one hundred precise definitions – here designated with his initials.

Full details of traditional Scots words and phrases included in Gibbon's distinctive lexicon can be found in *The Concise Scots Dictionary*, editor-in-chief Mairi Robinson (Aberdeen: Aberdeen University Press, 1985) and in the *Dictionary of the Scots Language*, available on-line at www.dsl.ac.uk. More specialised information is available in *Speak o' the North-east*, by William Morrice Wilson (NESP, 1993), and in *A Doric Dictionary*, ed. Douglas Kynoch (Edinburgh: Scottish Cultural Press, 1996).

affronted embarrassed and humiliated
agley skewed, wrong
argy argument; to argue
argy-bargy lively dispute

Auld Kirk, the literally, Old Church – archaism used for the Church
  of Scotland
awful extremely LGG
ay yes
aye yes; always
ayont beyond

bairn child
bap bread roll
beasts animals, especially farm animals – specifically, cattle
bed to make love with
ben within; through
bent hill-slope
bide to stay; to remain
bigging building
billy young man LGG
binder machine for cutting grain and tying it into sheaves
birn load, burden LGG
bit a mildly deprecatory adjectival handle LGG
black blood endemically evil disposition
blash to splash, to shower
blatter loud rattle; nonsense talk
blither blether, senseless talk
blow to brag
blow the organ to operate the lever pumping air to the organ's bellows
body person, somebody
bombast to brag, to exaggerate
bonny naturally beautiful
bothy bachelor farm servants' dwelling LGG
bout swath LGG
brae slope, hillside
brave fine; handsome
bree water, gravy, liquid LGG
breeked put into trousers; grown up
breeks trousers
brier type of thorny shrub
brose a sketchy oatmeal dish LGG
brose-cap bowl for preparing **brose**
bruise to squash corn by crushing or pressing
brute one mildly antipathetic to the speaker LGG
bubbly-jock turkey-cock
bucht animal shelter, generally sheep-pen

burn stream
butt and (a) ben single-storey cottage comprised of two modest rooms
by nearby, about
by his lone all alone, by himself
byre cow-house LGG

caller fresh, invigorating
callipers measuring instrument with two parallel legs
Candlemas 2 February, one of the four annual **term days**
canny cautious, natural (**not canny** suspicious, unnatural)
canteen presentation box with cutlery
canty full of life; pleasant
carle ordinary person
cateran (originally) outlaw; generally, rogue
cattle-court cattle yard
Chakie diminutive of Charles. The order is: Charles, Charlie, Chae,
    Chakie LGG
chancy fortunate
chap tap, knock; chime
chave to toil back-breakingly LGG
chief-like over-friendly, intimate LGG
childe a full-grown, responsible male LGG
chirawk throaty clucking noise
claik gossip LGG
clairted plastered
clamjamfried cluttered; caked
clart a byre implement LGG
clean completely
cleck to give birth to LGG
clip to catch, to hold
clip clouts to cut cloths
close courtyard; farmyard
clour/clout hard knock LGG
clout cloth
clown fool, idiot
clya(c)k end – specifically, of harvest
coarse wicked LGG
coin to earn
coldrife intensely cold
cole haycock; to put hay up into a haycock
come-up social climber, nouveau riche
conchy abbreviation for conscientious objector (derogatory)

cotter peasant farmer renting small plot from a landlord; married worker occupying cottage as part of contract

coulter plough blade

coup overset LGG

course/coarse rough, disagreeable

couthy known and kindly LGG

creash fat (adipose tissue) LGG

creature living thing – generally, contemptuous of a person

croft smallholding, smallest unit of subsistence farming: small enclosed plot of land, attached to the cottage, worked by the occupier and his family

Cruelty, the official body for investigating instances of cruelty to animals

cry to call; to proclaim

cuddy donkey LGG

curry-comb square comb with small teeth for grooming horses

cushat-dove wood-pigeon; ring-dove

daft silly, light-headed

daftie fool, imbecile

dander stroll; temper

daurna dare not

dawtie darling LGG

deave to annoy LGG

dicky false shirt front normally worn with evening dress; bow tie

dirk dagger

dirl racket; to reverberate

dirt rubbish; nonsense – generally, malicious

doiter to totter

doitered unbalanced; senseless

Dominie schoolteacher – usually, headmaster

dool pain, anguish

douce wholesome LGG

dour hard, stubborn, surly

dowp posterior LGG

dreich dull, dreary

driblet small dribble, trickle

drill furrow in which seeds are sown; to plant seeds in a row

drookèd deep-drenched LGG

dux formal title given each year to academically most successful pupil in school

dyke stone wall LGG

eightsome Scottish country dance, reel for eight dancers
Epilude postlude, concluding movement (*see* Epilude, note 1)
ere before
esparto twine thin rope made from grass fibre

factor manager, business agent – generally, on estate
fair quite, certainly LGG
fairlies fairies; wonders, imaginings
faith! hard to believe – generally, prefacing revelatory comment or punchline
fash fuss, worry
fauld pen, small field
feared afraid
feckless gormless
fee formal semi-permanent transaction of employment for a farm worker (*see* Prelude, note 21)
fee'd fixed up with a fee
feein' market recruitment fair for agricultural workers
feint hardly LGG
fell exceedingly LGG
feuch! yuck!
fiddley-faddles trivialities
fine! all right! – generally, challenging or sarcastic
first foot first visitor of the New Year
flail wooden handle with attached wooden or iron cantilever for threshing grain
fleer to scoff, to flare LGG
flite to scold
forbye besides; notwithstanding
freestone kind of easily worked sandstone
fusionless weak, feeble, unenterprising
futret weasel LGG

gabble babble, nonsense
gait way, road
gang to go
gear belongings, furnishings, chattels
gelding castrated male horse
gentry social class just beneath aristocracy
get on to prosper
gey (sardonically) rather, very LGG
gig light two-wheeled one-horse carriage without a hood

gillie gamekeeper; sportsman's attendant

gird to scold

girdle flat iron plate for cooking

girn to whine hardily LGG

glass looking glass, mirror

gleg horse-fly

glen hill valley

gley to squint LGG

glint glance; look slyly

gloaming twilight, dusk

glour black, viscid mud LGG

glower scowl, look fiercely

glunch to mutter half-threateningly, half-fearfully LGG

gnomon arm on a sun-dial that projects the shadow

go over the gate to go mad

goloch earwig, beetle; insect

gomeril half-wit LGG

good-son son-in-law

Gordons Gordon Highlanders

gowk fool

gowkèd stupid LGG

graip pitchfork

greet to weep

greeve good LGG

greip a kind of cow-shed drain LGG

gryphon mythical creature combining an eagle's head and wings with a lion's body

guerdon reward, payment

guff overwhelming smell

gutsy greedy

hackstock chopping block – often, a tree trunk

handless clumsy, inept

hantle a lot, very

hantle few very few

happed well covered LGG

harrow implement used to break up and flatten hard ground; to use a harrow

hauch flat land – generally, beside a river

haver/haiver to gibber, to talk nonsense

havers! nonsense!

haws hawthorn berries

heuch sickle; hollow LGG
hiddle huddle, shelter
hinder end back section
hippens babies' napkins LGG
hirple to limp, to hobble
hoar hoar-frost
hoast 'a hacking cough' LGG
hold over to walk over, to cross over
holding farm; tenure
hoots goodness gracious (generally dismissive)
hornbeam type of hardwood tree
hotter to simmer, to boil
howe valley flanked by hills
hubbley-jock a turkey-cock LGG

ilka each, every
ill badly, poorly; difficult, curmudgeonly (of people)
ill-fashione rudeness, nosiness, devilment
ill-like poorly
ill-reared roughly constructed; badly brought up
ill-use to abuse, to insult
in by inside, in here

jade disreputable woman
jing-bang total sum, whole lot
jobe probe LGG
jookery-packery jiggery-pokery; trickery, deception

kailyard cabbage patch, kitchen garden
keek to look slyly; an impudent, innocent girl LGG
kenspeckled prominent, ostentatious
kine/kye cattle
kirk church
kist trunk; box
kittle to tickle; the itch LGG
kittle up to rouse, to stimulate
knacker horse dealer specialising in slaughter and disposal of old animals
knap(p) hillock, knoll
knowe small hill; top of a hill

laddie boy, young man
laird landowner

laired bogged down; covered in mud

leet list of employment candidates

leggings over-trousers covering the lower legs (generally regarded as an affectation signifying social rank beyond the working class)

leman female lover; mistress

ley fallow land LGG

libbed castrated LGG

lilt song, rhythm, melody

limmer sharp-tongued woman LGG

lithe shelter, lee LGG

lone alone

long in the tooth getting on in years; elderly

long syne a long time ago; long before

longer languor, tedium; loneliness

loon boy; farmer's boy

loose untie, unyoke

Losh! Lord!

loup to leap, to jump

louring scowling; darkening (of weather)

lowe glow LGG

lug ear LGG

lum-hat top hat

made at moved towards threateningly; assaulted

mains home farm of an estate

malachite bright green mineral

mannie man (sardonic diminutive)

marled mottled

mart market; market building

Martinmas 11 November, feast of St Martin, one of the four annual term days

maw mouth; throat

meat food, nourishment; to feed

meikle great, much, large LGG

melodeon type of small accordion

Mem Ma'am (deferential)

mere marshy edge or inlet

mid amidst, in the middle of

midden dung-heap, rubbish-heap

minded reminded, remembered

mirk gloom, darkness

mischieve to hurt

mislike to dislike
moonlight flit surreptitious removal from area to escape debts
morn tomorrow (from the present); next day
moulder to decay, to crumble
mouser moustache
mow to communicate visually with mouth
muck to clean out
mucker a euphuism for 'bugger'; i.e. a Bulgarian heretic; i.e. suspected
    of nauseous practices LGG
mutch woman's tight linen cap

neb nose
nether lower – especially of two places
neuk nook, corner
nick steal
nicker whinny
not canny *see* **canny**
nozzle nuzzle

on the go busy; working
ongoing mischief, shenanigan
orra odd; untidy; wicked LGG
orraman farm labourer
out by outside; out there
over too
oxter armpit; to embrace

paich to pant, to gasp
park field
peasant member of rural society of low status, dependent upon subsist-
    ence farming
peely-wally unhealthily pale in complexion
peesie peewit, lapwing
penny smallest unit of British sterling, worth less than half a new
    pence
pernickety fussy LGG
Petronella classic intricate Scottish country dance
piece sandwich; cold snack
plaid woollen cloth used as a blanket; tartan shawl worn over the
    shoulder
plaint complaint; wail
plash splash; torrent

pleiter to wade aimlessly LGG
ploy enterprise, ruse – generally, sardonic
pother commotion, fuss
pouch pocket
pouches under his eyes bags under his eyes
pound main unit of British sterling, originally of equivalent value to modern decimal pound
pow head
Prelude preface, preceding movement
pretty handsome LGG
prig urge LGG
pringle tingle; to tingle

quean girl LGG
queered puzzled
quick alive; animated

rangy lanky LGG
rax to stretch, to strain
reaper (ancient) machine for cutting the harvest
redd to clear away LGG
ree pen
reek smoke
reischle rustle; noisy gathering
rickle/ruckle loosely assembled pile, jumble
rig ridge; strip of ploughed land
right really, strikingly
rill stream
rime frosty haze
rive to tear, to burst
road to drive; to travel along a road
roup public auction – generally, of a whole farm
roust to become busy; to move briskly

sampler intricate decorative work of embroidery
sappy plump, formless
sark shirt
scavenger person employed to clean the streets
schlorich a shapeless, unchartable sticky chaos LGG
schottische piece of music composed in style of nineteenth-century German dance
scraich to screech LGG

scud to slip quickly
scunner to disgust LGG
set(t) match; sexual intercourse
shake-down makeshift bed; digs
sharn dung in a semi-liquid state LGG
shaw vegetable leaf or stalk
shelvin section of a farm cart LGG
shilling small silver coin in British sterling, equivalent to five new pence
sholtie pony, young horse LGG
shover chauffeur
silver money
simple ordinary people
skelp to smack, to strike
skilly skilful; useful
skirl to shriek, to wail
skite daft (used flippantly) LGG
sleekèd sly, shifty, cunning
slippy smartly, promptly
slummock a lumpish slattern LGG
slump economic depression
smit to infect LGG
smore to smother LGG
sneck latch LGG
snicker snigger
sniftering snuffling LGG
snipe long-billed marsh bird
sock pointed end of a ploughshare
sonsy handsome; flattishly burly LGG
soom to swim, to float
sore made harassed, hard pushed
soss a static mess LGG
sotter to bubble stagnantly LGG
sough to sigh
sourock a little sour plant LGG
sow a long stack of straw
spate river flooding
speak infamy, scandal, subject of gossip; speech, saying
spleiter a wettish mess LGG
spunk essence; courage; grit. A lucifer match LGG
spurtle a stick for stirring porridge LGG
stamash blind fury LGG
stammy-gaster to puzzle LGG

steading farm outbuilding

stew dust; upset

stipend salary of Church of Scotland minister

stir trouble, uproar

stirk bullock or heifer LGG

stite gibberish LGG

stiter to lurch, to stagger

stock person LGG

stook loose tower of corn sheaves; to build a stook with sheaves

store the kin to keep the human race going; to survive (*see* Seed-Time, note 12)

stour dust; commotion LGG

strainer the main upright of a wire fence LGG

Strip the Willow popular Scottish country dance loosely based on traditional Hebridean weaving dance

sumph lout LGG

sutor cobbler, shoemaker

swack agile LGG

swede common Eurasian turnip, used as a vegetable in cooking and as cattle fodder

sweirty reluctance; laziness

swick sly cheat LGG

swither to swish draggingly LGG

syne since, then

tack sailing of a ship heading windward

taik stroll

take through hand to explore; to discuss fully

take up with to begin a romance with

tarn small hill loch

ta-ta good-bye (affectionate)

tee-tee teetotal, abstemious

term day/term-time one of appointed calendar days set four times a year for review of agricultural contracts

thole to suffer, to endure

thrapple throat LGG

thraw to strangle

thrawn stubborn; mean

tice to coax, to wheedle

time about taking turns

tink tinker, or travelling person – generally any socially undesirable person

tocher inheritance LGG
toddy hot drink made with whisky sweetened with sugar or honey
toff posh person – generally smartly dressed
toun large farm
tow twine, string
toward happening; unusual
trig neat LGG
trollop promiscuous woman; prostitute
try attempt
tune mood; temper
tuppence two pence – generally, an insignificant amount
turnpike junction or road – originally, for collecting payment of toll
twist small amount; broken-off piece
tyne to lose

Uhlans Prussian cavalry (*see* Epilude, note 3)
uncanny ominous
unchancy dangerous, foreboding
unco strange(ly), unusual(ly), extreme(ly)
uncouthy unfriendly
unsneck to open, to lift the latch
up to get up
up-jumbled mixed up, jumbled up
upprums upper settlement on poor farming land – originally, referring
    to 'rums', bituminous shale

villein peasant personally bound for rent and services to his lord in
    mediaeval Europe, in return for farming his land

wabble to shake
wame stomach LGG
wastry waste, extravagance
wean child LGG
wearing on passing; getting late; growing old
wee small – generally, affectionate
week to squeak, to whimper
well-kenspeckled trim LGG
wheeber to whistle birringly LGG
wheep whistling sound
wheest hush
whelm to overwhelm
Whiggam! historical Covenanting battle cry (*see* Prelude, note 9)

whimsy impulse, fanciful notion
whin gorse bush
whip sudden quick movement
whist! shoosh!
whoom to boom, to roar
wife woman
wight blame; fault LGG
winnow to toss grain in order to free it of chaff
wist to know
with bairn pregnant
without outside

yammer to talk relentlessly
yavil land in harvest the previous year LGG
yowl to yell, to howl

NOTE

1. The introductory note reads in full:

A Note the Reader is Advised to Read

Those who read and run – or who find all antique history a weariness – or have little relish for meeting the characters, one by one, in detailed biography, before the story begins – *are advised to skip the Prelude and begin the Song at page* 33. If they feel the urge, they may later delve in the Prelude as a handy reference to the off-stage history of this soul and that.

Similarly, should the context refuse to give up the meaning of a Scots word used, the reader may turn to the Glossary. But the author hopes that that will be seldom: the author, indeed, has quite failed in his purpose if the Glossary proves a pressing need.

For the author (whose humility may be taken for granted) can be best regarded as a sagaman arrived in the house of the English with the salvage of his own ruined house of words; and the tongue of his hosts, so it seems to him, may be yet enriched with this salvage of words that are only half-alien.

L. G. G.

THE STORY OF PENGUIN CLASSICS

Before 1946 ... 'Classics' are mainly the domain of academics and students; readable editions for everyone else are almost unheard of. This all changes when a little-known classicist, E. V. Rieu, presents Penguin founder Allen Lane with the translation of Homer's *Odyssey* that he has been working on in his spare time.

1946 Penguin Classics debuts with *The Odyssey*, which promptly sells three million copies. Suddenly, classics are no longer for the privileged few.

1950s Rieu, now series editor, turns to professional writers for the best modern, readable translations, including Dorothy L. Sayers's *Inferno* and Robert Graves's unexpurgated *Twelve Caesars*.

1960s The Classics are given the distinctive black covers that have remained a constant throughout the life of the series. Rieu retires in 1964, hailing the Penguin Classics list as 'the greatest educative force of the twentieth century.'

1970s A new generation of translators swells the Penguin Classics ranks, introducing readers of English to classics of world literature from more than twenty languages. The list grows to encompass more history, philosophy, science, religion and politics.

1980s The Penguin American Library launches with titles such as *Uncle Tom's Cabin*, and joins forces with Penguin Classics to provide the most comprehensive library of world literature available from any paperback publisher.

1990s The launch of Penguin Audiobooks brings the classics to a listening audience for the first time, and in 1999 the worldwide launch of the Penguin Classics website extends their reach to the global online community.

The 21st Century Penguin Classics are completely redesigned for the first time in nearly twenty years. This world-famous series now consists of more than 1300 titles, making the widest range of the best books ever written available to millions – and constantly redefining what makes a 'classic'.

The Odyssey continues ...

The best books ever written

PENGUIN 🐧 CLASSICS

SINCE 1946

Find out more at www.penguinclassics.com